Blue Monkey Quest

III

The Perils of Erebus

By Alex Ross Carol

Blue M Publishing

Library of Congress Cataloging-in-publication data
Names: Carol, Alex Ross
Title: *Blue Monkey Quest III -- The Perils of Erebus*
Description: First edition | Blue M Publishing, Chicago, IL [2020] | Series: Book three of
monographic series | Contents: The Perils of Erebus | Summary: Oliver and Gemma find
themselves in the kingdom of Frezia where Oliver is forced into a challenge that means life or
death. | Audience Note: Recommended for readers thirteen and older
Identifiers: ISBN 978-1-945385-20-9 (Paperback)
Subjects: LCSH: sh85047117 Fantasy fiction, American | BISAC: FIC061000 FICTION /
Magical Realism | FICTION / Fantasy Contemporary | GSAFD: 00000cz a2200037n 45 0 155
Fantasy fiction | 455 Fantastic fiction | Genre/Form terms: gf2014026333 Fantasy
fiction/Heroic fantasy fiction.
Classification: LCC PS370-380 | DDC 813/--dc23

Blue Monkey Quest III -- The Perils of Erebus
Alex Ross Carol
Contents: Part one—The Frozen Kingdom | Part two—The Challenge |
Part three—The Unexpected Challenge

Printed in the United States of America
www.blueMpublishing.com
Book Cover Design by Allendorf Vigenere
Blue M Publishing
Hinsdale, IL 60521

Contents

Summary—Books I and II

Oliver and Nikko strike out to find the fabled Map of Gneima. Nearly getting killed by a strange, squid-like beast, the duo opens an egg-shaped rock and discover a stone fragment inside. Returning to their homeland of Rootan, Oliver joins his aunt to visit her brother, the wise and gracious Sojourn. There, Oliver learns that the dark stone he found is, indeed, a piece of the Map of Gneima. Unfortunately, he also discovers that it is only one of twelve pieces.

Together with Gemma, a lady knight from the neighboring kingdom of Dulcenou, Oliver and Nikko travel to the Desert of Riakalah in Sanzotur. There they follow their mysterious clues to the giant Arch of Gaya in search of the next piece of the map. Meanwhile, the kingdom of Rootan is taken over by another – one more wicked than King Portenza. It is a young man possessed by an evil spirit named Barbarot who unleashes a terrible plague upon the former king and his kingdom. With the king dead, he quickly seizes power. Oliver, Gemma, and Nikko reunite with Donus in Dulcenou but are forced to escape as the plague seeks to destroy them.

and so, it continues …

*****

Summary - Book III

The Perils of Erebus

The third adventure takes Oliver, Gemma, Donus and Nikko into the cold tundra of the kingdom of Frezia. There, Oliver is forced into a deadly contest to track down another piece of the Gneima puzzle.

King Barbarot and his army are on a campaign of destruction and war to take over all the neighboring kingdoms and force them into slavery under his rule.

Meanwhile, Oliver's aunt and uncle are plotting to take back control of Rootan after another old foe—Viceroy Konjuur—slips into the kingdom and is leading its people in revolt.

*****

Blue Monkey Quest

PART I- THE FROZEN KINGDOM

CH 1 - The Forgotten Soul

Sojourn leaned precariously over the white, stone cistern that was balanced on top of a matching, carved pedestal. The liquid in the bowl was clear but jiggled on the surface like jelly instead of making waves as water might. He placed his wrinkled and spotted hands on the bowl's smooth rim and began tracing the edge with his fingers in a clockwise motion, going around precisely two times before reversing and going the other way once more.

After completing the ritual, Sojourn stood and watched. The basin began to vibrate and swirl on its own with steam beginning to waft from the surface. Then, as quickly as it started, the thick broth became smooth as glass once more, and an image appeared, slowly at first, but then condensing rapidly into a clear picture.

"I was wondering when you were going to contact me," said the face reflecting back from the cistern pool. It had long, gray-hair and a short-cropped goatee. The face was as aged as Sojourn's but was longer and narrower. However, it did share one common trait—it too showed deep wrinkles and lines of serious concern.

"Sage, how are you?" asked Sojourn with brotherly affection. "I hoped you were unharmed by recent events. So, I'm glad and relieved to see you are still alive and kicking."

"Alive, yes. Kicking? Some days I'm not so sure," Sage said, laughing. "But I was worried about you as well, Sojourn, my good friend. I heard a great deal about the ravages caused by the virus, and I tried to reach you several times," said Sage. "What is happening? Thank the God of gods you survived the canibola. Was anyone else in your household harmed?"

The canibola had come in on a silvery cloud from a distant kingdom. It had started as a small mist but grown large and traveled quickly. After destroying much of Rootan—eating everything in its path from the inside out—it left the kingdom and, as word later reported, it either dissipated into the mist of the night or floated back into the valley from where it came.

"Well, Sage, we managed to escape unharmed. But I must tell you that Cleora is in trouble. Barbarot took her and threw her in prison. I think it was revenge for her making him look bad in front of our former King Portenza," said Sojourn, his voice choking. "And, I don't know where she is now. She may be in the castle." He stopped and then continued after getting his voice back. "Do you know anything?"

The face and voice gazing at Sojourn out of the cistern pool softened, and a weak but clear smile shown back at him from the clear liquid.

"Yes, Sojourn. That's why I've been trying to reach you. I do have news to tell you."

The creases in Sojourn's face relaxed, but his eyes grew more intense, as if it would help him hear more clearly. "Tell me, then," he answered.

"It is both good and bad news, Sojourn. However, I think there is a chance … although a small one … of getting to your sister out from Barbarot's clutches. I know the locksmith who made all the keys to the castle. I will make the arrangements."

*****

CH 2 - Wild Ride

Aunt Cleora sat on the hard, stone floor of her cell. She was weak from the lack of water, and her crying had only made it worse. The putrid smell of the dark, dank prison was becoming too much for her, and she wished that either a miracle from the God of gods or her final end would come to save her.

"Scram!" she shouted, annoyed by a pair of white, blinking eyes that kept watching her through a jagged crack in the cell wall. She was sure it was a huge parathian rat.

The eyes were unblinking and only stared. Eventually, they went away, but she knew they were only waiting, patiently. Indeed, as the days passed, the eyes in the wall no longer scampered away when she yelled. They just stayed there—watching and waiting. She knew all too well what it was waiting for; she just didn't like to think about the enjoyment it would have once she was gone.

This time, the animal stuck its nose out of the fissure to sniff around. It was just as she had thought — an enormous parathian rat. It came closer now to see how much longer it would be before he could start working on what was left of her.

"I said, get out of here!" screamed Aunt Cleora, throwing a rock at the pink-whiskered nose but missing and only managing to scare it back into the depths of the walls.

Her eyelids drooped as the sunlight outside dimmed. She could tell that night was approaching from the fading light that came through small air holes leading to the surface above. Of course, by the time it reached her, a hundred feet below, it had none of its pristine, clean freshness. Yet, she was comforted by the coolness it brought with it.

Feeling tired, she felt the energy drain from her eyes. She fought the feeling but realized she couldn't win. The grips of something more powerful than her soul had her in its own claws and wasn't willing to let go so easily. The gray stones within her cell began to spin slowly in her mind, and darkness fell around her.

However, she found herself standing in the middle of a vast field. Suddenly, it was the middle of the day, as if her time and place had instantly changed. The field was covered with flowers—beautiful in color, ranging from amber and ambrosia to violet and vermillion. The trees surrounding the field wore luscious fronds and bore canary and honey-colored fruits hanging lazily from their branches.

The sun felt good, warming her arms and her neck, and she put her head back and closed her eyes against the brightest of light streaming down on her. The air was fresh, scented with the aroma of flowering didactics and dialectics—odd plants that talked to everyone who passed by. She felt at peace—a tranquility she had never felt before. She felt immortal, like her body had gone beyond life itself and was standing in a field on the other side of reality.

Aunt Cleora suddenly felt the urge to explore, so she walked around the field, looking here and there and taking in the beauty that was both large and small. She relished the magnificence of the sky, the clouds and the bliss that permeated everything. At the same time, she marveled at the intricate dances of the insects buzzing about, the birds flitting from branch to branch, and the small creatures scampering beneath the low-hanging leaves of scrubby bushes. Bedazzled in their coats of periwinkle, rouge and striking bands of yellow, the birds floated, as if suspended in mid-air with only a quick flap or two of their fluffy wings to get across the open space.

Looking down on it all, Aunt Cleora saw a hole—a curious hole—one that seemed unusually large for most of the animals she knew lived in the area. In the middle of the verdant field, the hole was an oddity.

It must be a very small tendoore deer or a very large, cartasian mouse, she thought. *Then again, it could just be a molemacaw.*

The molemacaw was a very colorful, furry creature that lived underground and came out at night to fly in search of food for its young. She had longed to see one as they were extremely rare.

Looking at an almonoot, a low-growing bush that bore heavy starchy, black nuts, Aunt Cleora grabbed one of the nuts and pulled it from the plant. She tied a thin, black thread to it and began lowering it into the hole. Although she didn't know why, she 'jerked' it a few times as if she were fishing in a small pond. Yet, there didn't seem to be any answer on the other end. She repeated this several more times. hoping to catch something on the other end. But still there was nothing.

Finally, she dropped the line several more fathoms, letting out all but the last yard, which she wrapped tightly around her hand.

"Cleora ... Cleora ..." came an echo that reverberated through the chamber.

Aunt Cleora awoke with a start. She was confused and disoriented, but she was sure she had heard her name bouncing off the walls. She sat quietly, listening again.

"Cleora ..."

That was it! she thought. *That was the sound!*

"Cleora … Cleora …"

But as soon as she heard it, the sound began fading away, as if it were moving on—leaving her desperate and alone in her cold, prison cell.

In a panic, she cried out, "Yes ... yes, I'm here! I'm right here!"

Her voice was strained, and she could only hope it was loud enough to be heard. The noises returned, coming from above through the same small, earthen holes that had brought her air and light.

"Cleora, are you down there?"

Aunt Cleora began weeping with relief.

"Yes, I'm here. I'm right here below you!" She waited anxiously for a reply. "Sojourn, is that you?" she asked, this time more urgently. But she heard nothing more—only more silence.

"Don't go! I said I'm right down here! Don't leave me!" she shouted in panic. "Sojourn! Don't go! Come back! Please come back!"

Then, she saw something glimmering in the dim light—something reflecting one of the moon's rays, spraying the yellow beams all around the prison cell. Whatever was in the hole was twisting— slowly turning back and forth until it popped out of the hole in the stone on top of the cell and descended to her eye level. She grabbed it and cradled it in her palm. It was a key.

Mustering her energy, she rushed to the cell door and pushed her hand through, angling it to insert the thin, metal key into the lock.

Click

The gate was unlocked, and Aunt Cleora quickly pushed it open, listening to it creak in final protest. Then, she ran down the hallway toward the main dungeon door and leaned against it, trusting it would open as well. But this one did not move. Again, she used her key, but as she unlocked this door and nudged it ajar, she saw something unpleasant on the other side—a guard.

Oh no, she thought. She began to turn away when she heard: *Zzzzzz … Zzzzzz*

He's asleep.

Quietly she pushed the door open the rest of the way and slipped past him, noticing his helmet had fallen over his eyes and his snoring was making his jowls jiggle. At the end of the corridor she heard the siren song of water splashing nearby. She followed the new sound, listening as it got ever louder until she saw a fountain. Water was pouring from a hole in the wall, nearly shoulder high, and streaming in a perfect arc into a crescent-shaped pool at her feet. Ravaged with thirst, she stuck her head into the flow.

"*Aah*," she said softly, wiping the drops from her mouth.

But as she turned, she kicked the bottom of a half-filled, rusted bucket, sending the water splashing across the stone floor. The noise was loud and echoed off the rocky walls.

"Who's there?" came a gruff voice from the guard she'd just passed.

She froze, hoping he would go back to sleep once he heard no more sounds. But she saw a shadow stealthily tiptoeing up the hallway toward her, its sword raised over its shoulder.

"I said, who's there?" repeated the guard, turning the corner and drawing closer to her. "I know someone's there! Come out, beforeı ..."

Aunt Cleora slammed the pale into his forehead as he rounded the corner, and she watched as his body crumpled to the floor. She didn't wait to see if she'd knocked him out. Instead, she dashed up the hallway through a series of meandering chambers.

I'm lost, she finally admitted, her eyes drifting left and right trying to figure out where to go. Panicked, she continued, but the light was so dim she stumbled over a large, flat table in the middle of one of the rooms. The old table was low to the ground, and she heard something heavy fall from it as she knocked it over. Squinting, she spotted a tattered book. Picking it up, she noticed there were silk ribbons marking pages within it.

What could this be? she thought.

Aunt Cleora opened it. The words were strange but somehow familiar to her.

Macaara, she realized. *This must be one of the mystical books.*

She read the words and translated as she went.

Conjuring Deadly Pestulances

These conjurings are most deadly and are most difficult to control. Great care must be taken, lest a contagion of catastrophic proportions is unleashed.

Not wanting to waste any more time, she moved to several more bookmarks within the tome, flipping the pages as she read the titles. Finally, she landed on another that caught her eye.

Drink of Compliance

This drink must be prepared precisely. Once imbibed, the person will fall under the complete and utter control of the one who prepared it.

Then later, it read …

There is no known antidote for this potion. Over time, however, persons with strong resistance will be able to overcome its power.

"What's going on down there?" came a voice rattling through the stone walls.

Aunt Cleora picked up the book and hurried through an open door and then up several flights of narrow, stone steps.

At last, she thought *… the castle.*

She was in the Hall of Portraits. It was lined with paintings of royalty, from men dressed in their finest garb to pictures of ladies wearing elaborate dresses with fine lace and high collars. Aunt Cleora didn't stop to look, but there were hundreds of them hung on the walls on both sides.

With the book still tucked under her arm, she finally found the central atrium and the massive front doors. They were closed, but she threw her body against them, and they grudgingly creaked open. Across the moat and the bridge were a sight for sore eyes: Sojourn and Amicus, each riding volarequi from Sojourn's personal stable.

"Sojourn, my brother! And my good friend, Amicus!" she cried out. But then she glanced around. "Where are the guards?" she asked.

"They are resting," said Sojourn with a smile, pointing to either side of the doors.

Indeed, there were four guards, all with small darts embedded in their arms or legs, and all fast asleep.

"It's a potion I created many years ago. I never thought it would work, but there you are," said the Librarian smiling.

"Cleora, come. We must leave at once," said Sojourn.

Just then, the bells in the tower began ringing. This only happened during royal celebrations, victories at war, or when a prisoner escaped. The purpose of this sounding was obvious.

Amicus' winged filly, Cheruba, reacted, first fidgeting nervously and then rearing back on its hind legs, making it difficult for him to control her.

"Get her under control, Amicus. You can't take off if she's not steady," said Sojourn.

Aunt Cleora covered her ears with her palms as the bells continued to peal. But it was what they heard next that sent ice down their spines. The howl of the kujopt hounds rose above the cacophony from the bell tower. These beasts were four-eyed canines that stood three feet high—nine feet on their hind legs, like tigers in the wild. Black and deadly, they could hear keenly, but could only see movement—even with all four eyes focused sharply.

Aunt Cleora panicked and darted across the bridge that spanned the castle moat. She ran; however, smelling fear and hearing her romp, the dogs sprinted after her, their fangs bared and mouths watering.

"Hurry, Cleora! Hurry!" cried Sojourn, steadying his mount. But he saw she was running out of time, as the dogs gained on her. With sweat pouring off her face, she was breathing heavily trying to reach Sojourn. Finally, she crossed the bridge and grabbed for Sojourn's hand. His fingers closed around her wrist, and he began pulling her up.

But a kujopt lunged and sank its teeth into the rear flank of Angele, Sojourn's winged horse, causing her to kick and then jump into the air to flee. Aunt Cleora held on with both hands as the steed rose quickly into the air, flapping its expansive wings feverishly. Dangling in mid-air, Aunt Cleora looked down and screamed.

"I can't hold on much longer!" she cried. "Pull me up!"

Because of the twisting and turning of his horse, Sojourn struggled to lift his sister's small body into the saddle with him.

Amicus was now aloft too, but he was unable to help as the brother and sister flew higher and away from him.

Sojourn leaned over, whispering into his horse's ears before patting her on the neck. Then he said, "Hold on Cleora. You're in for a wild ride. It's a good think I know you can swim."

"What?" she asked, not understanding.

Sojourn could tell Angele was hurting from her wound, and the weight of Aunt Cleora dangling along her side was becoming too much.

"Hang on girl," he said, comforting his horse.

Sojourn clung to his sister's arm another few seconds until they reached the Confuto River.

"I can't hold you any longer, sister. I love you!" he said, as he let go of her hand. He watched her fall, disappearing into the dark waters below. The next thing he heard was a splash ... it was over.

*****

CH 3 - A Cold, New Kingdom

The snow grew heavier, and the winds blew harder, forcing them to cover their faces to prevent frostbite. All around them was a sheet of pure whiteness.

The group had flown out of Dulcenou to escape the oncoming canibola plague which had ravaged Rootan and then veered into its neighboring kingdom to the south. Oliver, Nikko, Gemma and Donus had taken columbas from King Coraga's stables, hoping to divert the pestilence away from the Dulcenou castle and town of Treah. And, as Oliver predicted, the black death followed them.

So, Oliver steered a course north toward another kingdom, Frezia, where he hoped the ice and cold would kill the plague before it destroyed anyone or anything else. Although he believed the plague would die in the frigid air of the north, he didn't realize its effect on their columbas. They couldn't handle the frigid, blustery cold of Frezia and their wings began to freeze. Weakened by flying against the ferocious winds and fighting the intense cold, the birds faltered.

Oliver and Gemma had taken the larger bird to ride, while Donus had grabbed the smaller one. Nikko had hopped from Donus' columba to Oliver's when the bantam bird labored to keep up with the bigger one. But even with less weight on his ride, Donus' struggled to keep up with Oliver and Gemma, and he fell farther and farther behind.

"We have to fall back and help Donus," cried Nikko, pleading with Gemma, who sat just in front of him.

"Where is Donus?" asked Gemma. "He was right behind us."

"You must go back," said Nikko. "I don' see him now."

But Oliver's columba shook her head. "No, I land," she cried. "I sorry."

"You can't!" shouted Gemma.

Yet, the huge bird tucked in her wings and began to drop like a dead-weight stone to the wintery surface below. The treetops came at them quickly, and their small branches began whipping the trio across their faces on their way down. Covered with a light, white, blanket of snow, the trees and the ground were a stark contrast from the hot orange desert and searing sands they had experienced in Sanzotur.

"We going to crash!" shouted Nikko, covering his eyes.

"Brace yourselves," said Oliver, lowering his head.

The bird smashed through the trees and into a deep snowbank, spraying snow and ice. Oliver catapulted over the columba's head, narrowly missing a giant sequa tree trunk with a girth of over thirty feet. Both Gemma and Nikko were launched too, landing only a short distance away—unhurt but a little shaken. Getting up, they brushed off clumps of snow, scraping it out of their ears and nostrils.

"Oliver! Where are you?" Gemma cried out, looking for her friend.

Nothing stirred; nothing made a sound. All was deathly silent.

"Oliver! Oliver!"

Still, there was no sound.

Finally, Oliver popped out of his own snowbank a few yards away, spitting snow and shaking it from his long, red, matted hair.

Gemma laughed.

"What's so funny?" Oliver asked.

"That's what my dog used to do after we gave him a bath," she answered him.

Oliver grimaced, but then smiled. "Okay. Have a good laugh. But we can't stop here. We have to keep moving," he said forcefully and waving them on. He kept looking up into the white fury above them, hoping to see some sign of Donus.

"What about our columba?" asked Nikko.

It was sad, but she had perished. Her eyes were closed—her having been broken in the crash.

"I'm afraid she's gone, Nikko. Right now, we have to find Donus," said Oliver. "He won't make it in this weather alone."

"What we need to do is find a cave," said Gemma. "At least until this storm blows over."

"I don' see any rocks here," said Nikko. "How we find cave?"

"Well, if we stay out in this much longer, we'll freeze to death!" she answered. "Then it won't matter where Donus is."

Indeed, as Nikko looked at Gemma's face, he could see it had begun to turn a bluish gray and ice had begun to form on her golden blonde hair.

"This way!" Oliver shouted above the howling of the winds.

Walking stiffly through the snow, the group fought the urge to sit and rest – something that would mean certain death. Nikko, on the other hand, had a furry coat that helped keep him warmer. Gemma pulled her coat around Nikko so he could curl inside next to her and keep them both warm.

Hours passed, and their desperation grew. Gemma's feet began to grow numb, making it hard for her to keep walking. The light boots she had worn from the castle didn't seem like such a good idea now. And even though she had worn a coat, it was not nearly heavy enough to keep out the intense cold.

Oliver too began to shiver, although he was reluctant to show it. He hadn't worn anything heavy either—the wool coat he had on was enough to keep off a chill, but not fifty degrees below freezing, and soon, he couldn't feel his fingers or toes anymore.

Suddenly, Gemma collapsed unable to go any farther and lay unconscious in the snow. Nikko scampered out from beneath her coat and stood staring at her pale face.

"Master! It's Gemma!" shouted Nikko.

Oliver ran back to her and began warming her cheeks with his hands. He picked her up and cradled her in his arms to give her more heat, but she didn't open her eyes. He knew he needed to get her help.

"We have to find shelter, Nikko. Run ahead and see what might work for us."

Nikko vanished into the white curtain of snow that continued to fall around them. It seemed like an eternity, but he soon came back, his blue coat covered with white flakes and little icicles forming on the tops of his eyelids.

"Up ahead, master. D'ere's a shallow cave. Follow me—it's d'is way," said Nikko, hardly waiting for Oliver to readjust Gemma's limp body in his arms.

Trudging behind his pet, Oliver forced himself to keep moving one foot in front of the other. *Just one foot at a time*, he said to himself. Coming through a grove of trees, he saw the rock formation Nikko had described, and below it, a bear cave. Inside he lay Gemma and propped her head on his satchel.

"Look for some kindling, Nikko. I need to start a fire," Oliver ordered. "Oh, and watch out for the neolithican bear that lives here. He may want his cave back."

"A neolith lives here?" Nikko answered, trembling more from the name than the cold.

"Yeah, I'm afraid so."

"But d'er ..."

"Yeah, I know that too. They're about fifteen feet tall on their hind legs. We'd make a nice snack for it, that's for sure. So, hurry! We don't have a lot of time."

Nikko quickly came with some wood, and Oliver wasted no time to use his flint and ferro bar together with some pyrodust to get a small fire going. Slowly, the heat began to warm Gemma's hands and feet, and the rosiness of her cheeks began to return. She coughed and then opened her hazel eyes, trying to figure out where she was. The crackling fire and warm air helped bring her back to them.

"Good to have you join us!" said Oliver, smiling at his patient. "We'll rest here for the night."

"What about Donus?" Gemma asked weakly.

"I'm afraid he's on his own," said Oliver. "We could be out in this weather for days looking for him. We just don't have the warm clothes for it."

There was little chatter that night. No one was in the mood to talk, and as the snow continued to fall outside, their thoughts turned inward. The day had taken its toll on them. Yet, they were all hopeful for a sunnier, warmer day to follow.

Oliver gathered enough wood to last the night and stoked the fire, making certain it wouldn't go out before daybreak. To the haunting whistle of the wind howling through the trees and the fire crackling inside the cave, the three soon fell asleep.

***

Donus awoke with a massive headache. It throbbed through his temples as though he'd had too much to drink the night before. Slowly, he put his thick forearm against his forehead to see if he were still alive and try to make the pain go away.

"*Ow!*" he said to himself, gently touching the bruise on his head. He felt the lump and pulled away his hand, shocked to see blood on his fingers. *Great!* he thought to himself but otherwise with little emotion.

Looking about, he saw no sign of his ill-tempered columba which had been nothing but trouble since they'd left the castle. It was dark, and he didn't know how long he'd been lying there in the snow. He also couldn't tell where he was—the clouds hid the moons, and with the blizzard he couldn't see more than a few feet in front of him. Cold and hungry, Donus decided to strike out to find food and shelter.

Dizzy and disoriented, he couldn't remember much. In fact, the more he thought about it, the more he realized how empty his head had become. Not only did he not know where he was, he couldn't remember *who* he was or why he was there in the first place. They only thing he recalled was flying on a columba to escape something. Yet, even that, couldn't recollect. All he knew was this place was not his home.

Donus looked in all directions to figure out where to go to find help. He decided to head through the woods, moving south for no other reason than it just seemed like the right way to go. What Donus didn't know was that his friends had landed just *north* of where he was standing, and they had headed north—in the opposite direction.

Again, he would not see any of them for a very long time.

*****

CH 4 - Missing Men

The road north and west of the king's castle in Rootan was narrow and passed through dense undergrowth. But eventually the jungle-like foliage gave way to scrubbier brush and shorter trees as it approached the Frezian Pass. This pass led from Rootan, cutting between the kingdoms of Dulcenou and Frezia and into the western kingdom of Vaporia. The mountain peak of Mt. Aether loomed high above the pass, and the men thanked the God of gods that they could go through it and not have to climb the peak to reach the other side.

Rising only slightly higher than Mt. Gaia, the seven-mile-high peak of Mt. Aether was the tallest on the planet. No life could live at that high altitude where there the temperatures were brutally cold and there was little air for either plants or animals. The craggy blue-gray slopes of the mountain dropped precipitously into the Frezian Pass which stretched for miles between two kingdoms.

"What do the scouts report, Uzi?" asked King Barbarot, now commanding the mightiest army ever assembled in the Realm of Orphus.

Barbarot had taken over where Portenza had left off. However, after killing the former king, Barbarot wasn't interested in the power of the Map of Gneima as was his predecessor. Instead, his sights were more direct. He merely wanted to conquer all the kingdoms of the realm and rule them without challenge—and as soon as possible.

"The sky is clear, sire. The temperatures are right, and the winds calm. Do you wish to proceed?"

Uzi, always the obedient commander, did whatever his master ordered. He had seen the destruction and devastation Barbarot could wreak on people and the countryside, and he wanted no part of that.

"Yes. And make it quick. I don't want my men in that pass any longer than they have to be. It would be too easy for an enemy to ambush us in there," replied the king.

Whipping his volarequez, Uzi scrambled to notify the commanders of the orders. Once into the long and treacherous pass, the weather often became unpredictable, as wind gusts and sudden hail and ice storms could slow or even stop the troops from moving. Worse yet was the rare possibility of an atmospheric vacuum. These "atvacs," as they were known, occurred in strange, swirling wind eddies that suddenly arose and sucked all the air out of an area. If the air didn't return quickly enough, all animal life within it suffocated.

The severe V-shape of the cliffs on either side of the terrain was the telltale sign that the pass was directly ahead of them. It was a narrow passage—only twenty yards wide—making it easy for hostiles above to fire arrows down at them and then disappear into caves that lined the rocky formations above.

Obeying the order to move quickly once inside the pass, the leaders of the first infantry brigades pushed through. After thousands of foot soldiers entered the gorge, it was time for the mechanized divisions. These were led by the merakez attack animals and military assault chariots like the rollopods and argentamors that rambled into the canyon in single file. The merakez had the head of a lion, the body of a bull, and tail with a poisonous, scorpion-like barb. They were a formidable weapon themselves, but when combined with the machines of war, they made an unstoppable force.

Just as the first merakez plodded into the gorge, a roar sounded behind them.

"Stop them!" shouted Barbarot. "Don't let them into the pass!"

"What's wrong?" asked Uzi, startled by the sudden change in plans. "I thought you said to get through as fast as possible?"

"Something isn't right," said the young king. "Only send in one squad of beasts and machines at a time and see what happens.

Warn them to keep a watchful eye. Something's amiss; I can feel it."

Uzi gave the order to Commander Demood who rode to the front of his troops with his flag bearer beside him. Parading his winged, but mottled volarequez, the commander went ahead to lead his men through the pass. He proceeded into the gorge slowly, keeping his eyes peeled for anything that could pose a threat. Only five men, along with one merakez, moved through the narrow opening right behind their leader. The other three hundred rows of warriors, war animals and chariots from the division waited anxiously at the entrance, hoping for a positive sign.

Demood and his small squad was unnerved by the sudden change in plans, and all feared they were being offered as sacrifices to whatever evil or danger their king sensed ahead. Silently they walked, watching, listening, sniffing the air with their shields up and bows ready.

Every hundred yards or so, Cmdr. Demood stopped his men. *"Shhhhhh!"* he whispered. "Stop and listen!"

This went on for several miles; yet, each time they stopped, they only saw geiers, a vulture-like creature with four sets of wings, circling overhead. And aside from the faint smell of mintberries, which grew low to the rocky outcrops, nothing else seemed unusual or suspicious.

One soldier, Onus Yewts, a grade-two archer, stood trembling as he trekked through the valley holding his deadeye crossbow in his hands. He had only been with the king's army for a few weeks and was not hardened to the ways of war like others were. Most of the men in his company were forced to serve the king and were young and inexperienced, like himself.

Yewts' teeth chattered from fright. He jerked his head about like a red-tailed squirrel searching for nuts, making quick, jerky movements. His usually small, brown eyes looked large now as he braced himself for the unknown.

"Halt," whispered the commander again, this time holding up his hand to make sure they heard him. Everyone held their breath and watched as he sniffed the air like a marifian dog. Then, he motioned them onward as if nothing had happened.

After several hours, they reached the midway point of the pass without incident, and the commodore ordered Yewts to take one of the volarequi and fly back to Uzi and the king to let them know they had not encountered anything.

As Yewts left, he saw his squad following the wide trail that led down a tree-lined hill to the beginning of a long, stone bridge that spanned the vast chasm separating Vaporia from its neighbors. Most of the bridge was hidden behind part of the mountain and the bight in the trail itself. The remainder of the pass lay beyond.

The way back to the main army was easier as Yewts flew high above the treacherous pass he had just navigated. As before, he kept a close eye out for anything strange and out of place; however, as before, nothing seemed out of place. In fact, the worst part of the trip was coming out of the pass to the gaze of thousands of eyes watching him, waiting for his report.

Seeing the young lad, Uzi jumped onto his winged horse and flew to him at the pass's opening. Then, landing next to him, he grabbed Yewts by his chain mail,

"Well, what have you learned? Was there anything in the pass?" asked Uzi. "Anything unusual to report?"

Demood listened to the short answer before returning to tell the king.

"Sire," said Uzi, "Yewts reports that the way is clear. There wasn't anything unusual and nothing happened to them as the approached the Vadulroo Bridge, sir."

"Very good," said Barbarot. "Inform the others to move ahead—full speed."

Within minutes, Uzi gave the signal for all troops to begin filing through the pass. The long parade of men, machines and animals made Uzi nervous as he watched the plan of his king carried out. Getting the campaign through the pass would take the rest of the day, even though Yewts' squad would have exited the gorge by the time the rest of the army had entered it.

Yewts was granted permission to fly back to his squad, rejoining them on the other side in Vaporia. He left and traveled once more over the now-familiar terrain until he reached the entrance to the stone bridge. There, the weather turned foul, and a thick mist rolled into the valley below. Still, he could see the huge rocky span, and like others before him, he was awed by its size.

The Bridge of Vadulroo had been built by the peoples of Vaporia, Dulcenou and Rootan to help with trade in the area. It had taken centuries to lay the stones and cement the massive archways in place. Although heavy, gray clouds and fog covered much of the span, Yewts could tell the bridge was likely an incredible sight in the fullness of the day's rays.

Standing just below the trail and before it joined the bridge was the dark figure of a man, as if hiding in the brush. Yewts flew his volarequez down to the steep drop-off and landed only yards away from him.

"You there!" said Yewts, catching the man by surprise. Instantly, Yewts recognized him from his squad. "Shollip, is that you?" Shollip was another archer of the same rank but with more experience than that of Yewts.

Shollip shrank back into the thick underbrush trying to hide.

"Come out of there, Shollip!" shouted Yewts. "Why are you hiding like that? Where is the rest of the squad? Where is Commodore Demood?"

"Yewts?" said the man stumbling as he pulled himself out of the thorny morass. "They … they went across the bridge, Yewts. That's the last I saw of them."

"Why didn't you go with them?"

Shollip looked at the ground as if ashamed. "I … we … "

"I … we what?"

"Yewts, my friend, this is the last place I saw them. Well, actually, it was back there before the trail started. But I saw them go down the trail toward this bridge."

Yewts could see the twitch in Shollip's face get deeper and faster.

"Then?" asked Yewts.

"They just disappeared into a fog that suddenly rolled in. It was like it 'ate' them. I can't describe it."

"Did you go looking for them?"

"Yes."

"And?"

Shollip looked away, trembling.

Yewts looked at Shollip and wasn't sure what to believe.

"Okay," said Yewts, "then let's go and see where they are now."

Yewts pulled Shollip up onto his steed, and they moved onward across the bridge. Hoping things would clear and they could see better, they found instead the weather turning fouler as the mist grew denser. Soon the winds gusted, and the rains came, pelting them with pebble-sized hail from above.

They pushed on, struggling against the winds until they reached the bridge's midpoint. And, as if walking through a door, they found themselves in a column of brilliant light streaming through a vortex in the clouds. The air was still and calm, and the temperature was warm and comforting. But Shollip could sense something ahead of them.

"It's up there," he said to Yewts.

"What's up there?"

"Just keep going," said the other archer. "You'll see soon enough."

Their horse walked on until Yewts pulled on the reins. "What is that?" he asked, peering many yards ahead.

"That must be the edge of our paradise inside this vortex," said the other man. "But it's what's on the other side that … I can't. I can't go any farther, Yewts."

"You have to, Shollip."

"It frightens me."

"How can you see? All I see is a gray veil ahead of us."

"We will go back into foul weather, but it's then when we'll see it."

Yewts didn't understand, but he kicked his horse and moved along until they reached the odd, gray curtain that hung across the bridge span. He stopped and put his hand through it to be sure they could continue. Indeed, his hand and arm disappeared behind it.

"Are you sure you want to go on?" asked the other man.

Yewts didn't answer. He already knew the answer and so did Shollip."

They passed through the gray cloud, and the rain and sleet again began to pummel them.

"There," said Shollip, pointing. "Over there."

Along the side of the bridge were dark piles of something, but it was impossible to figure out that they were. The clouds were so thick and heavy there wasn't enough light to show them.

Coming up to the heaps, Yewts recognized equipment from their squad. There were tunics and weapon bags all over the ground, as well as a number of swords and shields. Several of the satchels had been blown to one side, and Yewts watched as they clung precariously to some broken limbs of a small quarterbush. He tried to pick one up, but the wind caught it, lifting it from the dead branch and tossing it over the cliff. He watched, helplessly, as it became smaller and smaller, before vanishing altogether.

"What do you think happened, sir?" asked Yewts.

"Dunno," was the only reply he got.

They continued across the bridge, when Yewts saw a sword abandoned near a large boulder. He picked it up; it had blood on it, smeared from the tip to the guard and grip.

"Look at this!" he said to Shollip. "What do you make of it? It looks like they were in a fight, doesn't it? But then, where are *they*? Where are the bodies?"

"What did you tell the king?" asked Shollip.

"I told him the way was clear—at least as far as the bridge."

"I see. Then, how do you think he's going to react to seeing this?" Shollip broadened his arms to show the carnage all around them.

"He's not going to be happy."

"No, and who do you think he's going to take it out on?"

Yewts now understood. "What do we do?" he asked.

"I don't see anything here, do you?" Shollip asked with a feeble smile. "At least, I hope not, and I hope the king doesn't when he arrives. Now, I suggest you help me clean up this mess, soldier."

Yewts watched as Shollip took piles in his arms and walked them to the edge of the bridge. There, he threw them out as far from the span as he could where they couldn't easily be seen.

Shollip looked over at Yewts. "Well?" he said to him. "Are you helping or not?"

Yewts began picking up everything in sight and tossing them over the side into the abyss below. The wind was picking up, and it became harder to get rid of the evidence, as some blew back toward the span. But when they had almost finished, Yewts saw something in the mud. He pulled it out and looked it over. It was a gray, slimy tentacle, some three feet long. It was blue-gray and had suckers all over it. It had been cut off from whatever had owned it. Yewts thought about asking Shollip about it but then decided not to. He then just shrugged and tossed it off the pier with the rest of the evidence.

After finishing, they waited for the first of Barbarot's mechanized army to come to the bridge. Uzi was with them.

"It's all clear," said Yewts to his superior.

"You didn't stay with your squad then?" asked Uzi, looking confused.

"No, they went on ahead. I'm sure we will catch up with them at the end of the pass."

"Yes, you're probably right," said Uzi. "We need to hurry if we want to get all these animals and men through before nightfall."

"Yes, sir," said Yewts.

Uzi chose to fly across the bridge on his volarequez instead of walking. Later, Yewts uttered a prayer of thanks for that. For as he walked with the next group over the span, he saw several more succors and tentacle arms they had missed during their initial clean up. *We were lucky*, he thought, *that no one else spotted them either—whatever they are.*

*****

CH 5 - A Conunder and a Stranger

The snow had stopped falling, and the winds had died down just enough for them to feel their fingers and toes once more. Oliver, Gemma and Nikko continued to huddle around the fire, not wanting to leave its heat or the protection of the bear cave where they'd spent the night. It was morning now, and the clouds were beginning to part in the sky. Gemma rubbed her hands and feet, feeling life returning in them. Although well-rested for traveling, they knew from experience that without food they would only grow weaker. Time was not on their side as they had no idea when the next storm might blow in and force them to find another cave. Food was a priority.

"Which way?" asked Nikko.

Oliver pulled out his compass and opened it as he had in the past. However, neither the rings nor the pointer moved—they were frozen solid. He gently placed the device near the fire, hoping to thaw it, but it heated too quickly and melted not only the ice but part of the casing, causing it to spin wildly out of control.

"Stupid thing!" said Oliver, finally putting it away.

"Maybe if you nicer to it, it be nice back!" said Nikko, grinning at him.

"Oh, shut up!" snapped Oliver, cranky after having gotten so little sleep the night before.

Gemma just shook her head and started walking out of the cave.

"Where are you going?" asked Oliver.

"This way. Do you have any better ideas?" she asked dismissively, not bothering to turn around and listen.

Hearing her tone, Oliver and Nikko followed her. It was the blind leading the blind, but Oliver just hoped that lady luck was with them that day. It was badly needed.

As they moved through the deep snow, Oliver noticed the tracks of small animals, like the nilithian badger, the white-horned ferret and the furry bundi, with its cat-like face and long, springy legs. But what troubled him were the much larger tracks—the twenty-inch paw prints of what he guessed was an arctic, yombatin tiger which grew to over eleven feet long in the more arid and warmer climates. But ones with this size, he figured, would be well over fifteen feet.

"What on earth are d'ose?" Nikko asked finally, pointing to imprints in the snow that passed between two, good-sized, spiritus fir trees. The markings suggested that the tiger had been moving through the snow to that point but had abruptly stopped. There were no prints going away from that spot in any direction, as if it had been plucked out of thin air.

"Odd," said Oliver, now more concerned.

"Which ones?" asked Gemma. "What are you talking about?"

"Oh, never mind. Don't worry about it," said Oliver. He didn't want to upset them until he knew more. There would be a time and a place—but he didn't think it was then or there.

But when he looked up into the trees, he saw it. Indeed, it was a yombatin tiger—an enormous specimen of over fifteen feet. Oliver took a quick breath—his heart almost stopping. But fortunately for them, it was fast asleep sitting on a thick branch high up in the tree.

"Let's move along," said Oliver, keeping a watchful eye on it. "We need to hurry if we want to find food somewhere."

The day wore on, and even though Oliver navigated by the angle of the two suns, it seemed like they had not traveled far. The snow drifts were getting deeper, making it harder to get through without sinking deeply into the light powder. Worse, they were expending a lot of energy.

Oliver stopped to let the others rest. He took a woody vine and made a noose. Then, he set two poles two feet apart, bracing each one. Stringing the noose between them, he made sure the opening was about the right height to snag a bundi. He made several more and place them around the area.

"Why you doing d'at?" asked Nikko. "We staying here tonight?"

"No, but if we come back through here and need food, hopefully, there will be a nice, frozen bundi waiting for us."

"Oliver, I'm tired ... let's stay here tonight anyway, okay?" said Gemma.

She was getting cold, and Oliver worried the frigid weather was not only taking its toll on her, but all of them. Nikko, too, looked bluer than normal—as if hypothermia were beginning to settle in. At the same time, if they stopped, Oliver worried they may fall asleep and freeze to death.

"No, Gemma, we must keep moving. We have to find another shelter where I can make a fire," said Oliver, lifting her to her feet.

Reluctantly, she got up, and Oliver helped her for a few steps until she was walking again. However, within a few seconds, he did not hear her behind him anymore.

"Master!" exclaimed Nikko. "She not waking up, master!"

Gemma was sprawled out on the snow; her eyes closed. Oliver went back and knelt, gently patting her face with his hands and trying to get her awake.

"Will she be okay?" asked Nikko, nervously watching over her.

"I'll just have to make a fire. Go find some branches, and we'll try to build a shelter right here," said Oliver.

It was the second time they'd been forced to stop by the freezing weather, but this time things were far graver. The wind began blowing stiffly again, making it hard to get a fire started. Nikko gathered small twigs and sticks, while Oliver found some dry needles that were still hanging from dead branches on some trees. The flint, ferro bar and pyrodust came out of his satchel, and he began striking the bar to get a spark to light the dust and pine needles. But as soon as the needles caught the spark, they went out—extinguished by the winds swirling incessantly around them.

"What we going to do?" cried Nikko.

Oliver remained hopefully, but even his ember of optimism was cooling quickly.

"What is it that you seek?"

It was a familiar voice and one which came from behind a nearby spiritus fir tree. Oliver didn't have to go searching to find the source; he knew the source would come to him.

Oliver smiled. "Our friend is back, Nikko, and its timing couldn't be better."

The Conunder was a strange creature. It had a baby's face but other characteristics of an old man. It hobbled and walked with a cane—slowly and methodically. It appeared out of nowhere and always came bearing a riddle. Its intent was to help, but the message was sometimes so obscure it was hard to know what it meant. Solving the riddle was the key.

The first time it had appeared to Oliver at the Gates of Kronos after a disastrous avalanche had killed many of his king's men. The second time, in the Riakalah Desert, it had helped Gemma by healing her wound, but then had given them a second riddle to solve. Both riddles had come from the *Book of Gneima*, the second book of the sacred *Tribal Noque Trilo*gy.

"My friend, my friend. It is good to see you again," Oliver said with a smile.

But the Conunder did not return the smile; it seemed never to show emotion. Instead, it merely repeated the question. "What is it that you seek?" This time, its voice was raspy and coarse.

"Can you help Gemma? She's starting to fade on us, and I'm afraid if she sleeps, she won't wake up," said Oliver, pleadingly.

This time the Conunder did not move toward her as he had in the desert. He merely looked down at her and said calmly:

> *Escape will be daunting, imperiled and grave*
> *Through the air both will fly far and wide*
> *A friendship's thread that holds them as one*
> *Will be cut as if thoughts have just died.*

> *The way for the other will be frigid and raw*
> *The ice will close in with disdain*
> *It is there that he'll search in a cave for the truth*
> *A secret that will bring him much pain.*

"That's exactly what Queen Clytie told Donus when they read from the *Book of Gneima!*" exclaimed Oliver.

Oliver took out the manuscript and unrolled it until he came to the section the Conunder was quoting.

"Here it is." said Oliver. "It says, *'Escape will be daunting, imperiled and grave ...'*" Oliver stopped and looked up. "It's just what's in the book."

"What's next part?" asked Nikko.

Oliver began reading again, but as he did, the Conunder joined him in delivering the lines from memory ...

> *By three he will find the prize that he seeks*
> *In the course of a quest he will strive*
> *But beware of the number that blocks his path*
> *His life or another's won't survive.*

> *The key may lie in the faith that one brings*
> *For after a war, what is left?*
> *Be grateful indeed if he lives through it all*
> *For the next trek may leave him bereft.*

"D'at not sound good," said Nikko.

"Hey, I don't choose them, Nikko, so don't complain to me," said Oliver.

It was then that the Conunder looked over his shoulder, hearing something the others hadn't. In an instant, he vanished as mysteriously as he'd come.

"Who's there?" It was a high-pitched and melodic voice from some distance away.

Gemma still lay unmoving. Her ashen-white face becoming more rigid as the minutes passed.

"We're right here!" yelled Oliver. "Right over here!"

Nikko whispered angrily to Oliver, "Are you crazy? How you know if d'ey friendlies? D'ey could be murderers just waiting to kill us and take everyd'ing we have!"

"Settle down, Nikko," said Oliver, still trying to make out the figure coming toward them through the woods.

"Hello? Hello?" said the voice as the shadow drew nearer.

"Hurry!" Oliver called out again. "We need help!"

Moving slowly through the woods came a tall, thin hunter carrying a long bow and a green quiver full of arrows on his back. The forager was wrapped from head to toe in heavy, dark clothing. His head was completely covered with a fur hat covering his head and ears and a black woolen scarf hiding his face and neck. It was clear the person was a native of the cold climate as his coat was thick, sewn from the skins of many animals, and his boots were lined with the same heavy, black fur.

"Who are you?" mumbled the hunter, who had not drawn his weapon.

"I'm Oliver, and this is Nikko. We're here with our friend Gemma, who, as you can see, needs to get help quickly. She's freezing, and I'm afraid she won't pull out of it unless we get her someplace warm."

The figure nodded and said abruptly, "Follow me."

Oliver picked up Gemma and followed after him.

"Wait up!" shouted Nikko, who was scampering behind.

The deep snow made it difficult for the little blue monkey, and he had to jump from spot to spot, sinking deeply into the powder each time. But Nikko's thoughts of a short journey were quickly bashed as the hunter didn't stop once to let them rest. He continued on through the snow and the forest, never looking back to see if they were still following.

"How are you doin' back there, Nikko," asked Oliver, laboring as he carried Gemma.

"I back here ... I coming."

They reached an open field where the winds picked up, making it harder to walk. It wasn't snowing, but it was still gray and overcast, with clouds so thick that little light was able to poke through. Finally, they reached a steeply-graded hill, and Oliver let out a moan, struggling to go on.

"Come on, master," encouraged Nikko. "I sure it not much more."

But the climb was painful, and the burning in Oliver's thighs only got worse as the snow and ice began to fall once more.

"How much farther?" Oliver shouted to the mysterious figure still plodding ahead. However, the hunter only turned around long enough to see if they were still close behind him and kept going.

As they drew closer to the peak, the figure slowed and then, reaching the summit, stopped.

"There," he said to Oliver, pointing downward.

"*Wow!*" Nikko exclaimed, looking out.

The snowy slope gently descended into a magnificent, basin— one horseshoe-shaped and ringed by a series of majestic mountain ridges. The whiteness of the wintery powder extended as far as the eye could see in all directions with the exception of one area in the center. Taking up most of the basin was a sapphire blue lake—unfrozen with a misty steam rising from its surface. Around the perimeter was a sandy shoreline, offering an other-worldly picture of something completely out of place with its surroundings. It was forty degrees below freezing, yet there was an unfrozen lake stretching out before them.

"And look d'ere!" said Nikko pointing to something for his master's attention.

At the far end of the oval-shaped body of water, stood a grand, white castle that glistened even though it was overcast. The castle looked like it was made of solid ice with three turrets that soared high above the valley floor and were capped with iridescent blue, cone-shaped bonnets with rings of gold around each one. Around the castle walls was a wide moat—again, strangely not frozen, but instead, glimmering with deep, azure water. The mist from the water made the castle loom high in a shroud of mystery and awe.

Just outside the castle, a village lay on one side of the lake, mostly in the lower levels of the mountain range around it. Outside of the village and surrounding the castle was a thick stone wall that offered a ring of protection for both the townspeople and royalty.

"Nikko! Let's get going before we lose sight of the hunter!" Oliver said as he stumbled down the slope, jostling Gemma's tiny frame as he lurched from side to side trying to balance her.

The village looked a lot farther away than it really was, and before long they entered through an arch in the wall. Oliver thought it odd there were no guards. The rocked street had already been cleared of snow and led directly into the heart of the village. It was a grand boulevard lined with tall, lush trees and shops that lay empty, presumably until the springtime. The road led to the great castle, where it widened—far different from the narrow lane that started down by the lake.

"So, what do you call your town?" shouted Oliver to the stranger.

However, there was no answer. The hunter didn't even turn to acknowledge he had heard him. Instead, he continued briskly ahead, not waiting for Oliver or Nikko but seemingly hastening his pace to get to the sentry station which came into view ahead.

The guardhouse was a small, cabin-like building with a chimney that belched black smoke and a roof-line that was made of red tile and brown walls from the stones of the nearby shoreline. Reaching the station, the hunter stopped, pointed at the three behind him and continued through. The guards inside merely peered outside the window and waved to strange figure, not stopping him to check his identity or his papers.

Oliver prepared to stop and put Gemma down onto the frozen stones to answer stiff questions about where he was from and why he was there. He was nervous. As he drew near, stumbling with his precious load, the guard inside the hut came out from the doorway. Wearing a brown, fur hat snuggly tied around his head and a heavy wool coat down to his knees, the guard looked at him without expression. Oliver smiled and nodded to him, pointing toward the figure who'd just gone through. The guard gave a quick smile in return and just waved them through, hurrying back inside the hut to get out of the subzero weather.

After passing through the wall, they approached the castle where Oliver looked up. It was, indeed, enormous—much bigger than either castle in Rootan or Dulcenou. With seven spires, it was a wonderous and humbling sight. Each spire was gilded in gold and two stood over one hundred feet in the air. There were three massive stone towers at the corners with slotted windows top to bottom for archers to fire on invaders attacking from below. Oliver counted over six levels of the castle, each with hundreds of wider windows peering out over the lake and the countryside. The lake drained into a deep moat that encircled the castle, and the stone bridge leading to the palace spanned the hundred feet to connect the king to the outside world. In the center of the bridge lay wooden planking that could be raised or lowered by a system of pulleys on the far side of the bridge by the castle's iron gate.

"Nikko! Did you see where the hunter went?" asked Oliver, frantically.

"I d'ink he went across bridge, master," said Nikko.

"I don't see him, Nikko. Do you?"

Nikko turned his head in all directions. "No, master. I don't."

Oliver groaned.

"Now what?" asked his pet.

"We have no choice, Nikko. Keep going." Oliver pointed straight ahead across the bridge and the moat.

The blue pithicaan monkey bounded across the bridge as the steamy mist rose from the moat. After reaching the other side, he found the gate to the castle, which was locked, but the road didn't end there. Instead, it split off in both directions going around the castle and its perimeter.

"How did the hunter get into the castle?" asked Oliver. "I know he went across the bridge."

"I d'ink he went d'is way," said Nikko, moving to his right around the path. Then, he stopped. "No, maybe he went back d'at way."

"Pick one," said Oliver, struggling a bit more with Gemma on his shoulder.

Nikko headed off to the right side of the fork not knowing if it was the way or not. The snow clung to most of the bushes and trees surrounding the castle, and icicles lined the lower roofline where the higher angles of the palace came down to the main level. Yet, the cascade of long stalactites hanging from the edge of the roof melded into the slick, wet stones the castle making them look part of the same icy wall.

They walked the path on the outside of the castle—all the way around—until they found themselves back at their starting point at the bridge. By now, Oliver's arms ached, and his patience was growing then.

"Where the heck is the entrance?" he shouted. "The castle has no doors!"

Curious, Nikko walked up to the castle wall and touched it. "It ice, master! It not stone!" he said, licking his fingers to warm them.

"It can't be, Nikko. It looks like stone," said Oliver.

"It not. It ice, master. I swear!"

At that moment, a door appeared where Nikko had touched the wall. It was built into the castle wall and was barely visible.

"D'is way!" cried Nikko, pushing with his tiny blue hands against the outline in the ice.

The door moved, as if on invisible hinges, swinging inward and out of the way. Oliver followed the little blue monkey through the entry, hoping to find warmer temperatures in the castle.

Once inside, they walked down a narrow hallway with walls made of sheer ice extending upwards forty or fifty feet. Mounted on the walls were lanterns that gave off an eerie, flickering light that gave off different colors at different angles. It was strange, though, that the flames didn't seem to melt the iced walls or the ice overhead. Although the building was cold, the fire from the iron lanterns was warm and danced as if delighted to have new guests to entertain.

Oliver put Gemma down on a long runner made of black animal fur that ran the length of the hallway. He rubbed her hands and blew his warmth onto her fingers to bring life back to her. She was still breathing, but her face was still and pasty.

"How is she?" came the same muffled voice that Oliver had heard in the woods. However, this time it easier to understand without the wind blowing around them.

The figure emerged from a hidden doorway in the corridor and was still covered with leather, fur and heavy wool clothing.

"I think she'll make it," said Oliver. Then glancing up at the hunter, he asked. "What's your name?"

The hunter removed his bow, quiver and other belts that held his knife and water skein. Then, he took off his hat and scarf and dropped them on the floor.

"My name is Corrival, but you can call me Cori," came the distinctively female voice.

Oliver gasped. "You're a girl?" he blurted out crudely.

The hunter only scowled at him. The voice had been so muffled under all the wraps it had sounded deep and masculine. All that had now changed.

"I'm sorry," said Oliver, "I just thought that ..."

 ... that I was a guy?" she said with a snap in her voice. "No, I'm not and never have been. Thank you very much."

"Sorry!" repeated Oliver. "Your voice was hard to understand, that's all. And, you were out hunting, so I thought ..."

"... only men like to hunt?" she asked, finishing his sentence for him.

Oliver felt bad. Standing over him was a petite young girl, not much older than he was, if at all. She was clearly no servant, as she held her head high and had the confidence of someone with much higher standing. With short, straight black hair and large almond shaped, green eyes, she was quite attractive. The redness in her cheeks only added to her beauty.

"I'm Oliver, and this is my best friend, Nikko," stuttered Oliver, his eyes fixed on her.

"Pretty girl," said the young woman looking down at Gemma, whom Oliver had laid gently on the floor.

"No, no ..." mumbled Oliver, "... this is Nikko," he said clumsily, bringing his blue pet monkey over to his side.

Cori rolled her eyes. "No, I'm talking about *her*," she said, pointing directly at the girl lying unconscious next to Oliver.

"Oh, dat's Gemma," said Nikko, filling in the gaps while Oliver sat speechless.

"Nice to meet you Nikko," answered Cori. "We'll have to get her upstairs and into a warm bath to get her temperature back to normal. Follow me."

Oliver was still mesmerized by her. There was something about those emerald eyes that drew him in. They showed strength and power but at the same time a remoteness Oliver had never seen before.

Cori led them up a winding staircase where they were greeted by two women attendants. Like Cori, they, too, were petite, although dressed in light, tan cloaks with white, furry hoods scrunched around their heads to keep warm.

"Margi ... Nupha, take this one for a warm bath—not too hot, for it could burn her," Cori instructed her attendants.

Oliver hesitated when they picked Gemma off the floor and carried her away. He started to follow them as they left the room.

"So, you two must be *very* good friends," said Cori, grinning mischievously, "because you know she'll be bare in the tub while you watch."

"Oh, of course," replied Oliver, turning lightly pink. He realized what she was saying and stepped back to where Nikko and Cori were standing. "We're friends, just friends."

Through an adjacent doorway cut into the wall came another young woman. She resembled Cori in many ways, except her hair was a reddish-brown. Her cheekbones were high and glowed a deep pink, either because of the cool air or a touch of rouge. Like Cori, her face was oval-shaped, and her eyes a brilliant green. Unlike Cori, she was dressed royally. Her gown was of an amethyst satin with gold stars of different sizes embroidered throughout. It flowed to the floor and trailed behind her a good two feet or more. Around her neck was a diamond necklace that sparkled in the light of the lanterns on the wall. Oliver guessed the two were sisters and that this one was Cori's older sibling.

"Well, hello!" said the young woman, checking out the handsome young knight. "And who have you brought home with you this time, sister?" she asked of Cori. Her eyelashes flashed and her smile broadened. It was clear she was not ashamed to flirt openly with newcomers.

"Don't start!" said Cori, belligerently.

It didn't take long for Oliver and Nikko to figure out that these two were, indeed, sisters but not friends.

Oliver greeted the young woman, introducing himself. "I'm Oliver of Rootan, and this is Nikko."

"Nice to meet you Oliver of Rootan," the young woman replied. "I'm Prima, and I see you've already met my little sister, Cori."

"Younger! Not, little!" Cori corrected her.

Oliver could see the animosity.

"Ladies, ladies!" said Oliver, trying to calm them. "Please, let's not argue, shall we!"

The cold stares between the two women continued despite Oliver's request.

"You're a long way from Rootan," said Prima. "In fact, I've never met anyone from there. What are you doing here in Frezia?"

Oliver went on to explain that they had been chased by a viral plague that had destroyed half of their kingdom. He told them how they had flown to Frezia, killing the disease before it killed them.

"But you say you lost one of your friends along the way—there was another?" asked Cori.

"Yeah," replied Nikko, sadly. "Donus and his columba crash somewhere between here and Dulcenou. We don' know where he is."

"Where we landed was far from here," Oliver added, "and even if we find him, we might freeze to death in the process."

"Well, at least you three are safe here," said Prima. "We have a fully-stocked kitchen and plenty of rooms to spare. We're happy to have you as our guests."

"Why don't you join us for dinner?" asked Cori. "Father would love to meet you."

"Splendid idea!" repeated Prima. "It's all settled. You'll come to dinner, and we'll talk more."

"Where would d'at be?" asked Nikko. "Do we have to go far?"

The two ladies laughed.

"I don't think so," said Prima. "Our father is the King of Frezia. This is his castle. You can also meet our mother, the queen." Prima clapped her hands twice. "Margi and Nupha will take you to your quarters, and we'll see you again in the dining hall."

"What about Gemma?" asked Oliver, particularly concerned with her welt being.

"Oh, she'll be fine," said Cori. "If she's up to it, we'll bring her down with us when it's time."

*****

CH 6 - Saving Aunt Cleora

"Let me get her!" yelled Amicus, riding behind Sojourn and seeing Aunt Cleora fall from her brother's grasp.

"No, Amicus! I can't lose you too. Be patient," Sojourn said calmly, "We'll find her ... we *must* find her."

The warriors on top of the castle walls continued to rain arrows down on them. One arrow flew so close to Sojourn's head that he heard a *zinging* sound that startled him. Reacting, he pulled on the reins jerking Angele, his horse, and making her buck, nearly throwing him off.

"Did you see where she fell?" asked Amicus, still circling the area where she dropped into the river. His volarequez flapped her wings quickly to stay aloft and hover over the rushing waters below.

"Yeah, I think it was over there," said Sojourn, "but she would have floated downstream with the current. She'd be farther that way," he added pointing away from the castle.

Sojourn and Amicus steered their volarequi downstream and away from the barrage of missiles coming from the castle towers.

Amicus' horse, Cheruba, followed the beating wings of Angele while her rider kept a close watch on the stream below for anyone moving in the currents or along the banks. Puffy black clouds were beginning to roll in from the west, casting dark shadows over the green grasslands of the kingdom.

"Drop down. I think I see her!" shouted Amicus, pointing farther down the river.

The darkness and mist surrounding the fomenting river made it hard to see clearly. However, there was something bobbing in the center of the fast-flowing stream. The water swirled and spun, twirling the object around like a silver top on a table.

"Cleora!" yelled Sojourn, hovering just above the white tops of the rapids.

"Here, Sojourn! I'm down here!" came the familiar voice.

Amicus followed the struggling figure in the water as the stream pushed it just out of reach. Yet, as he watched carefully, he spotted a mysterious, dark section of the otherwise blue river ahead.

"Sojourn, look there! What is that black area in the middle of the river there?" asked Amicus.

"Oh, no!" cried Sojourn.

"What is it?"

"It's a nether vortex," said Sojourn, gasping. "It sucks in everything that comes near it. The water reaches it and gets pulled down with whatever it's carrying. The water is usually spit back out, but not whatever went in with it. That can never escape."

"Cleora!" cried Amicus in despair. "Sojourn, we have to dive in and save her! Otherwise, she'll get sucked in!"

"Cleora, get to shore! You've got to swim to the shore, *now!*" shrieked Sojourn, kicking the sides of Angele to get her to drop down toward his sister.

"What?" she asked. "I can't hear you!"

The waves were rolling over her head, making her cough as she began breathing in water.

"Let's go Cheruba!" Amicus yelled as he leaned forward to push his winged horse down into the blackness. The filly moved faster than he'd ever seen her. She knew the urgency and dropped in near free-fall toward the raging waves.

Aunt Cleora floated closer and closer to the vortex, seemingly unaware of the fate waiting her. However, as the water began swirling more violently, she began to scream.

"Sojourn! Amicus! Help!" Her body kept bobbing up and down, and she began flailing her arms.

Cheruba swooped in low, and Amicus reached for Aunt Cleora's hand. But her fingers slipped through.

"Try again!" shouted Sojourn.

Amicus again dove, steering his winged horse even closer. This time, the roiling waters splashed up onto Cheruba's flanks and its wings were getting wet from the spray.

"Don't go too low or her feathers will get too wet, and you'll fall into the water!" shouted Sojourn.

The nether vortex started to tug on Aunt Cleora, pulling her in, and she began spinning faster inside the swirling blackness, closer and closer to the vortex's center and ultimate doom. Logs and other bits of debris that were already in the throes of the vortex and were quickly vanishing down the throat of this insatiable monster.

Amicus lunged for Aunt Cleora again, this time grabbing onto her wrist. "I've got you, Cleora! Just hang on!"

Aunt Cleora used all her strength to cling to her lifeline. Her arm began twisting in Amicus's palm as the current twirled her body.

"No, no …" Amicus shouted, feeling his grip loosen.

Finally, her small wrist was ripped away from him, and she resumed her death spiral into the blackness.

"Amicus! Don't leave me ..."

The two men watched as she entered the inner orbit of the whirlpool and began revolving around its eye, faster and faster as a fourth and final act of this tragedy.

"What else can we do?" screamed Amicus, his eyes imploring help from his friend.

"*Nooooooo!*" Sojourn shouted as his sister vanished into the maw of the rotating tornado.

She was gone, but the water continued to spin, falling into the black hole in the center.

"Cleora!" shouted Amicus, pitifully; then, he broke down and began to sob.

Sojourn too was struck with grief, and he motioned for Amicus to set Cheruba down on the riverbank. They dismounted and fell down on the wet rocks, crying like infants in a nursery. There were no words. There were none to be said.

"Sojourn!"

Sojourn looked up, hearing the voice.

"Sojourn! Amicus!"

Far downstream they saw a shadowy figure crawling out of the river and onto the shoreline.

Both of the men rushed to their horses and flew directly to where the figure lay. It was Aunt Cleora. Overhead, the suns were breaking onto a new day, signaling a change from the dark clouds that had been casting doom and gloom on them. Her eyes opened, but she grimaced, putting her hand to the back of her head, giving it a tender rub.

"Boy, does that hurt," she said, trying to lift her head. "What happened?"

"Not much," laughed Sojourn. "Sis', it was just the usual, you know. You nearly got caught getting out of the Forgotten Prison, shot at while hanging high-up in the air from a volarequez, escaped drowning in a nether vortex and got spit out onto the riverbank without completely splitting your skull open. That's all," said Sojourn smiling. "I think you used eight of your nine lives this time."

"I think I must have eighteen 'cause I think I must have burned through at least eight before this day even started," she said, still rubbing her head.

Amicus laughed. "I think you're right, Cleora. You must be up to at least sixteen or seventeen by now."

"Good to have you back, sis'," said Sojourn, putting his hand gently on her face and giving her comfort.

"We thought you were gone when you got sucked down into that vortex," said Amicus.

"You're lucky," replied Sojourn.

"I guess you just left a bad taste in that thing's mouth, the way it spit you out like that," said Amicus, chuckling.

"Yeah sis', and we always thought you were made of sweetness. Who would have known that wasn't true?" joked Sojourn.

"Very funny!" exclaimed Aunt Cleora, smiling.

"Good thing there was another port to the vortex tunnel," said Sojourn. "That's where you came out—just farther down the river."

"Well, good thing," said Amicus lovingly. "I … we would have missed you."

Aunt Cleora saw the love in his eyes, and it gave her comfort.

"So, what's next?" she asked still rubbing her head.

"What do you mean?" asked Amicus. "Wasn't this adventure enough for a while?"

"I dunno. As Nikko used to say, 'our adventure is only starting, I'm afraid'," she replied.

"At my age, dearie, this adventure better be *well* underway by now, or I'm never going to see it to the end!" said Sojourn, shaking his head.

*****

CH 7 - The Bridge of Vadulroo

As Barbarot's main army approached the Bridge of Vadulroo, Uzi raised his hand. Behind him, the troops ground to a stop, nearly bumping into one another with the surprise change in plans. He had flown back across the span to ensure the rest of his troops made it safely across.

"Why are we stopping?" demanded Barbarot, riding furiously up to where Uzi had given his order.

"I'm afraid there may be too much weight on this span of the bridge," answered Uzi. "If we send over a full division at a time, we will have problems. If it's only a brigade, I think we'll be fine. I just don't want to take the chance.

"I don't care what you think!" scowled the king. "I want the army across that bridge as soon as possible. Now, make it happen!"

Uzi swallowed and bit his tip. "Yes, my liege. As you wish."

He reversed his order and reluctantly gave the go-ahead for the troops to resume their march across the broad, expansive piece of rock.

The infantry divisions made their way over the bridge slowly and without incident. The archers and some of the lighter supply wagons then crossed; they too had no problems. Uzi badgered and threatened them to march faster to lessen the weight concentrated in any one point and allow the heavier, mechanized divisions to pass over as soon as they could.

Temperatures from the morning chill began to rise, becoming more temperate as the cavalry began to move over the span. Neither the volarequi nor the meraki had any difficulties navigating the narrowness of the bridge. The winged horses were accustomed to flying high over hills and dales, and although this pass was much higher, they seemed at ease with it. The meraki, a less intelligent animal, either didn't understand the danger or didn't care.

It was only when the mechanized divisions started across that the tremors began. At first, the shaking was minor, but as more rollopods and sinjay orb slings made their way onto the rocky overpass, the vibrations increased.

"My Lord," said Uzi to Barbarot, "I think we need to slow the crossing. Can you feel the shaking under our feet?"

The king only scowled.

Uzi sighed and went back to reprimanding his officers, pushing them even harder to get their men to the other side so they could regroup and set camp before evening came.

But the rocking of the bridge only worsened. After the vibrations started, they reinforced themselves—compounding the problem, making the shaking worse by the minute. Soon, the pulses had become so severe that the men could no longer walk. They fell and had trouble getting up again.

By then, it was too late.

The pods and slings flipped over or were tossed off the edge by the quaking bridge. Rock from the surrounding cliffs began tumbling down on top of them as small pebbles were followed by larger and larger stones loosened by the rolling cascade down the mountainside. Behind these rocks, however, was a sea of huge boulders baring down on the thousands of soldiers still standing on the bridge span.

"Land slide!" cried out one of the commanders. "Take cover!"

A huge rocky ridge from above, just under the towering mountain peak of Mt. Aether, cut loose. It thundered down the sheer cliff, taking out everything in its path. Thousands of tons of rock headed straight for the bridge and the helpless troops on it.

"This can't happen to me!" cried Barbarot. "I'm the king!"

No doubt, Barbarot couldn't help but think about the avalanche that had crushed his predecessor's first march through the Sythian Pass before he had reached the Gates of Kronos.

Turning to Uzi, Barbarot barked, "Fire the Lamers. Do it now!"

"I ... I don't understand," said Uzi, confused at the order.

Barbarot took command and shouted his orders directly at the Lamer sergeants. "Fire the Lamers at *that* rock ledge!" he bellowed, pointing to the other side of the pass. The ledge was far below that of Mt. Aether, but the boulders were much larger than those racing down on top of them.

"Ready them, now!"

The Lamers were fueled by lumidite bars and were quickly engaged, turning a bright green. The glow built fast, funneling energy into a series of coils and wires in front of a giant mirror. The green glow was blinding—its brightness so intense none could look at it without harming their eyes.

"Hold it, hold it," cautioned Barbarot, not wanting to shoot until the last minute. Recharging the bars would take too long. They would only have one try.

"Hold!" cautioned Barbarot with sweat dripping from the side of his face. He watched nervously as the rockslide moved closer and closer to them, like a rabid monster ready to pounce on its fearful prey.

"Now!" Barbarot shrieked, making sure all his commanders heard him.

It took three seconds for the energy to fire from the lumidite bars onto the reflective mirror on each machine. The energy condensed in the concave mirrors attached to the war wagons, bouncing around before shooting out.

The first green beam struck a point just beneath a giant, striped megalith. The rock layer below the boulder exploded into a mass of powder, dislodging the huge stone and letting it roll down the hill. Several more Lamer rays hit their targets too, letting loose large rocks that began teetering before cascading down the slope, picking up speed as they went.

Uzi looked on in terror. "What are you doing?"

"Wait and see," said Barbarot, calmly watching.

As the first avalanche of rocks bore down on the Rootanian army, another was coming from the side, perpendicular to it. The second avalanche of behemoths converged on the smaller ones from Mt. Aether, picking them off like a game of billiards, redirecting the entire flow down the other side of the valley wall and away from the bridge. The waterfall of solid rock from Mt. Aether was quickly overwhelmed, and all went over the other side of a steep cliff, falling short of the Bridge of Vadulroo. Thousands had been spared.

As the boulders and debris rolled over the side, flowing over the edge and dropping thousands of feet to the valley floor, the men on the bridge fell to the ground in praise and relief. Pieces of rock landed in the river below, causing it to rage with fury and turn into a fierce rapids. The rest of the rocky deluge fell to the water's edge and along the shoreline, crushing bushes and trees and clearing a wide swath in its path.

Most of the men were saved, there was one small group at the far end of the bridge that had not reached the other side. Unfortunately, the largest of the boulders had acted like bowling balls, knocking over men like pins, smashing wagons and destroying machines as if they were matchsticks.

"Good work men!" Uzi shouted to his commanders. "Nice work!"

Barbarot was not pleased. "Well, what are you waiting for now?" Barbarot barked to his second in command. "Get these men across this bridge or I'll chain you to one of those boulders and push you off this bridge myself!"

"Yes, sire," replied Uzi, before turning back to his officers. "You heard the king; let's get going, men!"

The men and machines once again resumed their march across the bridge. This time there was no need to scream at them to hurry. Once they reached the span, they did all they could to get across as quickly as possible.

Barbarot and his army found the border with Vaporia and crossed into the kingdom without detection. There were no guards or patrols at the passage, and they slipped in and continued their march on the capital without firing a single arrow. Yet, as they left the pass and entered Vaporia, they soon realized they were no longer in the familiar land of Rootan; this was a very strange and unfamiliar place.

While planning his strategy, Barbarot had sent scouting parties to survey the territory and report back. He plotted on his map all the major towns and route to the capital seat of the kingdom—Lagerfall.

"We will split our army into two divisions and attack Lagerfall from two fronts," said Barbarot, describing his plan to his commanders. "The first division will strike from the south along this line ..." he said pointing to a ridge that wound along the southern border of the capital city, "... then, the second will hit them from the east over here."

The king looked up to address Uzi. "I trust you can command the first army?"

"Yes, my Lord, but I'll need to know when you expect to attack from the east to coordinate our forces and take them by surprise!" said Uzi. "You do want us to surprise them, right?"

"You will receive a columba that will deliver the message to you. It will be in code, a simple cipher—one you were taught in the Knight's Observatory," said Barbarot.

"Yes, sir. And if the columba fails to reach me?"

"It won't," said Barbarot smugly.

*****

CH 9 - Finding His Way

Donus stumbled through the woods, making his way south. He didn't know which way to go, so he chose that direction to avoid even colder weather north that might freeze him to the bone.

Eventually, the snowstorm eased, and he could see more clearly even though the trees were still thick and dense. Here and there, he saw a tendoore and tried to shoot one with an arrow, but it scampered away before he could get close. He was hungry, and a roasted tendoore would have done much to improve his spirits and his stomach.

The snow, heavy underbrush and layers of trees finally gave way to a clearing where a group of shepherds were guiding their flocks of aries through a meadow. It was idyllic, but cold, and the breaths of the animals and the shepherds hung as a fog in the air, momentarily frozen in time, until they faded away into nothingness.

"Hey, there!" yelled one of the lads who was caring for the animals. "Do ya' need some help?"

The boy was older than the others but was still no more than fifteen. He had long, blonde hair that hung down the middle of his back. It was tangled and knotted, as if it had never seen the bristles of a brush. His face was long, his eyes close-set, and his mouth small and narrow. He had the start of a light beard that covered his thin lips and protruding chin—signs of budding puberty.

Donus stared at the boy, his face white and blanched from the cold, yet tough and thickened even at such a young age to withstand the ravages of the climate. Donus' mind was still hazy after the fall, and he wasn't sure what the older boy was saying to him.

"What?" Donus finally asked the shepherd.

"Are you all right?" asked the boy.

"Are ya' lost?" came another voice; this one higher-pitched from a younger boy, perhaps eight or nine.

Both boys were dressed in brown woolen trousers, black boots and heavy, gray coats with matching caps. Unlike the older boy, the younger one had a friendly face that was jovial and disarming. His black hair sprouted out from under his cap and curled up over his rather pointy ears.

"I ... don't know," Donus replied, stuttering and stammering. "I don't know if I'm lost. But, maybe that's because I am."

"We need to get him back to the manor," said the older boy. "I think he's got brain freeze."

"Not sure about that," said the younger one. "We don' know what we're bringin' back with us; now do we? You just don' know ... he could be a robber or even a killer!"

Donus became light-headed and began teetering. Then, his eyes rolled up into the back of his head, and he collapsed. The older boy tried to catch him, but Donus slipped through his fingertips and crashed into a pile of wood the shepherds had stacked earlier that day.

The next thing Donus remembered was waking up in a large room with many straw cots spread out over a wooden floor. Each cot was unmade with dirty navy or black blankets twisted into knots lying this way and that. Socks, mittens, trousers and other clothing were scattered about haphazardly as well. But what was worse was the foul smell, likely of mold or mildew from the clothes and beddings.

Donus was on a cot at the far corner of the room, isolated from most of the other boys. It was a residence hall of sorts—meant to board household servants and field hands. These were youths who toiled long and hard to make it through life. From sunup to sundown and with backs that ached and arms that grew numb from the work, these boys kept the place running.

"So, where am I?" Donus asked, his head clearing.

In front of him stood the two shepherds who had found him and carried him inside. The younger lad had taken off his heavy coat and gray cap. His face was narrow; his black hair matted down around his ears. Eyes of brown, he had a complexion that was pale, almost sickly.

"Why, you're with us!" said the younger boy gleefully. "Where did ya' think ya' were?"

The older one suddenly jumped in. "I think what he means is 'What town am I in?'" He then looked down at Donus and said, "You're in Ralop."

"Ralop?" asked Donus, blinking stiffly. "Where's Ralop?"

"Ya' don't even know what kingdom you're in, do ya'?" asked the younger lad. "This is Frezia—you've heard of that haven't ya'?" His youthfulness and impatience were beginning to show.

Donus looked about to see who else was in the room. "How long have I been here—unconscious, I mean?"

"We brought ya' in here about two days ago. We figured sooner or later you'd wake up," said the younger boy.

"What's your name?" asked the older one.

"I ... don't remember," said Donus, queasily. "I don't remember much of anything, I'm afraid." It suddenly dawned on him that he, indeed, didn't recall anything—including who he was or where he was from. Suddenly, all those questions flooded his mind and made him panic.

But then, another lad came to the bedside to see about the newcomer and find out what was going on.

"Who's he?" the boy asked. This shepherd was about the same age as the older boy and was chewing on a rasnut—a fruity morsel that had the crunch of a nut but the juiciness of a red, berry-like fruit.

"You hit your head pretty hard, so maybe you don't remember much," said the older one.

"Well, I'm Whaltooth," said the younger one, "and this is Blu-Ice," he added, pointing to the older boy next to him.

"And I'm Vinigreer," said the third boy, somewhat sarcastically. "But you can call me Vinigreer," he repeated with an impish laugh.

Whaltooth gave Vinigreer a friendly punch in the arm as they both chortled once more.

"Nice to meet you ... I think," answered Donus, rubbing his head some more.

"That's okay," said Whaltooth, smiling. "You can also call Vinigreer Butt-head if you want!"

This brought a roar from the other boys from across the barracks.

"We brought ya' here to the shepherd's bunkhouse to get you your strength back," said Blu-Ice, the oldest of the boys. "Ya' took a mean whack on the head, ya' did,"

"Ya' don' remember anythin'?" asked Whaltooth.

"No, unfortunately, I don't," claimed Donus. "Are you two brothers or something?" he asked, looking at the first two who'd brought him in from the cold. They really didn't look alike, but they had the same mannerisms.

Vinigreer laughed. "No, by all the gods, no!" he said. "They're about as close to being brothers as a raccoon and a skunk. In fact, ...," he said sizing them up, "they kinda' look like 'em."

"You can stop right there, V. You're real funny today," interrupted Blu-Ice. "I know what you were gonna say next, but don't go there." The others were already chuckling too. Blu-Ice turned back to Donus. "We're just shepherds who take care of the baron's flocks. In fact, most of us have been here as long as we can remember too. We all camp out here in the bunkhouse when we're not taking care of the flocks."

"How many of you are there?" asked Donus blinking stiffly.

"There are twenty-four of us right now," said Whaltooth, the younger lad. "We look after things during the day and at the night. But that's when the baron has a tutor come teach us about things that he says we're supposed to know. It makes for a long day, but it's worth it, I guess."

"Yeah, except, the tutor we had just left us ... family problem or something like that is what he said," said Blu-Ice, coldly. It was obvious from his tone that he didn't believed it.

"Oooooh," said Donus again, holding his head. He was getting dizzy and lay back down on his straw mattress.

"Just rest awhile. We'll come back and check on you later," said Whaltooth. He put his wool cap on and flung his scarf around his neck. The other boys in the cabin did the same, and they all left to go outside and finish caring for the sheep.

A short time later, the door of the bunkhouse creaked open and in came a short, small-framed, young woman carrying a basket. She wasn't much older than Donus and had the most beautiful blue eyes he'd ever seen. Her hair was shoulder-length with tight, black curls cascading around her ears. She brought with her several kinds of fruits that were in a basket that she cradled tightly against her body. Glancing around, she carefully placed two pieces of fruit next to each bunk making sure there was enough for everyone. It seemed routine for her—something she had done many times before.

As she approached Donus' bunk, she gasped, not expecting to find anyone there.

"Who are you?" she asked, frightened and backing away.

Donus was tall and husky, and even on the rather large cot he'd been given, his legs stuck out from under his blankets.

"Hello," he said in as kind of voice as he could muster. "I'm a friend of Whaltooth and Blu-Ice. Who are you?"

Immediately, the fear that had overcome her thawed. She came closer and smiled at him. "Oh, I'm Genona," she said glowingly. "But you must not tell the boys that I was here!"

"Why not?" asked Donus.

"Because I don't want them to know who's been giving them treats every day. I wait until they all leave to tend the flocks ... then, I come and give them a piece of fruit or candy or something to make their day a little better. I'm just trying to be nice—to ease the burden they carry by taking care of the flocks."

"You're a very kind, young lady," said Donus. "You're especially pretty."

Genona blushed.

"It's wonderful that you'd do that for them, though," Donus continued. "Is one of them your brother or part of your family?"

"I guess you'd say ... yeah, all are, in a way ... part of my family, that is," she said. "My father is the one who has the good heart, and he encourages me to do the same."

"Your father? Who's your father?" asked Donus.

She paused. Then, she said quickly, "I must go. You will meet him soon enough. In fact, tomorrow, I'll have you meet him tomorrow."

She was embarrassed, but Donus worried it was something he'd said innocently—without knowing he'd offended her. *She was so young and so lovely,* he thought. *It was hard to believe she'd have anything to be embarrassed about.*

She turned and scurried back toward the door. "Bye for now." And out the door she went.

Donus tried to get up to go after her, but his body made it clear that it wasn't going anywhere, and he slumped back in his bed.

Two days passed before Donus was feeling better, but he still didn't remember anything. His head didn't hurt as much, and he could finally move his arms and legs without pain. But what helped him the most were the young men in the barracks. They were full of life, and every evening they had some new form of entertainment.

After they returned from the fields, they got together and sang songs after cooking dinner and clearing the tables. Old Man Bonjo, who was only in his late teens, played a harmonica, and Sheepskin Ike played a lute. Together with Whaltooth, who banged a couple of sticks against some kitchen pans, they made a pretty decent trio—at least good enough to carry a tune.

The ale was mild, and only the older ones were allowed to have any. Mostly, they drank a wicked brew of molasses, sheep's milk, and crushed chacunuts—a little bitter, but the chocolate taste was just too good to pass up.

Although he didn't know where he'd come from or even what his name was, Donus somehow felt at home in this new place. The company was good, and the bunkhouse was warm and hospitable. He only hoped that his real home was as nice as this one.

However, the night's festivities were interrupted when there was a firm knock on the door. This late, a visitor was unusual, and the music stopped abruptly. Everyone looked at each other while one of the boys went to the door, opening it slowly.

"Good evening!" said an older gentleman, dressed in a fine, maroon velvet cape, gray jacket and white leggings. He was accompanied by two attendants who were bundled for the night's chilly air. Everyone in the room immediately jumped off their chairs or scrambled to get up from the floor.

Old Man Bonjo went to the door and bowed low and graciously. "My Lord, it is so good to see you, but what brings you out to our humble quarters this late at night?"

"Oh, Bonjo, you know I like to stop by every now and again to see how you boys are holding up out here!" the man said lightly. "I want to make sure you have plenty of coal and anything else you need for the cold night ahead."

"You're too good to us, you know that!"

"You all are part of my family. You help take care of things around here, and for that I'm grateful," said the old man.

The gentleman walked into the room where he was greeted by the other boys who bowed before him. There was a real compassion for this man and a genuine feeling of loyalty amongst the shepherds, Donus noticed. The man's tall, lanky frame covered the space within the room quickly, and he made his way to each boy, calling him by name and chatting briefly.

With his well-groomed, gray hair hanging long to his shoulders, the old gentleman held an air of confidence and dignity about him. His smile was broad and sincere, even though over many years creases and wrinkles had formed around his mouth and temples. His eyes were melancholy, but they embraced the moment and seemed to enjoy the company of others.

The old man's twinkling blue eyes were striking, and they reminded Donus of someone else he had met recently. She too had the same kindness, energy and sparkling eyes as this man.

"And who might this be?" said the old gentleman coming over to where Donus lay on his cot, now sitting up but unable to stand to show his respect.

"This is ..." said Blu-Ice, then he stopped. "Well, Baron Lukae, to be honest, we don't know exactly what his name is, and, I'm afraid, neither does he."

The baron stooped and looked at Donus, extending his hand in friendship. "Well, it's nice to meet you," he said. "You are certainly welcome here."

"They are right, my Lord. I'm ... I'm afraid I don't know who I am," replied Donus. "You see, I've lost my memory."

"Yes, sir," said Blue-Ice, "we found him wandering in the woods a few days ago. He had a bad bump on his head, as if he'd fallen on it somehow. He doesn't remember how he got into our kingdom, and there were no others with him."

"I see," said the baron. "We'll, I am Baron Lukae the fifteenth. My family has owned the land in this part of Frezia for thousands of years. It's nice to meet you."

He put out his hand again to shake Donus'. Donus returned the gesture, pumping the baron's hand vigorously and staring into his deep, mesmerizing eyes.

"I believe my daughter mentioned something about a young man who joined us recently, but she couldn't ... or wouldn't ... fill me in on any details," said the baron. "That's just like her, though. She's a bit shy around strangers."

Whaltooth and Blu-Ice stared at each other wondering how she knew anything about the newcomer.

"She asked me to stop by and see how you are doing. And, as I can tell, I think you need to come up to the main house with me, so we can better attend to your medical needs."

The baron motioned for the attendants to help Donus with his bag and give him support, if he needed, to walk. Donus, still weak, hobbled across the floor toward the rustic door. He knew enough not to argue with a baron, even though he preferred staying with the boys in the bunkhouse.

"It's okay," said Blu-Ice. "You'll be in good hands with the baron and his family. In fact, we'll see you again soon; I'm sure."

With that reassurance, Donus smiled and gave a brief nod goodbye as they led him out the door. The cold, brisk air slapped him sharply in the face, reminding him he was in a frigid northern climate. Strangely, though, it also triggered fleeting images of his past in his head. For a split second, he visualized a blue monkey hopping up and down on the ground and trying to talk to him.

Odd, he thought. *A talking monkey?*

It would be some time before he would fit that piece of his life back into the bigger puzzle—some time indeed. In the meantime, the footman opened the door to the baron's coach which was pulled by seven black steeds. However, instead of wheels, it had skids or runners, and within moments it began sliding across the snow and ice, back toward the baron's home. Donus could only hope that the baron's daughter would be there waiting for him. *That would make the stay much more enjoyable,* he thought.

*****

CH 10 - Dinner with the King

In another castle inside the kingdom, Oliver and Nikko were summoned by one of the maidservants. She was a giant of a woman who looked and acted like a drill sergeant in the kingdom's military rather than a household attendant.

"It's time you move to the dining hall," she snapped, talking to Oliver without any courtesy.

Oliver, who was cleaning himself after the torturous ride from Dulcenou, merely returned her brusqueness with a respectful smile.

"We'll be down shortly," he said.

It wasn't far to the dinner hall, and when Oliver and Nikko arrived, they found it completely empty. It was fashioned like an ice cave, and only slightly warmer and inviting. The walls were made of shear blue ice, but the texture and pattern were more akin to veined, aquamarine marble rather than of cold, crystalline water. Long, colorful rugs on the floors and the walls added warmth to the room; yet, Oliver noticed again that the ice was not wet and did not melt from the heat inside. The walls were a mosaic with blues in some spots and minty-green or pale grey in others.

Oliver sat in one of the dining room chairs and felt the hard, crystalline arms.

"Anything not of ice seems to be made of crystal," he said to Nikko, rubbing his fingers up and down one of the chair arms.

"Master, you shouldn' sit down before d'e king arrives!"

"But Nikko! I think the castle is made of crystal—not ice! That's why nothing seems to melt!"

Indeed, even the plates and goblets were translucent, made of blue crystal that glimmered from the light that shown down from the dancing flames flickering off the walls. The only things on the table that had color were the rich flower arrangements and the plates of fruit that were placed from one end to the other. Two enormous urns overflowing with colorful flowers graced each end of the long table. There were also trays filled with duexberries, naranjalas, orbanas and kiwellons, all scattered throughout the room with their unique hues of ginger, mustard, crimson, pink and emerald.

Nikko sat down, reluctantly following the lead of his master, and they waited patiently for their host or hostess to arrive. It wasn't long before Prima and Cori entered, dressed in elegant evening dresses. Prima wore a rose-colored, ball gown with a trimmed bodice and chemise ruffle; the matching jeweled trim and a tapestry overskirt made her look, quite simply, beautiful. However, she was evenly matched by Cori, who wore a plush, cobalt blue velvet gown and bodice with white satin sleeves. Oliver hardly recognized them, and he felt a bit overwhelmed and underdressed by their elegance and refinement.

The ladies came in and stood by their seats that straddled either side of Oliver. Oliver immediately jumped out of his seat and motioned for Nikko to do the same. Their manservants gently pulled the ladies' blue velvet chairs from the table, and the young women gracefully took their seats as they had rehearsed thousands of times before.

"*Wow!*" said Oliver, otherwise speechless. "I mean, hello ladies!", I'm very delighted to see you two. You both look *amazing*! Nikko thought for a moment that he and I would be dining alone tonight."

Prima smiled, her white teeth shimmering against her light, smooth complexion. "Oh, don't worry. You and Nikko won't be alone. Trust me," she said.

Just then, a maidservant came in with Gemma following right behind her. She walked to the dining table and gingerly put her hand on Oliver's shoulder, squeezing it ever so lightly--lovingly.

Gemma's long white and gold dress was beautiful, and she was absolutely stunning in it. Oliver had never seen her quite like that before, and his emotions stirred inside him.

"Gemma?" Oliver said in amazement. "You look …"

"Amazing …" said Nikko, sitting in his chair also amazed by the transformation.

In her gold, chiffon gown with sparkling sleeves, Gemma had no competition in the room. She looked every bit part of the royal family.

However, Gemma felt far from it. She felt awkward in such a dress—as she'd never worn such a formal evening gown before. She cast her eyes downward, timidly, unwilling to make eye contact with either Oliver or Nikko. But finally—when she did—she saw their reaction.

Her face softened as she saw that Oliver was enchanted—spellbound—by her. She saw an affection and a lust that she had only sensed before, but not seen. His smile told her that she was pretty, attractive, and alluring—irresistible.

"Gemma, you look ... marvelous. Is d'at really you?" asked Nikko.

"I'm so glad to see you, Oliver," Gemma said before turning to his blue monkey. "And you too, Nikko."

Gemma's face was naturally beautiful, but the young ladies had given her face a bit of blush and eye makeup that accentuated her hazel eyes and long lashes. Indeed, Oliver couldn't take his eyes off her. He was enthralled. He'd never seen her quite like *this*.

Gemma sat down across from Oliver, having a seat pulled out for her as she scooted in her chair.

"Uh, how are you ... uh ... feeling?" asked Oliver, trying to find the right words and getting over how beautiful she looked.

"Better, thanks," she replied, blushing a bit.

Gemma had enjoyed the attention of men, but in a different way. It had been when she was dressed as a warrior and 'in charge.' She couldn't remember the last time she had worn a ball gown, and she felt uncomfortable with her growing femininity. Her breasts were filling in, and her curves were much more noticeable with the gown she was wearing—a far cry from chain mail she was used to.

"Uh, well, you look … rested," stuttered Oliver awkwardly, as if he'd never seen her before.

The frown on Gemma's face told him instantly that he'd said the wrong thing.

"Uh, I didn't mean well-rested ... I meant nice," he corrected himself. But the frown didn't go away. "How about pretty? I really meant to say pretty, even beautiful!" he said, attempting to get closer to the right answer.

"Stop it!" she answered him. She clicked her fingers once or twice in front of his face to get his attention. "It's me! It's the same old Gemma! They told me it was required that ladies wear gowns to dine with the king. The men are supposed to wear jackets ... so where's yours?"

As if on cue, a manservant came over to the table and whispered in Oliver's ear. He rose unceremoniously, and the servant helped him on with a dark gray jacket with brass buttons.

Gemma grinned at him, but Oliver wasn't sure whether she was smiling because he was now as uncomfortable as she was, strapped into the ball gown, or because she thought he looked handsome. He rather hoped it was the latter.

"So, where my coat?" asked Nikko, pouting.

The other four at the table burst into laughter. Oliver consoled Nikko and offered to loan him his jacket if he really thought he needed one.

"All rise!" bellowed the sommelier, and a sudden silence fell over the table. "I present the King of Frezia, His Majesty, King de Riguere, and his lovely queen, Her Majesty, Queen Yamina."

Prima leaned over and whispered into Oliver's ear, which Cori and Gemma could easily hear, "That's the first time he didn't say, 'and the more honorable queen.'" She giggled. "It's a little joke we have that drives our father crazy."

The king entered the dining room dressed in an exquisite burgundy, velvet surcoat with white breeches and long, silk stockings. Around his neck lay layers of gold and ruby-encrusted chains. But most magnificent of all was the enormous green emerald pendant he wore that dangled just under the other jewelry. By far, it was the largest gem Oliver had ever seen, easily the size of a giant naranjala fruit from Rootan.

Directly behind the king came Queen Yamina. She was adorned like no royal Oliver had ever seen. Her dress was elegant, gold and burgundy and made of silk and velvet. The lace around her neck was of a design so intricate that even Gemma, who typically wasn't impressed by such things, marveled at it. Like her husband, Queen Yamina had a smaller version of his emerald around her neckline. By contrast, however, it was the only necklace that graced her slender and delicate neck.

The queen was striking, yet not beautiful. Still, her upright bearing and grace put her squarely in the realm of high royalty. Her magnificent cheekbones and sunken, amber eyes exuded a sensual quality, one more rounded and refined than that of the king. Short, but well-endowed and curved, the queen was younger than her husband by many years. Her straight black hair glistened in the candlelight and hung down the middle of her back, suggesting an informality to her that was not shared by her husband.

"Welcome!" said the king, making a grand gesture with his hands. "My queen, Yamina, and I are so very pleased to have you as our guests for dinner. You have met our lovely daughters,

Primavetta and Corrival. It is too bad my son is not here tonight—you would have enjoyed meeting him as well."

The king appeared in good spirits. Like his queen, he was not tall, but unlike her, he had a belly that made his presence large. De Riguere's pudgy body didn't stop at his midsection. His fingers, hands, arms and legs were also chunky. With large, black eyes that were set far apart, and a broad mouth lined with plump lips, his features were distinctive. Like his bushy eyebrows, his hair was dark and thick, curling slightly at the end of the long black strands that flowed down to his shoulders.

"Now, please enjoy our feast and our company," the king added.

The queen's reaction to his remarks was stiff and aloof. She produced a smile, but it looked forced and unnatural. There was something unsettling about her that Oliver sensed. She was quiet and emotionless, watching what was going on around her rather than participating in it.

With the stiffness still lingering in the air, the servants began serving the dishes of each course to all at the table, starting with the king and queen as was tradition and custom. Meanwhile, the two daughters laughed and giggled, whispering back and forth.

To break the awkwardness, the king spoke as he raised his glass for wine to be poured by one of his attendants. "We'd like to know more about both of you. What can you tell us?"

The queen peered intently at Oliver and Gemma. "Please, share with us ... will you?" she repeated, the corners of her mouth turned up slightly but offering no more comfort.

"Well, I am Nikko," said the blue monkey, from the opposite end of the table, interjecting awkwardly into the dialog.

Startled, the queen turned unexpectedly toward the monkey. She gasped, not having noticed the little blue fur-ball who had seated himself at the royal dining table.

"Oh, my!" she said with alarm. "What is that *thing* doing at my table?"

"It's all right, mother," said Cori. "He talks. He's almost like one of us."

Although Nikko didn't appreciate the remark, it was enough to calm the queen. She continued to stare at him suspiciously but finally sat back in her chair and raised her cup too, hoping for a speedy pouring of wine herself.

"I didn't quite expect that!" she exclaimed. The look on her face was priceless—so much so, that both Prima and Cori began sniggering quietly.

"This is my very good friend, Nikko," said Oliver. "He's a pithicaan monkey from Vaporia."

"Nice ... to ... meet you?" Yasami replied haltingly. "I guess your friend is dining with us, then?" she asked distastefully, suggesting that it was neither appropriate nor welcome.

Oliver looked at Prima and Cori for guidance. Sadly, they shook their heads.

"Usually, my parents don't permit animals in the dining hall," said Prima. "I guess we forgot to mention that."

"But ..." started Oliver but stopped abruptly. He understood. It would just be hard on Nikko to have to eat elsewhere.

Oliver looked at Nikko and smiled, nodding to him that it was better if he left. Nikko's lowered his head, sad but accepting of what his master was telling him. He slowly jumped down from his chair and followed one of the servants outside into the hallway, his tail tucked between his legs like a hurt puppy.

"They'll take good care of him, don't worry," said Cori, reassuringly.

Fortunately, the rest of the dinner went better. The servants brought out roasted seal with red olives, sautéed vegetables of spiky squash, tarrocs, pineplums, and walnut mixed gifs. Fresh fish was served, head, tail and all, and the mounds of sweet yams with deuxberry sauce were something neither Oliver nor Gemma had ever had before.

The brawny, white candles on the candelabras burned low as the night drew on, dripping tearfully down the sides of their gray pewter holders. The king was charming but drawled on about his journeys as a young man and his many far and distant exploits. He had hunted fallubs in the southern sector of Frezia and somme in East Vaporia. He'd been to Chasmia and Sanzotur but never to Oliver's kingdom of Rootan or Gemma's Dulcenou. Yet, he claimed his barons often hunted with him, and he promised to show Oliver his trophy room where all his prize catches were mounted.

Although parts of his stories were engaging and fascinating, most were about his own achievements and his greatness as a hunter, explorer and leader. It didn't take long to understand that while there were likely truths buried within his tales, there was also great fiction. However, both Oliver and Gemma endured them, being quiet and respectful in the great man's home.

Meanwhile, the doting queen watched her husband lovingly, as she took small bites of roasted seal and sips of green wine brought in from Vaporia. Even though she'd heard the stories countless times before, she truly seemed to love the man.

On the other hand, Prima and Cori did not hide their boredom— pushing pieces of spiky squash and morsels of neebs around their silver plates, they cradled their chins in their palms, hoping they would be granted a reprieve by their mother.

When the desert was served, the discussion finally shifted to Oliver and Gemma. "So, you never did tell us about yourselves," the queen said to Oliver. "What brings you to our kingdom, my dear boy?"

"Our kingdom was being attacked by a plague that had spread through Rootan. It killed many there and then drifted into the mountains near Treah in Dulcenou," Oliver said, describing the events. "We were afraid it was coming after us, so we fled north to escape it and found ourselves here."

The king immediately raised his voice in alarm. "You mean, you brought a plague with you into my kingdom?"

"No, no, Your Majesty," Oliver said quickly. "It was a disease that came in on a cloud, but it can't live where it's cold. It can't survive in your weather here. That's why we flew north. The thing died once it hit the frigid air of Frezia."

"If I may, Your Majesty," interjected Gemma, "you and your people have nothing to worry about. You are quite safe here."

"You're saying that this thing was coming after you?" asked the queen. "That seems odd; don't you think?" She looked at them more suspiciously. "How could something like that target you as if it had a brain of its own?"

"Actually, there were four of us," Gemma replied. "One of our friends didn't make it. He fell out of the sky south of here, but there was a blizzard and we couldn't find him.".

"You still didn't answer my question, young lady," said Yasami, impatiently, and ignoring the subtle plea for aid.

"We think the plague was conjured and guided by someone within my kingdom—inside Rootan," said Oliver. "There is a new king there, and we think he deals in black magic and sorcery."

"Really?" the king said skeptically.

"What he's really after is the Map of Gneima," said Gemma.

"*Ha!*" laughed the king, pushing his chair back from the table. "Ah, yes, the great and mysterious map ... How many times have I heard that talked about over the years?" Then, his faced sobered, and he looked curiously at Oliver. "So, tell me, Oliver, why would such a king believe you have the map, *eh?*"

"You don't believe it exists then?" asked Oliver, sidestepping the question.

"I didn't say whether I did, or I didn't?" parried the king.

"There are people who believe it does not, my king," Oliver answered.

"But I know the answer, my young lad. Come, let me show you."

Gemma and Oliver looked at each other in stunned amazement. To their surprise, the king got up from the table to leave the room, and they hurried after him. He led them to another room, just as large as the elaborate dining room, but far more interesting. Nikko had seen them pass down the hall where he was sitting and quickly jumped in behind them to join the group.

King de Riguere grabbed the thick, iron handle on the wide, royal door and swung it open with as much pomp and ceremony as he could.

"*This* is my trophy room," the king said proudly.

The candles illuminating the room revealed walls chocked full of stuffed animal heads. It was an amazing display of creatures from throughout his kingdom and many others, all frozen in time. There were wild chimeri, a blinoplast with two horns instead of the usual one, a tendoore head so large that it looked like an alturian elephant, and also smaller mounts, like a rare, teal nilithian badger and a red raptor, a deadly and smart mammal that ran upright on its large hind legs and hunted in packs. In the corner of the room was an enormous, perfectly-preserved, ursidian polar bear. White with massive incisor teeth that hung below its jaw, the bear had a twisted horn on the top of its head and stood over fifteen feet high.

Gemma shuddered as she looked at it. "*Oh,* that must have been something to bring down."

"That one almost got me," said the king, puffing out his chest. "We were hunting up near the polar triangle. There's nothing there but mountains and glaciers. I wanted to bag one of these, and we spent two weeks in sub-zero weather tracking him. We knew he was big from his massive paw prints in the snow and hoped we could get him before he returned to his cave.

"Alas, we trekked up a steep mountainside and found he had already gone back into his burrow. The cave was deep and dark, and it would have been suicide to venture inside, even with all my men at my side. So, we waited outside, hoping it would come out, but it didn't. Three days we waited. Finally, my patience ran out, and I marched to the front of the huge opening."

"What did you do?" asked Gemma.

"I called out to it, demanding it show itself to me. The huge beast came out bellowing and snorting. It took its big, white paw and swung it at me, missing my head by inches. That's when I pulled back on my bow and let my arrow fly."

The king went on to describe how he needed two more arrows to finish the job and how his men struggled to pull the massive weight of the bear back to his castle.

"There are many other great hunts in this room," bragged the king. "For example, take that yombatin black panther over there. I was on safari in …" The story went on for what seemed like an hour before the Riguere finished. Then, he looked confused. "Oh, now what was I was going to show you here? I forget."

"I believe you brought us in here to show us something having to do with the map," said Gemma, flattening the front of her dress.

"Oh, yes. This way."

He walked to one of two tall, crystalline cases. They were beautiful, yet odd. Not the typical, four-sided kind, one had five sides and the other seven. They stood only three feet high and each held only one thing inside – something that lay on a red, velvet pillow with gold fringe and tassels on the corners.

Nikko watched as the king opened the top of the pentagonal stand, lifting the heavy crystal cover and placing it on another table beside him. He looked down and exclaimed, "*Ah,* there is my beauty!" Reaching in, he pulled out something wrapped in a garnet cloth and placed it on the tabletop next to the cover.

"Now, what I'm about to show you is *very* special. It has to do with the Map of Gneima."

And with that introduction he unveiled a small, very smooth piece of stone—very much like the others Oliver had found. This one was light gray but darker than the ones Oliver had. And although roughly the same size, it was a different shape.

Riguere held it up as if he were holding a fragile egg. "This ... this is the Map of Gneima."

"How do you know?" asked Oliver, feigning ignorance.

"While I was hunting in Edenot, I was in the village of Evydam where the chief asked me to find and kill a wild ambore ... you know, the pig-like creature with a long trunk nose, tusks and claws. It had been attacking some of the children in the town. You probably noticed it on the wall under the nilithean badger over there," he said pointing to the far end of the room. "Yep, I shot that bad one with my cross bow in the hills near the town. I had a tough time tracking him, I did. First, I had to ..."

"Uh, I'm sorry to interrupt, Your Highness, but you were talking about the map piece, I believe," said Gemma, gently bringing him back to the point.

"Oh, yes. Well, the chief was so pleased with me that he gave me this piece. He said it was the Map of Gneima, and he showed me the markings on it where it says, 'Gneima' ... See right here." The King pointed to the picture of the eye and the word *Gneima* right under it.

"*Wow*," said Gemma. "That's amazing! Can I see it?"

Oliver watched her carefully, nervously. He was afraid she may say something about their map pieces. Revealing too much about what they understood about the map was dangerous, as they well knew. It was even more dangerous to talk carelessly around a powerful king like Riguere.

"No, I keep it protected in here. No one touches it but me," said the king, pulling it back.

He rewrapped the bundle and put the piece back into the case. Then, he walked to the other case—the seven-sided one—and took off its glass top. This cloth covering the item was royal blue. It was about the same size and shape as the other, and as the king unwrapped it, another small stone emerged. This piece was also a medium gray, but slightly darker than the first. Both were smooth as silk and glistened, reflecting the candlelight flickering from the chandelier hanging overhead.

"And *this* is the other one," said the king proudly.

"Where did you get that one?" asked Oliver.

"This little gem I discovered in Vaporia, also while I was hunting ..." he stopped and looked at everyone staring at him. He cleared his throat and began again. "As I recall, we were hiking through the geyser fields near Lagerfall when one of my knights stumbled on a deep depression. We thought it was just another extinct geyser hole. However, I saw the top of a white object sticking out of the ground. It had a smooth, rounded top."

"You just saw the piece sitting there?" asked Gemma, skeptically.

The king laughed, "Oh no, my child. It was nothing like. You see, what we found was the top of an egg-like stone. I ordered my men to dig it out so we could look at it, and when they pulled it up, the ground shook and a crack ripped open in the earth. I shouted to everyone to run! But we hadn't gotten very far, when the biggest geyser I've ever seen blew on that very spot. It shot into the air sending hot water and spray at least five hundred feet into the sky. Unfortunately, some of my men were scalded, but the rest of us only got some minor burns."

"How did you get the stone out of the egg?" asked Oliver, curious. It had been an ordeal for him to get the stone out of the first egg he'd found inside the cave in Dulcenou. The only way he had managed it was by using his very unique Annihilation Blade.

"Actually, it was quite easy," replied the King. "The bottom part of the egg was already cracked—probably because of the forces building up underneath it for so many years. We just broke off the rocky shell, and out it came. Since I had the other piece from Edenot, I knew immediately what it was."

"That's impressive! You have two pieces of the map," Oliver said, enviously.

"Two pieces, yes. But this *is* the map," said the king emphatically. "I have the Map of Gneima right here."

"There aren't any other pieces of the map?" asked Gemma, baiting him to see how much he knew.

"Oh, I don't think so. I think it's all right here – safe and sound with me," he said proudly.

The king re-wrapped the second piece and gently placed it back into the case where he'd gotten it.

"So, you have power of map too," said Nikko from behind his master.

Riguere smiled. "Yes."

"Have you used that power?" asked Gemma.

"No. I don't believe in using such power, even though I have it."

"Why not?"

"Let me say that I haven't had the need to," answered the king.

Oliver grinned and nodded, but he was doing it only because he understood much more than what the king was saying. He knew the king did not have any powers and the king knew that too. He only said he did to keep others in line—to fear him.

"I think that's enough for me this night," Riguere said. "I'll have my attendants take you back to your rooms now."

Before retiring for the evening, Oliver, Gemma and Nikko talked about what they had seen. Aside from enduring the boredom of the dinner and the endless stories of the king, they were, of course, most interested in the pieces of stone.

"I'm sure those are real map pieces," said Oliver. "They look just like the others we've found—the right size, the right shape, the right color ... everything matches."

"Yeah, I agree," said Gemma, mournfully. "But they are very important to him. I'm afraid, there won't be any way of getting him to let us have them."

"Why didn' you tell him you have some too? Maybe he give you his," said Nikko.

Gemma shook her head. "The king isn't the kind of person to be generous with things like that. They mean too much to him. He was very proud of those pieces—that was clear enough."

"Maybe we trade him somed'ing we have d'at he wants instead," said Nikko.

"Like what?" asked Oliver. "What could we possibly have that he would want?"

"For one d'ing, you have all d'ose 'gadgety' d'ings—you know, de' compass, Fortunuts, and ... of course!" Nikko said, hesitating.

"What?" asked Oliver, puzzled.

"You can offer your Annihilation Blade! He like hunting. I'm sure he love to have d'at!" said Nikko.

"He's a bowman, an archer ... not a swordsman," said Oliver, dismissing Nikko's idea. "They are two very different types of people. A bowman would never hunt with a sword or use it that way at all. Swords are for ... well ... for dueling and war stuff. It's just different."

Gemma shook her head. "I think you're underestimating the man. I think he'd really like something like that. I agree with Nikko."

"I don't think so," said Oliver, rather coldly.

Fatigue was setting in, and Oliver was becoming stubborn. Gemma could tell and decided to address the subject again in the morning when they had gotten some sleep. She too was still recovering from the cold and dehydration she'd suffered while outside.

"Okay, well, I'm tired, and I'm going to bed. Good night," Gemma said with a bit of an edge. She got up and left the room, moving quickly down the hall and out of sight.

"I d'ink you made her mad," said Nikko.

"She'll get over it," replied Oliver, getting grumpier by the moment.

"What if you ask Prima or Cori to ask de' king?" asked Nikko.

"I couldn't do that. It wouldn't be right. I mean, what do you want me to say to them? 'Hey, we are guests in your father's castle and, by the way, can we have your father's two most prized things in his trophy room?'" Oliver said sarcastically, mocking a conversation he might have with the two daughters. "I don't think so."

Nikko just lowered his head. He hated to see his master so down.

"Goodnight, Nikko. I'm sure tomorrow will be a better one."

He left his pet and headed toward his own bedroom, a separate room off from the sitting area where they'd been talking.

***

Oliver had dozed off even though his bed was lumpy in spots making it hard for him to stay asleep. He had tossed and turned but finally had shut his eyelids and let them stay closed.

However, in the middle of the night something stirred him. Suddenly, Oliver heard the rush of feet down the hallway which passed his room. The guards were yelling and banging their sabers against the cold, icy walls of the castle as they passed. It took a minute for him to regain his senses, but now sitting upright in his bed, Oliver was alarmed. The noise and confusion grew as more guards ran down the hall, their swords rattling in their sheaths.

"Nikko! Get up!" Oliver shouted. But there was no reply. "Nikko!"

Oliver checked the sitting room where Nikko was staying. "Nikko? Nikko, where are you?" *****

CH 11 - Vaporian Geysers

The road that led to the east side of Lagerfall was not difficult for Barbarot and his men. It was wide, and although it had many ruts and holes, the wagons and animals easily navigated around the them, often moving just off the path onto the hard clay along either side, to avoid getting stuck.

When the ruts were the size of gullies or small canyons, the king used other means. He created a unique group of men for these times—he called them his "engineers." They were the ones ordered to solve these any many other problems of this kind for the king. Besides these problems, they were told to figure out how to move the huge army so the enemy couldn't hear or see them coming. There were many war machines that were big and sometimes squeaked and creaked on their wheels as they rolled along.

The engineers redesigned the equipment to move silently and greased the axles with animal fat to keep them from squeaking. To cover their tracks, they used wagons with rakes dragged behind, erasing their wheel and animal marks as well as the boot prints left by the thousands of soldiers. After they'd gone through an area, they left no tell-tale signs they'd ever been there. And, finally, the king ordered special camouflage uniforms to make it difficult to spot them along the road. His soldiers' colors blended in with their surroundings, making them look like bushes, and his war animals like large rocks or decaying tree trunks.

Yet, Barbarot still moved his army swiftly because he knew the Vaporian King Ferox would find out sooner or later that he was coming. It was only a matter of time. His engineers were good, but his army couldn't be made completely invisible.

Meanwhile, along the southern border of Vaporia, Uzi and his army made their way along the tough and inhospitable range of the western Yasalimah mountains. The road was seldom traveled, and as they moved into higher elevations along the desolate path, the trees thinned and the number of boulders in the roadway grew. The steep drop-offs and narrowness of the trail made detours impossible. So, the rocks had to be cleared by chaining the larger merkezi to them and pulling the huge stones out of the way. But this took time. Hours turned into a full day, and Uzi had not yet reached his mark on the outskirts of Lagerfall. He had sent several columba's to the king telling of his slow progress but had received the same number of nasty replies back.

"I don't want excuses! I want action!" read one. "If you can't get your men to the south post of the city by tomorrow night, you will be replaced. I don't have to tell you where you'll be spending the rest of your days," read another.

Finally, after working his men all day and night clearing the road to get to the city, Uzi arrived outside the southern wall. King Barbarot held his army hidden just east of Lagerfall, and when he learned of Uzi's position, he prepared for his attack.

Between the city wall and the tree-lined hills that extended miles north and east toward the mighty range of the Yasalimah mountains, was a vast area of flattened earth. This was an expansive geyser field, and scattered throughout were holes that spewed hot, scalding steam. These columns of hot water were unpredictable. Without warning a blast would erupt from the ground and shoot high into the air. Anyone unlucky enough to be walking over the spot at the time would be burned alive. Closer to the city wall there were even more vents. In fact, it was surrounded by them. It was one of the great defenses nature had offered the Vaporian king's ancestors when they had decided to build their castle on that location.

The white plumage of steam erupted here and there, shooting into the sky before slowly and quietly sailing off to the east, over the treetops of the Vaporian forest and Barbarot's army. The earth hissed and groaned from the stresses and strains under the surface, while on top the rocks sweated like dew settling on a grassy meadow in the early hours of a cold, clear morning.

From the southern side, Uzi's army had far more land to cover to get across its geyser-pocketed landscape to reach the city walls than did Barbarot's. Worse yet, Uzi had been given far fewer wall rams, the slingshot devices Portenza had used to crash through the Gates of Kronos.

Uzi issued the order for the few wall rams he had to be rolled across the dangerous geyser plain as quickly as possible and pushed up against the towering stone walls of Lagerfall Castle. All twenty began advancing, slowly at first but then picking up speed as they made their way toward the perimeter of the city. The way was rough, and the axles jerked and jostled as the wheels ran over the irregular and uneven stones.

"Ahhhhhh!" cried one of the ram drivers as his machine turned over after hitting a break in the stones and splitting the axle in two. At the same time, he landed on top of a geyser hole. The earth began shaking almost immediately, and he lay there holding his leg in pain. "No, no," he mumbled as he felt the tremors. He tried to crawl out of the depression where the hole was, but he only made it to the rim.

It was then that the hot water pocket erupted, throwing his body into the air and over the heads of the others who were still advancing toward the wall. His screaming could be heard as it sailed over a hundred of feet, landing with an unremarkable thud. There were no more screams.

"Get on with it!" yelled the commanders, pushing their men to stay disciplined and not panic.

It was no surprise when the young men on top of the castle turrets heard the cries, and soon there was a loud blaring of horns echoing off the walls surrounding the city and bouncing among the distant hills. The warning siren had not been heard in Vaporia for hundreds of years, so most of the citizens inside the city walls didn't realize what was happening. However, the Vaporian soldiers who manned the turrets had been well trained, and the archers scurried along the top of the catwalk to get to their posts.

The first of the wall rams made it across the plain, rumbling up the castle. Covered by a thick, wooden canopy to protect the men inside from arrows and hot tar falling from above, the wheeled ram stopped just outside the city's perimeter. Soldiers began setting the timbers in place to catapult into the twelve-foot-thick walls. The commander would then crash them into the wall, over and over until it buckled and collapsed.

From the turrets above, volleys of arrows rained down on them as they readied their machines. The air was thick with the long darts as they hit the wooden canopies and the shields of men advancing behind them, sinking deeply into both.

Uzi ordered the catapults with the greatest power to be positioned within firing distance of the wall. These heavy catapults began hurling fiery balls of molten metal through the air, smashing holes in the city walls and turrets and forcing the Vaporian archers to run for their lives. The sky was soon filled with blazing, iron missiles that pounded the stone and spread fire and destruction everywhere.

From across the geyser plain, Uzi could see Barbarot's huge army advancing from the east. The geysers were less active there, making it easier for the king's rams and wagons to cross without casualties. Unchallenged, some of Barbarot's volarequi began flying in dropping lumidite bombs. The green fires quickly spread inside the castle grounds, igniting the thatched roofs on the shops, homes and animal barns inside the walled perimeter.

Next, Barbarot let loose a volley of Sinjay orbs, which flew in mass by the thousands. The small, silvery, razor-sharp disks sliced through the archers atop the towers and sent a wave of terror throughout the Vaporian ranks. They had never seen things as sophisticated as these, and they had no way to defend themselves against them. They had not been at war for a long time and hadn't developed anything more than their swords and crossbows. Now, they found themselves completely at the mercy of their Rootanian marauders.

"Send in the ground troops," barked Uzi, "and ready them to run through the breaches in the walls once the rams have broken them!"

Three brigades of infantry, nearly thirty thousand men, began crossing over the plain—bows and battle axes readied. But just as the bulk of the forces made it to the middle of the plain, chaos broke loose. Boiling hot water suddenly began shooting up from holes within the rock below, rising hundreds of feet up into the air. It was as if a switch had been thrown from inside the castle, as geysers were triggered throughout the deadly field. Men were blown to pieces by the force or cooked alive as they walked across a geyser hole when it went off.

"No!" cried Uzi, "The geyser field is erupting! Break off the attack! Retreat! Retreat!" he yelled.

But it was too late. Thousands of his men were vaporized as superheated geysers went off one by one. It was bizarre—as if each pocked geyser hole could sense when footsteps were trampling over their sacred ground above. The white vapor from the steam turned red, and the body count grew.

Uzi's men threw down their weapons and began running back toward the defensive line of troops Uzi had held in reserve. At the same time, the men who were already beating their rams against the walls turned to see what was happening. What they saw were their reinforcements abandoning them. They knew they didn't stand a chance without the support of those fresh troops behind them. And, in a chain reaction, they began leaving their machines and running for cover across the geyser field. Most didn't get far. They were either struck down by the arrows from Lagerfall archers or killed by the hot water blasts from the steam vents. Uzi looked on in disbelief. His entire army and his plans were falling apart before his very eyes.

On the east side of the battlefield, Barbarot's men ran into the same problem as steam shot up from the ground, roasting many of his best men. The geysers began popping off as if the army stumbled across the watery, mine field.

"Shall we retreat, Your Majesty?" asked Seber, his grand commander, as he watched Uzi's men run from the field of battle south of their position.

King Barbarot exploded. "If you do, I will roast you myself over one of those geyser pits. Do you understand me?"

"But, what about Uzi's army?"

"I'll deal with Uzi. You deal with your troops, commander. If anyone tries to retreat, order your archers to shoot them on sight before they reach our lines."

The grand commander gasped at the cruelty of the king.

"You heard me, didn't you commander?" screamed Barbarot.

"Yes, Your Majesty. I ... I …"

"Do I need to replace you as well?"

Seber shook his head and flew off on his steed to execute the order he'd been given.

Seeing Uzi's troops in retreat, Barbarot's infantry began to do the same as the hot water claimed more victims. Like Uzi's reserve units, Barbarot's men threw down their weapons and made a run for it. However, they were unaware of the king's order. The archers on the front line waited—their bowstrings pulled, and arrows steadied.

The first wave of retreating infantry didn't know what to make of their own archers aiming at them from the front lines. They thought they were going to give them cover as they ran for their lives. However, when the archers released their volley of arrows, they watched in terror as their comrades fell by the hundreds. None of the fleeing soldiers had any chance to raise his shield in defense.

"What are they doing?" yelled one of the retreating soldiers. "Are they mad?"

"Maybe they just missed. Maybe they just aimed too low?" said another, trying to decide what to do.

"Let's keep going, then," said a third.

But the arrows kept flying right at them, and they watched their friends continue to fall. Quickly, they realized this was no mistake, and the rest of the men turned and ran back across the geyser field toward the arrows from the castle, many dying along the way.

Watching the massacre unfold, Uzi knew his fate was sealed as well. He watched as Barbarot's archers took down his own retreating men. He knew that he could not go back and face his king. Taking out his knife, Uzi knelt down on both knees. The end came quickly.

Barbarot's men saw they had no choice but to return to the city wall and fight. There they resumed pounding the walls with their rams, continuing to beat on the dense, stone perimeter. Soon, the tree-sized battering devices finally pushed through the thick wall and a large section collapsed. The main turret swayed and then caved in, breaking into pieces and crushing many flimsy, wooden buildings below inside. The mighty, "invincible" perimeter wall—manned by the noble nights of the Vaporian order—was no more.

The Rootanian infantry and then the cavalry poured through the gap, riding their meraki with their lion-like heads roaring and barbed tails thrashing. The knights galloped onward as if possessed, swinging their swords and goedendags at anything that moved. The vicious spikes on the chained ball goedendags sent panic into anyone in their path, and they all ran for cover.

Riders of the second cavalry, mounted on wingless sensavols held their torches high and set fire to anything they thought could burn. Soon, homes, stables, stores, and anything else made of wood or straw was afire. The smoke turned dense and black and began billowing up from the city, darkening the skies. From a distance, the Rootanian king viewed his battle scene and smiled. The smoky plumes were a sign of success. Lagerfall had fallen.

The battle inside the city went on for a few more hours and then was over. When all was calm, the king and his commanders entered triumphantly through the front gates, parading as conquerors of the new kingdom. The fires had taken their toll, and the charred remains of the buildings looked like picked-over carcasses of animals after the cathartes vultures had finished with them.

Lined up on both sides of the street were the high-ranking officers of the opposing Vaporian force. With hands strapped together with metal bands, they were rounded up to be locked away in the kingdom's prison cells. Their faces were blackened by the smoke and ash, and they had been stripped of their swords.

Barbarot stuck out his chest like a peacock proud of its plumage. This was his triumph. It was the first of the kingdoms to fall, and the young king knew it would not be his last.

"Where is the King of Vaporia?" he shouted to his grand commander. "Bring him to me!"

"I am here, in front of you," came the voice.

Barbarot looked into the ranks of officers chained together like animals. Short and stout, the king looked like all the rest of his officers—nothing in his uniform distinguished him from the others.

"Bring him to me," ordered Barbarot, curious about this unusual man who chose to be among his men.

The Vaporian king was brought forward and pushed down into the dirt, his knees grinding into the ground after a loud crack as he knelt. Pain flashed across his face momentarily, but he showed no more emotion after that.

"What is your name?" asked Barbarot.

"I am Ferox, King of Vaporia," he said without expression.

"Well, Ferox, *former* King of Vaporia, you have chosen to reveal yourself to me as the one in charge of the kingdom. Do you know what I do with rival kings?" Barbarot said sneeringly.

"Do as you wish. But I am among my men—we live together, and we die defending each other. I am nothing more nor less of a man than they, and I expect no better treatment. If my treatment is worse, as I am their king, then so be it. If your punishment for me is death—so be it. I only plead for the lives of my men, who have fought bravely and were willing to die to defend their kingdom and their king," replied Ferox.

Barbarot raised an eyebrow. He respected a man such as this— someone willing to sacrifice himself for his men. This was something Barbarot would never do, and he admitted it to himself. But for someone else of lesser talents, such as this king, he thought it admirable.

"Well, well. So, we have someone who believes he is brave and righteous, do we? Do you know what I do to those who also believe they are morally superior?" asked Barbarot.

"Again, My Majesty. You may do with me as you wish. You have beaten me and my men. Our fate is in your hands."

Barbarot moved his face close to that of the Vaporian king's. He took out his sword and pushed the blade up against the nobleman's throat, but Ferox did not move, nor did he blink. Receiving no satisfaction, Barbarot jerked the sword slightly and drew blood that dripped from the cut on his victim's throat. Yet, still there was no flinching from fear.

"Humph!" grunted Barbarot, who withdrew his sword and pushed it into its sleeve. "Ferox ..." he said looking down at the man kneeling before him, "... you have earned back your life and that of your men. I have found few men of your caliber who were willing to face death so directly and not blink."

The Rootanian soldiers lifted the former Vaporian king to his feet and dragged him away with the rest of his men.

"Commander!" Barbarot shouted to his grand commander, Seber. "We're going to move out. Take enough men with you to secure the city and maintain control over the rest of the kingdom. You shall remain, as governor. Suppress all resistance with force — be vicious and remorseless. I will send further instructions to you later."

"But, where are you going now, Your Majesty?" asked the grand commander.

"We continue on to our next conquest, of course ..." Barbarot replied. "... the Kingdom of Chasmia!"

After completing the campaign against Lagerfall, Barbarot directed his troops south, across the remaining geyser fields. There he picked up Uzi's men who had begun the attack on that side of the city but had fallen back. Riding on his mount, the king pranced through a rift in Uzi's army. Like a sea parting, the men moved to the side as the king rode his magnificent volarequez, its wings flapping proudly as it trotted along. Behind him were the legions of soldiers he had just led to victory, and their rows and columns formed up sharply behind him in his wake.

Slowly, the king reached Uzi's encampment and his command post. Although most of the men had deserted, running off into the countryside to escape the fate they knew was coming, some remained. Now, they trembled with fear. They didn't know what would happen to them having witnessed the massacre of the king's own men for having done the same. All kept their eyes on their leader as he entered the campsite.

Barbarot rode forward, coming up to the body of Uzi, which lay crumpled on the ground under a white-canvassed, command tent. The king passed it, glancing down at the corpse and spitting on it before moving on.

"Scum!" he cried out.

Then, as if changing his mind, he stopped his winged horse and turned to face his troops. All could see the anger in his face, and they braced for the explosion. Standing up in his saddle, Barbarot addressed the thousands lined up around him.

"I have only a few words to say," he barked.

Breathing quickened throughout the ranks, and sweat trickled from foreheads and beneath helmets secured tightly by chinstraps. The stirrings and movement of the soldiers stopped abruptly as the king began again.

"We have won a great victory over the Vaporians. It has come with great loss and much sacrifice, as many of your comrades have fallen. Yet, they died for a noble cause. Without their courage, we would not be standing here now. More importantly, we would not be able to continue our quest for what is right and righteous.

"We Barbarotons are a mighty people," he said, referring to the new name he'd given the Kingdom of Rootan. "Ours is a lineage of masters of our planet. We are superior to others and other kingdoms. We were born as higher beings and must exert our power over those with lesser talents. We must preserve our kind at all costs. We cannot, and will not, permit anyone to threaten our way of life and our way of being. In this way, we will succeed. We will destroy all who stand in our way—who may wish to take all we cherish from us.

"We are threatened by people on all sides of Barbarotus. They are all plotting to invade and destroy our kingdom and take your wives and children from their homes. We are attacking now only to prevent them from doing this to us. We must protect your families from them. No one else will do it for us. The task is left to us and to us alone."

The troops were roused, and the emotions began to swell. The warriors slowly, but cautiously, raised their voices and then with his last remark, they roared their approval, shaking their spears, flashing their swords and rattling their shields. But the king was quick to temper their enthusiasm.

"However, there is one thing I will not let happen during my campaign," Barbarot bellowed, his anger spilling out of him. "I will *not* permit the weak and cowardly to lead my valiant troops," he said, pointing his sword at the body of Uzi. "You deserve better than this. You are the strong ones, you are my fighters, and you will ultimately be the winners!"

With that, the roar from the men was deafening. The valley shook as the sound of their voices echoed off the hills and mountain sides. The thousands before him, whipped into a frenzy, were ready for their next mission. They were ready to do anything their king asked of them.

Barbarot smiled. He had them right where he wanted them.

*****

CH 12 - A New Mission

It had been weeks, and Konjuur had still not been able to figure out the piece of stone he'd taken from the Arch of Gaya in Sanzotur. It was large, heavy and had symbols of people hunting animals and playing festival-type games all over it—something he'd never seen before. He hoped he'd be able to decipher the ancient drawings, and they would lead him to the secret treasure and ultimate power within the Realm that he believed was rightfully his.

His one source to find the answers to the stone was in the *Book of Gneima*. At one time, he had held the book in his hands. Even worse, he had taken possession of both the book *and* the stone at the same time. But that was then, and this was now. Donus had taken the book with him when he escaped from the cabin where they were holding him. They didn't know where he'd gone or what he'd done with the book.

"I need that *damned* book!" growled Konjuur. "We must get it back from that Donus lad who comes from the Rootanian kingdom."

"What if we track down his family and hold them hostage?" asked one of his knights. "I'm sure he'd give up the book if he thought his family would be harmed."

"He has no family," said Konjuur. "At least that's what I've been led to believe. But your right about one thing … he likely has friends still there. Perhaps we can find some of them and hold them ransom in exchange for the book."

"And what of Barbarot, my liege? He will return to the kingdom after his campaign. Then what will we do?"

"That is of concern, my Lord," said another. "A lady in town told me of strange powers the king has. They are far beyond those of any normal man, and no one can figure out where he gets them."

100

"Is he a sorcerer?" asked Konjuur.

"More than that, I believe. They say he created the plague that killed thousands in their kingdom recently. He's also put many people inside the castle under his spell. He controls their minds somehow, sire. It's black magic. Of that, I'm almost certain."

Konjuur brooded.

"Sire, it's as if he's already ...

"What? Found the map and its power?" said Konjuur amused. "Not likely. I've got the only map."

"We *think* it's the map, sire," his officer replied cautiously, knowing the danger of angering his lordship.

"It *is* the map, I say!" Konjuur screamed. "Don't you utter another word that this is not the Map of Gneima. Do you hear me!"

Konjuur sat and stared at the large rock leaning up against the wall in the corner of the cabin. They had been there weeks now after he had arrived back from Sanzotur and Donus had made his escape with the book. The viceroy got up and went to the stone, looking again at the strange symbols and letters engraved in its gray, smooth surface. He ran his fat, dirty fingers over the ridges and valleys as if it would come to life and begin speaking to him, revealing all its secrets.

"If the power is already in the hands of this new king," he said, musing, "then there is only one thing to be done."

"Yes, my Lord?" asked Malrod, his first knight.

"How long will it take to ride to Rootan?"

*****

CH 13 - Troubles at Home

At the newly-named Telic Castle—previously Claustrus Castle—the mood was subdued. A runner had returned from Vaporia with news. He rode in and dismounted quickly, running into the castle and finding the royal throne room.

"My Lord, my Lord!" the rider cried out, pushing aside the doors and barging in without waiting to be announced.

"What is it?" came the reply.

"I have news from the front in Vaporia."

"Go on …"

Baron Marbray, the father of the young man possessed by the darkness and now king, sat on the throne. His fingers gripped the broad, carved ends of the chair's arms. He had a dazed look—one of somebody being held in a trance and under the control of another.

The messenger read from a short scroll.

"Our troops engaged the enemy at Lagerfall, in front of the walls of the city. They fought for over six hours, taking heavy casualties. When the southern front faltered, the eastern front pushed ahead and took the city. Our magnificent king, Barbarot, was victorious and has seized the castle, the king and his army. Lagerfall is ours."

"I am very proud of our king," said Marbray. "He is a fine man, and very brave."

"Yes, my Lord," said the runner. "Are you not afraid for your son?"

"He is the king. He is not my son!" said the baron.

"Yes, my Lord, as you wish."

***

Meanwhile, Sojourn and Aunt Cleora were traveling to visit another of their countryman and former friend of Sojourn's. Weeks earlier, all had gone to Barbarot to change his mind and see if they could bring him back from the dark side of sorcery. However, Baron Marbray and Sir Montoi Leedsom had drunk from a spiced chalice offered by the king. Instantly, they had fallen under the spell of his potion.

"How are you doing, Cleora?" asked Sojourn. "We're almost there."

"Has he returned to us? Has he recovered from the spell?" asked Aunt Cleora.

"Montoi? I'm not sure, but we'll know more after we see him at his manor house. I've been speaking with him over the Nunzio Tablet."

"How did he seem?" asked Aunt Cleora.

"At first, he was still under the hex of the king. However, each day he continues to fight it. I've heard changes in his voice every time we talk," said Sojourn. "But we'll know for sure in a few minutes, won't we?"

It had been hard on Sojourn. Both his friends had gone to Claustrus Castle to convince the king. They had done it at Sojourn's asking. They had done it to try to save the kingdom. They had done it for many reasons—all unselfish ones.

The second hardship for Sojourn had been his sister's imprisonment. At least he had gotten her out. Now, he had to get his friends back.

Sojourn landed his volarequez, Angele, just inside the estate grounds with Aunt Cleora putting hers down behind him. They walked their horses up to a wide and squat konig tree just outside of view from the manor. There they tied their rides and went cautiously up the cobbled path to the main house. As uninvited guests they had to be wary, not knowing if Montoi had recovered enough to welcome them warmly or whether he would turn on them and have them arrested for the king.

Sojourn scanned the grounds nervously as they approached the house, deciding not to go in through the front but rather circle around to the back. They entered the manor through the narrow, green but peeling, servants' door and quietly tiptoed down the short hall leading to the kitchen.

"Shhhh!" said Sojourn, putting his finger to his lips.

They heard voices. But the sounds were coming from upstairs, and none were those of Montoi. Aunt Cleora continued down the hall, but Sojourn grabbed her elbow and shook his head. "Wait," he whispered.

After a few moments, Sojourn's eyebrows lifted, sensing something Aunt Cleora had not.

"What is it?" she asked, seeing the change in him.

But Sojourn only put his finger to his lips once more to keep her silent. They listened for a few more minutes, and then he motioned for her to follow him. He moved around the corner and next to a doorway, which he gently swung open. Only then did Aunt Cleora hear what her brother had sensed minutes earlier— it was Montoi. But there wasn't just one voice; there were two.

"I don't understand why you continue to badger me with this!" said Montoi, his voice escalating.

"You just aren't acting like yourself, sire. You haven't been yourself since ... since you came back from that blasted castle!" exclaimed the other man in the room, a voice Sojourn didn't recognize. "Why do you continue to defend him? He is bringing nothing but pain and suffering to our kingdom. Now, he's involved us in a war against our neighbors—why?"

"It doesn't matter! He is the king! We must obey him," Montoi responded.

"Ugh! You're infuriating!" the other man said before they heard the door slam on the other side of the room.

"That's all right, Bubba, he just doesn't understand, does he?" said Montoi to another in the room. "But I must tell you I've begun wondering the same thing during the last few days."

There was silence, as if the other stranger in the room were mute.

"So, boy, what do you think about this, *huh?* Perhaps the king isn't what he seems," said Montoi, continuing to babble. "Yes, that's a good boy."

"I think he's lost his mind," said Aunt Cleora. "He may be beyond saving, my brother."

Sojourn shook his head a smiled. "No, I think he's coming around."

Bark! Bark!

Sojourn wasted no time and stepped into the room, seeing his old friend. Beside him was his favorite pet kujopt, a miniature, but beautiful in its silky, black fur coat.

"Hello, Montoi," Sojourn said.

His friend looked up from his desk with a start. "Sojourn! Why are you here?"

"I've come to reclaim your soul, my friend," he replied.

Montoi looked puzzled but determined.

"You know there's a bounty on your head. The king wants you and your sister. He's willing to pay up to 1000 unio pieces. That's quite a sum, you know," said the nobleman. "So, why shouldn't I have my men arrest you now and claim the reward?"

"Montoi, we have been friends a long time. Why would you do something like that?" asked Sojourn.

"You are a traitor to Rootan. You defy the king. You must be arrested. You must be punished!"

Sojourn grabbed his friend and shook him. "Didn't you just hear that other person in the room here with you? What did he say? He said you are not the same person, Montoi! You're under the king's spell. You must fight it! You must free yourself! The king has drugged you. He's controlling your mind. You can't let that go on!"

Montoi shook his head, confused. "No," he said abruptly, pushing Sojourn's arms away. "No, I … I don't think ... I don't think that's right!"

Aunt Cleora came up to him and slapped him in the face.

"*Ow!*" Montoi shouted. "Why did you do that?" He pulled his arm away from Sojourn and began rubbing his cheek.

"I just wanted to see if you were still in there—at least the person we used to know," she replied.

"What?"

"What is your name?" asked Aunt Cleora.

"I am Nastasi Barbarosa," he replied.

"No, you're not.

"Yes, I am."

"No, you're Montoi Leedsom. You've always been Montoi Leedsom."

"I am Nastasi Barbarosa!"

"All right, Nastasi. When were you born?"

Montoi stared at her. "I was born …"

He stood bewildered, blinking furiously trying to remember.

"Who were your parents?"

"Uh, my parents? Well, my parents were of course, uh, they were …"

"Where is your wife? Where are your children?"

Aunt Cleora continued peppering him with questions.

Montoi began to get agitated and then angry. His face grew red with rage, and it was clear he was about to strike back.

Instead, Aunt Cleora slapped him again—this time harder. Montoi stumbled backwards. He grabbed for the desk, but his hand slid over the top, and he fell backwards onto the floor hitting his head.

"Montoi!" shouted Aunt Cleora, realizing what she'd one.

Sojourn ran to him, but his friend was out cold. His eyes were closed, and his head turned at an odd angle.

"Oh, my!" cried Aunt Cleora. "I didn't mean to hit him that hard. Is he … is he?"

"He's fine," said Sojourn. "You just knocked him unconscious." Then he picked up Montoi's head and gently tapped him on the side of his cheek. "Montoi? Montoi? Can you hear me?"

Eventually, the elder knight opened his tired, sagging eyes. He tried to focus on the person kneeling next to him but was having trouble.

"Where … where am I?" he asked.

"Montoi?"

"Yes? Who is there?"

"It's me, Sojourn. I'm here with Cleora."

Montoi sat up, rubbing the back of his head. Still groggy, he turned to his old friend and frowned.

"Why did you do that?" he exclaimed, looking at Sojourn.

"Do what?"

"Why did you hit me?"

"I didn't hit you. My sister hit you. If I had hit you, we wouldn't be having this conversation, Montoi. I would have decked you even harder."

"Do you remember who you are now?" asked Aunt Cleora.

"Of course, I do."

"You're the Queen of Edenot, then?" asked Sojourn, smiling.

"Very funny," said Montoi.

"Well?" asked Aunt Cleora still waiting for an answer.

"I'm Sir Montoi Leedsom if you don't remember. Sojourn, you of all people should be able to remember that! You're not that old and senile, are you?"

"No, not yet," answered his friend. "Welcome home. We've missed you, but now, we have much to do."

*****

CH 14 - High Stakes Trial

The noise faded as the guards cleared the passage at the far end of the west wing of the castle. Oliver jumped off his cot and ran to Nikko's bunk.

"Nikko!" he said anxiously.

Oliver poked the lump that was under the wool covers, but the shape didn't move. Oliver pushed on it again, and when nothing moved, he pulled back the blanket only to find two lumps of clothes bunched up to make it look as if a monkey were sleeping soundly beneath.

"Nikko!" Oliver yelled louder, looking around the rooms. "Where are you? We have to go!"

Not finding him, Oliver threw on his trousers and a white tunic and rushed down the hallway to follow the commotion he had heard earlier. He entered the dining hall, but it too was empty.

"I think it's coming from the trophy room," said Gemma coming up behind him. Her hair was disheveled, and her eyes were still sleepy and at half-mast.

They marched down the hallway, tracing the same route they'd taken the night before with the king after dinner. As they approached the room, they could hear loud voices. Inside, there was a small crowd of guards and servants gathered by one of the two crystal cases.

"What's going on?" Oliver asked.

But before Oliver could enter, two guards drew their swords and pointed them at his throat.

"Stop right there!" shouted one of them. "You cannot enter here."

"Let him through," came another voice—one higher-pitched—from within the room.

As Oliver walked in, he could see glass scattered all over the floor near where some maids and manservants were talking with the commander of the guard unit.

The crowd parted for Oliver, and he saw Cori kneeling down over the body of Nikko, which was laying still on the floor.

"Cori! Nikko! What happened?" shouted Oliver, who started to go to them. He knelt by his pet, putting his hand on Nikko's neck to check for a pulse. "What happened?" Oliver asked.

Cori was stone-faced and silent. She sat, stroking Nikko's body gently and combing the blue fur in the same direction down toward his tail.

"Nikko, wake up," she said softly. She looked up at Oliver unsure what to do.

"I think he's okay," said Oliver. "His heart is beating, and he's breathing. What was he doing in here?"

"They said he was trying to steal the map pieces," said Cori. "I don't know if that's true, but I can't understand why Nikko would be in here, do you?"

Oliver shook his head.

"Oliver … Gemma … Cori … why are all of you down here?" asked Prima coming into the room. "What's wrong with your pet monkey?"

Nikko stirred.

"Come on, Nikko. Wake up," coaxed Gemma, watching him.

Nikko opened his eyes. "*Oh,* what hit me?" he asked, rubbing his head.

"Nikko, are you all right?" asked Gemma.

"What were you doing down here, Nikko?" asked Oliver, scolding him but relieved that his pet was not seriously hurt.

"I … I …"

"Were you trying to steal the map pieces?" asked Cori. "They say that's when they caught you—when you were trying to take them."

"Steal d'em? No! I couldn' sleep! Dat's all! I came down to look at d'em again. Dat's all." He looked forlorn. "Honest, I didn' try to steal!"

"Then how did the crystal pedestal get broken?" asked Prima, accusingly.

"I dunno. I heard guards rushing down hall to da room. I guess d'ey t'ought I trying to steal d'em so d'ey came in. D'ey chased me, so I jumped on top of stand over d'ere. D'en one of d'em took his battle ax and raised it over his head. I jumped, and ax landed on top of stand, barely missing me!" He paused to catch his breath. "D'at could have been my head all over d'a floor d'ere, you know!"

"Take that blue thing away!" came the gruff voice of the guard commander.

"Where are you taking him?" asked Gemma.

"None of your business!" snarled the commander.

Prima stood next to Gemma and put her hand on her hip. "What happened here, Bromus?"

The guard commander stared at the daughter coolly. "That monkey was trying to steal the map from the king. We came in and stopped him."

"How did the case get broken?"

"That monkey jumped on it trying to break inside. He pushed the whole thing over trying to crash it so he could take the map piece."

"D'at not true!" shouted Nikko.

"We're going to take that creature away, Your Royal Highness," the commander said haltingly "It will be up to the king to decide what to do with it."

"Where are you taking him, then?" Oliver asked.

"I'm taking him to a prison cell. He'll have to wait for a hearing before the king in the morning," said the commander. "He'll have to stand trial for trying to steal the map."

"I didn' do d'at!" Nikko shouted angrily, the redness in his neck turning his blue face purple. "I swear, I didn'!"

"Sorry, but the laws of the land say he has to go to trial! The king will decide whether he's guilty or innocent," said the head of the guards. He turned to Prima as he left, bowing slightly and saying respectfully, "Your Highness."

Oliver watched as Nikko was chained and led out. The blue monkey looked back at his friends with a sad, mournful face. Then he disappeared down the hall.

***

It was early in the morning, and the first sun was rising. However, Oliver and Gemma had not slept a wink since the incident. Prima and Cori came by and tried to give them comfort, but neither sister knew much about how trials were conducted in the castle or what they might expect.

"Father is a fair man," Cori began, "yet not always the most understanding. When it came to rules and abiding by them, he is very strict."

"She's right," added Prima. "He can be rigid. When he disciplines us, he rarely makes exceptions for something that happened we had no control over. It's Mother who sometimes steps in to set him straight when he gets like that."

"But she probably won't help you with Nikko," said Cori. "He's not part of the family." Then, she said, "I am worried. I love my father, but I know how he can get. I also know how important those map pieces are to him."

"Why would the commander of the guard lie?" Gemma asked.

"Bromus is arrogant," Prima answered. "He can't admit that he made a mistake and destroyed the glass case. The king would be furious with him. It's easier for him to lie and pin that on Nikko to avoid punishment."

Cori went on to tell them of a time the king heard a case where a farmer's ulmpig had escaped and destroyed a neighbor's watermelon. However, during the trial, they found that the neighbor had gotten into an argument the day before with the farmer's wife. They had quarreled about the smell of the farmer's pigs drifting onto his land and into his house.

After the incident, the village constable had found the fence on the farmer's property broken, letting the ulmpig run into the neighbor's land—right where the watermelons were growing. In fact, the watermelon that was destroyed was small and had been fenced off from the others—the neighbor's best ones.

Yet, with all the evidence that the neighbor most likely staged the incident to get the neighbor's pigs taken away, the king ruled that the law was the law and that since the pig destroyed the property of another, it should be removed along with all the others.

"What can we do?" asked Gemma.

"I don't think there is anything we can do," said Cori. "Father certainly won't listen to Prima or me."

"What about your mother, the queen? Could she talk to him?"

"No, like I said, she'll only get involved when it's family," said Cori. "Mother won't waste an argument with Father over total strangers. She's not like that."

When the time came, the four walked into the royal throne room to await the trial. They took their seats at the back of the room, while the members of the court entered and found their assigned seats up front and along the sides. Eventually, the kingdom's chief prosecutor came in, dressed in pantaloons and a plum doublet jacket made of ruffled velvet and bone buttons. Ranking below the aristocracy, but above the commoners, the prosecutor managed the affairs within the castle walls and brought to justice anyone within the kingdom who violated a law, regardless of how minor or trivial—that was his job, and he took it very seriously.

He even looked like a prosecutor. Wiry with silver spectacles, he had large hands and wore white gloves as if he were going to a formal ball. His black boots were either too big for his feet or unusually long for the rest of this body. His narrow, black eyebrows stretched continuously across his forehead, spanning both of his soulless, black eyes.

They called the chief prosecutor "CP" for short. Some said it stood for *cold pirate*; others suggested simply *cruel person*. In either case, his face was cold and emotionless, as if he lived in a freezer and came out only when there were cases to prosecute for the king. He also looked as though he spelled something foul, but that was his usual demeanor. With pointed ears and a piercing gaze, there was little that he didn't see or hear. And when it couldn't be seen or heard, people said he could sense it. There was little that went on in the kingdom of Frezia that he wasn't aware of.

The side door to the throne room opened, and the guards brought Nikko in, still chained like a vicious mass murderer. Rather than placing him in a chair as they did with most defendants, the sentries threw him in a cage that had been brought in especially for the trial. No sooner was he shoved inside than the door was slammed shut and locked. Nikko put his head down. He couldn't bear to look at his master or Gemma.

CP stood by his table studying some papers when the twin doors opened, and two guards came in taking positions on either side of the entryway. CP then unrolled a short scroll, holding the top in his right hand while his left steadied the parchment.

"Hear ye! All rise for the King of Frezia. His Royal Highness, King de Riguere," he called out dramatically with flair and gusto.

Everyone in the crowded room rose as the king strutted in wearing a black, billowy robe with white cuffs on the sleeves. He entered walking briskly and sat down in his high-backed, royal chair—a large, stone throne with navy cushions piped with gold fringe to protect his back and seat from its hardness.

"So, what do we have here?" asked the king looking down at the little blue monkey trapped in the wire cage. "I believe we just dined together with you and your friends last night. How quickly you've found your way to my trial room? You don't seem to be a very grateful guest, now do you?"

The king's stare was not warm and compassionate, and Oliver felt a shiver go up his spine as he watched. It was not a good beginning.

CP went before the king and handed him the scrolled parchment from which he'd been reading. The king took it in his stubby hands which were well-manicured and had never seen a day of hard work. He quickly scanned it, familiarizing himself with the contents before handing it to the court crier.

"Read the charges," the king ordered in a booming voice.

The diminutive crier cleared his voice and began.

"The charges against the accused are as follows. In the case of the people of Frezia against the accused …" He stopped and looked at the blue monkey as if to connect the two before he continued. "… Nikko, you are charged with attempting to steal the priceless pieces of the Map of Gneima from the King and Queen of Frezia."

He looked up from his reading. "How do you plead?"

Nikko glanced at Oliver. He didn't understand what he was being asked.

"What you asking me?" he blurted out.

"If I may ..." said Prima, standing at the back of the courtroom.

The king nodded and motioned for her to help the little blue monkey. His daughter went to the cage and knelt down beside him.

"Nikko, what he means is ... do you say you're guilty of trying to steal the map or not," she said to him.

"No! I didn't do it!" shouted Nikko firmly. "I didn't!" His face was tight and animated; every muscle was moving or twitching.

"I see," replied the king, unmoved. "Well chief prosecutor, present the evidence, then," he said to CP in a monotone voice.

"The people call Commander Bromus to the witness stand."

Commander Bromus went to the stairs leading up to the witness chair where he took his seat.

"Commander, please explain what happened last night in the trophy room."

Bromus pointed his long, but crooked finger at the cage that held Nikko.

"That creature was in the trophy room when we arrived. It was trying to push over the case that holds one of the map pieces. I knew what it was trying to do—to topple it over so it would break, and it could grab the treasure inside."

"What happened then?"

"The monkey started scampering all over the room to get away from us. He jumped on top of several other cases before hopping back on one with a map piece. Then, it took its hand and tried to break the top of it. When it wouldn't break, it started rocking the case back and forth on the pedestal. I attempted to stop it, but by the time I reached the case, it had pushed it over, shattering it in a million pieces. Then, it started to reach in to take the blue package that holds the map piece. One of my guards lunged to grab it, but it jumped out of the way. However, I caught it with my net and made it drop the bag."

Oliver shook his head. That story was not the same one he had told them the night before.

Nikko shook his head, muttering, "No, no, no! It didn' happen d'at way!"

The King smirked. "You swear you're telling the truth, commander?"

"Of course, Your Royal Highness. Of course," said the commander solemnly.

"I see," said CP. "That is all I have, Your Majesty. I think that's all we need."

Cori got up from her chair. "Father, that's not true!"

"Sit daughter!" shouted the king.

"There was no net in the room. I was there. They had no net, Father. What they're telling you isn't the truth."

"It seems pretty clear what happened here," said the king. "The monkey was caught in my trophy room. It matters not how he was captured."

Suddenly, Oliver jumped up in the middle of the courtroom. "I protest!" he yelled.

All eyes turned toward him, including those of CP and the king.

"Young man, you are out of order!" barked the king. "You have no claim to make in this case. This matter is between the kingdom and the accused!"

"I do have a claim, with all due respect, Your Highness!" said Oliver loudly, wrought with emotion. "Nikko is my property. I own him. Therefore, I am part of this case whether you know it or not."

"So, your property inflicted damage on mine?"

"Yes, Your Majesty. If you wish to look at it that way, yes."

The king glanced at CP who shrugged and then nodded in agreement.

"But you haven't permitted me to defend myself or my property. You haven't heard *our* side of the story. You must hear from the defendant for this to be a fair hearing!"

The king sat back in his chair. He was not used to such thoughtful challenges.

"Fine!" he said. "Let's hear from the furry, blue creature. Open the cage. Allow him to take the witness stand."

A long chain was attached to Nikko before he was let out of the cage. He climbed the stairs and sat on the same chair the commander had held only moments earlier.

"You have only two minutes," said the king. "Tell us why you were in the trophy room and what happened."

Nikko explained that he had only been looking at the museum piece through the glass top of the stand. Then, according to him, the guards rushed in, swinging their swords and battle axes and chasing him around the room. Nikko claimed that one of the guards swung his battle ax, accidently hitting the pedestal and shattering it. Then, one of the sentries struck him with the grip of his sword, knocking him out.

"That's all I remember," said Nikko, hoping the king would believe him.

"*Mmmmm...*" said the king. "But, why would you have been in the room to begin with, except to steal them?"

"I told you. I just looking at d'em. D'ey are amazing!"

"Why should I believe you? I took you and your friends into the room only hours before to show you something very precious to me. And only a short time later, you are in the room, alone, looking at them. What else would you make of this?"

Nikko said nervously, "I ... I don't know what else to say. I couldn't sleep and got up to walk around. I went down de' hall, passed dining room, and then to trophy room. I saw door to room already ajar, so I just went in ... d'at's all."

The king frowned. "I don't think so. That room is never left unlocked."

Nikko could see that the king's black eyes were unsympathetic. In fact, they were harsh and unmoved.

"Father," said Prima, respectfully.

"Yes?"

"I don't believe this little blue monkey would try to steal something like the map," she said. "How would a monkey like this know how valuable those pieces are, and why would he want to steal them? Anyway, both pieces would be much too heavy for the little creature to get them out of the room by himself. And about the case, Father—it is very heavy. I don't think that little monkey could rock the pedestal back and forth. The case didn't look like it fell over—it looked like it had been hit by something.""

"I think what you're saying is that this monkey could not have done it on his own. Is that what you are saying, my child?"

"Uh, no. I wasn't trying to say that ... what I was trying to say is that ..." she stuttered, getting confused by how to answer the question.

"If that is true," said the king, "then you are suggesting that your friends helped him with it?"

"No ... I don't think that at all!"

"Then, I suggest we stick to the facts at hand, shall we?" said the king.

Prima sat down. She knew when her father got angry, it never helped to argue with him. He rarely backed down when he was put into a corner. Getting him more upset would only make matters worse.

"I have reached my decision, then," said the king. "The accused will rise!"

One of the guards motioned for Nikko to come down from the witness chair. Then, he put Nikko back in the cage to await his sentence.

"As king and the ruling sovereign of the Kingdom of Frezia and as representative of the people of this kingdom, I hereby sentence you, Nikko, to death."

Oliver and Gemma gasped. They had no idea that the sentence could be that severe—that Nikko could be sentenced to death for attempting to steal something.

"You can't be serious!" yelled Oliver.

But Prima put her hand on Oliver's shoulder. "Sit, Oliver, or you and Gemma will be the next ones sentenced," she said.

"Take him away!" bellowed the king, pointing to the door that led to the prison cells.

Oliver ignored Prima's warning and marched to the front of the courtroom. There, he put his hands on his hips and challenged the king directly.

"This is not right! It isn't fair!" Oliver shouted, the redness building in his face. This was a side of Oliver Gemma had never seen before.

"How *dare* you challenge me!" roared the king, his formalness evaporating.

"You have no right to condemn him to death based on the evidence—the word of one man? Especially, when several others are telling you it's not true and the actual evidence of the room doesn't support it."

"Silence!" shouted the king.

"Then take me instead?" said Oliver defiantly. "Take me as prisoner and let my pet monkey go."

"Why would you do that, boy? Is it that my daughter, Prima, was right ... that you and your lady friend were helping him and all conspiring to steal the map pieces from me?"

"No. You know that's not true. You know you have no proof of that!" Oliver spouted back at the ruler.

The king stopped. "Interesting. So, you're telling me that you would sacrifice yourself for your pet?"

"Yes. I believe he is innocent," said Oliver, who then corrected himself. "No, change that. I *know* he's innocent, and I believe in the justice of law. It's the principle of it. Law without justice isn't a worth the paper it's written on."

The king sat thoughtfully about the proposal. "Well, what are you willing to wager then? I am not just going to put you to death instead of your animal here. I'm a sportsman, you see. I'm willing to make you a bet. The question is what are you willing to give me in addition to your life, if you lose?"

Oliver stood looking at him, unprepared for the question.

"I tell you what," said the king, not waiting for an answer. "I will agree to free your little friend; however, you must win my Frezia Challenge. If you win, then you will win your pet's freedom."

"And if I don't win?" Oliver asked hesitantly.

"Then you and your friends will *all* be put to death."

"*All* of us?" asked Oliver, glancing over at Gemma.

"Yes. All," replied the king.

"Father, no!" shouted Cori, but he ignored her outburst.

It was now clear there was an even darker side to this king than they had known. Both his daughters looked on in horror as their father issued the challenge. Perhaps this wasn't a side of him they knew either.

Gemma was worried, but she nodded her consent for Oliver to go ahead. But Oliver shook his head. "Your Majesty ..." Oliver began.

"He will do it!" Gemma blurted out, not letting Oliver sacrifice himself alone.

Oliver stared at her in disbelief.

"Accepted," said the king joyfully.

"No!" said Oliver. "This is my trial and my pet. I must agree to the terms."

"I heard the answer from one of your party who was included in the wager. Since she would be affected by your winning or losing, she has the right to speak for the group. She has done so."

"If this is the wager," said Oliver, "then it must be three for three—that's only fair."

"What do you mean?" asked the king, confused with Oliver's answer.

"If you are going take all three of us if I fail, then we should get three of something in return if I succeed," said Oliver.

"What are you saying?"

"I'm saying that a fair wager would be to trade our lives for the freedom of Nikko and the two map pieces you have in the other room," said Oliver.

The courtroom gasped. Prima and Cori looked on ... they couldn't believe the audacity of this young, red-haired knight.

The king smiled, confident in his challenge. "I like someone who is bold and gallant—someone who believes in themselves so completely. Interesting, your offer is." He stopped for a moment. "Yes, I will accept your terms. You have a deal, Sir Oliver."

Oliver wasn't sure whether this was such a good thing, especially when the king was so quick to agree to it. The young knight was nervous and fidgeted, but he did his best to put on a brave face.

"However, I must tell you something, Sir Oliver. You are foolish and reckless with your life and those of your companions. There are two things you must know about the Frezian Challenge. First, you must be *very* smart and have the answers to almost any question you may be asked. In fact, I'm told the questions are so hard that few have returned from that part of the challenge."

"And what's the second thing?" asked Oliver.

"There are many who start the challenge believing they have what it takes to win," the king laughing. "However, by the time it ends, none feel that way any longer."

"And why is that?" asked Oliver.

The king laughed more loudly this time. "Because they're likely dead!"

*****

CH 15 - A Threat

Baron Lukae's manor was modest by the standards of many others in Frezia, but in the southern part of the kingdom, it was grand enough to make him an aristocrat. Known for his hospitality and kindness, the baron took painstaking measures to make sure his new guest was comfortable and welcome. However, all that charity didn't go over well with someone else in the family. Unfortunately, the baron's son, Parogild, did not see his father's kindness in the same way, and he became jealous.

Parogild had been born with one leg shorter than the other, which gave him a discernable limp. However, neither his father nor his mother had let that affect them. They had still loved him as if he'd been born the perfect child—which, in their minds, he was. It was Parogild who carried the guilt and shame, thinking others believed him something less than a whole person.

Despite the challenge, the boy was very smart and remarkably handsome. Broad-shouldered and muscular, he could do what most other boys could do except run as fast or jump as high. He had dark, wavy hair that fell to the middle of his back and by the age of eighteen had a full, ebony beard. Parogild was much like his sister. His sapphire blue eyes were deep set and wide, and his nose was royal—strong but narrow. Yet, he was more darkly complexioned than his sister, and he carried the stigma of self-doubt.

Increasingly belligerent, Parogild watched as the baron placed Donus in charge of tutoring the shepherds who worked his flocks in the pastures. It hadn't been that Parogild was incapable; rather, he had been indifferent toward the boys and hadn't wanted to. They saw him as arrogant and, at times, mean. As a result, they didn't like or respect him.

Donus, on the other hand, was jolly and good-natured. At the end of each day, he would march out to the shepherds' quarters and begin teaching them. Although he didn't remember much about himself or where he came from, he did recall the things he'd learned at the Knight's Observatory back in Rootan. Donus took pride in helping boys who didn't have the same opportunity to learn as he apparently did.

The days were short but getting longer every day as spring was coming. It was a wonderful time of year as the ice began to melt and the plants and flowers began to spring back to life. The life of a shepherd was wonderful in the springtime. The temperatures were not too hot, the soft breezes kept the bugs away, and the animals were happy to be out of their pens and free to roam and graze.

Yet, the young boys still had hard work to do. The baron relied on them to repair fences, clear brush, maintain the main house and their own quarters, while at the same time tend to the herds. By the time they returned from a full day's work, the boys struggled to stay awake during Donus' classroom at night.

"Blu-Ice, what is this letter?" asked Donus, showing them a capital *A*.

Blu-ice was sound asleep even though he sat upright on the wooden floor. Whal-tooth nudged him, and he woke up, startled.

"What?"

"I asked you what this letter is?"

"Uh, it's a … it's a letter. I think," answered Blu-ice, disappointing Donus.

"Yes, that's true. I already told you that. But which letter?"

"It's an *A*," said Urchin, another boy, who was younger than most, but one of the brightest in the room.

"Very good. And what about this one?"

"That's an *E*," said Urchin, smiling broadly.

"That's right," said Donus. "Is there anyone else in the room besides Urchin who knows what this letter is?"

"Is it a *U*?" asked Blu-ice, trying.

"No, it's not a *U*, but good try. It's an *O*. Now, we have a few more letters in this group—the *I*, the *O*, and sometimes the *Y*. *A, E, I, O, U*, and sometimes the letter *Y* make up a group called what?"

Again, it was Urchin. "Vowels," he said.

"And why are those so special?"

No one in the group raised their hand.

"Well, it's because every word has to have at least one vowel in it to be a word. Sometimes the vowels are at the beginning—sometimes at the end. Sometimes, a word is only one letter, like *I* or *A*."

Donus continued a little longer but found it hard to keep the boys' attention.

"All right. That's enough for one night. We'll start fresh tomorrow," he said.

Walking back to the manor house, Donus found Parogild in the doorway.

"I bet you're real proud of yourself, aren't you?" Parogild asked Donus.

Donus looked at him curiously, not knowing how to answer. "I'm not sure what you mean?"

"You and father. You're best of chums, aren't you?"

"I think you misunderstand," said Donus. "I'm only trying to help. I'm glad I can teach the boys something. They're eager and hungry for it, you know."

However, Parogild was not amused. He had gone out of his way to be nasty to the visitor. Once while Donus had been out teaching the boys, Parogild had slipped into his room and let loose several parathian rats, which quickly destroyed Donus' bunk, blankets and satchel. It took Donus several weeks to catch all them and get a full night's sleep without waking up in the middle of the night, staring into the eyes of one of the vermin. They usually crawled up on his bed and sniffed him, poking his face with their foul whiskers.

However, these minor pranks had only increased, and Parogild now confronted Donus directly, pushing him up against the wall inside the manor house and bullying him.

"You already know how much I don't like you!" he threatened, with anger and malice in his eyes. "No, that isn't true ... I actually despise you!"

"I don't understand. What have I ever done to you?" asked Donus, staying calm.

"You exist!" spat Parogild, jealously. "I want you gone from this house by the end of tomorrow, or else!"

"Or else what?"

"You don't want to know. You'll regret it if you don't leave."

Donus snapped. He'd had enough abuse coming from this lad. He grabbed Parogild's smaller hands and ripped them from his tunic. Donus was much larger, and he straightened his shirt to remove the marks left by his attacker. Then, moving toward the baron's son, Donus smiled disingenuously.

"Parogild, I have gone out of my way to be nice to you. You are the owner's son, after all. However, I will *not* continue to be bullied by you. If you *ever* touch me again, I will tear your arms from your body and feed them to a cerberian wolf in the woods. Two of its heads can chew on your arms while I find another piece of you to feed to its third. Do I make myself clear?" Donus then turned and stomped away.

Later that day, Donus saw Genona near the stables and approached her. She smiled at him as she always did, looking up from her chores as she heard him coming up the stone walk. Even though she was the daughter of a baron, her father believed it was important that his son and daughter do work around the estate. Genona, the obedient one, always had hers finished before noon; however, Parogild rarely even started his.

"How are you?" she asked Donus, who reached down to help her up.

"Fine," he replied. "I'm having a wonderful time teaching the boys. I think they really want to learn."

"They say nice things about you."

"That's good to hear."

"By the way, what name should we call you?" Genona asked. "I've been saying 'hi' to you for some time, but I never know what to call you."

Donus was stumped. "Well, I guess ... maybe ... You know, I don't know. What do you think you should call me?"

Genona thought for a moment and grinned. "I think you look like a 'Reginald.'"

"Reginald?"

"Yeah, don't you like it?"

"It's okay, I guess," responded Donus uncertainly.

"All right, well, how about Volcom?"

"Do I look like a Volcom?" he replied, scrunching his face up to look mean and nasty.

She laughed. "I don't even know what a Volcom looks like. I've never met one."

"Then where did you come with that!" said Donus, smiling.

"I dunno. What about Arifarious Morgenstern?"

At that, both began laughing heartily.

He was fond of her—very fond of her—and his liking grew every day. Most of all, he loved her sense of humor which she rarely had a chance to show him.

"Since I don't know what I am, I guess whatever you come up with is as good as anything," said Donus.

"I like the name Benigno," she stated, putting the final exclamation point on the argument.

"Then, Benigno it is," affirmed Donus.

Genona smiled as if she'd won the grand prize at the shire or county fair.

"Okay, Benigno. It looks like you've got something else on your mind. You usually don't come down to the stable to talk to me. Is there something bothering you?"

"There is something I'd like to talk with you about, Genona."

She looked at him intently. Her eyebrows raised wondering what he was about to say or ask.

"It's about your brother, Parogild."

"Oh, Pari?" she said, acting as though she wasn't surprised. "What's he done now? Has he been a horse's butt to you?"

"Yeah, how did you know?" asked Donus.

"He can be a real jerk sometimes. He is so conceited and arrogant. He thinks he's an only child, and if anyone tries to come between him and father—well, it's not good!" she warned.

"So, this isn't the first time he's been like this?"

She shook her head. "Oh, no. In fact, I even have to be careful not to make him angry. He's got a bad temper, you know."

Donus nodded, having witnessed it firsthand.

"But you shouldn't worry too much about him, Benigno. You're a lot bigger than he is. He won't push you too far."

"What happened the last time he got this way?" asked Donus.

"Let's see. It was a few years ago. There was another boy from the village who was having problems at school. He was getting into trouble all the time, and the teacher didn't know what to do with him." She stopped and looked at Donus.

"What is it?" he asked.

"The teacher looked a lot like you. He was wonderful with the kids and also helped out around here as a tutor for the shepherds," she said. "Anyway ... where was I?"

"You were talking about ...

"Yes, yes, I remember now," she interrupted. "The teacher was talking to Father about how unruly the boy was. Father invited both of them to come to dinner one night, hoping he could help. I recall that dinner very well."

"What happened?" asked Donus.

"It didn't go well. Father spent the entire dinner talking with the boy—you know, asking him what he liked and didn't like about school, who his friends were, and other stuff. I could see the look on Pari's face as Father gave all his attention to this boy, ignoring Pari completely.

"So, Pari began interrupting their conversation for meaningless—really childish—things. And then, without saying a word, he stood up and threw his goblet across the dining hall floor. I remember him saying 'Am I now invisible to everyone?' before storming out of the room and slamming the door."

"How old was the boy?"

"He was young—probably about ten," said Genona, "but that was the last time I ever saw the boy."

"What happened to him?"

"Someone told me that Pari confronted him a few days later in town and told him *never* to come to the castle again if he knew what was good for him."

"Did the boy ever go back to school?"

Genona answered, "I don't know. We never talked about it after that."

"It doesn't sound like I'll be able to change Parogild's mind about me, then. He's threatened me too. He wants me out of the manor and out of the kingdom by tomorrow. But the problem is I don't have anywhere I can go."

"What?"

"Yeah. He said he'd do something to me if I don't leave," said Donus.

Genona shook her head slowly. "Don't worry," she answered him. "I'll talk to Father and see what he says. Father likes you; he enjoys your company. Besides, you're helping his cause by teaching his field crews."

"What do you mean his 'cause'?"

Genona took him by the arm and began walking with him. They left the stables and began wandering down a path that led to a small, frozen lake nearby.

"You see," she continued, "Father likes helping those who are disadvantaged; you know—the peasants. He's always trying to give them chances to improve themselves and give them hope. He's a good man, my father. Of that, I'm certain. Anyway, he hired each one of the shepherd boys because they wanted to learn and do better in their lives. He's told me he's not going to *give* it to them—they have to *earn* it—but he does want to give them every chance in life. And now, you're part of that."

"I see," Donus said. "Quite admirable, I'd say."

"Yeah, my father is like that—always has been. But at the same time, he also believes we should do the same thing. That's where the problems lie."

"What do you mean?"

"Well, now that you understand a little about my brother, you know he's not the most ambitious person in the kingdom. In fact, he relies too much on Father to get him through things. He's always needing money and getting into trouble. When he does, Father bails him out, of course."

"Why does he do that if he believes each of us should work our way up?"

Genona nodded. "I think it's because he's a cripple. Father feels guilty about that—like it's his fault. He tries to make up for it all the time, and Pari is all too willing to take advantage of it."

Donus hadn't said much but was taking it all in. He was beginning to understand what was going on and that he was caught in the middle of something that had been there long before he had appeared on the scene. Suddenly, he too felt a pang of guilt.

"I was a bit short with your brother this morning when he tried to bully me. Now that I see where he's coming from, I feel ..."

"No, don't. Don't feel bad. That's the problem. Everyone feels bad. We need to treat him like everyone else. That's what he needs. He doesn't need our pity. He needs our respect. That's what I would want."

"Yeah, you're right."

"Pari and I get along fine because I don't cut him a break. I treat him like a full brother of mine—not someone I need to take care of."

"I just hope we can get beyond this, then," said Donus.

"Benigno, it's nothing to worry about. We'll sort it out. I'll see what I can do, okay?"

Donus squeezed her arm. "Thanks, Genona. I'll owe you one!"

The rest of the day passed without any sign of Parogild. Donus spent the time working around the manor house doing most of the chores the baron's son was supposed to do. After his talk with Genona, he knew that wasn't the best thing to do. But the baron had asked him, and he had told him he would.

132

That night, Donus headed away from the manor house toward the shepherds' quarters for their nightly lesson. But as he left, Genona caught up with him.

"Have you seen Pari?" she asked, obviously upset.

"No, I haven't seen him since our little run-in this morning," replied Donus.

"No one can find him. He's left the manor and didn't tell anyone where he was going!"

"Who saw him last?"

"I don't know, but father wants to see you right away," she said.

They went directly to the baron's private quarters, and Donus knocked respectfully before going in. The room was surprisingly small and sparse. The furniture was plain, as if it had been made by the hands of one of the shepherd boys during their time at the estate. There was a crude, wooden bookcase in the corner, several chairs without arms but with caned seats and backs, and a massive, rustic table that was triangular, rather than the typical square or rectangle.

"Come in, come in," said the baron with an urgent voice that showed concern.

Together, Donus and Genona went in, closing the door behind them. Sitting next to the baron's table, Genona moved the red candle that had burned down a third of the way so the smoke wouldn't float into her eyes. There were a few papers scattered in front of her father, together with a pen and a porcelain cup of sand which he used to blot the excess ink from the page. Between his fingers, the baron held an iron seal that he was steadying over a glob of yellow wax ready to emboss it with his sign of rank and authority.

"Thank you for coming so quickly, Benigno," said the baron. "I just wanted to talk to you about my son, Pari."

"What's happened to him?" asked Donus.

"That's why I asked you to come. But since then, I have found some answers." The baron put his hand to his forehead as if he were in pain.

"Father, what is it?"

"Pari came to me this morning to talk about you," he said pointing to Donus. He then smiled and added, "Don't worry, Benigno. You must hear the entire story first. You will see that I understand a great many things about my son."

"What did he say about him?" asked Genona, defensively.

"Pari said that was 'tired' of the way he's been treated by all of us, and he wanted 'out,'" the baron said.

"What did he mean by 'out'?" Genona asked.

"He told me he was finished with our family and with everything else going on around here. He asked me for his inheritance—now—before I died. He said he would take it and leave, never to return and never to ask for anything else." There was genuine sadness in his voice.

"What did you say, Father?" asked Genona.

"Genona, I want you to know that I love you, and I love your brother very much. I did what I would do for you as well."

"What was that? Did you tell him to grow up?" she asked, getting emotional.

The baron was calm, and he took her hand. "I gave him what he wanted," he said and then paused. "I tried to persuade him not to go, but he was ... well ... you know how he can get."

"Yes," was her only reply.

"So, I told him that I loved him, and I wished him the God of god's speed."

"What?" said Genona. "You gave him his inheritance and let him go?"

"Yes, my dear. He has wanted to go for many years. He has held a grudge against anyone I showed any interest in. It was time for him to go and strike out on his own."

"Father, how could you?"

"Genona, it was the right thing to do. I know it, and you know it. It was what I was supposed to do," he said.

The baron tried to take her hand, but Genona pushed it away. She stormed out of the room, angry and in tears.

"Genona!" Donus called after her, starting to leave.

"She will be okay," said the old man. "Just give her time."

"You are right about her," said Donus. "She is stronger than she looks, but it will take time."

"Yes. I know. I also know that what I did was the right thing," said the baron. "When the time is right, I will explain to her that I will make good on my word. My son has received his inheritance and will not get a token more. She will be looked after and taken care of after I'm gone. I will make sure of that."

Donus replied from his heart, "I believe you. You did what you thought was best. And as for Genona, I think she'll be just fine on her own. She can take care of herself."

The baron smiled. "Yes. You know her well too. You are, of course, right. You have feelings for her, yes?"

"I like your daughter very much, my Lord."

The old man grinned. "The feelings are mutual, I'm sure."

*****

PART II - THE CHALLENGE

CH 16 - On to Erebus

Oliver arrived in front of the crystal castle, where he was told to come and where the challenge would begin. However, when he got there, he found he was far from alone. There was a throng of people wearing their thick, fur coats and rubbing their leather mittens together to keep warm. The temperature had dropped during the night, and the snow had started to fall again in earnest. With the winds gusting, it felt far colder than at any time since they had crash-landed in Frezia to escape the virus cloud.

An area was roped off next to a large, ice-block building, and in front were twelve sleds, each with a second sled tethered behind it. These second sleds held a few lumpy, silver bags that were strapped down with heavy, coarse ropes.

The king and queen were not there, but it seemed like the rest of the town was on hand. Even Prima and Cori were standing in their white fur coats and hats with their arms around each other to keep warm.

Cori approached Oliver and gave him a feeble, but sincere, smile. Then, she gave him a kiss on the cheek.

"Oliver, the God of god's speed to you. I pray you will return safely to us." Then, she choked back tears and looked away before more came flooding down her reddened cheeks and froze to her skin.

In a rare moment, Prima put her arm around her younger sister to console her. She too was sad and found it hard to control her emotions.

"Oliver," Prima said, "we *will* see you again; I know it." She took her other arm and gave Oliver a soft, loving pat on the shoulder.

Oliver looked around to find his friends, but they weren't there. Surprised, he asked Prima, "Where are Gemma and Nikko? I thought for sure they'd be here to see me off."

However, it was Cori who answered him.

"Oliver, they *can't* be here. They're in prison. They were taken in the early morning hours and won't be released until you cross the finish line and win this thing."

"They're already in prison?"

"Yes. I'm sorry. So, you see, you must return to us … to them."

"And if I don't?" he asked, upset by the news.

Cori and Prima could only look down at the snow.

CP was again the center of attention and master of ceremonies. He stood in front of the ice building directing the comings and goings of people and equipment. He was all in his glory, enjoying every second of the limelight.

"Hear ye! hear ye all!" CP began as he had in the courtroom. "It is with great excitement that I announce the start of the biannual Frezia Challenge. This year the competition is keener than ever before as we have someone outside our land as an entrant into our famous race. His name is Oliver—Oliver of Rootan."

With that introduction, the crowd began cheering and whistling their enthusiasm. Even some of the huskies that were with their owners began barking loudly, jumping up and down.

CP continued.

"Oliver of Rootan will be joined by many others who have come to the capital to compete against him."

At that moment, the king's guards opened the doors to the ice building, and eleven men, all cuffed in arm and leg irons were brought out from their cells. Dressed in thin, white leather jackets, the men looked rough and ... mean. Oliver had expected a group of hardened and well-experienced competitors. What he saw instead was a group of hardened criminals. If he had any thoughts this would be a clean and fair race, they immediately evaporated.

The guards took each man and chained him to the railing of a sled. After all men were secured, they were handed a whip. And even though many were tempted to use it on their overseers, none raised a hand. They all knew they wouldn't get far.

"Now it's time for the dogs!" shouted CP with glee. "Strap them to the sleds. Make sure they're locked on and can't escape."

From the other side of the ice building, towering iron gates squeaked open, and the animal handlers struggled with their keeps. Their arms jerked violently as the animals strained against the black chains, snarling and barking.

But these were no ordinary dogs. In fact, they were not dogs at all. These were wolves that made the kujopts Oliver was familiar with look like puppies. It was a wild breed of wolf that he had never seen before—far nastier than anything he knew. These were the famed cerberians—three-headed beasts with fangs that stuck out of each sides of their mouths, hanging a good four-to-six inches below their lower jaws. This made them look like prehistoric sabretooth cats, but without the charm. The wolves' heavy coats of white fur blended with the surrounding snow; yet, some had spots or stripes of black or brown, making each different and distinct.

Lovely, Oliver thought, rolling his eyes. *What else could happen to make this any worse!* Then, a little voice went off inside his head. *It's a challenge, Oliver. Not a curse! It will be whatever you make it to be. The choice is yours.* Oliver smiled. That was what Nikko would tell him if he were there.

"Over here you!" growled one of the sentries, motioning for him to get into the last, empty sled. "We ain't got all day!"

The guard started to shackle him to the sled when Prima yelled at him. "That is not necessary," she said. "He is not a prisoner, like the others."

"Not yet," snarled CP, grinning.

Oliver got on the long, wooden sled. It looked solid, but when he stepped onto the footboards, they wobbled and creaked. The handlebar on the platform was no better, jiggling from side to side and forward and back as if it hadn't been attached right. He glanced down, expecting a tether for braking the wolves, but when he pulled on the cord, it broke, frayed completely through.

"Competitors ready?" shouted CP.

Grabbing the reins, Oliver pulled them tight.

His wolf turned its three heads and each one snarled at him, showing Oliver who they thought was in charge. But Oliver yanked on the reins harder, pulling it until the wolf let out a yelp. Then, he let them go, tying them around the sled's rail in front before reaching to grab his satchel. He threw that into the second sled with the other silver bags behind him.

"What do you think you're doing?" yelled CP, pointing at the bag Oliver had tossed. "You can't take that with you!"

"What?" Oliver asked, surprised at the order.

"That!" shouted CP, shaking his finger at Oliver's satchel. "You can't take that bag with you! Nothing can be taken with you except what we provide. That would be cheating!"

Oliver started to hand over his satchel, but as he did, he slipped another, smaller bag, out of the side pocket. This one he slid calmly underneath his jacket. Then, he handed the large bag to CP, who looked at it before hurling it carelessly to the side of the ice building.

"You all know the rules!" CP said to the group. "You must go to Mount Erebus. There you will find the Rebus, which will ask you some questions. You must answer all correctly. If you don't, bad things are certain to happen to you. If you make it past the Rebus, you must find the right path to find a treasure. You must return with the treasure to the castle. We have the only keys to your chains. If you don't return to the castle, you will never be freed from your sleds.

"You have exactly three days—no more and no less. If you return without the treasure, you will be killed. If you try to escape and free yourself from your sled, the dogs are trained to attack and kill you; otherwise, we will track you down and do it ourselves.

"If you think you are too smart, let me warn you. No participant has ever left the contest alive if they did not win. There is, of course, only one winner."

CP stopped and surveyed the group, sneering. "Do you have any questions?" But he didn't wait for any. "Have a nice race," he ended sarcastically before nodding to the starter.

"Ready?" came the starter's voice, shouting above the crowd. "*Oshva!*" he then said, a word from an ancient Frezian language which simply meant 'go.'

The cerberian wolves took off dragging the long sleds behind them. Some had rather light loads to carry—those with prisoners who were small and thin—while others had far heavier payloads—those with huge, muscular prisoners who could have easily pulled the sleds themselves.

Oliver had a cerberian that was larger than most and also more vicious. It seemed to dislike everything and everyone, and, in particular, it did not like being chained to a sled. With its three heads, the dog was mostly white but had two black stripes that girded its midsection and three that wound down its back. Its tail was completely black and wagged incessantly, even though Oliver sensed it was not out of happiness or joy.

Grabbing the reins, Oliver instinctively cracked them, snapping them against the back of his cerberian canine. It snarled at him and bit at the reins in anger. But Oliver stood firm and cracked them again, inflicting no pain but still getting the beast's attention.

The wolf took off, pulling the sled forward. Quickly, all the sleds began bunching together into the narrowing path, becoming just wide enough for one or perhaps two sleds to run abreast. Farther along the trail, it shrank further to a single lane, and everyone formed a single line with Oliver second to last in the pack.

"Come on, Snarlface," shouted Oliver, making-up a name for his wolf. But the cracking of the reins and all his shouting didn't push his animal any faster.

The snow continued to fall making it difficult to see, and, worse yet, Oliver didn't know where he was supposed to go other than follow the trail like everyone else. The only thing for sure was he needed to keep his mind sharp and try to anticipate whatever might come his way. He knew the types of people he was up against, and whatever they were plotting, it would come suddenly and without mercy.

It was soon clear the wolf knew where to go. Oliver wasn't guiding the sled; rather, the wolf was leading him. He held on for his life as the sled screamed through the snow at high speed, following closely on the heels of the prisoner in front of him. Through the driving snow and the cold, he pushed. His face numbed, and his eyes dried, both to the point they hurt. He was, however, thankful for a small thing. Cori had given him a pair of specially-lined gloves to keep the frost off of his hands; otherwise, he would have been left with little hope at all.

Then, out of nowhere, the sled from behind slammed into his, causing it to veer dangerously off the main path. Oliver steered it back onto the trail, but the dark image of the same sled appeared again, careening into his.

Bang!

This time, the other sled smashed the back, sled rail and breaking off a piece of his runner. But not satisfied with merely hobbling Oliver, the attacking sled came back for another hit—this time to finish him off.

Oliver watched carefully to his side, waiting for the rogue sled to reappear out of the blinding snows storm. Again, he saw the three-headed wolf come into view with the hulking prisoner madly whipping his lead.

"Run, you lousy mut!" shouted the prisoner, cracking his leather reins.

He moved up quickly and at full speed next to Oliver, ready to push him off into the steep ravine below. But at the last minute, Oliver yanked back on the reins causing his cerberian to snap his heads, stopping immediately in its tracks and nearly throwing Oliver over the top of his sled bar.

The prisoner shrieked, missing the final hit on Oliver and his sled. He veered wildly off course, overshooting Oliver and the trail and launching off into the ravine. He plummeted hundreds of feet down before slamming into a huge altimont pine tree. Oliver didn't see what happened, but he heard the huge crash and splintering of man, beast and sled.

Oliver took a deep breath. *So, this is what's to come,* he thought. *This will be a very challenging race indeed.* He was about to crack the reins to get going again, but his wolf was already moving—facing ahead faster than before, getting back on the path and chasing after the other sleds ahead of them.

Now damaged, Oliver's sled shook without part of the runner in back and steering became harder. His wolf seemed completely unfazed by the incident and quickly resumed its torrid pace, closing in quickly on the rest of the group.

At last, through the pelting sleet and snow, Oliver could see the sled in front of him. It wasn't more than twenty feet ahead, but after his run-in with the last prisoner, he wasn't ready to do battle with another so soon.

Yet, the musher ahead of him looked over his shoulder and saw Oliver following behind. Moving to the side of the trail, the man waved for Oliver to come up and pass him, but Oliver knew better and hung back. When the musher saw that Oliver wasn't biting on his ploy, he jerked on the reins slowing his wolf instantly, just as Oliver had done. Within seconds, Oliver found himself side-by-side with the short, thin prisoner, who started to laugh and then curse at him.

"You're never gonna' make it!" he shouted. "We're all gonna make sure you die before you even get to the mountain. The king said whoever does it gets an extra hundred talends. You're a marked man."

Then, the toothless musher smashed his sled into Oliver's, pushing it sideways.

Bang! Bang!

Again and again, the wooden sled bashed against Oliver's. Then, the prisoner's wolf snapped at Oliver's beast, sinking its fangs into his neck.

"*Whoa! Whoa, there*!" Oliver yelled to his cerberian lead. Frantically, he tried to keep his balance on the footboards as the sled started to whipsaw back and forth, out of control. The prisoner to his side only laughed.

"Get him, boy! Get him!" the prisoner shouted to his wolf.

Ahead, Oliver saw that the ravine on the one side of the trail grew deeper while a steep cliff began to rise on the other. As the two fought, the pathway merged into the growing mountainside, hugging it like a collar around a kujopt. But on the other side was a steep drop-of—so steep that Oliver couldn't see to the bottom of it.

"Crap!" he said, realizing he was on the wrong side for his fight with the other prisoner. His sled was headed off the edge.

But just before the thick grove of trees dropped off into the ravine, Oliver spotted one last, narrow opening that led out to a promontory. It was just enough room for him to pull off. He steered his sled abruptly off course, sliding between two more altimont pines before bringing it to a stop. He looked back and watched as the other musher laughed and waved as he went by, pushing up the trail to wait for another chance to collect his talends.

Oliver hopped off his sled and ran to his lead wolf, which was lying motionless, panting in a drift of snow that had helped stop them. He brushed off the snow and went to his supply sled to see if he had anything in one of the silver bags they'd been given. He untied a few to see if there was anything he could use, and in one bag, he found a large, heavy wool blanket.

His cerberian was breathing heavily when he covered it with the blanket. Shock was setting in, and he didn't want to lose his only way to get through the race alive. Then, he went back to see if he could repair the sled's runner.

It took a while, but Oliver found a long branch from a yamich tree to lash to the fractured runner that was left. As one of the hardest woods, the yamich could hold-up better against the hard ice than any of the softer pines in the forest. Using a knife he had hidden in his tunic belt, he shaved down one side for a sharp edge to cut through the snow cleanly.

Ooooow! Ooooow!

The sound was coming from the front of the sled.

"Hey, buddy. You'll be all right. Just hang in there," Oliver said, giving words of comfort to the nasty beast that had taken him this far.

Oliver looked into the eyes of each of the three heads and saw fear. He wasn't sure if the animal was afraid of him or dying in the woods. So, he stroked one of the wolf's noses.

"Settle down, now. It'll be okay. You're not hurt badly ... just a little banged up. That's all. We're going to make it out of here, Snarl ..." But Oliver stopped. Looking into the wolf's eyes, he began to understand it better and he couldn't bring himself to finish the nickname.

"You know, I'm going to give you a new name," said Oliver, still stroking the beast's nose. "I'm going to call you Tristyx instead. How's that? Do you like that better?"

Oddly, the wolf whimpered but began licking Oliver's hand like a domesticated dog. Even its solid black tail began to wag again—this time out of contentment.

"I guess that's a yes," said Oliver, smiling.

Kneeling down next to his wolf, Oliver stroked its middle head. This time, it purred almost like a kitten.

"It looks like no one has treated you this way before," Oliver said. "I bet you've had a hard life. Well, I'll take care of you, if you promise to take care of me. Together, we'll be fine."

Tristyx barked and pushed one of his noses into Oliver's chest. Another one of his heads began licking Oliver's face in gratitude.

"Okay, okay, I got it," said Oliver. "I love you too."

After another hour Tristyx began acting more normal.

"What do you say we try for a few more miles, before nightfall, *eh* buddy?" said Oliver, patting him on the neck.

Oliver turned the repaired sled around, and they started back on the trail they'd been forced off. The snow had stopped since they'd left the trail, so they could still see clearly the grooves made earlier by the other prisoners as they'd continued on their way.

Soon, both suns had dropped out of the sky bringing nightfall and its icy cold fingers. And although the stars would be out by the billions, that also meant no clouds to hold in the heat of the day. The evening would be cold—quite possibly, deadly cold.

Hoping to find a clearing to camp for the night, Oliver spotted another sled parked deep into the woods off the side of the path. He could tell the driver had intended to hide from anyone else coming, but Oliver had seen his wolf move and then give a low howl.

Oliver pulled back the reins on Tristyx, slowing him to a walk and letting the sled glide into the woods a short distance from the other sled. Careful not to give himself away, Oliver went back to his supply sled and got out the blankets he would need for the night. In one of the bags, he found what looked like dried, brown food he hoped was for the wolves and not for him. Grabbing some, he returned to Tristyx, who looked at him with each of his three heads, uncertain about the food he was carrying.

Oliver put down a generous portion and stroked each head that wasn't eating. Finally, the food was gone, and one of the animal's tongues began licking Oliver's hand. Tristyx let out a soft howl of his own, wagging his tail and lying down to rest. But the sound was enough to echo in the deep canyon.

Oliver jerked his head up to see if the person in the other sled had heard them, and, indeed, the dark figure looked up to see where the sound was coming from. Oliver froze, not wanting to invite trouble and hoping the person would think it was just the howling of the wind or some other animal in the woods.

"Who's there?" came the voice Oliver had not wanted to hear. "I said, who's there?" There was more fear in the voice than a threat. "I've got a knife, and I'm not afraid to use it!"

Oliver sensed the fear and finally answered. "Don't worry. I'm not here to hurt you. I'm resting—just like you!"

"Who are you?" asked the voice.

"I'm Oliver of Rootan, and who are you?"

At first there was no answer; then he heard the voice again.

"I am Fermat." Then, there was a pause before he added, "So, you're the one CP talked about at the start of the race. I don't remember seeing you at the prison. When were you brought in?"

But before Oliver could answer, Tristyx started to yelp.

"What's wrong with your mutt?" asked Fermat, referring to the wolf.

"He's hurt."

"So, you can't finish the challenge, then."

Oliver wasn't sure whether it was said out of pleasure or concern. He ignored it and went to attend his lead.

"I can't release you, Tristyx. I don't have the key," said Oliver.

But Tristyx continued to moan, and Oliver worried that his injury was bothering him. He searched through the bags to find something that might free his wolf but found nothing.

"You trying to free your mutt?" asked Fermat from across the way.

"Yes," was Oliver's short reply as he continued to look for something.

"This might help ya'."

"What is it?"

Fermat held up a skinny, dark piece of metal. "One of the guards gave it to me. My sister always brought him food from town to keep me on his good side. He was quite fond of her, ya' know. You can use it if you want."

Oliver hiked through the deep snow toward the other prisoner. He stopped a short distance from Fermat who appeared still chained to his sled. Oliver noticed that he was much smaller than many of the other prisoners in the challenge. In fact, he looked like a young boy of no more than fourteen or so. Bushy black, stringy hair with white stripes running down the sides, the lad had deep blue eyes and a badly crooked nose, as if he'd broken it or someone had punched him. Then, there was that thick ring that pierced through his bottom lip.

"You have a ring?" asked Oliver, pointing to Fermat's lip.

"Yeah, it's part of my tribe. We're native Frezians. My people date back thousands of years in this land. Most of us were taken prisoner when the king's family arrived on the shores long ago. Are you not from this kingdom?"

"No, like CP said, I'm from Rootan—just over the mountains."

"We call your land Nede for we think of it as being lush and green."

"It is beautiful," said Oliver.

Fermat held up the key again. "Do you want to use it?"

"Sure. Thanks."

Oliver took the key and started back to his lead, but then he stopped and turned. "Why haven't you freed yourself if you have this?" he asked.

Fermat laughed and easily pulled the manacle away from the sled rail.

"I just make it look like I'm still attached—just in case another prisoner comes for me."

Oliver freed Tristyx who bounded over the snow piles toward Fermat's wolf, pulling on Oliver's leash and easily strong enough to pull his new master along with him in the same direction. The two wolves began sniffing each other and then nipping at each other's flanks, playfully.

"I guess they know each other, *huh?*" quipped Oliver.

"Oh yeah. These two are best buds, I think. I can tell by how they're licking each other instead of going for each other's throats," said Fermat. "So, how did you get into this thing? You couldn't have volunteered for it."

"Yes and no," replied Oliver. "You see, a friend of mine was arrested for something he didn't do, and I bet the king that if I win this challenge, he will release him."

"And the king agreed?" asked Fermat.

"Yes. He said he'd be happy to take that bet. I can see now why he did. I didn't know what I was getting into at the time. It was only after I agreed that I learned that few come back from it."

"Oh, that isn't true!" said Fermat.

"It isn't?"

"No one does."

"What?"

"The rules say that the king has to grant freedom to *anyone* who returns with the treasure—or *a* treasure. It's in the ancient rules of the challenge that go back centuries. Those who don't come back almost always freeze to death out here. But if they do try to escape, the king sends his guards out to finish them off, so they never come back. It's quite clean that way."

"Then, *no* one has lived through one of these challenges?"

Fermat replied, "See, that's the thing. I've heard that's right—no one has *ever* returned from the challenge."

"No one?"

Fermat just shrugged.

"Why are you here?" Oliver asked him, digging through his bag. "What did you do?"

"My family has been in the king's prisons since the beginning. I thought I had no choice but to try. If I find the treasure, I can free my family from years in a freezing cell."

Fermat stopped and looked puzzled as Oliver continued rummaging through his bags. "What are you looking for?"

"I thought there might be something in here to eat. There was food for the wolves, but I don't see anything else."

Fermat laughed. "You really think the king cares that much about us that he'd pack us a lunch? I don't think so. The wolves—yes; us prisoners—no."

Oliver threw the bags back onto the sled in disgust.

"Is there anyone else we can trust on this little adventure of ours? Do you know any of the other guys?" Oliver asked.

"I think there is one other that is a pretty good guy. That's Wylie. He and his family have been in a cell as long as we have — probably longer. I don't know him that well, but he may be worth talking to. The only thing is, I haven't seen him since the start of this race. I think they may have gotten to him already."

"Who got to him?"

Fermat looked at Oliver as if he didn't understand the question. "Are you kidding? The others. It's every man for himself out here. I'm sure the others knocked him off into the ravine or something."

"Someone tried to do that to me already."

"Yeah? Me too. Good job, then. You've made it through your first day," said Fermat, yawning. Then he added, "Why don't you get some sleep while I keep the first watch?"

Although Oliver didn't think there was anything to fear from this man, he couldn't be sure, and he wasn't willing to bet his life on it. He decided he was done betting—at least for one day.

"Let's both watch. Okay? What do you think?" asked Oliver.

Fermat understood and shrugged his shoulders. "Sure, no problem. You know there are other things to worry about—more than just the other prisoners."

"What do you mean?"

"You're not from here, so you probably haven't been out in the woods here at night, then?" asked Fermat.

Oliver shook his head.

"Well, just tune your eyes and ears into anything that's, well, unusual."

"Can you tell me what I'm watching and listening for that might be 'unusual'?"

"I think it's best if I don't. You'll know it when it happens."

Oliver sat silently in the cold, his eyes twitching left and right as if he had a nervous tick. He knew that by the time 'it happened' it would be too late. At first, every sound, movement, and breeze caught his attention. Each time a twig snapped, his neck almost snapped as well, swiveling to see what menace might be approaching. But as the night drew on, Oliver's anxiety gave way to heavy eyelids. Fermat was already snoring soundly, deciding Oliver wasn't much of a threat and was capable of keeping watch for both of them.

"I'll just rest my eyes for a moment," Oliver said to himself.

Oliver snorted loudly, waking himself up. He didn't know how long he'd been asleep, and he sat up startled. But the darkness of the forest still wrapped around them, as threatening as it had ever been. Yet, there was something in the distance—deeper in the woods—that caught his eye. It looked like a blue campfire, burning but without flickering or giving off a reddish or yellowish glow. Instead, it was an iridescent and shimmering—something that sparkled in the snowy depths. Far off among the trees, it was something out of place, yet mesmerizing.

Oliver got up and noticed that Fermat and the two wolves were all still asleep, unbothered by anything strange going on in the woods. So, he struck out on his own, trudging through the thick, wet snow toward the dancing blue light. He pushed back tree limbs as he went and rubbed a circle of snow onto some of the tree trunks to mark his way in case the wind picked up and covered his tracks.

As he drew closer, he saw the light was coming from a translucent ball suspended in mid-air. It floated there as if by magic. Inside was a black thread that vibrated and glowed like a fulgent beetle in a dark cave. The blue light was sparkling, tantalizing and beautiful. It overwhelmed Oliver's mind, drawing him ever closer.

He raised his arm and stretched out his hand to touch the orb, trying to see of what it was made. But before his fingers made contact, a drop of sticky, white slime splattered the side of his face. Oliver wiped it off with his hand and instinctively looked up.

Above him were a set of massive, razor-sharp teeth and huge black eyes that were cold, heartless and unblinking. With the head of a snake and the body of a giant spider with its eight legs protruding out its sides, the creature was hairy and had a rattler's tail. Like a tightrope walker, it had wrapped tree vines around its legs for support, enabling it to hang motionless underneath the limbs until a victim, unaware of its trap, came calling.

"Oh my ..."

But those were the only words that left Oliver's mouth. Before he could run, the creature dropped from its place, missing him by inches, its teeth only catching only the left side of his arm. It tore away part of his coat and pierced the skin on his shoulder. Yet, the monster's other legs quickly grabbed him and began wrapping an invisible wire itself around his body, yanking him off the ground and drawing him up into the trees above.

An angler! Oliver realized.

Oliver swung his legs and body violently, doing all he could to twist his way out of the deadly grip that was cutting off his airway. Tighter and tighter the line wrapped around his body, rapidly sealing him up in his own cocoon.

He kept fighting, but he was losing his strength, growing weaker by the second. The more he fought, the tighter the clear line bound him, and as the seconds ticked by, the grains of sand in his life-clock were falling too. Soon, the time would run out.

*****

CH 17 - Condemned to the Canyon

The army lined up at the edge of the canyon. Commander Seber looked across the mile-wide gap between the canyon's two rims. Over five miles deep, the bottom wasn't visible from that height as clouds had formed part way down the canyon walls. There was a reason why the natives called this place the Canyon of Perdition, and only time would bear that out.

"How are we getting across this?" Seber muttered aloud, as he stood next to Yewts. Seber didn't expect an answer, but Yewts was there with one anyway.

"I don't know, sir," replied Yewts, who was just as puzzled as his commander. "Maybe we're expected to fly our volarequi across?"

"That would be great, but not all of us have a volarequez, son," the commander replied.

The day was late, and Barbarot gave orders to make camp for the night. Around the camp, stretching for miles in all directions, was a flat plateau that held only tall, dried grasses and a few stubby, brown trees that looked like they had died long ago. Each brigade commander directed the heavy cloth tents to be unpacked from the supply wagons and setup to make a temporary city for the thousands of soldiers—all within a matter of hours. Smoke rose from the many campfires burning around the makeshift town, in an attempt to ward off any wild animals considering an unwelcomed visit.

In front of Seber's fire sat seven of his commanders who were finishing up their supper of roasted tendoore and chicobeets. At that time, a black-and-white dappled volarequez unexpectedly landed near the commander's tent. The messenger, a squire who's master had been killed in battle at Lagerfall, tipped his hat to the commander before speaking.

"Commander, as you know the king has ordered all of us to bed down here for the night. However, he has commanded that you take a small band of men and scout the valley to find a quick passage across. He said you have three days find it and return. In that time, you are also to provide him a detailed map of the entire canyon. Remember—you have only three days."

The squire saluted again before flying back into the night's sky, presumably returning to the king's command tent. Only five miles away, Barbarot was encamped with the rest of the army. All had followed behind a division of men led by Seber which were to clear the way. If there was trouble, Seber would bear the brunt of it until the king could arrive with the main force.

Seber assembled a small group of his best men and told his commander the king's order. Although he did not look happy, he nodded his understanding. However, one lieutenant took exception.

"But grand commander," said one of the lieutenants, "how can that be done? The canyon is five miles deep, a mile wide and possibly tens of miles long. It would take all of our men years to scout and map it—not three days!"

"We will do the best we can do," said Seber. "That's what I ask of each of you. Give me one hundred percent. Think critically and don't waste time on anything that isn't important. Do you understand?" Seber then summoned Yewts, the archer who had helped Uzi at the Bridge of Frezia. "Yewts, I hear you have a keen eye for details. We will need your help in constructing a map for our king. Have you done that work before?"

"No, sir. Well, at least not recently, sir. I drew maps when I was in school, but ..."

"That's good enough for me. Get some drafting tools. You'll be needing them."

As a lowly ground archer, Yewts had been just one of many thousand in the service of the king. However, his hard work ethic and smarts were becoming known among the commanding officers, and he was now more valuable than ever.

"Yewts!" said Seber, "Or should I say, Sir Yewts."

"Sir? You mean …"

"Yes, I'm knighting you on behalf of the king. Now, let's get to work."

"Thank you, sir!" replied the new knight, beaming with pride.

Yewts couldn't help but smile. He'd dreamed of becoming a knight, but never thought it would happen so quickly and in this way. This was not the normal way to knighthood, but the pressures of war often changed rules—rules of all kinds.

As Yewts was learning most of all, rules were made by those in power, and the rules were usually written to benefit those in power. He knew he had to play by the rules if he wanted to win this game—*the game they call life*, he thought, beginning to understand. Yet, at the same time, he hated having to keep his mouth shut about things he thought were wrong. *When I'm in a position of power, I'll change all that,* he hoped. *It will be different, then.*

Seber let the men sleep until an hour before the first sun rose and got them on their way by the time the light began cracking through the darkness. By the time Duex was up, he had them marching down the rocky trail that lead to the bottom of the canyon. Progress was slow, as men and animals kept slipping off the trail—a few falling to their deaths below. They had also not counted on the change in temperature, which by the time they had reached the halfway point, had risen from 45° F at the surface to nearly 100° F and growing hotter by the minute.

Yewts could feel the rough, scratchiness in his throat and was rationing his water. He'd only had a few sips on the way down, and he knew he'd need a lot more at the bottom and during the long climb back up.

With only a few pack mules in tow, the troop was traveling light to speed the trip along. Seber knew surveying the entire canyon was not possible in three days, but if he could find a short, safe way to the other side, the king would likely forgive the other half of the mission.

Grand Commander Seber led the way atop his volarequez, Nimbus, with the rest of his men following, carrying their bows and swords. Seber had ordered them not to take shields or their heavy armor because he knew the trail would be strenuous and the extra weight would likely kill most of them from exhaustion and dehydration.

They marched quickly to make up as much ground as they could before the suns got too high into the sky. By noon, the temperature was a scorching 125°, and they stopped to let the suns fall and temperatures cool. Then, they would start again.

Circling overhead were two geiers. Vulture-like birds, they used their two sets of giant wings to stay aloft and watch the small ant-sized figures moving along the dusty trail below in the canyon. They were patient, and they waited for anyone to fall or drop. Their wings beat with alternating rhythms that were unmistakable to the men on the ground. They knew they were up there incessantly buzzing around; they were also aware that the sign of geiers was often viewed as a bad omen of things to come.

It was mid-afternoon now, and there was no breeze, no relief from the brutal heat. The heat waves made the steep canyon walls look like they were rippling in the hot air—like waves in a pond after a stone is dropped in the middle. Everything pulsed and vibrated with heat, and as the men started up again and continued marching to the bottom. There, the heat soared, rising to over 135° F—enough to cook a man's brain.

Two men collapsed, and Commander Seber quickly got off his horse to see to them. He called for more water which was brought quickly from one of the burros. The first man had difficulty gulping down the few drops he was given, as if he had swallowed sand instead of aqua. Seber turned to help the other man, but it was too late. Heat had overcome him, and he was gone.

Once they reached the canyon floor, there were no trees anywhere to give needed shade and no river to offer fresh water. Although there was a riverbed, it hadn't seen flowing currents in years, perhaps centuries.

Seber let his men rest and wanted to wait until the evening when the suns would be low in the sky and take the edge off the extreme heat. But as the suns fell, the heat didn't, and Seber had to consider what to do next. Certainly, they could wait for nightfall, but then it would be more treacherous and harder to see. They were also running low on water and without finding any in the canyon, the commander knew many of his men wouldn't last the next day.

"Yewts!" yelled Seber.

"Yes, sir."

"We will be leaving in a few hours, but we don't have enough water for all of us to make it if we search for a passage up the other side of this canyon. We may need to leave some of the men behind."

"If I may speak freely, sir?"

Seber nodded.

"Even if we all do make it to the top of the other side, we still might not find water. Someone will need to return to the king with a map of how to get across. Who will survive that?"

"I understand what you're saying, and I agree, Yewts. However, let's focus on escaping the first grim reaper before worrying about the second one. If we don't make it past the first, then the second doesn't really matter, does it?"

*****

CH 18 - By a Thread

As the beast drew the dangling, cocooned body of Oliver toward its gaping mouth, another animal came running through the woods, jumping high into the air. It struck the angler's snake-like head, sinking its fangs deep into its skull. The angler let go of Oliver, dropping his body into the snow below.

"Tristyx!" Oliver shouted.

His wolf mate shook his head back and forth, fighting the spidery creature for a moment before releasing its bite. Injured, but not killed, the angler scrambled up into the tree limbs above to recover and wait for another day and another victim.

Oliver smiled as he got his face licked by three different tongues. "Tristyx! Good boy!" he said. "Buddy, you saved me, that's for sure. I thought surely I was gone that time."

Oliver put his arms around the middle head of the huge canine and gave it a hug. It returned the affection by taking its long, slobbery tongue and giving Oliver another lick across the face.

"What's going on?" Fermat shouted from across their camp. He had just woken up and heard the commotion nearby.

Oliver came back with his three-headed friend and plopped down next to Fermat.

"My friend here just saved my life. Why didn't you tell me not to chase after strange lights in the woods at night? Why didn't you warn me?"

Fermat laughed. "If I warned you about everything there is to worry about out here, you'd never leave this spot. You're just lucky that angler didn't get you. They usually don't let go so easily."

"Thanks, I think."

They packed up the few things in their camp and threw their silver bags into the back of their sleds, harnessing their cerberians to the front. Then, they mushed them to the trail above.

"So, where do we go from here?" asked Oliver. "Do we just stay on this trail? I don't even know where we're going—where Mt. Erebus is—do you?"

"You don't know where we're going?" said Fermat. "You are a mystery, Oliver from Rootan."

"Why do you say that?"

"For as smart as you may be, it doesn't seem like you thought through this very much, did you?"

Oliver realized he had been impulsive at the trial, and now—almost constantly—he was being reminded of how foolish that had been.

"So, you know where we're going, then?" replied Oliver.

"Uh, no," admitted Fermat. "I really don't either, except it's to that mountain—Ebus."

"It's called Erebus," said Oliver, correcting him. "See! You don't know either."

"Well, at least I knew more about the rules of the thing than you did!"

"How does that help if you don't know where you're going?"

"I was just going to follow everyone else."

"What if everyone else was going the wrong way thinking everyone *else* knew the way?"

Both were frustrated, and it was starting to show.

"Listen," said Fermat, "we have to get to a place called Mt. Ebus or Erebus and go inside a cave there. I don't know where it is, but I know this trail leads the way."

It was then that Tristyx started whimpering to get their attention.

"What is it, boy?" Oliver asked.

Tristyx began shaking his three heads and pawing the ground.

"What is he trying to tell us?" asked Fermat.

Tristyx began whimpering, trying to pull the sled forward.

"I think he's saying it's time we got on our way," said Oliver. "It will probably take several hours this morning to get to the cave. Then, of course, we have to get home. It doesn't leave us much time for anything unexpected along the way."

"You mean, the Rebus."

"Yes."

"But all we have to do is answer a bunch of questions, get the treasure and bring it home," said Fermat. "It seems easy enough."

Oliver laughed. "Of course," he said, "You've forgotten a few things. For starters, we've got nine or ten other competitors out here trying to do the same thing, all who are trying to kill us and each other. Second, we don't know what the Rebus' questions will be but do have a good idea of what happens if we can't answer them. Third, we don't know where the treasure is. And, lastly, we still have to make it back and figure out how to keep the king from killing us. Does that fill in the holes for you?"

"Yep, I think that just about covers it," said Fermat.

*****

CH 19 - The Game

While Donus was helping with the shepherds, teaching them the fundamentals of writing, mathematics and the world, Parogild was striking out on his own. First, he went to the nearby town of Kafar, but there were no vacancies at the inns and no shops open for a wayward traveler. So, he traveled on to Ralop. There he went to the local tavern and hobbled in to take a seat on one of the benches inside. Quickly, he found himself ordering too many beverages that left him feeling light-headed and care-free. He reveled in being out on his own—no worries, no concerns and no one to tell him what to do. He figured he had all the money he needed to live well the rest of his life—the money his father had given him as his inheritance. So, he threw caution to the wind.

The bartender opened a new keg of suds, sticking a spout in one end and screwing it down until it locked in place. He turned a knob to let the green ale slide into a partially-cleaned, wooden goblet. Then, when it reached the top, he turned the knob off, taking a knife to skim off the suds before slamming the mug down in front of one of the patrons. The man had obviously had too much as well but continued drinking anyway.

After a sip of the green draft, the man looked over at Parogild. His face was old and wrinkled, and his peppered hair hung in greasy strands along one side of his face. Wearing a black eyepatch, he had only one good eye which was blood-red, matching the tip of his nose as if he'd been out in the suns too long.

"Hey, buddy," he whispered to Parogild. "Do you play games?"

"What?" asked Parogild, thinking the man was referring to children's games. "Of course not! I'm too old for that sort of thing."

"No, no. I mean do you like to gamble?" said the old man.

Now, he had Parogild's interest. The young man had never gambled before, but he knew of it, and knew it was what real men in the world did to entertain themselves.

"What kind of gambling?" the baron's son asked, finishing his drink and ordering another.

"Well, there's a little game that's played just down the street," the man said, eyeing him. "You dress like you could afford it. It's for rich people, you know." He took another drink and put the mug back on the table. "You should try your luck there. I think you'd be good at it."

"What game is it?" asked Parogild, beginning to have a little trouble talking.

"It's called Prime. I'm sure you know of it. Only the most distinguished men in the kingdom play it, you know," said the man playing to Parogild's ego.

Parogild nodded. "Yes, of course. I fancy myself an expert at such games," he said pompously.

"Good, I heard they had room for one more at the table tonight. It's at the back of the Golden Lair. Knock twice, then again. You'd better hurry, though. I think they're going to be starting soon."

Parogild finished his drink. "Thanks, old man," he said, getting up but catching himself before he lost his balance.

With his money purse in hand, he stumbled down the main road bumping into a few other townspeople along the way but not apologizing. He finally reached a small store at the edge of town that had a sign that read simply "Golden Lair Inn" with an arrow pointing down a narrow alley. Reaching an unlit black door, he knocked twice and then another time before waiting.

The code worked, and someone answered, inviting him in. The guard manning the back door was a big lout with forearms the size of Parogild's legs. After letting him in, the man slammed the door and locked it behind him.

"Back there!" he grunted, pointing to where Parogild was supposed to go. "Back room."

The front of the tavern had many tables—all crammed with middle-aged and old men playing cards, smoking long pipes and drinking green ale. Each held a stern, serious look as they carefully watched the other players at the table and the cards they held in their hands. There were no spaces available at any of the tables, so Parogild made it through the tavern area, past the men and down a short flight of uneven stairs toward the back of the establishment.

There was only a single room at the bottom, and it was small— far smaller than the one in the front of the saloon. In the middle of the space was an oddly-shaped table—like a horseshoe—and there were eight men sitting along the outside. A woman, wearing a white robe with her head covered by a matching hood, sat in the center of the horseshoe by her own smaller, triangular table. On her table was a white, velvet bag trimmed in gold and cinched with a gold cord. The woman in white held a bag too—a gold one.

The men around the table didn't notice Parogild when he came in. Even his marked limp didn't draw their attention away from the game they were about to play. He took the last empty seat around the table and looked around at his competitors. These were wealthy men, draped in luxurious silks, gold chains and jeweled rings. Behind each stood a beefy knight who was there to protect them. However, it bothered Parogild little. He was a baron's son, after all, and with that title came certain privileges and rights. Like the others at the table, he was arrogant; unlike the others at the table, he didn't know his own limitations.

There were two others in the room—another woman who was dressed in a black, hooded robe and carrying a black box painted in gold trim as well as a woman wearing a red, hooded robe and carrying a red, velvet bag. However, unlike the black box and white bag, this bag had no gold on it.

The lady in white stood up. "Welcome," she said. "As I'm sure you know, we play Prime at this table. The rules are known to all. If they must be explained, we ask that you leave the table and the game. This is no place for amateurs." She looked directly at Parogild, but he did not flinch.

"I am the White One, and as you know, there is a Black One and a Red One. If there is a dispute, others will join us immediately to escort you from the room. There will be no incivility. Do I make myself clear?"

All the men at the table either nodded or grunted.

"Good. Then, let us begin."

The Red One, short with long red hair, approached the first player at the end of one leg of the horseshoe. He was a black-haired man with a tricornered hat and a brilliant blue sapphire pendant around his neck. His eyes were black as coal, and his sour disposition seemed eager to drain the room of any joy or humor. He snapped his fingers, and his knightly attendant placed three gold coins inside the opened, blood-red bag. The man next to him did the same, and around the table the woman went, collecting coins—until she reached Parogild. Parogild had no assistant; so, he pulled out his own coin bag and dropped three gold coins into the bag as well. The Red One gave him a curious eye and then opened the bag wider to check if the coins were real. Satisfied, she continued on to the others at the table, collecting the ante from each as she went.

After finishing, the Red One went to the triangular table next to the White One, who remained motionless, still holding the elaborate gold bag in her hands. There, the Red One placed her bag on the table where all could see it. Then, she bowed to the group and to the other two women dressed in the white and black robes and returned to the far end of the room. After bowing in return, the White One opened her gold bag and the Black One reached inside, pulling out five triangular pieces of bone—each with a number written on it.

"Tonight's primes are five, seven, thirteen, seventeen and twenty-three. Choose wisely," said the Black One.

Several minutes passed. While the Black One was busy doing something inside the black box, the other players seemed deep in thought, perhaps considering the numbers and what they would do next. Since Parogild did not understand the game, he had no idea what he was supposed to be doing.

"Time is up," said the Black One, closing the lid on the black box.

She lifted the box from the table and went to each player, opening and closing the lid each time. The first man picked two square pieces of carved bone and placed them in front of him on the table. The next player did the same. This continued around the table until the Black One reached Parogild. He looked in the box and found five sections divided equally. Within each section were square pieces of bone that had one of the five numbers inscribed—either a five, seven, thirteen, seventeen or twenty-three. Parogild chose a five and a twenty-three and placed them on the white, velvet-covered table surface in front of him.

The Black One returned to the front and again bowed to the other two women.

"We play," the White One murmured softly, without emotion.

The Black One now picked up the white bag from the table and held it out for the White One, who reached inside and withdrew a flat, round piece of bone—also with a number on it.

"Two," she announced, glancing at the number. She then placed it on the first, white square drawn on a red, velvet cloth that lay across her table.

There was no reaction from the group, and Parogild began getting nervous, wondering if he had already made a mistake.

Of course, there were rules, and like all games, knowing them would make the difference between winning and losing. As the other players already knew, this game called Prime was simple—or so it seemed. Players picked which, if any, of the five key prime numbers drawn from the gold bag would be "hit" as the dealer pulled numbers from the white bag. There were only three different kinds of numbers in the white bag; they had either a one, two or three marked on them. There were no others. There could be equal quantities of each number within the bag or different ones, depending on how the bag was filled before each night's contest. Since there were hundreds of flat circles in the bag, it was difficult to predict from the drawings what numbers were most or least included.

But the game continued, and the White One picked the next number.

"Three," she said, reading the circle.

That made the first "hit" a five—the two plus the three. This was a prime, and it was one of the prime numbers drawn from the gold bag at the beginning of the round. Those who had chosen a five were still in the match; those who hadn't were out.

Only one of the men had not chosen a five, and he took his thick, long arm and swept the two prime numbers he had picked violently off the table in front of him, sending them flying across the room. Then, he got up from his seat and stomped up the stairs, leaving the room for either a breath of the chilling night's air or to go home and lick his wounds. The other men at the table didn't react—not seeming to care in the slightest one way or the other. This was the way the game was played—winners kept their calm, while losers ... well ... did as they wished.

"Three," came the next call.

The total was now eight, and Parogild was still in the game as he had not selected the number seven; however, four of the other players had picked the seven, which meant they too were out. That left two other players still in the hunt.

The next numbers came quickly as the game gained momentum.

"Three" the White One called—which triggered the eleven prime. But that was not one of those picked at the beginning of the round, so no one was penalized. Then the woman picked several more in quick succession. One, two, and one came next in sequence, totaling fifteen. None of the totals had been prime numbers.

"Three," said the White One.

Eighteen was not a prime, but seventeen had been. The other two players had picked seventeen. They were out. The round was over.

Parogild wasn't sure what had happened. It was only when the Red One picked up the red bag and came to him with it did, he understand. He had won.

It was the White One who rose from her seat and announced, "You have won this round. Do you wish to roll your winnings over to the next round or take the gold coins in the red bag now?"

"Uh, …" Parogild wasn't sure what to do and in a moment of panic said, "… I will continue."

"Very well," said the White One, nodding to the Red One who handed him a round, blue piece to keep in front of him indicating his decision. "For rolling your winnings, you will have two hands for the next round. All others will ante six gold coins each," she added.

The second round went as the first one had with the new primes announced: seven, eleven, seventeen, twenty-nine and thirty-one.

Parogild chose the seven and twenty-nine for one hand and the eleven and seventeen for the other. He placed both sets of flat circles in front of him on the horseshoe table. The first player, whom Parogild referred to as "Blackeyes," sat thumping his fingers against the table waiting for the number draw. But there was another man, standing just behind him and beside the knight bodyguard who puzzled him more. He looked familiar to Parogild, but he couldn't place him. The man had fine features and soft, gray eyes. He had returned Parogild's gaze as if he recognized him too but quickly turned away to watch the game.

After the first three draws, the seven was hit, and Parogild breathed a sigh of relief. At least one of his two hands had that number. Three other players were not as lucky and left the game. Two more draws pushed the hit number to twelve, missing the eleven. Likewise, the seventeen was passed as the hit number jumped to nineteen. At that point, only two players remained – Blackeyes and Parogild.

The game continued. The White One again reached her long, slender hand into the white bag, pulling out piece after piece.

"One," she called—then "three," "two," and "one." The hit number was now twenty-six.

Parogild looked at the number Blackeyes had left. It was the thirty-one. If Parogild did not win on twenty-nine, Blackeyes would automatically win the pot as he would be the last one still in the game.

"One," said the White One.

Now, the hit number was at twenty-seven. A three would sink Parogild, but a couple of ones or a two would work nicely.

Blackeyes stared coldly at the young man. There was a lot of money in the red bag now, sixty-six gold unios. Even for someone as well-off as Blackeyes, the money must have been important.

"One," said the White One.

At twenty-eight, the odds were against Parogild. A two or three would end his chances. He held his breath as the next number was pulled and read.

"One."

Parogild jumped up, shouting and clapping. "Yes!" he yelled. He was thrilled. He had just won sixty-six gold coins – instantly doubling his original inheritance.

The White One again asked if Parogild wanted to roll his bet to the third round. Without hesitating he said, "Yes!"

Blackeyes had not reacted—seeming neither disappointed nor angry. He merely snapped his fingers and directed his attendant to produce gold coins for the third round. As they waited for the others to return to the table, he again stared menacingly at Parogild.

This time when the Red One came to collect gold pieces she required twelve—again, double that of the prior round. Although surprised at how quickly the *ante* had gone up, Parogild felt confident in his luck that night, and he quickly took another round, blue disk from the Red One adding it to the other already sitting in front of him.

"The primes are: thirteen, seventeen, twenty-three, twenty-nine, and thirty-seven," was the announcement. "Choose wisely," again said the White One.

This time Parogild had three hands to play, increasing his chances significantly. His hands were thirteen and twenty-three; seventeen and thirty-seven; and seventeen and twenty-nine.

"We play," said the White One before pulling the first number. "One," she said. Then, there were several more numbers drawn, reaching the hit number of twelve. This was the first critical point in the round.

"Two," was announced. Two players had chosen the thirteen and were out. Five remained.

"One," the White One said, followed by "Two."

"Yes!" said Parogild, savoring his two hands that had the hit number seventeen. However, Blackeyes was still in the hunt, having chosen seventeen and twenty-nine.

The next numbers called were three, two and two, bringing the total to twenty-four—skipping the next prime of twenty-three. Two more players left the game. This time, they packed up everything to go home and took their entourages with them.

The next prime target was twenty-nine—a number Blackeyes had chosen for his hand and Parogild had picked for only one of his two still-live hands.

One, one and two were the next calls. The total was now twenty-eight. Blackeyes needed a one.

For the first time that night, Parogild heard a guttural growl coming from Black Eyes. His face was distorted with an internal rage and fire burning inside him. It was a hate so great that Parogild could feel it sink into his bones.

The White One picked the next number and looked up, pausing before announcing it.

"Two," she said.

The total was thirty. Blackeyes had lost. Parogild had won. Both Blackeyes and the other player had picked twenty-nine.

This time, Blackeyes pounded the table with his fist causing the pieces to jump off the surface and onto the floor. He grabbed his mug and emptied what remained before getting up and storming out.

Parogild shouted in glee, jumping up and down like a child and making a complete fool of himself. Yet, he had won over one hundred fifty golden unios. This was a significant sum; he was a wealthy young man.

The other players rose from their chairs and left hurriedly from the room, leaving Parogild with only the ladies who had pulled the numbers and held the coins for each round.

The Red One took the red bag from the table and walked to where Parogild was sitting. She opened it, showing him the large number of coins inside. His eyes glistened with excitement, and he dipped his fingers into it and pushing them around, feeling their smoothness and listening to their clarion call for wanting even more.

After dumping the coins into his own bag, he cinched the top. The bag bulged and was heavy—very heavy.

The Black One came to Parogild and said, "Nice job. You seem to be new at the game, but very lucky. Your name is ...?"

"Parogild. I'm the son of Baron Lukae."

"Well, Sir Parogild, it is nice to have you attend. It is customary for the winner to offer something to those who have served you tonight. May we count on your generosity?"

Parogild reached in and pulled out three gold coins—one for each of the ladies—and handed them to her.

"Thank you," she answered, smiling. "Now, you know there is another game to be played here tomorrow night if you'd like to join us. The ante is lower for each round, but I think you will still find it entertaining."

"Lower?"

"Yes," she answered. "Tonight's game has the highest ante of all the games played each month. You were lucky on many counts tonight."

"Let me think about it," he said. "Right now, I think I'll find an inn. It's been a long day."

Parogild left through the front door and headed back toward the center of town. There was an inn not far away, and he had more than enough money to cover an extended stay.

As he approached the door of the Zero Tundra Inn, he was met by three men who came out of the shadows to block his way.

"So, we meet again, eh?" said a voice.

Parogild saw the familiar face he had seen at the Prime game standing behind Blackeyes. He came out of the mist and gloom of the night's air. But he wasn't the only one; there were two others—the knight and Blackeyes himself.

"What do you want?" asked Parogild, in no mood to talk.

"Looks like you did pretty well tonight, wouldn't you say?" said Blackeyes moving toward him.

"Yes, I won fair and square."

"Yes, you did, my friend. But you missed the *fourth* round of the game."

"What do you mean? There was no fourth round."

Blackeyes' two guards surrounded the young man.

"Oh, there's always another round, and in this one you lose." He nodded to his men, and they moved forward threateningly.

"My father's the baron of this region. He'll have your heads if you come near me!" shouted Parogild.

Blackeyes laughed. "I'm sure he is, lad. I'm sure he is."

One of the bodyguards was big and muscular and picked Parogild up quite easily while the second punched him in the stomach.

"Ugh!" groaned the young man, doubling over.

They continued hitting him in the face and stomach with their fists—over and over again. The pain was terrible, and each blow broke a jaw, a lip, a tooth or his nose. He fell to the ground and rolled in the snow in agony. He could feel the warm blood oozing from his nose and mouth and see it as it dripped onto the white canvas of the road, staining it a sickening crimson.

"And this is for threatening me those many years ago after I had dinner with you, my teacher and your father!" said the familiar-looking young man, rearing back with his fist to strike once more.

It was the grownup version of the boy Parogild had threatened for stealing the attention of his father at supper. This was the one-time boy who had desperately needed the kindness of the baron to give him a chance at a good and decent life. Instead, Parogild had told the boy never to step foot in their castle and village again. Apparently, the boy had not gone back to school and had gotten in with a bad group and learned some very bad habits. He had grown up but had also grown mean and spiteful.

The boy—now a strong, young man—kicked Parogild in the face. That was the last thing the baron's son remembered. When he awoke, he was still lying in the snow, shivering and in terrible pain. His body was now more broken than ever before.

Parogild checked his tunic pocket. The bag, of course, was gone. *All* his money—every coin given to him by his father and won at the game—had been stolen. He was penniless and homeless. But what was worse was that he no longer had his family, either.

*****

CH 20 - Knowing the Law

Abandoned, Nikko and Gemma were stuck in separate cells in an underground dungeon at opposite ends of the castle. Although cold, the dungeon was warmer than the frigid weather above ground outside. The underground cells held the temperature at a constant and comfortable 50° F, but it was damp too. To Gemma and Nikko, it was anything but warm, particularly to Gemma whose teeth chattered incessantly. Gemma spent her days exercising, trying to keep her body active and fit. As for Nikko, he mainly slept. Without a window to the surface, they had no idea what time of day it was, and boredom set in quickly for both.

It was late one day when Gemma heard a noise at the far end of the dungeon. There was a clambering of keys and the squeaking of a door before it slammed shut. Gemma listened, hoping to hear what was happening, and within minutes, a fresh face appeared at her prison door, peering in through the barred window. It was Cori who had come down to see her. Carrying fresh bread and some grapes, Cori avoided being accosted by the outstretched arms and hands of the other prisoners along dungeon's hallway and slid the food through the bars and into Gemma's hands.

"Thanks," Gemma said, her teeth clicking and her body shaking.

"I really feel badly about this. You know that, don't you?" asked Cori, her face sad and droopy.

"Yes, of course. I know this has nothing to do with you or your sister. I just wish your father saw things differently."

"Me too," replied Cori. "But my father has always been that way—strict and domineering. Growing up wasn't easy in this castle with him as your father. My sister and I had many nights when we cried, having been smacked around by him. If you did something he didn't like, you soon found out about it."

"That's awful," said Gemma.

"Yes. It really was."

"So, tell me, Cori, what will happen if Oliver comes back with the treasure? Will your father be true to his word? Will he let us go?" Gemma asked, uncertainly.

"He will be true to his word, but that doesn't mean he'll do what you think," said Cori, cautiously. And without waiting for a reply, she added, "You see, there are parts of our laws that are subject to interpretation, if you know what I mean."

"No. What do you mean?"

"It means that the laws are written to benefit the king—my father. That doesn't mean my father won't free you, but it does mean there may be conditions attached."

"Like what?"

"He's been known to find loopholes in the law. Like if the person doesn't do *exactly* as agreed or what he *thought* was agreed, then he might go back on the agreement or make you do something more to gain your freedom—something that will benefit him more."

"How can we find out what the law permits, then?" asked Gemma.

"You'd have to go to the castle library. There are a lot of books there. There are many on the kingdom's laws too. It might take a while to go through them, though."

"It's going to be even longer if we can't get out of here," said Gemma.

"I may be able to help," said Cori. "I can't let you go free, but I can ask Mother to let you out of your cell to exercise … and, of course, make a run through the library."

"Okay then," said Gemma. "Ask her. I can't stand it in here anymore."

Cori left and came back later that day.

"You're in luck. Mother was in a good mood, and she said you could leave the cell to exercise. She only told me not to tell Father. So, neither can you."

"Lips are sealed," said Gemma.

Cori called over one of the guards, and he unlocked the cell door. Gemma came out and walked to the far end of the dark, rocky hallway where they passed Nikko's cell.

"Where are you going?" Nikko asked, seeing her outside her cell. "And how did she let you out?"

"Sorry, Nikko. I can't help you," said Cori. "Mother is a little more sympathetic to Gemma than she is to you right now."

"Trust me, what I'm doing will help all of us," said Gemma. "At least I hope so."

Cori took Gemma to the castle library. In many ways it was like Sojourn's but far larger. There were sections on philosophy, art, poetry, warcraft, and myths and legends. There were also sections on religion and law. Within the large area for law there were many books and scrolls on the laws and proclamations of Frezia.

"How am I going to do this?" cried Gemma. "I don't have a lot of time—only two more days before Oliver comes back. Where do I start?"

"At the beginning, my dear," Cori said smiling.

Gemma laughed, but then returned to staring at the many shelves and many more rows of books.

"Here," said Cori, pointing. "This is where you'll find laws on crimes, like stealing. There is where you'll find laws on games and betting, and finally over there you'll see laws on general agreements. I think they call them contracts."

"It's too much!"

"No, I'll help you. We can do this. We must have confidence in ourselves," said Cori. "Now, let's get busy. We're not going to get anywhere unless we start opening some book covers."

*****

CH 21 - Recruiting

Creatures large and small will seek shelter, yet its force will overwhelm them. Life giving and life taking will the power be. A strength and might only from the God of gods could it come. It will be the end for many, but the beginning for a few—a few who will forge the future for what is left behind.

The Book of Gneima

Konjuur's band of men entered the town of Emani near King Barbarot's castle. They were a mangy-looking bunch, not having had a decent place to stay for many months. In front of the Boarswag Inn, they stopped and tied up their sensavols which they'd stolen from a nearby farmhouse. Fireplaces blazed inside the inn to keep the patrons warm as the nights were getting colder with the advancing change in seasons.

By now, Konjuur had recruited or coerced more men to join him, and his group had almost two dozen, unknowing stooges of his cause. It wasn't mighty, but it was enough to attract the attention of others who were angry at what was going on in the kingdom. While Barbarot was away from the kingdom, his people grew increasingly restless and resentful.

Instead of going directly to the Boarswag Inn, Konjuur led his men into the Noctair Tavern next door. When the saloon doors opened, no one took notice of the group at first; however, after the huge girth of Konjuur waddled in, followed by the tenth man in his clan, people there began to take notice.

"A round for the great people of Rootan!" shouted Konjuur, trying to get the attention of more than just the bartender, who was busy preparing drinks for everyone.

"Hear, hear!" came the answer from a few closest to their table. But most of the others in the tavern either weren't paying attention or thought he was only referring to his own group.

"I said," Konjuur tried again, "I'm buyin' a round for the great people of Rootan—that is for *anyone* who agrees with me!"

This time there was a greater wave of voices. "Hear, hear!"

One man at a table next to theirs leaned in toward Konjuur with mug in hand and whispered, "You must remember. We are not Rootan anymore. The king changed the name. We are now Barbarotons. It is dangerous to say the word Rootan these days."

"Barbarotons!" said Konjuur loudly, sensing ire in the new name by the man next to him. "We are not Barbarotons! We are Rootanians! We have *always* been Rootanians!"

At that, there was a roar of cheers and whistles.

"I say again. Ale for all the Rootanians here!" shouted Konjuur.

The froth was passed around to anyone who wanted one, and after they had gotten theirs, Konjuur stood once more. He raised his wooden mug high.

"To Rootan! May our people someday get our kingdom back!"

He threw his head back and sucked down the last drop. Then, he slammed the mug down on the table and wiped his black goatee with the back of his sleeve.

"Hear, hear!" all in the tavern cried out.

Konjuur ordered another froth for himself which the bartender quickly delivered. With all eyes on him, he stood and proposed one last tribute.

"This time, I toast to the spirit and fight of our people. We know what's right and what's not. We have always believed in our kingdom and our long heritage of greatness. We are a great people—a great kingdom. Why does a two-bit despot think he can control us? Why should we let a two-bit despot do this to us? Would our fathers and grandfathers have let this happen? I don't think so. They would have stood up to him. They would have fought back."

Everyone in the place was now cheering him on.

However, there was one older man, tall and slender with a short-cropped beard, who stood in the corner listening intently. He shook his head at every word Konjuur spoke, as if in disagreement. Konjuur saw this and called out to the man.

"Hey, you over there! You're shaking your head. You don't believe what I'm saying? You don't agree that the new king has turned us into slaves? Think of all of the wealth he has ... think of what luxury he lives in while you live in squalor and poverty. Is that fair? Why should he have it all and then order you to do his bidding? Why should your families suffer and starve while he's living without worry or care—spending the money you worked so hard to make?"

"Because it's always been that way—that's why," replied the old man. "He's the king!"

"Does that make it right?" questioned Konjuur. "Is it right that one person should have so much, and you have so little? Haven't you all worked hard all of your lives? And for what—for the scraps that he gives you. He doesn't work—he merely taxes you and spends your money on more gold for his castle!"

"But he has an army," said the old man, continuing to challenge. "And if you hadn't noticed, we don't."

"You are very smart," said Konjuur, playing on the man's ego. "But he is not here now, is he? Your king is off on some campaign with his army, trying to take over other kingdoms and enslave other peoples just as he has done with you. He's spending your money so he can get more power and more wealth and control more and more. And when he returns, he will need even *more* from the sweat of your brow and aching backs. You and I both know ... that he must be stopped."

Many wanted to agree but now feared being blackmailed by others there. They worried for themselves and their families. If word got to the castle and the king that they were against him, they all would be in great danger.

"So, how can we do as you say?" asked the old man. "How can we do something about this king who is bringing misery to our people?"

"Not only misery," spouted another, much younger man in the group, "but what about the plagues and diseases that have come to our kingdom? How do you explain them?"

"Just a few weeks ago, he ordered that anyone speaking out against him would be imprisoned!" cried another. "It's too dangerous."

A middle-aged man with ragged clothes and knotted hands said, "Not only that, but he put my brother in prison for being late paying his taxes on the few crops he harvested this year! My sister-in-law and their five children live in fear at home without food."

Konjuur smiled but was patient. He was too smart to rush things. He knew from experience it would take several more meetings in other taverns and inns to convert the number of people he needed to take control. Yet, he couldn't wait too long either. Barbarot would return home soon with his army, and Konjuur knew he had to have the support of the people before that happened.

"Until tomorrow, then," Konjuur said to the crowd. "We will be in town for a while, but we will continue to talk about what is happening here in our kingdom with others too. We are not afraid, nor should you be. We believe in our kingdom. We believe in Rootan!"

*****

CH 22 - The Trek Up

The day was passing quickly, and Duex—the first sun--had already dropped below the far horizon in the west. Seber and his men had begun the hike up the far side of the canyon, hoping the temperature would drop enough to make the climb survivable. With Piquet's rays streaming in at a sharp angle, the canyon's layers of stone were a rare sight in the natural world. The beiges, tans, and pale yellows of the daylight hours had disappeared, and the brilliant colors of ochre, orange, plum, and pink were seeping out of the rocks. They were magnificent, but no one on the climb could appreciate their splendor. They were merely trying to do whatever they could to survive.

Yewts noticed the spectacular show of color; yet, he felt uneasy. He knew the dangers of the steep canyon embankment when the light was fading. One wrong step and the loose gravel along the side could give way, sucking the person over the edge and down into the abyss below. As the path steepened, the hazard only grew worse. In some places, the drop was thousands of feet. When someone did lose their footing, no one heard or saw the person's body hit the bottom. It just vanished.

Hours passed, and the platoon trudged steadily upward. Water was in short supply, and the dehydration of the men was taking a toll. The heat had dropped, but only a bit; it was still 100° F.

Wolmer, another archer, did not look well. His face was hot, red and dry, and he began shaking uncontrollably. As he continued the climb, he became weaker and his breathing shallower.

"Here, Wolmer, take some of my water," Yewts offered generously. But Wolmer shook his head; he was delirious and not thinking clearly. However, after three more steps he collapsed.

Yewts ran to Seber, pleading. "Commander, your men need to rest. Can't we take a few minutes?"

Seber shook his head. He didn't look much better than Wolmer, but at least he didn't have to walk. Looking down at Yewts from Nimbus, he said, "I wish I could Yewts. But if we stop now, I'm afraid none of us will make it to the top. We just don't have enough water."

They marched onward, trudging after their commander, whose volarequez could no longer stay in the air for lack of water. It was still light out, but it was dim and becoming harder to see the edges of the trail. The dust, which had been thick on the way down, was billowing, making it even more difficult to see and breathe. More ominous were the geiers. Still circling above they waited until a man dropped and then fell out of the sky to take advantage of easy prey. There were many now flying about, as they knew there would be more for them if they hovered long enough.

As Yewts struggled to keep his footing, he watched as two more men in front of him staggered and slipped on the fine gravel of the trail. He lurched forward to reach one of them who clung tenuously to a rock just over the edge, but the man's fingers, weakened from the lack of water, let go. He frantically pawed the powdery earth, digging grooves into the cliffside, trying to regain a grip. But it was in vain.

"No!" mumbled the man as he fell.

It was a cry Yewts would never forget as it then became muffled and silent. The man vanished into the canyon.

The other man also struggled to keep his grip. His body dangled over the same chasm that had claimed the other man. This time, Yewts used both hands to grab onto him. He was heavy, weighed down by a quiver of arrows and a thick sword he had brought. Sweat dripped off Yewts' face, rolling down his arms and onto his clenched, white fingers. He tried re-gripping his hold, but it only made things worse. Finally, the young man gave up and let go. Yewts choked back a tear and sat in disbelief.

How could this be happening? he said to himself.

Darkness fell, and the feeble light from Titan, the largest moon, flickered on and off from the passing clouds overhead. The trail was hard enough to follow with a full Titan moon, but the clouds now made that nearly impossible.

The relentless heat and lack of water was taking its toll on all them. Seber saw a soldier fighting to squeeze one last drop from his water skein. The commander took his own water bag from around his neck and handed it to him. The young warrior looked up at him with surprise.

"Here," said Seber. "It looks like you could use the extra drop right now."

The young man smiled feebly and nodded. His thirst was so great that he couldn't refuse the offer. Grabbing the skein, he quickly lapped down what was left inside.

They hiked up the far side slowly, deliberately, all night, trying to be as safe as they could. By morning, Seber glanced behind him to see how many men were left. Exhausted, he finished his count. It didn't take long—only six of the thirty-five men who started with him were still alive.

Finally, they reached the top, just as the heat began to build. However, it was cooler than it had been deep in the canyon. There was still hope—but only for the two who were left: Commander Seber and Yewts.

"Do you think there is another way?" asked Yewts.

"I don't know," said Seber, "but it really doesn't matter. We don't have time to find another. We're out of water, and unless we find some up here, we're not going to make it back anyway."

Yewts understood. "So, are we heading back or finding water, sir?"

"We have no choice."

They began their search along the rim of the canyon in search of water. It was as hot and dusty on that side as it had been going into the gorge. They only hoped they would see an oasis with fresh water soon.

It was late morning, and Yewts' head was bouncing up and down as he rode with Seber sitting behind him on Nimbus. He had dozed off in the hot suns and had lost track of time and place.

"Commander? Have you seen any place to get water?"

Yewts waited for an answer, but when he didn't get one, he turned around. Commander Seber had slumped in the saddle behind him.

"Commander?"

"Yes, Yewts?" said the officer, reviving.

"Have you seen anything that looks like it might have water?"

"No, not yet."

"Do you think we'll find our way back?"

"You must keep your faith, lad. It is important to remain positive."

"How can you?"

Seber smiled weakly. "You just do."

"But what if we don't find it?"

"I hear doubt in your voice, young knight. There is no room for doubt. You *must* believe. That is your only hope."

Yewts nodded. His throat hurt, and his skin badly burned by the suns' rays. Yet, he understood what the commander was telling him, and he tried to stay positive.

Hours passed, and Nimbus continued to plod along. Yewts patted its neck and offered encouragement.

"Come on boy. We only have a little farther to go. I know you can make it. Just keep it going—one foot in front of the other. We can't let your master down, now that we've come this far."

But as the lazy suns drifted across the sky, Yewts fell asleep again as Nimbus continued to rock to the left and then to the right, still following along the canyon's rim. He awoke only when he felt the horse stop and snort.

"What is it boy?" asked Yewts.

Ahead of him along the rocks and scrub trees was a man standing along the side of the trail. He wore an officer's uniform and carried a sword in his belt. Yewts drew near the man, and soon realized he knew him.

"Commander?" said Yewts. "What are you doing down there?"

Yewts turned around. Seber was no longer in the saddle behind him.

"Yewts," said Seber smiling, "you are a fine soldier and a fine man. You listened to me when I told you stay optimistic, and that has saved you, my friend." Seber looked refreshed and strong, no longer dehydrated and weary.

"But how did you get ahead of me?" asked Yewts.

Seber grinned. "Son, you must go that way." He pointed to his right side, away from the canyon. "Do you see that cliff less than a mile from here?"

"Yes," said Yewts. It was a grand, outcropping of stone with many trees around it. It would have been easy to miss even if he had been awake on the horse.

"Ride there. You will find the water you need. Then fill my skein and return to the other side of the canyon. You will not find there what you expect, but it will be better for you."

"But I don't understand," said Yewts.

"You will."

Then, the image of the commander vanished like a desert mirage.

Yewts rode Nimbus in the direction the commander had pointed. There, under the cliff, he found a small, but deep, pool of cold, blue water. It bubbled up from the depths like life bursting from a seed.

Yewts jumped off his horse and ran to the pool. Jumping in, he sucked down the cool water and splashed it on his face and body. It was pure joy. He had never felt happier in his life. Next to him, Nimbus lapped up the water too, taking in gallon upon gallon.

"Ah!" Yewts sighed, closing his eyes and feeling a light breeze blow through his hair. But it was only a moment later when he heard a voice.

"What is it that you seek?"

Yewts opened his eyes. "What?"

"What is it that you seek?" came the voice again.

In front of him along the edge of the pond was a Conunder. It was something Yewts had never seen before and knew nothing about. With droopy eyelids and wrinkles around its temples and forehead, the Conunder also had rosy cheeks that were plump and cherubic. It was both old and young at the same time. Its eyes were snow white; its ears pointed and smooth, and its scalp wrinkled and spotted with dark brown, irregular-shaped splotches. In its hand was a white cane which it grasped with fierce tenacity.

"What is it that you seek?" it asked again.

"I just want to go home," said Yewts.

"Yes," said the Conunder. Then, strangely, it smiled. "You have seen my brother. He has guided you here."

"Your brother?"

Not answering him, the unusual creature continued. "You are only beginning your journey. You have a long way to go. Yet, you will find your way. I have no words to help you at this time, but rest assured that we are always with you."

"We?"

But just as the commander had vanished before his eyes, so too did the Conunder.

Now, Yewts was truly alone, except for his new friend Nimbus. The sound of the wind gusting up from the canyon and whistling through the caves and holes in the cliffs was an unsettling reminder of how vulnerable he was. There was no one to help now—or was there?

***

Meanwhile, King Barbarot and his commander stood at the rim on the other side of the canyon looking across at the switchbacks and meanderings of the trail that went down into the gorge. He had given his other grand commander, Seber, orders to find a passage around or through the canyon and had told him he had three days. One day remained.

But the king was impatient.

"Commander Sterinis," said Barbarot, calling to his other grand commander.

"Yes, sire," came the reply.

"We will break camp immediately and head east along the canyon rim. Seber went down this path and has not returned; therefore, it must not be the right one. There must be another way to cross farther along the plateau. We've already wasted a day, and I'm not going to wait any longer."

"But Your Highness, you gave them three days. They have another day. We should at least wait until ..."

"I gave him orders to find a crossing as soon as possible—clearly, they failed. I'm not waiting for them. Ready the animals and mount your men ... we leave within the hour."

*****

CH 23 - The Law

Gemma returned to King de Riguere's library with Cori leading the way. The king took great pride in his room of books—as much as he took in his trophy room. Although the library was much like Sojourn's, the king's collection had many more books on the law. As king, de Riguere was particularly interested in it. He had appointed himself head of the courts and maker of all laws. Although others enforced them, he took pleasure in drawing up rules that favored him and his family. He also liked playing supreme judge of the land and passing sentences on those he considered criminals against him.

"My father tracks all his books here," said Cori. "So, when you're finished, you *must* be sure to put them back *exactly* as you found them." Then, she added, "And whatever you do, don't make a mark in them! He gets very upset about that."

"Thanks," replied Gemma. "I will ... and Cori?"

"Yes?" Cori replied.

"Thanks for being a real friend. I really needed that right now."

Cori smiled and left the room, closing the arched door behind her.

Gemma poured over the law books and read all she could on the statutes having to do with theft and agreements. They were thick and, she thought, very boring. Page after page described different types of stealing, depending on the value of what was taken and the type of thing stolen. The books on agreements covered all types of those as well.

In a book called *The Kingdom of Frezia: Statutes before 2890 YOL*, she found references to the punishment for stealing a volarequez or a sensavol.

> *"The punishment for stealing livestock, a volarequez or sensavol valued at more than 25 unio is a mandatory 40 years in prison and 1000 unio fine."*

Whoa, pretty stiff! she thought.

But the laws and sentences for violating them were very strict and clear in their meaning. Each law spelled out the precise punishment if it were violated and gave little room for interpretation.

Gemma read on, flipping to another page where she found another entry.

> *The punishment for anyone stealing something with a value that cannot be determined, that is, something irreplaceable, will be one of the following as selected by the presiding judge:*
>
> - *Death*
> - *Life in prison*
> - *As otherwise determined by the judge*

Gemma got up from her chair and wandered through the sea of bookshelves. It took hours, but at last she found what she was looking for and pulled a brown-leather book from its resting place. It was small and thin but more important to her than any other in the room: *The Frezia Challenge—Rules and Regulations*, by G. de Riguere.

Just as she opened the cover, Cori came in.

"It's time to go," she said to Gemma.

"Just another minute or so, Cori. Look what I found?" Gemma held up the little brown book.

"Oh, yeah. That little gem," replied Cori. "You're not going to find a lot about the challenge in that, you know."

"Why not?" asked Gemma.

"It's just a list of the rules for the challenge. That's all. And, there are only a few."

Gemma frowned. She opened the book and found there were twenty pages of introduction and only two pages of rules. The first one read, simply:

- Shall be held one time every other year
- Shall last precisely three days
- No help shall be given to any competitor
- Treasure to be retrieved shall be chosen by the king
- Rewards and punishments shall be determined by the king

"That's it?" exclaimed Gemma.

"Yep. It means that it's a free-for-all out there! Those guys can do just about anything they want to to each other. That's why it's such a vicious competition—a deadly competition."

"So, they just have to survive against the other prisoners, find the treasure and come back. Right?" asked Gemma.

"Has anyone told you about the Rebus?"

"No."

"I've only heard stories, Gemma, but they say the Rebus, is a mysterious creature that's the keeper and guardian of Erebus Cave—where the treasure lies. He asks questions of all brave enough to try to get into it. The cave holds many secrets and many things of great value. His questions have to be answered precisely and correctly, otherwise ..."

"What? Otherwise, what?" Gemma asked nervously.

"Let me just say it this way ... no one has *ever* returned from the race."

"No one?"

Cori shook her head. "Nope. I'm afraid not. That's why you won't find many rules in that little book of yours. If the Rebus or one of the other prisoners doesn't get Oliver, there are plenty of other things out there that can."

"Like what?" asked Gemma, her full attention glued to her friend.

"Monsters in the woods near the mountain that even I have a hard time believing exist. I've never seen them, but Father has prohibited Prima or I from going anywhere close to Mt. Erebus. He says it's haunted."

"My god," said Gemma, putting her hand over her mouth in disbelief. "And Oliver's out there all by himself."

"Yes, and he doesn't even know the terrain. I don't know how he will make it."

"He will. If anyone can, he can," said Gemma, although she was now far from certain.

As the two ladies began putting away all the books in exactly where they had found them, Gemma looked again at the little brown book. Then, as Cori started to leave the room, she quietly tucked it under her arm. *Who knows,* she thought, *it might just come in handy.*

*****

CH 24 - Not Quite Right

Vacating the camp and going back on his promise to Commander Seber and Yewts to wait for them to return, Barbarot moved his army onward, following the rim of the canyon farther into Vaporia. The trip was long, taking several more days, but he soon found fresh water springs that began popping up from time to time to keep his men and animals well-watered. Around the pools were bushes and trees, and around them were sources of food. Once he found fresh water, Barbarot had little trouble keeping his army fed too.

Without any noticeable landmark, they marched from Vaporia into the neighboring kingdom of Chasmia. The long, dry canyon that had started in Vaporia stretched into Chasmia where it narrowed and then ended. At the end, they found a middle-sized village filled with peasants who toiled for their Chasmian king, watching over his herds and preparing the meats used at the castle and other castles throughout the kingdom.

Barbarot knew that bringing his entire army up to the edge of the village would only strike fear into them and sound alarms back at the king's castle. Instead, what he needed was their cooperation. He needed their help with his plans to attack the king and the kingdom's capital of Gilabend. So, he hid his army in the hills beyond view from the town and took a small band of men with him to find its leader.

Acting like a commoner, Barbarot got the people there talking about their kingdom, the ruling king and the capital city. He offered them spices, uni-horn goats, pelichiks, and fine fabrics for clothes he had brought from Rootan. He convinced them he had come in peace and friendship, and that he wished to help their kingdom and its people. Barbarot also promised them much more if they helped him.

Eventually, word spread through the town that a group of merchants had come to visit and were handing out fine gifts.

Soon, the elder leader of the town—referred to as *The Chief*—came to see what all the interest was. He greeted Barbarot, welcoming him and his men and hoping to get some of the bounty for himself.

"They call me The Chief," he said smiling. "It is not often we have visitors from outside our kingdom. Are you from Vaporia?"

"Yes, we are," said Barbarot, lying. "Of course, our kingdom and yours has had a very good relationship over the years. Your king is a wise man and a good friend of our King Ferox."

"How are things in Vaporia? I heard there was a plague was spreading through the realm. Were you infected by it?"

"No, we are on the other side of the mountains from where the plague was. I understand it hit Barbarotus hard."

"Barbarotus? Where is that?" asked The Chief.

"That is the new name for Rootan, or so I've heard. There is a new king there, a mighty king, named Barbarot. He is said to be a wise and fair ruler."

"I see," said The Chief, growing more suspicious. "Well, in honor of your visit, I invite you and your men to a dinner tonight. We of Aleguma wish to feed you properly while you are here."

"Thank you chief. Perhaps we can talk more about the kingdom then?"

"Yes, of course."

Clever and confident, The Chief didn't let this sudden chain of events unnerve him. He sent out several scouting parties to spy on Barbarot's little band and report back. Soon, he learned their true nature and discovered the vast army that was camped in the hills just outside village. The Chief knew he didn't have the warriors to fight Barbarot's army of thousands, so he had to come up with a different plan.

It was a marvelous feast. There were fresh obanas and naranjalas, which had been imported from neighboring Vaporia, and oosegi, a black, long-necked, red-crested bird that was roasted to perfection. The fruits were carved like forest animals, and the center piece was a blue watermelon, fashioned to look like a geier with its wings made from the broad, dark leaves of a plant Barbarot had never seen before.

During dinner, the two leaders chatted about their kingdoms and their cultures—mostly inconsequential matters that made only for passing the time more quickly. Of course, there were many things Barbarot said that The Chief knew could not be true about Vaporia, but he feigned ignorance and merely nodded and smiled.

After dinner, Barbarot sat next to The Chief as the guest of honor. They watched as the beautiful village maidens danced to the pounding beat of drums and the older women in the village played melodies on their recorder pipes. Next, came The Chief's small passel of young warriors.

"They are young," said The Chief, "but they are eager to learn."

One young warrior of only sixteen took his bow and as another threw a nut the size of a Fortunut high into the air, he fired his arrow. It hit the tiny nut fifty feet above them, showering them with brown shell fragments. He did this several more times to the delight of the crowd.

Then, they brought out a jug and put it on its side on a table several yards away. Immediately, a droplet of water began forming at the top of the jug and then, after many seconds, fell to the ground. The young warrior took his bow and aimed it just below the jug.

Everyone held their breath and watched.

The droplet began to form again, and when it started to fall, the marksman let go of the string. The arrow flew through the air and burst the drop before it reached the ground.

Barbarot was impressed. Never before had he seen such abilities.

"And he has one last trick to show you," said The Chief smiling.

This time, the men set up a post with a crossbar at the top. To it they tied a three-foot rope and to that they attached a horseshoe.

"*Ah*," said Barbarot, "This is a good trick, but even my archers can hit a swinging shoe from a distance."

The Chief only smiled and turned back to watch.

The young warrior had disappeared, and it was a few moments later that they heard the beating of hooves coming toward the viewing area. Another young man started the horseshoe swinging back and forth on the post and ran to see cover. The archer appeared on horseback, riding backwards and aiming his bow. Galloping past, he let the arrow fly.

Clang!

The arrow hit the swinging horseshoe on the post and stopped it cold in midair.

Barbarot was angry. He had been embarrassed in front of his own men, and it was something he could never forgive.

He gritted his teeth. "Not a bad shot, I must say," he commented. Then, he rose and extended his hand. "Thank you chief. This has been very entertaining, but now we must return to our camp. But before I do, I have a few more questions for you."

"I will answer what I can," said The Chief.

"Tell me. How far is the capital city from here?"

"Gilabend?"

"Yes."

"It's only a day's ride, if the weather is good," The Chief replied. "We're in the dry season now; so, the trail will be hard-packed and easy to travel. You wouldn't be able to get your sensavols through it during the wet season. The rains are too heavy."

"And King Scorche has an army of only ten thousand or so. Is that right?"

The Chief had never told Barbarot this, so he assumed he had heard it in the village. It was something The Chief really didn't know the answer to, but the stakes were too high.

"I believe they are over one hundred thousand, but I wouldn't be the one to ask. All I know is that many warriors are scattered throughout the countryside in small fortresses. We haven't had to battle anyone for hundreds of years, so there may only be that many troops in the capital city. Yet ..."

"Yet, what?" asked Barbarot, curious about the sudden hesitation.

"Yet, history has been kind to Gilabend. Do you know the history?"

Barbarot shook his head.

"The castle they call Captivus was built nearly two thousand years ago. The ancient peoples of Orasceum first settled here but were driven out by the Chasmians, who then built the castle. It was King Scorche who led the Chasmians to victory over the Orasceums and had the palace constructed. It took thirty years to build, and once completed, the king moved in with his queen, the magnificent Queen Hollythorn."

"Yes, yes, well what is the meaning? What does this have to do with the castle?" Barbarot asked, impatiently.

"Well, the king and queen were only in the castle one month before they were murdered. Both of them were slain as they slept in their bed."

"Who could have done such a thing?"

"Their son—the prince. Only fifteen, Prince Faregon, killed both of them, wanting to take over the castle and have the kingdom for himself."

Barbarot smiled. "It sounds like the young lad had ambition," said the king, grinning. "I like his initiative. So, what happened to the young man?"

"He was killed by his uncle, who also wanted the throne. The house of Chasmia was tossed into chaos for decades until members of the first family came back to claim it. This was the family of Scorche—the current ruler."

"I see. Then why is this story a warning?" asked Barbarot.

"Because it has been the history of that castle that whoever tries to take it from the family that holds it falls victim to—let's say—unfortunate circumstances. No one has taken the castle or the kingdom in over a thousand years. Some have conquered it for a short period—for a few months or even years—but none for longer. They say the spirits of the first king and queen haunt the halls of the castle and drive everyone who is not a Scorche mad very quickly."

"Ha!" said Barbarot. "That is a wonderful story, chief. But it is just a story. No sane mind would believe in it. If a kingdom exists, it can and will eventually be conquered. It says so in the *Book of Iuratis*. The one who holds and controls the Map of Gneima and discovers its secrets will rule the realm, and that includes Chasmia. Isn't it so?"

"As you say, my Lord," said The Chief, not wishing to irritate someone who had a vast army waiting in the hills just outside his village.

But being curious, Barbarot pressed further. "When was the last time you were there, then? In the castle, that is."

The Chief thought for a moment and then answered.

"It must have been three years ago. The Chasmian king invited the local leaders to his castle. I don't remember exactly what it was about, but I do recall that everyone had the same strange sense about the place."

"You don't remember what the meeting was about?" asked Barbarot.

"Like I said, that's not important," said The Chief with irritation. "What was important was there seemed to be no one there. The

198

royal family and a few of the court were in the castle, but the town around it appeared empty. There wasn't anyone there—it was a ghost town. And then, there was that other thing ..."

"What?"

"It seemed like we were being watched the whole time. You know, like we were being followed. But there was no one there."

"Did anything happen to anyone?" asked Barbarot, growing weary of the conversation and the dramatic way The Chief was describing things.

"No, not that I know of."

"Well, it should be of little concern then," said Barbarot.

The merriment of the evening went on well into the night with both the villagers and Barbarot's officers enjoying themselves. However, the king retired early, telling his host he was tired from the long trip into Chasmia and wished to be ready for another the following day.

***

The next morning, a warrior ran into The Chief's quarters, panting to catch his breath.

"Chief, I have troubling news!" said the knight, trembling.

"What is it? Speak up?"

"All our sensavols are gone! Barbarot and his men took them along with our livestock and much of our grain. We have little left. The stockyards have been cleared, and our grain bins are empty," said the warrior.

"What about the royal granary?"

"Empty."

"And the guards?"

"Dead."

"Unfortunately, I'm not surprised," said The Chief. "With an army of thousands just outside our gates, I was thankful they didn't kill us all. It's an inconvenience to have some of our crops and animals stolen, but it is not a disaster."

"But what will we do for food?" the soldier asked.

The Chief laughed.

"What's so funny?" asked his commander.

"I expected this and had nearly all the sensavols and grains moved yesterday afternoon when I found the king and his men were plotting against us. He only stole a small portion of what we had. There was much more he didn't find, I assure you."

"But why would you let him take any?" asked the warrior.

"That is easy, my friend. If we had resisted, he would have burned our village and taken what he wanted anyway. So, letting him have what he took was better than losing it all, wasn't it?"

The Chief smiled, proud of himself for having spared his people and, it appeared, deceived Barbarot and his army into believing the kingdom wasn't worth the trouble of a fight.

But that day, Barbarot drove his army out from the hills and onto the road toward the capital city of Gilabend. Behind him, lay The Chief's village with fire spiking high into the air and black smoke drifting east toward the far coastline. The Chief had been wise, but Barbarot had been even more ruthless. He wanted to leave nothing behind that might later cause him a problem. So, he wiped out The Chief and his village.

***

Once Barbarot and his army reached the perimeter of the castle they camped. Like many castles in the realm, Captivus was formidable with walls twenty feet thick and thirty feet high. Although many of his rams and boring machines had been damaged or destroyed during the attack on Lagerfall, Barbarot still had enough to move against this capital city. This was the castle of the Scorche family, and even with The Chief's warning of a dark and mysterious past, it was not going to frighten Barbarot away from conquering it and the other kingdoms.

Nightfall came, and the Rootanian king ordered the army to light as many campfires as they could.

"Set as many campfires in the camp as you can. Build three or four more too, and light them all. We need them to believe there are not just a hundred thousand of us, but a million!"

The following day, Barbarot ordered his commanders to ready the men for an assault. The archers would go first and launch their volleys of tar-soaked, flaming arrows, hoping to catch the dry, wooden rooftops of the buildings inside ablaze. Then, they would ram the massive doors in front with the battering rams they had used to great success against Lagerfall and King Ferox. Lastly, they would send a huge number of troops to scale the walls and open the gates from the inside, just in case the rams couldn't punch through. This plan had worked before, and the king was confident it would work again.

As the Rootanian army blew their conch shells to signal the attack, the archers ran to the front and lined up, twelve rows deep and two hundred men wide with their bows drawn and flaming arrows readied.

"Fire!" yelled the commander in charge, watching as the first volley of blazing arrows flew through the air, disappearing somewhere behind the city walls.

"Fire!" shouted the commander again. This time more arrows were launched, and a rain of terror blanketed the inside of the town. Soon, the sky was black and orange with soaring fire arrows as they flew through the air, gracefully arching to reach their zenith before bending to gravity and falling inside the city.

These volleys went on for an hour, and Barbarot expected to see some sign of a counterattack or the scurrying of defenses in or around the capital. However, none came.

Cautiously, the king sent in the "ladder climbers"—wagons with twenty-foot ladders lashed to their sides. In front of them were the rollopods with their huge shields ready to block any attack from archers mounted around the high walls and towers of the city.

Quickly, the troops crossed the dusty, rocky plain between the red hills that protected the troops and the white, compact, sand dunes that were built-up in front of the walls to guard the capital fortress. Barbarot's men ripped the ladders from the wagons and pressed them against the outside of the fortress walls, leaning them so the tops were just below the armaments. By the thousands they scurried, scaling the height and then jumping down onto the guard's walkway on the inside of the wall.

But eerily, they found no one there. No one was guarding the city. There were no sentries watching from the towers, no marksmen ready to shoot the marauders who were trying to take control of their capital. No one.

Barbarot watched the scene unfold, and the creases on his forehead became more pronounced. In the pit of his stomach, something told him all was not quite right.

"There is something about that place that has spooked me for years," The Chief had told him. *I think the place is haunted of the spirits of the dead king and queen*, he had suggested. These words now rang incessantly in Barbarot's ears.

"What's wrong, my king?" asked Commander Sterinis. "You don't look pleased at our progress. We should be able to take the town very shortly—and with no loss of men."

Barbarot didn't answer. Instead, he kicked his volarequez and galloped to another one of his officers. "Commander, I want you to take a squad of volarequi and scour the inside of the city. See if there is anyone there and report back to me as soon as possible."

"Yes, Your Highness," came the reply as the commander dashed off to carry out the mission.

Minutes later the massive wooden front doors to the fortress opened, and out came several of the first swordsmen who had climbed the ladders and gone into the city. Their bows held no arrows—in fact, their arrows had been put back safely into their quivers.

"Your Royal Highness," said one of the knights, "there is no one inside. There is no one in the castle and no one in the town. Everybody's gone!"

"They must be hiding inside somewhere, waiting to ambush us," replied Barbarot. "You didn't look hard enough. They are there. They must be there! You must find them!"

"They are not, Your Royal Highness," came the reply.

The same report came from the commander of the volarequi squad Barbarot had sent to search the town and the king's castle. There was no sign of the king, the queen or any of the army. In fact, the only ones inside the city walls were goats, chickens, and dogs.

"It's a trap!" yelled Barbarot. "Pull out your men now! Get them out of the city!"

Soon, his men came running out from the city gates and the ladder wagons and supply units were loaded and rolled back to the hills outside. As if they were running from a major offensive attack or a deadly disease, the brave men of the army ran faster than their commanders had ever seen.

"There's something in there," said one swordsman, running back to the front line. He was shaking hysterically. "It's cursed! It's cursed!"

Word spread rapidly, and by the time the last of the troops got the message, they indeed believed there was some curse within the city of Gilabend.

"Order the army to move quickly east and around the city," said Barbarot. "We will station a few troops outside of the city to keep an eye on things until we come back. They are not to go into the city or try to take it on their own. Do you understand?"

The officer, Commander Dedman, hesitated. "You just want us to wait out here even though there isn't anyone inside to stop us?"

"Yes," said the king. "You're not afraid, are you?"

"Of course not, my king. Never."

"Good. Do you have any family, commander?"

"Yes, Your Highness," answered Dedman.

"Wife and children, I suppose?"

"Yes, my Lord," the commander said nervously.

"Good, then you'd better hope the evil of this place doesn't possess you," said Barbarot laughing wickedly. "I'd hate to think you'd be taken over by evil and take it home to your family. Wouldn't that be a shame?" Then, he turned to his other commander. "Now, Sterinis, let's get going. We need to move our army on to Vinedria ... time's a wasting!" ordered Barbarot, galloping away.

*****

CH 25 - The Wrong Path

The cerberian wolves growled as they guided their sleds across the white glaze of snow, cutting dark furrows into the hard, crusty surface as they plowed ahead. It was a clear day, but also very cold. Without the buffer of clouds above, the heat quickly reflected off the white surface and back into the atmosphere, leaving little behind to keep either man or beast warm.

Oliver could see the white vapor spewing from his mouth every time he exhaled and could feel the ice forming on his eyebrows and around his nose. Ahead of him was Fermat and his female cerberian, which he had named Sedah. Oliver's sled was still broken with a rear runner that wobbled so badly it barely stayed on. It was only a matter of time until the supply sled behind him fell apart, but he was trying to go as far as he could with it even though he knew it put more strain on Tristyx.

High overhead flew a white-crested whirlidood, an odd bird with white-and-blue-tipped wings that rotated around its tail. Its largely-stationary main wings stretched stiffly to either side taking in the flowing air currents beneath them. Oliver had always heard these birds were good omens, but he'd never seen one because they lived in much colder, northern climates.

Soon they came across other sledding tracks that crisscrossed the trail as if there had been a battle of sleds going on earlier in the day. The good news was they were not lost; the bad news was they might soon run into the other unsavory prisoners who were all vying for their freedom and were willing to kill them to get it.

Smaller and lighter than most of the competitors in the race, Oliver and Fermat easily gained ground on them, and within a short time they could see a small pack of sledders just ahead. Knowing it wasn't safe to engage with them, they held back, keeping their distance.

As they reached the tundra, the land became more open. But this was only a prelude to more mountainous terrain and steeper hills ahead. Soon, they were mushing through the low-lying hills that bordered the taller mountains farther north. And soon they would find them—the Laru Mountains with its highest peak: Mt. Erebus.

Suddenly, the trail grew very steep. Even with the muscle of the cerberian leads, the load of the supply sled and the musher was a lot to pull up the grade. The rockier cliffs often obscured the view Oliver and Fermat had of the leaders ahead, and they struggled to keep their distance. However, as they grew closer to them, Oliver saw there were only three dogsleds left, which meant that of the twelve that had started, only five remained. He hadn't seen anyone else along the trail—only the occasional sled ruts that went off course. It wasn't hard to assume that all must have met an untimely end.

Rounding a bend and making their way up the slope to their first checkpoint, Fermat pulled his sled to the side of the trail and stopped. He turned back to Oliver and gestured with his hand for him to stop too.

"This is the first checkpoint," said Fermat. "I was told this is where we'll find The Scorpio." He looked around nervously as if something might jump out at him at any time.

"The Scorpio? What exactly is The Scorpio?" asked Oliver, with the same curious emphasis that Fermat had placed on the name.

"Oh, that's a rock formation we're supposed to see once we reach the mountains. Someone told me it looks like a long spider with a barbed tail and pincers. If we don't see it, we're lost."

They both looked around but saw nothing that remotely looked like a spider.

"Maybe it's farther ahead," said Oliver, trying to be optimistic.

"Yeah ... maybe," replied Fermat.

They continued on, keeping their eyes peeled for the elusive "Scorpio" formation. Later, they found another stretch of open snow on the steep path, but Oliver noticed something had changed.

"Weren't there *three* dog teams ahead of us?" Oliver yelled up to Fermat who was still ahead.

"Sure, why?"

"Because I only see two of them now!" said Oliver with concern.

Indeed, they came up to the body of a prison inmate and his broken sled. His cerberian wolf was standing nearby, still chained to it and looking lost.

Fermat stopped and hopped off his rig, moving to the body. He rolled it over and put his fingers against his neck.

"There's no pulse," said Fermat.

"Nice bunch of guys you hang out with," said Oliver.

"Hey, they aren't *my* buddies. I was just lucky enough to survive that place—only to be thrown into this. Do you think I'll be lucky enough the second time around?"

"I don't know, but I hope neither one of us has to go there after this is over," said Oliver.

Fermat trudged through the snow and grabbed the leash of the dead owner's three-headed wolf. It tried to bite him, turning one of its heads and nipping at his hand, but he grabbed it by its snout and shouted, "No! Bad dog!" giving it a sharp smack.

Once untied though, the wolf settled down and followed behind Fermat, prancing on top of the snowy surface with its big, furry-white paws.

"What are you doing?" asked Oliver, as Fermat began hooking the beast up to Oliver's sled, just behind Tristyx.

"I'm giving you another dog, of course. Can't let a good dog team go to waste, now can we?"

"Why don't *you* take him?"

"Listen," said Fermat, finishing the last knot to secure the wolf, "if there is anyone who's going to make it through this, it's you. Even if I make it back with the stone, there's no guarantee the king will let me live. You have a better shot at it than I do."

Oliver was speechless. He knew Fermat was right, but he didn't know what words to use to make his new friend feel better. Finally, he said, "We'll both get through this. You'll see." Then, he held up his hand, stopping Fermat before he started out again. "Wait!" said Oliver, surprised at what he'd heard. "What did you say about a stone?"

Fermat didn't realize that Oliver had no idea what they were supposed to find at the far end of their expedition.

"What? You don't know?" asked Fermat in astonishment. "You mean to tell me that you don't know where you're going or what you're supposed to find once you get there?" Fermat started to shake his head. "Maybe I got this wrong. Maybe you're *not* going to be the last one standing after all."

"Well, it did happen very quickly," said Oliver. "You know—when your friend needs your help, you just do whatever it takes, and you think about the consequences later."

Fermat sighed. "Okay, let me just say this. We have to find this 'stone' that the king is after. Apparently, it has some sort of power, but I don't know if that's true. As a kid growing up, we used to hear stories of some map that had powers. I'm thinking that's what this is all about. But you know, guys say a lot of things when they're cooped up in a cell for years at a time."

"Does everyone know about this?"

"Of course. We all were told that we have to find a certain stone in the Rebus' cave and bring it back to the king, if that's what you mean," said Fermat.

"No, I mean, do the others know about the power of the stone you're talking about?"

"I don't know. Maybe not, because all we were told was that we had to bring back this white or gray stone. Someone said the king has two other ones, so I don't know why this one is so damned important. Maybe having three makes a difference. You know—three times the power or something."

"Do *you* know where this stone is?" asked Oliver.

"Yeah, it's in the cave just under Mt. Erebus. Supposedly, it's been there for thousands of years, and all we have to do is find it and bring it back to the king. Sounds easy enough, right?"

Oliver looked at Fermat knowingly.

"What?" asked Fermat. "You mean because no one has ever returned alive from this challenge?"

"Well, yeah."

"I dunno. I realize it's cold out here, and we could have nicer company, but it doesn't seem that hard to go to a cave, grab a stone and bring it back. We're given three days to do it. Is there a dragon guarding it or something?"

Oliver laughed. "There's no such things as dragons. Have you ever seen a dragon?"

"No, but that doesn't mean there aren't any."

"Okay, fair enough. But in this case, there must be something more sinister than a dragon."

"The Rebus," said Fermat flatly.

"What is it? That's all I've been hearing—Rebus this and Rebus that. How bad could it be?"

"The Rebus ..." thought Fermat, "... no one knows because they've never come back to tell about it. Anyone who gets to the cave never comes back."

"No one?" Oliver asked haltingly.

"Nope. Why do you think the king wants us to go after the stone for him? Everyone thinks he's this great hunter—bah! He's not!

He supposedly has a trophy room filled with animals he didn't shoot. He had others to it for him. This is no different. He's not going to risk his life for this thing. He's only hoping someone will breakthrough and get it for him. Then, he can make up some crazy story about how he discovered it." Fermat climbed back onto his sled and picked up his reins. "The king isn't going to go after the stone. He made up this wild biannual hoax to get us— the desperate ones—to get it for him. But make no mistake—he wants it, and if he has to kill a hundred men trying … well, he'll send another hundred."

"So, no one has *ever* returned from this challenge?" asked Oliver mumbling to himself.

"Yep, that's what I'm saying, Oliver." Fermat paused and added, "That is, not until now." He then gave a wide, confident grin.

Oliver smiled back. He liked that about Fermat—his confidence. It was something he had but didn't always show.

"Now, let's get going before those idiots ahead of us get there before we do and take the prize from us, *eh?*" added Oliver's friend.

And with that, Fermat cracked his leather reins and his sled gave a sudden jolt forward as his cerberian canine dashed onto the grooved trail that had been left for them to follow. Oliver did the same but had more difficulty managing two wolves instead of one. Growling distrustfully at each other, the two surged on, unsteadily, hauling the sled.

Eventually they came to a curvy part of the trail, and as they rounded a bend, they found that the grooved tracks of the sleds ahead of them had abruptly stopped. Fermat halted his sled quickly and looked about anxiously.

"What's wrong? What is it?" asked Oliver.

"Shhhhhh!" Fermat whispered, holding his finger to his lips.

Fermat made a motion with his fingers to his eyes and then outward around where they'd stopped, signaling for Oliver to keep a watchful eye. He got off his sled and knelt by where the tracks had ended. Nodding, he pointed to where the snow had been brushed over, covering the tracks which had led off to the side.

Suddenly, two inmates sprang out from behind a large boulder jumping Fermat and pushing his body into the rocky cliff beside the trail. Each prisoner had sawed through his own restraints to the sleds and now used their muscle freely to try to crush their two remaining opponents.

Both were big men with stout, hewn forearms the size of a large kao tree. It only took one blow across the front of his head to send Fermat down into the snow. He didn't move.

"Come on Tristyx, let's go!" cried Oliver, and he slapped his reins just as the other one—a tall, hairy man with a greasy, gray beard and missing front teeth—leaped across the path in front of him. Menacingly, he pointed a spear at Oliver—one he'd fashioned as a weapon along the way. Oliver tried to run him over, but he jumped out of the way and then heaved the sharp weapon at him, narrowly missing Oliver's head. Instead, it hit a small pinot tree with such force that it split it in two.

Oliver sped ahead down the trail with the two convicts in close pursuit, yelling and whipping their lead wolves. As Oliver had problems steering his sled with two wolves, the prisoners gained on him, and soon, they were within striking distance.

Ahead, Oliver could see the trail veered sharply to the left, and he couldn't slow down for fear the men behind him would catch him before he made the turn. Thinking quickly, he yanked both his wolves to the right—away from the trail and directly into the thick woods. Surprised, one of the inmates behind him—frozen by Oliver's sudden move—smashed headfirst into a large boulder at the junction, unable to make the turn. The other also took his eye off the turn, looking at his buddy collide with the rock and flipped over on his own sled. He was thrown off, but his sled continued, twisting and spinning in midair.

Oliver didn't wait to see what happened to either of them but, instead, doubled-back through the woods, avoiding fallen trees and rocks to get to where his friend was lying in the snow.

Fermat wasn't moving, but his chest was heaving up and down in pain.

"Fermat, get up! We've got to get out of here!" Oliver shouted, watching for the other two prisoners to appear on the trail, coming for them.

Fermat moved his arm and then lifted his head. Snow was caked onto his face giving him a full, white beard of frozen crystals.

"What happened?" he asked, bewildered.

"Don't worry about that now! Climb on!" yelled Oliver, giving Fermat a hand and heaving him onto the supply sled behind him.

"We can't leave Sedah," groaned Fermat.

"We don't have time!" said Oliver.

"We *do*. I'm not leaving without her."

Oliver ran and unchained Sedah, reattaching her to the other two on his sled. Now he had three wolves to manage.

The three cerberians took off again, going back down the trail where Oliver had left the two attackers. They passed the splintered remains of the first sled that had been destroyed in its fight with the boulder. But the second man, although shaken, was not hurt and was brushing the snow from his white coat as he yelled obscenities and shook his fist at them.

But Oliver steered the sled onward, up a hill and deeper into the mountain range. As they moved swiftly up the cliffs, they could hear a sled behind them, and the obscenities coming from the musher that told them all they needed to know. All three heads of that sled's dog were barking ferociously, either out of pain from the whipping by their master or out of a viciousness they wanted to unleash on Oliver and Fermat if they were caught. Oliver didn't want to find out which.

"Get going, you mangy mutt!" they could hear the prisoner shout behind them.

"There! I think I see it up ahead!" said Fermat excitedly. He was still nursing a cut on the back of his head, but his attention was all on what lay ahead.

"What is it?" asked Oliver, trying to focus.

"I think it's Mt. Erebus ... it's the one with the smoke coming from the top of it."

"You mean, it's a volcano?" asked Oliver, alarmed.

"I guess so. All I know is that it's the only mountain peak up here. If that's true, then it's got smoke coming from the top of it."

They pushed on toward the smoking peak, taking the path that seemed to lead directly to it. But just as they were putting a little distance between themselves and the prisoner chasing them, they reached another split in the trail. One path went to the right of the peak, while the other seemed to go left of it. Neither pointed directly to the mountain top.

"Okay, any ideas?" asked Oliver. "If you've got any, you'd better let me know now!" His voice was quivering as he watched behind him.

"None are any better than yours, I'm sure," said Fermat.

Oliver slowed the sled to a crawl to give them a little more time to figure out which way to go. They could hear the approaching wolf—the growling and snarling growing louder with every moment they waited.

"Got anything yet?" asked Fermat.

Oliver reached in his duffel and pulled out his Eripio bag to see if it held anything for him. He had secretly stuffed it into a pocket when the rest of his duffel had been taken from him. But time was running out, and he didn't have enough to wait on the bag to do its magic.

"We're on our own, I'm afraid," he said to Fermat, throwing the Eripio back into his silver bag.

"Just slap the reins and let the dogs decide then," said Fermat.

And that's exactly what Oliver did.

"Okay, Tristyx. It's up to you."

The dogs chose to go to the left—whether due to the more powerful pull of Tristyx on that side or due to instinct, neither Oliver nor Fermat knew. But whichever the case, the sled pulled forward without any hand from Oliver. They were on their way down the left track, but Oliver listened intently to hear whether their chaser veered right or chose the left trail as they had.

Soon, Oliver had his answer. It was both good news and bad. The prisoner was no longer chasing them, as the snarling of his wolf faded into the distance. But that also meant they had probably chosen the wrong trail.

Oliver stopped the wolves.

"What do you think?" asked Oliver. "Do you think he knows something that we don't?"

"Most likely," said Fermat. "That's Bratworm. He's always been one of the guards' favorites—probably because he paid them off with sweet, Chacunut bars he had smuggled into the prison. But worst of all, he's cunning and has no remorse for anything. Let's just say, you don't want to get on his bad side."

"It looks like we're already on his bad side," remarked Oliver.

"I think we'd better follow him," said Fermat, pointing back in the direction where Bratworm had split off.

They waited a minute for their challenger to get far enough down the trail so he wouldn't see them doubling back and then followed him. Oliver didn't want to be surprised again by Bratworm jumping out in front of them like he'd done earlier; so, he was careful to stay out of sight.

The three dogs pulled their sled, following in the ruts created by the one ahead of them. This time, they were careful not to go too fast and overtake Bratworm, or worse, miss any other signs or splits in the path.

The winds began picking up, and the snow started blowing, drifting and making the going even harder. As the temperature dropped, ice began building up on the sled's rails, slowing it even more. Oliver's face felt like it would never move again, while Fermat's fingers and toes were growing blue from frostbite.

"I can't feel my face," said Oliver.

"I can't feel much of anything," said Fermat, sitting up on the back sled and watching for signs of an ambush or a hidden exit off the path.

As it grew colder, it also grew darker, and the second day was coming to a close soon. They had only one day to find the treasure and return. Time was running out.

"Stop!" yelled Fermat.

Ahead was a sled. The cerberian was munching on some chum that Bratworm had left for him, but Bratworm was not there. Oliver stopped quite a distance behind it, making sure they couldn't be easily seen. But then it wasn't the sense of sight that became front and center—it was that of sound.

The wind was howling, making it difficult to hear. Yet, there were voices not far away—not one, but two. The first voice was familiar—it was that of Bratworm. But the second voice was deep and resonated with power and authority.

Oliver and Fermat inched forward in their sled to hear better, but the gusts only blew harder. So, Oliver got off and helped his friend Fermat who was holding his hand to his head in pain. Together they moved to where they could hear what was going on. Crouching behind a pinot tree that had split into two trunks that curved away from one another, Oliver and Fermat got a clear view of the scene. In front of them was the cave—the Cave of Erebus.

"That's it!" said Oliver excitedly.

"Shhhh!" Fermat whispered, his face unhappy. "It is. That's true. But that's also a voice we should fear."

"The Rebus?"

"Yes. I think it's the Rebus," said Fermat nervously.

*****

CH 26 - Missing in Action

The army of Rootan moved out, and within hours the entire force vanished from the plains of Chasmia, leaving behind the strange and empty fortress of Gilabend. The remaining commander, Dedman, and his small battalion of archers and swordsmen stayed in their camp just outside the castle walls. Dedman set up the camp with the tents close together for protection and ordered massive bonfires to be lit to scare away wild beasts as well as any ghostly ones.

Numbering only three hundred, the warriors lined up at the makeshift mess tent for their dinners which consisted mainly of roasted desert rarebit and dried bobpta leaves. It would fill their stomachs but little more. As always, the part of the meal the men enjoyed the most was the last one: the froth. They drank with gusto and laughed and told stories well into the night before turning in.

Commander Dedman gave orders for several of the men to keep watch, positioning them at various points around the camp. But much to everyone's relief, the night was quiet. It was only the chirping of the sand crickets and the occasional flapping of pigmy owla wings that kept the guards entertained.

As morning dawned, and the trumpet shells blew their revelry, the men lined up for the roll call. Well disciplined, the men had risen soon after the call was sounded and had dressed in their military tunics to be ready for the new day's events.

Leading the roll call was a stocky knight of some age who had been with the brigade for years. He was the senior-most man and someone the commander could always rely on. His name was Sir Oscar Rollins, and his gray mustache bent around the corners of his mouth like a handle on a mug of froth. Always with a positive attitude, he smiled even though there were times it didn't seem to fit the situation. Hanging over his blue eyes like baggy curtains were wrinkled eyelids that ballooned out from sunken sockets. Those eyes had seen much during their lifetime, and they were about to see even more.

"Fifth Brigade line up for roll!" said the old knight with his baritone voice.

The men got in rows, as they always did, and awaited the call.

"Aber?" came the name.

"Ya!"

"Acerban?"

"Ya!"

"Argo?"

"Ya!"

The names continued through the roster.

"Edwardi?"

"Ya!"

"Epinold?"

"Ya!"

"Farinow?"

No answer.

"Farinow?" repeated Rollins. Yet, still there was no reply.

"Where's Farinow?" asked the knight. "Will somebody go and drag his butt out of bed."

"Gaelic?"

"Ya!"

"Gornig?"

Silence.

"Gornig? Where the heck is Gornig?" shouted Rollins, becoming upset. He nodded to another of the soldiers to go find Gornig.

"Hamergild?" ...

"Hamergild? Where the heck is everybody?" screamed the old man, now more irritated.

The roll call went on, and men were sent to find those who hadn't reported for the morning lineup.

"Rollins, what seems to be the problem?" Dedman asked coming up behind him to check on his progress.

"Sire, there seems to be some men ... *uh* ... missing."

"What do you mean missing?"

"I mean we can't find them, commander. They're just not in the camp with us this morning."

"So, they abandoned us in the middle of the night? They deserted? Don't the men know that is punishable by death?" asked the commander. "They're traitors!"

"I don't think they left like that, commander. These were some of our best men—some highly decorated with battle honors. I don't think they'd just leave, sire."

"You never know, Rollins. War does strange things to men. I've seen it over and over again. Today they're great heroes; tomorrow they're lowly cowards. The shock of war can't be underestimated."

"But sire, there are so many missing that I ..."

"How many are missing?"

"Of the three hundred, we only accounted for two hundred fourteen this morning, sire," replied Rollins. "That means we lost a lot of men."

The commander stood, silent and stunned. "Did you say we only have two hundred and fourteen?"

"Yes, sir. We've lost ... let's see ... eighty-six, sire."

"That can't be. Double check and report back to me as soon as you've found the men. They can't just vanish like that," barked the commander as he stormed away. Then he stopped and added, "And when you find them, I want them breaking rocks until they can't stand up anymore!"

Dedman wasn't happy about being stuck there, and he certainly wasn't pleased with losing men. What worried him most was what his king would do to him when he returned if he weren't able to find them.

However, no rocks were broken that day. There was no trace of the men despite all the efforts of the brigade to find them. The night sentries and others within the camp were interrogated on what they had seen and heard the night before. Some were even threatened, but none knew anything. The tents of the missing men were empty, and their beddings only slightly disturbed. There were no signs of a struggle. It was as if they had just evaporated into thin air—unseen and unheard.

That night, there was no revelry as the men worried about what had happened to their comrades and, worse yet, what might happen to them. Rollins divided the ranks and chose more men to stay up, on watch, while the others slept. He planned to rotate the groups during the daytime and nighttime hours, so he had sentries who were more alert and awake to spot deserters. He was determined to find out why the men had vanished and where they'd gone.

The second morning, roll was taken again.

"Aber?"

"Ya!"

"Acerban?"

"Ya!"

"Argo?"

No answer.

"Argo? Where is Argo?"

It quickly became obvious that more men were missing. When the final roll was completed, there were only one hundred seventy-five soldiers in the camp.

Angry, the commander threw the old knight into the brig and appointed another, less senior, man to conduct another search for the missing men. The hunt continued throughout the day but resulted in the same dead ends. No one had any better idea after the second day than they had after the first.

That night, Dedman ordered half-day shifts—half the men would watch during nights and half during days. They were fully armed and ready to strike at anything that came into the camp. Yet, they were scared. They knew their friends were disappearing, and no one had answers.

All night, the sentries stood watch. They were quiet, not uttering any sound for fear they might miss hearing or seeing something. They had built their bonfires even larger and put many more along the perimeter of the camp to illuminate every inch of the perimeter. The night passed, and again, nothing seemed to happen.

In the morning, the new knight in charge, Sir Olin Magnus, reported to the commander that there had been no usual activity the night before, but he had yet to call roll.

"We shall find out once you assemble your men," said the commander.

"Men, fall in!" shouted Magnus. Then, after they were in there proper rows, he yelled, "Attention! We will call roll."

The second sergeant pulled out a long scroll and began reading the names. But as he looked out over the group in front of him, the blood quickly drained from his face. He could tell he had far fewer men than before.

"Aber?" came the name.

"Ya!"

"Acerban?"

"Ya!"

"Amergo?"

"Ya!"

"Apri?"

"Ya!"

The names continued to be called, and all seemed to be going well.

"Melod?" was the next name called after several minutes of running through the first part of the alphabet

There was no answer.

"Megami?"

No answer.

"Moliss? Nazirey?"

Still nothing.

"Nazirey?" ...

"Does anyone know where any of them are?" asked the knight.

The men just shook their heads. The tenseness returned, and their hearts started beating quickly again. It was one thing to miss a few here and there, but now whole sections of names weren't answering.

"Nonnu?" ...

"Nonnu?" ...

Again, there was no reply.

"Oreon?" ...

"Oreon?" ...

"Where the heck are these guys?" shouted Magnus in frustration.

Dedman quickly called Magnus to his tent. "Are more men missing, Magnus? Have you let more men disappear under your watch?"

"There appear to be a few more missing, sire," said Magnus not wanting to reveal how bad it was.

"How many?"

"I don't know. We haven't completed the count yet."

Dedman motioned for the scroll which Magnus reluctantly handed him. The commander looked at it and the markings that indicated who was there and who wasn't. All the names beginning with the letters N through W were left unchecked.

"How did you divide the troops up into shifts last night, Magnus? Which ones were awake and on guard?"

"I split them alphabetically, sire."

"So, I presume A through M were awake and on guard, while N through Z were sleeping?" asked the commander.

The knight said nothing. His face was as white as a clean, cotton sheet.

Commander Dedman spoke sharply. "Order your men to brake camp immediately. We are getting out of here!"

"Yes sir!" said the knight with relief.

Magnus eagerly marched to his troops which were still in rank and file and gave the order to break camp and prepare to move out. Within the hour the camp was gone, and so was the only foothold Barbarot thought he had within the kingdom of Chasmia. As if the disappearing men weren't haunting enough, Dedman now had to fear the wrath of his king. All he knew was he had to leave that place if he wanted his men to live to see the next morning. He would give more thought to what he would do next.

***

As the daylight hours drew to a close and the night's curtain began to fall, the area around the Chasmian fortress grew still. Nothing moved on the plain outside the castle of Gilabend where Dedman had made his camp. The air was calm and eerie. The cold chill wasn't from the temperature outside—it was from something darker and more sinister.

As the large moon, Titan, began rising in the east, there were small stirrings in the desert sands around where the tents had been. Soon, small holes the size of round meat platters began forming, as bone-colored grains of sand started draining down into the ground as if a huge cavern had opened up below them. Like sands in an hourglass, the pockets appeared—first by the dozens, then by the hundreds. When the holes stopped forming, something emerged.

Out from the holes crawled tiny creatures—manlike, but yet very different. Strange and ugly they were, with waxy faces that looked as though they had been melted by the intense heat of the desert sands. Their skin was thick and wrinkled like a berhino's, and their eyes were pure white as if they lived permanently underground—never seeing the radiance of the daytime suns. Their eyes glowed but only when viewed head-on. Silent and nearly invisible, these creatures were the ultimate warriors. With skin the color of the night's desert hues, they were difficult to make out from the land around them. Only when Titan's light struck their faces at just right angle, could their presence be known.

However, this night, the creatures came out to find more victims in tents—invaders who had come to take their lands from them. But when they saw no one to drag from their tents down into the earth with them, they crawled back into their holes and disappeared. Then, only the ghostly images of a murdered king and queen remained, hovering over the site and smiling in contentment.

*****

CH 27 – Abandoned

Coaxing Nimbus, Yewts returned to where the trail had come up from the canyon and began its slow decent into the inferno. This time, however, he had water. Above him he heard the cries of the geiers circling and hoping for one last snack; he shivered at the thought of their enjoyment if he didn't make it to the other side.

It took another day, but he followed the path down the cliff into the canyon and up the other side. The heat at the bottom was as bad as it had been before, but the water he had with him made it bearable.

Popping out of the gorge, Yewts looked across the wide, expansive plateau. There were few shrubs and trees nearby, even though there were denser forests of tall pines in the distance near the capital of Vaporia. However, there was one thing he expected to see that wasn't there. The king and his army.

The campsite—with its still-smoldering fires and trenched sand dunes where tents had been raised and lowered—was abandoned. All the men, animals, weapons, and equipment were gone. The smoke from the burning fires trailed off into the mid-morning sky as he approached—dissipating just like the army had done. It was only the third day; he had nearly killed himself to return in time, and it had all been for nothing.

Angry at the deceit, Yewts kicked a smoldering log, and watched as it skidded along the rocky ground. He didn't have the energy to go after Barbarot and his men, even though their tracks in the sands showed him which way they'd gone. Instead, he walked around the camp and found a few water skeins carelessly left behind and strung them around his neck. Then, he hopped back on Nimbus and headed out. But he did not follow the trail of the army—this time he went in the opposite direction.

***

Two days passed, and Yewts had gotten lost. Out in the desert, he was tired, thirsty and now ready to give up. He had been wandering along the rim of the Canyon of Perdition, riding his commander's volarequez, and had once again run out of water. He lifted his water skein again putting it above his lips and hoping it held one last drop, but not even that came out. He forced his mind to concentrate on Seber's words. "Always be positive," he had said. "Never give up."

"*Whoa,* boy," said Yewts as he glanced up at the beastly sun of Duex that was bearing down on him. "I'd say this is about as good a spot as any to lie down and take a long breather, don't you?" His words were faint and halting, strained with the effort it took to form them.

His winged horse whinnied a bit but did not protest. It stopped and knelt like a two-humped soccamel that was accustomed to the hot, dry landscape of the Chasmian desert.

Yewts fell off his mount as Nimbus got comfortable in the dusty, bone-dry surface of the plain. Both lay there, delirious and numb. Eventually, Yewts rolled over, face down, into the sand. He could feel the hotness burning the skin on his face, but he no longer cared.

"Hey! You there!"

It sounded like gibberish to Yewts as his mind began to fade.

"*Uhhhhhh*?" Yewts groaned mournfully.

"Are you all right?" came the voice again.

This time a hand touched his shoulder and rolled him over on his back.

"Get some water, quick!"

A splash of water hit Yewt's face, and his eyes snapped open. "Where am I?" he mumbled.

"Let's get him back to the house, Bubba."

Those were the last words Yewts remembered.

Sometime later, Yewts opened his eyes again. This time it was nightfall, and he was in someone's house. There was a fire crackling in one corner and a woman, clothed in a long, blue dress with a wrinkled, taupe shawl wrapped around her shoulders stirring a thick, black pot suspended over the fire. Yewts couldn't see her face, but her straight, black hair hung below a scarf that she had wrapped around her head. Clutching a long-handled ladle, she stirred whatever was simmering inside the cauldron.

"Oh, it's nice to see you've finally awakened, young lad," she said kindly as she looked over at him.

She was middle-aged with the start of an extra chin under the one she was born with. Her eyelids too had grown another flap over the original which covered a pretty, green pair of irises beneath. Yet, her face was serene with a friendly glow that seemed as warm as the fire she was tending.

"Can I get you something to eat?" she asked him softly.

Yewts was still dazed—still trying to recover his strength from the trauma of the canyon.

"*Uh*, no ma'am," he replied. "But, perhaps, if you have some water?"

"Of course," she answered and grabbed the animal skein that hung over a beam at the far end of the room. Uncorking the end, she poured a generous amount into a silvery, metal cup before resealing it. She then brought the cup to Yewts who took it eagerly in both hands. He gulped the water down quickly, licking the sides of the cup for the last few drops as if he were still at the bottom of the canyon and on his last legs.

"Easy, easy, young one. There's plenty more. You don't have to squeeze the turnip," she said as she took back the empty cup. "I guess you had some trip. The boys told me they found you by the rim of the canyon in the middle of the day without water.

That's not the place to be, you know. Not many can survive out in that for very long, especially without water or shade."

Yewts looked into her clear, green eyes. "I … I've had a hard journey, ma'am."

"Take it easy. You aren't going anywhere anytime soon. You'll need to stay here with us 'til you get your strength back. Meantime, I'll tell one of my boys to take news of your recovery to The Chief. He's been asking how you are; you know."

"The Chief?" asked Yewts.

"Yes, The Chief. That's what we call him. He's the elder in a village not far from here. His village was burned to the ground by a murderous savage and his army a few days ago. He and a few others managed to survive, though. In a lot of ways, we think of him as our true leader. For us, he's the king of Chasmia."

"So, you don't have a king?"

"They say there is one inside the walls of Gilabend, but many of us aren't so sure. I think it's The Chief who's the real king, as do many others. He's a good man, The Chief—a good man." She giggled, "Oh, there I go. I can go off on such stories. But, that's enough for today anyway. It's time for bed—for you anyway."

She tucked the rough, olive blanket under Yewt's chin and walked toward the door.

"Perhaps tomorrow, we can have a better conversation—like, well, finding out what your name is for starters!"

And with that, she closed the door behind her.

*****

CH 28 - A Son Returns

Donus returned from the shepherds' cabin after giving his tutoring session and found Genona at the door of the castle waiting for him. She was anxious and began waving her arms excitedly.

"Benigno! Come quickly! I think it's my father. He's not himself. Something's wrong!"

Genona seized Donus' arm and dragged him out of the doorway. Together, they ran down the three hallways to the baron's chambers, where they found him lying in bed with feather pillows piled high around his head. His face was gaunt, and his eyes sallow and dark.

"What's wrong with him?" Donus asked. "He was fine just yesterday?"

"Yes, it came on quite suddenly. This morning he was fine; then, this afternoon he began complaining of pains in his chest. He collapsed, and we carried him in here. We've sent for the village doctor, who should arrive any minute. Father's never been sick a day in his life! He's never needed anything or anyone before. Never!"

A knock at the door was answered by one of the baron's attendants. The gentleman standing before them was short and balding with a slight build. His shaggy gray eyebrows and matching beard held more hair than his shiny head. Yet, what was most striking about him was his air of self-confidence which made everyone instantly feel as though things would be all right now that he was there.

"Where is the patient?" the man asked directly, not bothering with introductions.

"He's here, doctor," said Genona, waving him over to the bedside.

The doctor went to the bed carrying a small bag and a black, hour-glass-shaped jar with lids on each end. The baron barely moved, moaning mildly and moving his mouth as if he were trying to say something.

"Dr. Wom, what do you think?" asked Genona, her face full of concern.

The doctor leaned in and put his ear to the baron's chest. For only a few moments, he remained motionless, listening to his heart and lungs and thumping his chest lightly with his fingers. Shortly after, he stood back and shook his head.

"It doesn't sound good," said Wom. "It's his heart; I'm afraid. It's failing him."

"No!" shouted Genona. "I can't believe that! He's too strong. He's ... my father. He can't be going now. It's too soon!" She broke down in tears.

"I'm afraid, it is, dear child. Your father doesn't have that much time left," stuttered the doctor. He opened one end of the black jar and reached inside, scooping out a thick, pasty cream. Gently loosening the baron's shirt, he began rubbing the remedy on his chest, continuing until the cream had been absorbed into the skin.

Genona began sobbing softly and then more dramatically, her shoulders heaved up and down as she cried. Suddenly, she put her hands to mouth and began swaying. Seeing what was happening, Donus put out his arms to catch her but missed. She collapsed onto the wooden floor, her head hitting it with a dull thud. There she lay motionless.

Hours passed before she came to. Opening her eyes, she glanced around the room, startled and confused. The images were blurred, and the voices echoed in her head like tiny bells ringing beside her ears.

"Where am I? Was I out very long?"

"Yes, my dear sister. I am told that you fainted and knocked your head—that's all." It was Parogild.

Stroking her hair and holding her head gently with his other hand, he smiled down at her.

"So, I'm not dreaming? You've come home?" she asked.

"Yes, Pari has returned to us at last," came the weak voice of her father from the bed. It was trembling but now had a joy it hadn't had for many weeks.

"Father, I'm sorry. I am *so* sorry," said Parogild. "What I did was wrong. I know that now."

"Are you asking me for forgiveness?" asked the baron.

"If it were only that simple, Father, but yes, of course, I am. I don't expect you to grant it. I know what pain I've caused you," replied Parogild, embarrassed and humbled. "I've lost all my inheritance, Father. I squandered it. How can you ever forgive me for that?"

The baron reached out to embrace his son, and Parogild put his arms around his father. It was a poignant moment for both.

"You need not ask for forgiveness. You should know by now that I forgave you the minute you left my house. You are my son, and I love you," said the baron with a smile.

Donus helped Genona to her feet, and she went to the old man's bed where he lay quiet and breathing shallowly.

"Father, you can't leave us! What will we do without you?" she cried, a handkerchief trembling in her hand as she dabbed her eyes.

The old man took her hand and squeezed it. "I taught you all that you need to know. Now it's up to you and your brother to do with your lives as you will. As your mother said before she left us, 'You will always be in my heart, wherever I am and wherever you are.'"

And with that, he was gone.

Donus took Genona and hugged her tightly. Parogild bit his lip to keep from crying. His eyes were wet, and he swept away a tear that had begun to form in one corner. He leaned over and kissed the forehead of his father, stroking his long, gray hair.

"I love you, father ... and I finalize realize how special of a man you were ... and will always be," said Parogild softly.

Parogild looked at his sister. He could see the genuine affection Donus had for her and nodded his approval. It was time he assumed the mantle of the family, and he finally realized he was ready—his father had prepared him well.

*****

CH 29 - Start of a Revolution

Although they had reclaimed one of their own from the evil grip of Barbarot, they still had much to do. Montoi Leedsom had completely recovered after being slapped back to reality by Aunt Cleora. The Barbarot spell had been broken, and Montoi was slowly regaining his old self. Yet, there was another that Sojourn and Cleora needed to save ... to bring out of the darkness. They knew the challenge would be tough, but the sudden appearance of Konjuur and his men would make things even more so.

One day, while at her general store, Aunt Cleora overheard talk about someone new who had arrived in Emani.

"Patsima Tunos told me she heard this large, rotund stranger talking about a revolution against the king of all things! Can you imagine? Rebelling against the king!" It was one of Aunt Cleora's least favorite people, Lady Turbe.

Lady Turbe was middle-aged and a widow. Her husband had been killed in a tragic accident when both had been young. She was a small figure but more than made up for it with a ferocity unmatched by anyone one else in town. The baroness was always beaming and sociable, but this was deceiving. It was merely a mask that hid a treachery that lay just below the surface. As Aunt Cleora knew, Lady Turbe bought and sold gossip. That was her trade, and she did it very well. The juicier the gossip, the more she demanded in payment. It was known that she often used information to blackmail those who wished it kept hidden. And this was the way she paid for her lavish lifestyle.

"Haven't you heard about this?" Lady Turbe asked, now turning to Aunt Cleora while shopping in the store.

"Why no. When did this person show up in town?"

"Oh, I believe it was only a few days ago. How dare anyone defy the king! King Barbarot is our new leader. Think of him as you may, but you must always obey." Then, she giggled, realizing what a cute, rhyming phrase she had spun.

Aunt Cleora only smiled. She knew how dangerous it was to disagree with the baroness. The other woman with her also merely grinned and nodded.

But it wasn't long before Konjuur had begun stirring things up in Aunt Cleora's town of Omehya as well, and unrest was spreading across the kingdom. With Barbarot away, it seemed another evil had slipped in to fill the gap.

Aunt Cleora was familiar with the antics of Konjuur and knew he could be dangerous. She was afraid that the dark days of Rootan would only become darker if he gained the power of the kingship, while Barbarot was fighting his neighbors. At least with Barbarot's father, Baron Marbray, in control of the king's matters, things in the kingdom were not terrible. After all, he remained under his son's spell, so there was little he could or would do to make any changes. The Rootanian people had little freedom left and couldn't say anything negative about the king, but otherwise, they could go about their lives as they always had. For his part, Marbray was never seen by anyone outside the castle, and most people believed he merely kept the king's throne warm all day, sitting there and staring out the window.

Still, Sojourn, Aunt Cleora and now Montoi were determined to bring the kingdom back to the way it was—even before the rule of King Portenza. Those had been the good-old days, when King Greybeard, Portenza's father, had ruled with caring and kindness. He had respect for all his people and gave them the freedoms to choose their own paths. Freedom of speech, freedom of assembly, freedom of religion ... these were during the finest times the people had ever known. However, these freedoms had gradually disappeared, as Portenza, and now Barbarot, had put their own desires for power and riches above the happiness of their subjects.

For now, the three were being patient, as Konjuur's influence was something they had to consider as they prepared for what lay ahead. Desperate times called for desperate measures; they only hoped things wouldn't come to that. So, the watched, and waited.

***

The pounding of a hammer shook the Wayward Traveler's walls and woke the caretaker, Amicus, from his afternoon nap. He opened the wooden front door and saw a short man with grungy, gnarly hands finish pounding a long nail into it.

"What do you think you're doing?" shouted Amicus. "This is my tavern! You can't post a notice here!"

The man ignored him and walked off, down to the shop next door to repeat the same action.

Attached to the tavern door was a notice, written in black script and in large letters so anyone could read it from a distance. It read:

Notice

Meeting of Townspeople

To discuss the future of our kingdom

Tomorrow, Saturday, at dusk

At the Bridled Horn

"What?" exclaimed Amicus. "Hey, you!" he shouted again after the man who posted the notice. "What's this all about?"

But the man continued to pay no attention and kept walking, hammering more notices on more doors down the way.

Amicus learned from the shopkeeper next door that Konjuur was holding meetings throughout the kingdom. At the first ones, only a few people had attended, but as word spread, the gatherings got larger. Soon, people were anxiously anticipating a meeting in their little village—hoping to see the *Big One*, as Konjuur was becoming known.

Making their way from Oxbeard, Konjuur found the Bridled Horn, a competing tavern to the Wayward Traveler in Omehya. It was late in the day when he and his knights rode into town and tied up their sensavols just outside the tavern under a squat, konig tree.

The bar filled up quickly just before Piquet set in the western sky. Amicus sat at a long narrow table where customers ordered their beverages and drank in the late hours of the evening. He was talking with an old friend about the weather and the man's crops that he expected from his farm that year when Konjuur opened the door and strode to the front, slamming his fist down to get attention. Of course, such a demonstration wasn't needed— Konjuur's huge girth was enough to set him apart from everyone else.

The owner of the Bridled Horn was also a friend of Amicus', a man named Rufus Crofton. Older and well aware of what was at stake, Crofton had been a friend of Amicus' father before he passed on the Wayward Travelers' Tavern to his son when he died. Amicus and Crofton had remained friends ever since.

Surprised at the large man's actions at the counter, but not offended, Crofton interrupted his conversation with Amicus to attend to the new patron.

"Welcome to the Bridled Horn. What can I get for you?"

Crofton suspected the large man was Konjuur, but he never liked to make assumptions.

"I'm giving the meeting tonight," said Konjuur, "and I demand six froths on the house." Portly with black hair and white goatee, his orange-yellow eyes burned through Crofton as he looked him over.

"Oh, Viceroy Konjuur, I see," said Crofton. "I'm pleased that you picked my place for your meeting. Please have a seat anywhere, and I'll bring your froths out to you."

"You should thank me. You and your little tavern here will be part of history, you know," replied Konjuur, cocky and assured.

The bar was already packed with townspeople, and Konjuur's enormous size made it hard for him to maneuver between the cramped, wooden tables inside. Yet, he pushed his way through, acting as a celebrity—shaking hands and making small talk. He was clever and knew this was how he would get what he wanted in Rootan.

Crofton opened a couple of casks and let the froth drain from each into the metal goblets that were being passed around. The froth was black and tar-like, yet it had a light-tan foam that rose to the surface and sat on top of the mug like soap bubbles in a bath.

As for Crofton, he was a simple man. He didn't understand the ways of politics and how someone could persuade people by merely looking like a leader and being enthusiastic about a cause—regardless whether it was a good one or bad one. It was all in the presentation.

Konjuur stood in front of the group and made a quick quip to one of the patrons, loudly enough to be heard by others. "Did you hear about what the king's planning to do to us next? I heard he's going to take a third of everyone's land to help pay for his wars," he said. "Heck, I heard he's even thinking about outlawing froth and taverns!"

Of course, there was no truth to these things. It was like all the lies Konjuur was spreading throughout the land—just to get people angry and willing to fight back against their ruler. People believed just about anything and the more often the lies were told the more people believed them.

"What?" cried Crofton. "I haven't heard that. Where did you hear such things?"

"Oh, so you haven't been keeping up with the news, *eh?*" asked Konjuur taunting him. "You should listen more or ask more questions if you know what's good for you. If all this comes to pass—you'll be out of business, my friend."

Crofton's face became beet red. The anger made him tremble, and he pounded his fist on the bar counter in disgust. "That's outrageous! I won't stand for that!"

It was the same at each meeting. Konjuur started them in low tones, pointing out problems everyone knew were there or even better—making them up. Then, he got more animated, raising his voice and saying triggering words that got the people's emotions stirring. As the night wore on, the affairs became raucous and rowdy and by the end he had just the angry mob he wanted. The goal was simple—to incite them and move them toward revolution.

"Oh," said Konjuur, fanning the flames of Crofton's outrage, "you and a lot of others throughout the kingdom will be out of business. That would be very sad indeed."

Konjuur then turned to another young man sitting next to him. "So, what is it that you do, my dear fellow?" he asked.

"Well, thank the God of gods I'm not a tavern owner. No, I raise horses—sensavols and volarequi mostly. I've got a ranch just outside of town," replied the man, proudly.

Konjuur shook his head. "Oh, that's no good," he said with feigned despair. "The king's planning to make it illegal to raise those too—sensavols and volarequi. They will be bred on special farms run by his kingship. Anyone caught with any young animals will be arrested and imprisoned ... I just don't think that's quite right, do you?"

At that point, Aunt Cleora and Montoi came into the tavern and took a table in the far corner, away from the spotlight and the commotion Konjuur and his group were causing. At first, Aunt Cleora tried to get Amicus' attention but saw he was talking to someone else. So, she settled into her seat and enjoyed watching the show that was unfolding in front of them.

"I have to make an announcement," said Crofton, fomenting more rage. He banged a mug on the bar several times, getting the immediate attention of all in the room. "Who has heard that the king is going to outlaw froth and taverns? This gentleman here claims that King Barbarot wants to close down this establishment and all others like it. He also says the king wants to make it illegal for us to raise volarequi and sensavols, and if we're caught, we could be sentenced to prison. Has anyone else heard this?"

There were rumblings in the tavern. People whispered to each other anxiously. It was one thing to talk unfavorably about the king in private, but in public—every knew that was dangerous.

"I must say, I haven't heard this," said Amicus, defiantly.

But one of Konjuur's men, who had been inconspicuously sitting at another table, spoke up, "Oh, yeah, I heard the same thing—that those were going to be illegal soon—very soon."

Then another bloke from his group stood. "I heard it too, and I think it's an outrage! I'm not going to stand for it!"

"No!" shouted Konjuur, finally getting off his seat and taking the center stage, "I don't think any of us should put up with this. King Barbarot is a tyrant, and he must be stopped! Only we, the people of Rootan, can stop him!"

There was a great eruption in the hall—the shouting and shaking of fists in the air. People were now doing more than just growling and mumbling. They were energized and moving to do something about it.

Konjuur waited, but only for a moment before saying, "I think we should band together and fight him. We must unite! That's the only way to take back our kingdom! He should pay for what he's doing to us. It's not fair that he gets everything, and we have nothing. Why should we be slaves to him—giving him our sons for his army and our money to feed his campaigns of war? If he's not stopped now, when will he be? If we don't revolt now, we may never be able to stop him. He'll only grow stronger and, before you know it, it will be too late. Do you want that to happen?"

"No!" came the cry from those there.

Aunt Cleora and Montoi just watched, horrified at the angry mob Konjuur had created. They were likely to become violent, and if things went badly, there would be much bloodshed in Oxbeard, Omehya and throughout the rest of the kingdom. They knew the power of Barbarot, and they knew he would not back down when faced with a revolution. People would die, and with black magic behind him, the king would certainly try to make examples of many in that tavern so no one else defied him.

"Then, join me!" shouted Konjuur. "We must unite all the people of Rootan to fight against this menace. We must stop him, and if we stick together, we shall. We will retake the kingdom that we love and have devoted our lives to. We must fight for this land for the sake of our children and our children's children!"

"Yes! Yes!" was the sound that echoed through the room and spilled into the roadway outside and to the surrounding stores. Others passing by the tavern came in to see what was going on, and soon, they too joined in the madness.

"Take it back! Take it back now!" The people shouted in unison, stomping their feet and clapping their hands. The tavern was rocking, and the emotions and the drinking were in full swing.

Aunt Cleora and Montoi sat quietly, conspicuously the only ones who were not on their feet. Even Amicus was wrapped up in the moment. Instead, they watched with concern as Konjuur manipulated the crowd like trained seals barking for another fish.

"Should we leave?" Aunt Cleora asked her partner.

She looked in his eyes and saw fading hope. Yet, she was not about to give up—that much her brother, Sojourn, had always taught her. All hope was never lost.

"There's not much we can do here now," said Montoi. "This is going to get ugly, fast. Maybe not tonight but sometime very soon. And when it does ... well ... we'll need the God of gods on our side, I'm afraid."

Eventually, the meeting concluded, and Aunt Cleora and Montoi snuck out before anyone else reached the doorway. They were eager to share what had happened with Sojourn back at his manor.

***

Sojourn sat impassively as they told him about the meeting at the Bridle Horn tavern. Aunt Cleora described the frenzy Konjuur had created—whipping up the people's furor as they had never seen before.

"He's dangerous, this one," said Montoi. "He's getting everyone on his side to revolt against the king. Then, after they spill their blood for him, he will sit on the throne and rule over them. It will be going from the frying pan into the fire, I'm afraid."

"Sojourn? What do you think?" asked Aunt Cleora, hopefully.

Sojourn sat in thought. Then, he answered, "Perhaps it will be a big problem—perhaps not." He often summarized complicated problems in this way, making them seem much less threatening and then going on to give a simple solution.

"What do you mean *perhaps*, my dear friend?" asked Montoi.

"I say *perhaps* because I think this may be a blessing in disguise."

Sojourn got up from the table and walked into the hallway, pacing back and forth as he continued to think.

"A blessing? How could you *ever* think that?" asked his sister.

"The king's forces are much more powerful than we could ever hope to overcome on our own. Isn't this true?"

"Why, yes," replied Aunt Cleora.

"And do you think that if we united all the people of Rootan that they could overcome the king's army?"

"The army wouldn't fight their own families," said Montoi.

"Precisely," answered Sojourn. "They wouldn't, would they?"

"So, Konjuur is doing us a favor by bringing all the people together for a single cause—to fight against Barbarot," said Montoi. "Is that what you're saying?"

"Yes, and if the emotions of the people are already stirred up, why can't we redirect them toward a better purpose than to put Konjuur on the throne? So, the problem isn't that he is stirring up a revolution. The problem is that he wants the revolution to end with his being put on the throne. Am I right?"

"You are," said Montoi.

"What we need to do is change that outcome, then. We need to make sure the revolution occurs, just as Konjuur wants, but that it does not result in his becoming king."

"And how do we do that?" asked his sister.

"I may have the answer," Sojourn said with a wry smile.

*****

CH 30 - Stormy Future

In the center of the Aramus Ocean, a storm was brewing in intensity and strength and had passed across a series of small islands that dotted the shoreline but otherwise were of little significance. However, what was important was the direction the storm was heading—southeast across the Sea of Jaspar and the kingdoms of Chasmia and Vinedria.

Some of Barbarot's advance scouts had continued along the coast to watch for any ships that might signal an invasion by another kingdom trying to stop the king's march across the lands of the realm. Camped on the beach, the commander grew restless as he watched the storm clouds grow thick and the winds gust with more power and frequency, giving him the signs that a massive storm was making its way to shore.

"We must alert the king," said the commander, seeing the tall flags bearing King Barbarot's colors whipping stiffly in the wind.

Farther inland, even Barbarot noticed the changing weather. His army had left the desert-like canyons of Chasmia and crossed into the bordering and lush kingdom of Vinedria. The way had been easy for them—mostly downhill from the high plateaus of Chasmia. But what did follow them was the heat. Combined with the more humid air of Vinedria, the weather wasn't much better. The men continued to complain—especially about how sticky and uncomfortable it was in the heavy uniforms.

Soon, the gently rolling hills and grassy plains of northern Vinedria gave way to heavier undergrowth and dense trees to the south that clogged the trail. Unable to push the trees and shrubbery aside with his heavy wagons and plows, Barbarot was forced to use his engineering corps again to cut away the entangled vines that prevented him from moving his army forward. Like a spider's web of wood, layered one upon another, the vines were nearly impenetrable. The engineers had to use thick, broad swords to hack their way along to clear the trail.

But the deeper the army marched into the rainforest, the more dangerous it became. Not only were there monstrous spiders, snakes and vambats, there were deadly plants that could pop out of the ground without notice, swallow a man whole, and disappear back into the depths.

As the storm from the ocean moved in, the rains began to fall and the winds pickup. Within a day, the long arms of the hurricane began pummeling the kingdom, and creatures large and small scurried to find shelter. The commonly-seen warblingas and e-kranos—a long-legged, sticklike bird that foraged in deep ponds—were now nowhere to be seen. Vinedria's vast monkey population had also vanished from the treetops. Nikko's family members, which lived deeper in the rainforest, also left their stick homes in the tree canopy and secured themselves in the hollows of the trees below.

At first, it was the long-trunked palms that started swaying, their fronds rustling as if they had caught fire. But within a short time, the full fury of the storm made its presence known, and the same palm trees were bowing nearly perpendicular to the ground—hit by the ferocious winds that began ripping them up from the earth as if being plucked for a harvest. Coconuts flew from the treetops like balls exploding out of a canon, hurling through the air and smashing everything in their way.

But the storm was only getting started. The fiercest part was yet to come.

"You look scared, commander. What are you afraid of?" Barbarot asked Commander Sterinis.

"It's going to be a bad one, Your Majesty. I'd say we should stop and batten everything down before it hits."

"We have to push on. We only have a few miles to go to get through this mess. I want to be at the doorstep of Knotsbow and have King Viridius in chains before the day is out," said the king. "We need to pick up the pace. Get more of your engineers to whack away the brush alongside the trail to widen it so I can get more men moved through."

"Yes, sire," replied Sterinis, grudgingly.

Sterinis repeated the orders to the other commanders, making it clear what the king wanted.

"We've got to move faster! Get those lousy engineers off their butts and start cutting away at the vines to clear a wider path!" he yelled. "Then, I want the cavalry to lead the rest of the infantry. They must get to Knotsbow by sundown."

"But with this wind, there's no way we can ..." began one of his commanders.

"Shut up! Did I ask for your opinion commander?" Sterinis yelled. "Now, do as you're ordered, or I'll have you replaced with someone who will!"

It was then that the storm struck.

The winds howled, snapping tree trunks and overturning horses and wagons. Equipment flew through the air as if they had wings and disappeared into the deep foliage. Rain pounded the troops, coming down in heavy sheets so thick no one could see past five feet in front of them. The trail that had been thick with vines and roots was now worse—a sea of water and deep mud. Quicksand formed in small pools sucking down men and beasts. Men cried out for help, but others were too busy trying to find shelter themselves.

"Get your volarequi into that cave over there and order your men to lash everything down!" yelled Barbarot, as he jumped off his volarequez and dragged it by the reins into the large cavern that lay along a creek they had been following.

The king wiped the water from his face and tied his winged steed around a log just inside the entrance to the cave. He peered out into the tempest, wondering what, if anything, would be left of his mighty army after the winds and rains subsided.

"Crap!" he shouted, pounding his hand against the cave wall.

He looked out into the black sky and scowled. "Curse you!" he screamed, shaking his fist in the air. "You will not defeat me! Darkness is more powerful than light will ever be!"

*****

CH 31 - A Concerned Lady

She was outside on her balcony overlooking a sea of white and blue. A flock of long-necked oosegi were flying along the coastline forming their customary "V" pattern with a leader at the point and the others trailing off its flanks. The flock swung overhead before moving south, anticipating the change of seasons that was about to begin.

"Your steed is ready, my Lady," said Gabby, who had just come up from the stables.

Lady Sudé was the empress of the entire realm. She took responsibility for what happened there and for what didn't happen.

She left the railing and followed the beautiful stone path that led to the stables where her great white dularequez awaited her. This was not like the normal, winged horse—the volarequez—found in most kingdoms. This one had two sets of enormous wings that flapped in alternating waves. The huge expanse of its wings allowed these creatures to grow half again bigger than even the largest volarequez with only its single set of wings.

"Let's get on with it," said the Lady, talking to Gabby. "This is not a trip to which I'm looking forward, but it is one I must take."

"I understand," answered her trusted servant.

"And my knights ... where are they?"

"They will join us once we are out over the Sea of Jaspar. We didn't wish to be spotted by having too many riders at one time in the sky."

"Quite right. Well, let's go."

The duo glided effortlessly above the clouds at altitudes unattainable by any other creature. They looked down at the curved rim of the planet—its blue waters in sharp contrast to the greens of Vinedria, Rootan and Dulcenou and the tans of Sanzotur, Chasmia and Vaporia.

Farther out to sea and closing in on the west coast of Vinedria, they saw the spinning ball of white fury. It was a dense pack of billowing clouds rotating at high speed in a counterclockwise direction. Some one hundred miles across, the winds below were gaining strength, nearing one hundred eighty miles per hour.

"There it is," commented the Empress, pointing down to the fast-moving mass of clouds. "It is becoming a monster."

"Where is it heading?" asked Gabby, directing the other knights as they joined them in looking over the storm.

"Based on the ocean currents, winds, and temperatures, it should make landfall in Vinedria within the hour," she said.

"Shall we sound the alarm to warn them?" asked Gabby.

Although sympathetic, the Empress was not moved. "Only a few. We will not warn the masses. It will be as it will be. There is always some good to come out of a tragedy, and this case shall be no different. No, we will wait and watch."

"Can you tell me what good will come from this? I can't understand."

"Patience, Gabby. All in good time. Right now, we must continue to monitor it. This thing will continue to gain strength and will strike the west coast of Vinedria. Then, it will pass over and strike the east coast with even greater destruction. There will be a terrible tsunami, I'm afraid—a wall of water will come with terrible wrath."

"How can this be?" asked Gabby.

"Gabby, my trusted one, it is and must be. You know that. Now, let us get going. I do wish to warn those of Knotsbow, so they may seek protection. King Viridius is a good man and deserves a notice."

Lady Sudé flew onward, down through the milky white clouds that were darkening and growing in intensity. Gabby and the rest followed, hoping the king would hear her message in time.

*****

CH 32 - The Rebus

Above them was a vast cavity that looked like it had been dug out of the side of the mountain. The mouth of the cave was tall and wide with long, cylindrical icicles that hung like the fangs of an unsympathetic monster waiting to devour anyone entering.

"Well, what is your answer?" It was a deep, full, growling voice—one both threatening and impatient. It shook the walls inside the cave and rattled the snow-covered rocks above it.

Oliver and Fermat couldn't see the figures that were talking—their view blocked by several large rocks. However, they could hear every word.

"Please repeat the question," was the reply. This was the voice of Bratworm, the nasty prisoner who had chased them up the mountainside. Yet, in this moment, his voice trembled like a little child's. There was no doubt that for all his meanness and strength, he was melting before the force and might of the Rebus.

"That was your second question. You have only one remaining. Question two:

> *What can run but never walk?*
> *What has a mouth but never talks?*
> *What has a bed but never sleeps?*
> *What has a head but never weeps?*

"You have thirty seconds to answer."

"Oh, that would be a river," said Bratworm, nervously.

There was a hesitation, then the thunderous voice said, "Yes, you are correct. Question three:

> *The more that there is*
> *The less that you see*
> *Squint all you wish*
> *When surrounded by me.*

"That would be ... uh ... wait a minute. I know this. That one was ... darkness."

"Yes, you are correct. Question four:

> *I am nothing more*
> *I am nothing less*
> *Between a square and a cube*
> *My prime I express."*

There was silence for a moment, and then Bratworm shouted, "That wasn't one of the questions the guards told me about!" He then lashed out in defiance. "This isn't fair! You're trying to trick me! Why are you trying to trick me?"

"You were told you had but three questions you could ask. That was your third and your last."

"Then repeat the damned question ... I know I get that much!" shouted the prisoner, growling with contempt.

"Question four," said the Rebus.

> *"I am nothing more*
> *I am nothing less*
> *Between a square and a cube*
> *My prime I express."*

This time, there was no reply, and instead, Oliver and Fermat heard the panicked shuffling of boots through the snow, as if Bratworm were trying to make a run for it. Seconds later, they heard another sound, more chilling than before, followed by a low, rasping scream.

"Ahhhh!"

Then, there was silence.

Terror came over Fermat's face. He looked at Oliver in disbelief.

"So, what do we do now?" whispered Fermat, his eyes wide as saucers and his cheeks draining of their optimism. "Do we take the chance, or do we make a run for it too—before we go up there?"

"I have no choice, I'm afraid," replied Oliver somberly. "I have to bring back the stone or my friends will die or be imprisoned for the rest of their lives." Oliver paused and then looked his friend. "But you, Fermat, *have* a choice. Although it will be hard out here on your own, your chances are better than what you'd have up there with me. You should go."

Oliver could tell Fermat didn't want to leave him.

"Fermat, you don't have to do this for me. I'll be okay. You should go," coaxed Oliver.

Deep down, Oliver hoped Fermat would stay and go through the trial with him to give him support and perhaps help in answering the questions. Yet, he didn't want his friend to risk his life when he didn't have to.

Fermat smiled. He looked up and saw the rays of sunlight fading behind the mountain peaks above him and took a deep breath.

"Let's go answer some questions," he said firmly.

Fermat started walking up the trail toward where they'd heard the voices, and Oliver scrambled to keep up. It was getting difficult to see, but some light was still filtering through the trees and reaching the ground around the cave entrance.

They hiked up the tight, narrow passage and came to a clearing in front of the mouth of the cave. More than just the chill of the air struck them as they walked into the opening. In front of them was a vast, open space. It was then, they realized what the Frezia Challenge was all about.

To their shock, they saw the meadow was filled with hundreds of frozen bodies—all strewn about in different poses as they were in the process of running away in fear. Each had tried to escape from something but had clearly failed.

Oliver and Fermat passed by them—one after another—until they reached one whom they recognized. It was Bratworm's. His mouth was open and frozen in mid-scream, caught in the moment of utter horror as he tried to get away.

Shaking, the two young men walked farther up to the mouth of the cave, where a strange creature with large white eyes and a head that was twice the normal size for its body emerged. Walking on all four legs, it occasionally sat upright on its hind legs, sniffing the air with its long, whiskered snout. It had devilish ears—ones that looked more like horns coming from the top of its head. Icy blue in color, its skin was bare and scaley, and there were countless layers of folds and wrinkles cascading off its bones.

The Rebus was not huge, nor muscular. Instead, it was small and compact, but it had a large mouth it had not yet opened. On each hand were seven short fingers with long nails and in each arm, protruding black veins that moved as under its skin as it walked. It ambled out of the cave toward them, swishing its thin, whip-like tail behind it—non-threatening and calm.

Both young men were not deceived; they knew what this animal was capable of for they could see it for themselves all around them. And when the creature opened its mouth, they saw black, needle-like teeth and long fangs that emerged, dripping a red mucus onto the snow.

"You seek the stone, do you not?" asked the animal.

Fermat looked at Oliver, scared to reply.

"Is this one of your questions?" asked Oliver.

"Indeed, it is one of my questions," came the response. The animal's eyes opened wider.

"Are you the Rebus?" asked Fermat.

"I am," said the animal. "You have just used two of the three questions that you may ask of me. Now, I have five of my own to ask of you."

"But you never warned us we could only ask three questions. This cannot be a fair test and is therefore invalid," said Oliver.

The Rebus thought for a moment. "Indeed. You are correct. So, I will now give you your instructions. I will ask you five questions. You must answer each correctly and within thirty seconds. You may only ask me two questions."

"Wait a minute! You said three earlier!" said Fermat.

"Easy, Fermat. Let's not accidently waste our only question now. Just back off," said Oliver. "I need you to help me with this."

"Question one," said the Rebus, coldly.

> *"What lives in the winter,*
> *But dies in the summer.*
> *What has roots that grow upward*
> *And dies as it cries?"*

Oliver had heard this before, but he couldn't put his finger on it with all the pressure he was feeling. He looked at Fermat, who was about ready to speak. Oliver shook his head violently trying to shut him up before it was too late, but out came the words anyway.

"Oliver, don't you think it's ...?" asked Fermat.

"Your trial is over!" yelled the Rebus. "That was your last question, and you must suffer your fate!

"Wait a minute!" said Fermat, pushing back. "Now it's my turn to tell you it's not fair! That was not a question directed at you ... I was asking my friend that question! You specifically said they were questions asked of you!"

"And we weren't out of questions!" Oliver chimed in.

"Fine," said the Rebus, "but his answer will count as the answer to my question!"

Oliver looked at Fermat hopefully, yet frightened his answer would mean the death of both of them.

"You were going to say..." the Rebus prompted Fermat.

"Icicle. I'd say it's an icicle," said Fermat with confidence.

Oliver winced, but there was no reaction from the creature who stood in front of them as their judge, jury and executioner.

Fermat too held his breath waiting for the judgment.

"Yes. You are correct," said the Rebus.

Then, the strange animal continued, "Question two ...

What can run but never walk?
What has a mouth but never talks?
What has a bed but never sleeps?
What has a head but never weeps?

"You have thirty seconds to answer."

Having heard the answer only moments earlier, Oliver was quick to recite what had been said.

"It's a river," said Oliver with a bit of confidence.

"Yes, you are correct. Question, three ...

The more that there is
The less that you see
Squint all you wish
When surrounded by me.

"That would be darkness," said Fermat, also knowing the answer from before.

"Yes, you are correct. Question four

I am nothing more
I am nothing less
Between a square and a cube
My prime I express."

Oliver had read about this in one of his classes at the Knight's Observatory, but he struggled to remember exactly what the answer was. He pounded his head with his fingertips, hoping to dislodge it from the tangled cobwebs of his memory.

"Oliver!" said Fermat, nervously.

"Be careful what you say, Fermat. He may take anything we say as another question," said Oliver nervously, "or worse—our answer."

The Rebus smiled—his razor black teeth dripping with anticipation. He was hoping he had stumped the young knight and his friend and could add them to the other victims that stood as stone monuments in his garden.

"I would have to say, it's got to be twenty-six," said Oliver with more confidence than the Rebus was used to for that question. However, at the same time Oliver put his hand on his satchel, where the Eripio bag lay—just in case. He hoped to feel the lump of a sharp sword or some sign that the bag was coming to his rescue. But unfortunately, he felt nothing.

The Rebus' eyes drooped, and the corners of its mouth gave it away. It was disappointed.

"*y Primo y primo! Yes, you are correct*," it said sadly.

It had been a difficult question, but Oliver had remembered it from his math class at school. He had learned the little saying at the Knight's Observatory— "The square of five is twenty-five; the cube of three is twenty-three [then, hesitating] plus four." It was meant to be awkward, but that's what had made it memorable. So, twenty-six was the number that lay between them, and that was the answer.

"But now for your fifth and last question. Answer this, and you may enter the Erebus Cave. Get it wrong, and you will join those who have tried in the past and fallen short of their goal," said the Rebus with less certainty than he'd had with his other questions.

The cold night's air could not keep the sweat from bubbling up from every pore in Oliver's body. Each droplet, however, froze almost as quickly as reached the surface, creating a nice coat of ice that made him shiver even more. Out of the corner of his eye, he could see Fermat looking around for an escape route that hadn't been tried by one of the other victims in the clearing. But there were few options as the bodies lay everywhere around the snowy meadow.

"Question five, then," said the creature.

Oliver closed his eyes and listened carefully.

> *"What is always coming*
> *But never arrives*
> *What is always of hope*
> *and something all hope to see?"*

Fermat looked at Oliver and saw the blank look. He started to move ... started to make his escape ... when Oliver put his hand on his shoulder. Oliver knew their chance of making it out of there was zero if they tried to run, but they had some chance if he made a guess.

Oliver repeated the question to himself, mumbling the sentence over and over.

"What is always coming, but never arrives?" Then, he said, "always of hope and something all hope to see." Oliver thought immediately about the challenge and how he hoped to get back to the castle to see Gemma and Nikko. But that wouldn't be until ...

Then, a smile broke across his face, and he said, "I believe I can answer that for you!"

The Rebus looked at him quite shocked. "You must be a very smart lad to answer that question. You see, no one has ever answered *all* my riddles. In the end, I believe I will have the last laugh in this contest."

Oliver started to answer, but Fermat had already started to run. Chasing after him, Oliver tackled him, and they hit the hard ice.

"Stop, Fermat!" cried Oliver. They were both on the ground, rolling over and over fighting each other like two small boys on a playground.

"I said stop!" repeated Oliver sternly, pinning Fermat's arms to the snow. "If you run again, you'll kill us both. If you let me answer, we at least have a chance."

They got up.

"Okay, Oliver. I have no choice now but to trust you. Your life is in my hands."

They quickly returned to face the Rebus before their time ran out.

"Your time is up. What is your answer?" asked the Rebus.

"Tomorrow. The answer is 'tomorrow,'" said Oliver staring boldly into the eyes of the Rebus.

The Rebus had no expression on its face. Instead, it raised its hand and spread out its long-nailed fingers before them as if trying to decide what to do. Then, it glanced out at the red and violet hues of the last setting sun and sighed deeply.

"You are correct." There was sorrow in its voice as if it would be punished for being defeated.

Fermat jumped up and down in the snow and leapt on Oliver dragging him down too. This time they rolled around together, pounding each other on the chest in happiness, not anger.

"You did it!" cried Fermat. "You got it right!"

Oliver couldn't help but smile. He grabbed Fermat and gave him a hug too. It was a relief. The fear and stress seemed to drain away completely, and he almost collapsed again from the release.

The Rebus turned his back on them and sulked slowly back into the cave.

Fermat turned to Oliver. "What do we do now?"

"I guess we follow him," said Oliver, pointing toward the cave.

They began walking toward the opening having conquered one test but unknowingly entering the fury of another.

*****

CH 33 - New Alliance

"So, what does your king have in store for us now?" asked The Chief, his face scarred from the flames of his village.

"I don't know," replied Yewts, honestly. "As I've told you, he sent us into the canyon to find a way across. When we got back, he'd gone—he left us. I don't know where he went or what his plans are."

"*Humph!*" said The Chief. "He destroyed my village, killed many of my people, and tried to kill me. What would you think about that?"

"Chief," said the middle-aged woman, "I think he's telling the truth. I've been with him for many days now taking care of him. He's a kind, young man ... I just don't think he's lying to you."

It was the middle-aged woman whom he had come to know and trust. She was motherly and had cared for Yewts like he was her long, lost son.

"Eringca ..." said The Chief, beginning to chastise her.

"Now Chief, I've told you what I think, and you know I'm right," she replied. "Sometimes you just have to get past your pride and listen!"

The Chief lowered his head as if he'd been spanked. He leaned over the bed where Yewts was sitting up and gazed deeply into his eyes. He said nothing but just stood there, studying him.

Finally, he muttered, "Yes, Mother. I believe you're right about this one." He said it as though he were admitting he'd committed a terrible crime.

"That wasn't so hard, was it?" she asked, smiling at him.

Yewts could tell that she was poking fun at him but that he was taking it well.

"So, are you part of our team or part of *their* team?" The Chief asked sternly.

"What do you think? My king left me for dead to rot in the canyon where the blistering suns would bake me for the enjoyment of the geiers circling overhead. Which team would you choose?"

The Chief grinned. "You know, I felt the same way about him when he was here, dining lavishly at my expense." He paused, "I think you and I will get along just fine, Yewts. I can help you and you can help me ... Deal?"

"Deal," said Yewts extending his hand.

*****

CH 34 - A Wall Water

The rain was coming down horizontally with coconuts and tree limbs hitting the men like rocks from a catapult. Splinters from trees snapping in two flew through the air as if a giant were hurtling six-foot lances at the army, spearing them and leaving them for dead.

Wind gusts blowing at more than one hundred fifty miles per hour upended wagons and any materiel that wasn't securely lashed down. Some men and animals found sanctuary under rocky outgrowths that were otherwise hidden beneath the dense jungle floor. Stripped bare of brush and other foliage, these shelters were now easier to spot, and it didn't take long for them to get crowded with the troops trying to squeeze inside.

While inside the scene was heated with tempers flaring from agitated men, the outside was raging with an agitated Mother Nature. The wrath of the elements went on for what seemed like an eternity. But after a few hours, the winds calmed, and sunlight came out as if the sky had sudden amnesia. It was a strange serenity and oddly unsettling.

"I don't think this will last, my king," exclaimed Commander Sterinis. "We'd better stay sheltered and safe. I've heard stories of these types of storms, although I've never been through one myself. They say there is sometimes a 'calm before the storm'— even right in the middle of one."

"Or maybe," said Barbarot, "the god of darkness is sending us help so we can continue our campaign of war against our neighbors!"

The king stepped out from the rocky overhang when another mighty gust nearly blew him off the ledge. Barbarot sulked back into the cave and untied his saddlebag. He sat down and pulled out a very old book. The crusty tome was another like the one he had used to conjure the virus in the depths of the dungeon in his

Rootanian castle. With it, he had unleashed a terrible plague on the kingdom—one that destroyed everything in its path.

The mysterious virus had found then-king Portenza in the mountains, destroying the ruler and all his army within minutes. Only a day later, Barbarot had gone to the War Council to have himself declared ruler of the Rootan. He had not given them any option— "Declare me king or die."

But things were different now. Barbarot opened a conjuring book again—this time not to create chaos but to stop it.

He uttered his incantations with staccato sharpness as he followed the lines written in the book. Tracing the words with his finger and mouthing them carefully, he continued to the end of the page. When he had finished, he looked outside the cave and noticed the winds subsiding and the skies clearing. Soon, a blue sky returned and with it a hot, but humid, day.

"There," he declared. "It is done."

Yet, Sterinis was still concerned. He still felt the strangeness of the calm, an eerie quiet, like nothing he had sensed before. Even though the winds had stopped, there were no sounds of animals moving about, of insects buzzing in the trees, or birds flittering through the sky. *They must know something we don't,* he thought.

"Let's get going!" ordered Barbarot, barking commands. "I want to reach the capital city before sundown."

While the men got their supply wagons back on the road and moved the rollopods out from the caves, Barbarot poured over his maps trying to find the quickest way to Knotsbow. He knew King Viridius would not let him conquer his fortress easily, and the sooner he got there, the faster he could prepare his plans for the attack.

Knotsbow was located near the coastline along the Sea of Crisium. The castle was considered one of the most fortified in the realm and one of the most difficult to reach. It was surrounded by waterways and moats, making a direct assault nearly impossible. Located just inland from the salty waters of the sea, the twelve-feet-thick walls of the castle were built to last a millennium. It was intended to fend off invaders from outside as well as the relentless elements of nature surrounding it.

With his other bags of tricks and arsenal of weapons, Barbarot had brought his lumidite guns to blast holes in the castle's walls, but he had to get close enough to use them. With his mobile bridges, he planned to span the moats and bring his guns right up to the base of the walls where they could punch huge holes through the stone, allowing his army to rush inside. It would be a fast and painless operation, and it would give him control of yet another kingdom.

Still miles from the castle, what remained of the army began slogging through the knee-deep mud. The vines that had hung so harmlessly from every tree and bush when they were dry were now clinging to everything moving past them. They wrapped themselves around legs, arms, wheels and anything else that passed by.

The weather was clear and calm, and all were in better spirits. But the merriment lasted only an hour. Looking skyward, they saw unsettling changes in the clouds. The bright, blue sky was growing dark and windy again. Leaves were rustling more, and tree limbs were bending as they had before the most violent part of the first wave.

"Oh, no!" muttered Sterinis as he watched conditions worsen. "Your Majesty, I believe the storm is returning."

"Shut up!" snapped the king. "I have summoned the dark forces and they will stop this. It will not strike us here; it will pass over and let us be."

But when the storm returned, it didn't skip over them—it hit them harder. Trees snapped and began pulling out of the ground. Rocks—even boulders—began moving, rolling down hills or flying through the air. Barbarot saw his men hanging on to anything they could find to keep from becoming a human spear. Bodies of men were flying through the air, as were merkezi, volarequi and the few chimeri that Barbarot had managed to find and force into service.

Visibility dropped to zero as the rain hammered them. And it wasn't long before the rain turned to sleet and then to hail. Hail the size of orangeries fell from the sky, killing just about anyone unfortunate enough to be in the wrong place at the wrong time. As if the Vinedrian archers were firing at them, Barbarot's men fell by the thousands.

Meanwhile, moving slowly, the hurricane was stirring up the deep waters of the Sea of Crisium not far offshore. The waves far out to sea began growing as they came closer to shore and the shallow reefs along the coast. Waves of only a few feet in the middle of Crisium rose to heights of twenty and thirty feet by the time they reached the shoals off the eastern coast of Vinedria. Even the castle of Knotsbow was now in the storm's crosshairs.

A tall, sturdy breakwater had been built several decades earlier by King Viridius in case a small hurricane came through the area—but none had. The rocky barricade had eroded over the years but would finally be tested like it never had before.

The first surges of the sea were held back by the breakwater; however, within hours, it was overwhelmed by the twenty-foot waves and fierce winds pushing water over the top of its wall. By the time the tidal wave hit, the breakwater was broken. Over forty feet high, the surge of water became a sheet of pure, blue death. When it slammed ashore, it shoved sand, trees, rocks and debris ahead of it like a glacier carving a canyon. The water covered the tops of trees and spread inland, extending its arms in every low-lying direction.

Not far away, Barbarot's men heard the thunderous roar as the tidal wave breached the wall. The sound was getting louder as the waters rushed toward them.

"What's that noise?" asked one of the men.

"Dunno'," said another. "But it don't sound good."

The sound became deafening, and it was then that all could see a mountain rising above the treetops in front of them. It was dark gray with white, frothy peaks on top. However, this was no mountain of rock.

"Oh, my god!" exclaimed the first man.

He tried to pull his boots out of the mud, but he was stuck, caught in one of the quicksand pits that had formed from all the rain.

"Help me!" he screamed, reaching out his hand for someone to pull him loose. But his comrades were too busy running for their lives as the wall of water sped toward them.

Much of the rest of the army was also stuck in the mud or caught in the vines of the dense foliage. Those who had been lucky enough to survive the horrific winds and flying wooden spears, now had to face the gray curtain rising over their heads.

"Get the volarequi and anything else that will fly into the air, at once!" ordered Barbarot.

The command was too late. A few of his officers got their winged steeds off the ground, but most did not get high enough into the air to avoid the wave when it hit. The rest of the men and beasts did not stand a chance.

The water crashed down on the army with no mercy. The sound of the rushing wave was unworldly—as if the entire planet were coming to an end. Many took their lasts breaths before going under, pulled down by the force of the wave or killed instantly by the trees or rocks swimming in the torrent. These were thrown about by the wave like a child playing with toys in a bathtub. Later surges of water came, but by then there was little left of the king's once-mighty army.

Barbarot was in the air on his volarequez being buffeted by the swirling winds. Stunned, he hovered above one of the few places of rocky land not yet covered in roiling gray waters below him.

"I don't understand it," he said, unnerved. "It didn't obey me. It didn't bend to my commands," He paused and looked to the heavens. "You deceived me!" he shouted, shaking his fist. "I will not be controlled by you any longer! I will make my own destiny! I am greater than you and will be the sole ruler of the realm and everything above and below it. You will see!" He turned to his commander who was flying next to him. "Take a count of what's left. We will regroup before we head on to Knotsbow."

"But sire, there is nothing left! You have no more army to fight with? It's gone!" said Sterinis.

"I *will* fight them," said Barbarot. "My power is greater than that of my army anyway. I will take the kingdom myself."

"As you wish, Your Highness," replied Sterinis, and he flew off to execute his order.

Barbarot pulled out the volume of the *Book of Spells* and clenched it in his fingers. Then, leaning back, he hurled it into the air and down into the deep waters below. He watched as the ancient and powerful book bobbed up and down a few times before sinking beneath the foamy, frothy waves.

"I don't need you. I only need myself," he said, bitterly. "I am the one who will conquer and rule this planet, and I will do it my way—with or without the dark one beside me."

*****

CH 35 – A Second Test

The Rebus was sad, but Oliver and Fermat felt no pity for him. The garden outside the cave was evidence enough that no pity was warranted.

Oliver and Fermat entered the cave following the Rebus.

"So, where is the stone?" asked Oliver anxiously.

The Rebus said nothing, but only turned and shook his head.

"I could not tell you, even if I knew," it replied.

"Why not?" yelled Fermat. "We beat you ... we beat fair and square at your little game. Now you have to tell us where it is!"

"Only the one inside knows. You must seek him." Then, the Rebus disappeared, magically walking through a rocky wall as if it didn't exist.

It was darker the deeper they went in the cave, and the two young men finally stopped.

"We need some light," said Oliver. "Look around for something we can make a torch out of."

Finding some old, dried brush that had blown in from outside, they made two torches and lit them, bringing light back to where there was once darkness.

"Where do you think it is?" asked Fermat. "It really could be anywhere in here."

"There *must* be a clue," Oliver answered, "It wouldn't be a challenge without some sort of clue, But what?"

They looked up and down each of the moist, gray, cave walls but found nothing unusual. From the high ceiling hung long, jagged stalactites that threatened them like Damocles swords. Finding nothing, they searched deeper until the light from their torches dimmed. Oliver wished he'd been able to bring his ferro bar and pyrodust, but they were taken from him at the start of the race.

As he thought about this, the Eripio bag he'd hidden away finally began to move. Its silence was finally broken.

"What's that?" asked Fermat, looking at the small nut Oliver had taken from the bag.

Oliver was puzzled by finding the nut in the bag. He didn't remember any being left in his satchel. *Did the Eripio bag make it for me?* he thought. *Or did it just roll into the bag somehow?*

Oliver pressed the tips of the tricorner nut, letting it open. Then he shut it and pressed the corners again to release what was inside. With the gray mist came a puff of smoke which he sheltered with his hands so he could see what it looked like.

"What does that look like to you?" asked Oliver.

"What does what look like?" Fermat answered, confused with the question.

"That! The smoke! What does it look like?"

By then, the smoke had changed color and shape, turning white and wavy.

"I think it looks like a river," said Oliver.

"No, I don't think so. To me it looks like an icicle."

"That was the answer you gave to the Rebus' first question, wasn't it?" asked Oliver, starting to piece things together. "So, if that's the first clue, and my river was the second, then …"

"… darkness would be the third," replied Fermat, following the thought. "So, what were all our answers in order?" asked Fermat.

Oliver began reciting them. "The first was the icicle... the next was river, then there was darkness, then twenty-six …"

"… and the last was tomorrow. I'd say the first thing to do is to find the icicle," said Fermat, looking at each of the icicles hanging from the top of the cave.

"It's got to be one that's different from the others in some way," said Oliver looking at each carefully.

"Find anything?" Fermat asked after nearly an hour of searching.

"What about this one?" Oliver pointed to a massive icicle that could have easily been mistaken for part of the cave wall. From a distance it looked like ice, but close up, they realized it was a wet rock. It partially blocked a narrow slit in the cave wall that extended all the way from the floor to the ceiling.

Fermat watched as water streamed down the outside of what they realized was a stalactite, running to the tip which almost touched the ground. It dripped steadily, almost closing the final gap needed to join with the cave floor.

"It's unusually cold inside this cave—below zero, even," said Oliver, "yet, water is streaming down this stalactite. That's weird."

"It's supposed to be warmer than freezing underground. Isn't it?" asked Fermat.

"Yeah—both things are strange."

"What are we supposed to do, now that we think we've found it?" Fermat asked, scratching his head.

"We've found the 'icicle,' but I'm afraid we're a long way from finding the stone," said Oliver.

He reached up and touched the long dagger-like piece. He pushed and pulled on it, hoping it would do something—anything—but it didn't.

"Try pulling down on it," said Fermat.

Oliver tried, but that too failed.

"I don't suppose you can try pushing it back into the ceiling?" He laughed, watching Oliver shake his head.

"I don't think so, Fermat. That' makes no sense."

But Oliver tried anyway, wrapping his arms around the huge pointed rock and pushing up. To their astonishment, the entire stalactite began to retract slowly into the ceiling on its own, as if a cave ogre lived in the ceiling and was pulling it up and out of the way for them. When it had completely disappeared from sight, the two looked at each other with astonishment. Moments later, two stalagmites grew up from the floor of the cave, reaching the shoulder height of Fermat before stopping.

"Well I'll be a joker's peacock," said Fermat.

"You and me both," added Oliver.

"Do you feel something?" asked Fermat, his eyes growing bigger.

The floor of the cave began to rumble, and ice and snow started to break away from the slit in the wall next to where the stalactite had been, revealing an opening. Steam poured from it, blasting out like a caged tiger leaping from a pen. As the steam faded, darkness filled the void.

"It looks like the path slopes sharply down through that crevasse there, Oliver," said Fermat, fearfully. He pointed nervously at the dark crevasse that replaced where the stalactite had been.

"We've come this far, Fermat. We can't stop now. Are you going first, or am I?"

Fermat gave him a feeble grin and slipped through the widened crack and into the unknown.

It wasn't long before the way got so steep that they found themselves sliding down it instead of walking. The chill only worsened as they wandered farther into the depths.

"Do you hear something?" asked Oliver, pausing to listen.

"I hear it, but I can't see it," said Fermat.

The sound was muted and tempting them until they went some distance farther. Rounding a bend, they smelled a sudden burst of Sulphur and saltwater, and the breeze was warm and inviting.

"It's got to be just up ahead," said Oliver, watching the flame on his torch shrink lower. "It smells like an underground spring."

"It's getting so dark!" said Fermat, also noticing that his torch was going out. "Does this count as the river or the darkness?"

"Perhaps, both," said Oliver, now feeling his way along the wall. It reminded him of the other caves he'd been in—too many, as far as he was concerned. "I think it's just ahead. If we just take it easy on this ice, I think we'll …"

At that moment, Oliver lost his footing. He hit an ice sheet, skidding down the hill on his butt like he was on a runaway sensavol, galloping off at high speed.

Startled by Oliver's fall, Fermat fell face-first on the same ice and then half-rolled and half-slid right behind him on his backside. At the bottom of the icy shoot, he slammed into his mate, nearly pushing him into the rushing river below.

"This can't be happening again," Oliver said.

"What do you mean, again?"

"Oh, never mind. We've just got to figure out where we go from *here*. I'm thinking that the third clue of 'darkness' is more than it just being in the dark. I mean, it's been dark almost the whole time we've been in this cave, hasn't it?" Oliver stopped to think. "No, it's got to be something else."

Fermat just shook his head. "Boy, that's a tough one. I'm not sure, either. Darkness … darkness … *Ummmm*."

"Let's walk along here and see where this goes," said Oliver. "It's got to lead us to something,"

"Yeah, something, Oliver. Thank goodness you know where that is," said Fermat smirking.

Oliver put his hand on Fermat's shoulder to give him what comfort he could but then struck out ahead along the riverbank. They hadn't gone far when they spotted a faint glowing blue light.

"That isn't one of those spidery things is it?" asked Oliver, stopping dead in his tracks.

"An angler? No. Those things only hang out in the forest. They'd never come down here," said Fermat.

"What if it's a rare species that just happens to live in a cave!" said Oliver.

Fermat just stared at Oliver. "You're not being reasonable, Oliver. Calm down."

It was a rare moment when Oliver was suddenly struck with a fear he couldn't control. The angler had gotten to him. It had stressed him—traumatized him. It had become his phobia.

But still, the blue light was eerie, and as they approached, they saw that it was suspended in mid-air, just like the angler in the woods.

"I don't like this, Fermat. I can't go on," said Oliver, frozen by fear.

"You're not afraid of anything, Oliver."

"I didn't use to be. Now ...?"

Fermat grabbed him by the arm and began dragging him along the trail. "You just told me up top that we'd come too far to give up ... Now, it's my turn to tell you, Oliver. Buck it up!"

Oliver took a deep breath.

"All right. Let's do this," Oliver answered him.

But as they neared the blue light, they found it was a small momatu bush burning with the blue flame. The fire gave off light but no heat, and it wasn't burning the bush.

The river that ran next to them had narrowed to a small stream, and they could see the white, foamy surface vanish only a short distance away. Oddly, there was no sound of a roaring waterfall; it seemed to just end abruptly.

"Is that blue light beyond where the river ends or before it ends?" asked Oliver. "I can't tell."

"Neither can I."

"Well, what do you want to do, then?"

"As you said, Oliver. We've come this far."

They approached the blue flaming bush; yet, the river continued a little farther downstream. Oliver touched the bush, expecting to be burned, but instead it just went out. Now it truly was dark all around them. There was still the sound of the river next to them, but no other.

"Have you changed your mind?" Fermat asked, no longer visible to his friend.

"I …"

Then, there was another sound—that of rock moving or sliding next to them. Another flaming bush appeared—this one orange and below it was a stone table—something very much out of place deep inside a cave.

"That's really weird," said Fermat.

But what was more weird was what they saw next.

*****

CH 36 - Uprising

They few survivors of Barbarot's army marched on. The hurricane and accompanying tsunami had wiped out most of them. As for the typhoon, it had continued out to sea where it had turned north and headed into the countryside of Dulcenou and Rootan, causing further destruction.

This disaster followed so quickly on the heels of the *canibola* plague that the people of Rootan were left reeling from the chaos caused by the storm. At the same time, it made them angry. They were tired of not being in control of anything in their lives, and they wanted change.

Many shook their fists at the God of gods for bringing these calamities upon them. Yet, it had the opposite effect on others who drew closer to their families in a way they hadn't in years.

It was all written. It was all prophesied in the *Book of Iuratis* thousands of years earlier.

> *Creatures large and small will seek shelter, yet its force will overwhelm them. Life giving and life destroying will the power be. A strength and might only from the God of gods could it come. It will be the end for many, but the beginning for a few – a few who will inherit and forge the future for what is left behind.*

Those who understood would turn to the light and the goodness that exists in everything. They would make a new beginning and toil to rebuild and make things better. For buried within the Book's texts were the lessons of justice, temperance, prudence and courage. These were life-lessons that had held communities and peoples together throughout the ages.

But there were also those who did not understand. They would turn away from the light, embracing something far more sinister. These were the ones who saw the force as only a destroyer, not a life giver. They believed the end of times was coming, and since the Book's predictions were inevitable, there was no reason for them to continue following the path of goodness. A crisis was upon them, and so was someone more than willing to take advantage of it and them.

***

Konjuur sat and waited. Holed up in the Boars Wag Inn, he plotted his next moves. He had traveled from town to town, sowing the seeds of revolution and seeing his magic work. He now had a core group of disgruntled followers who were ready to do his bidding—for the good of the kingdom, of course.

"Yes, the time is right," Konjuur said to his inner circle.

"So, what's next, sire?" asked one of his knights.

"You'll see, soon enough. Be patient," Konjuur replied.

And he was right. It took several days to pick up after the hurricane blew through the kingdom, and many more for the people of Rootan to put their lives back together. Once the skies cleared of the black, swirling clouds and were replaced by puffy, white ones, there seemed to be a new hope and optimism. Yet, this hope meant different things to different people. For some, it was to rebuild their lives and go on their way; for others, it was an opportunity to seek revenge for their misery. However, these two groups could agree on one thing—they both wanted to stop the madness of the current king.

Konjuur sent a notice to all the towns and villages asking the people to come to Emani and assemble just outside the castle. Carrying homemade weapons—farm tools, old swords, clubs and knives—they came by the thousands. Emotions ran high, and the viceroy was only too willing to encourage it. The crowd moved closer to the base of the cylindrical stone tower that stood in the middle of the town square. Anyone looking out a window in the king's castle could see a tea pot boiling in the town square below.

"My friends," Konjuur said to the growing masses. He stood on the uppermost step of the stairway that wound its way to the tower's top. "It's time we march on the one who has caused us so much pain and suffering. The hurricane of the last few weeks and the plagues and diseases of the last few years were caused by our king."

The mention of the king's name brought loud and thunderous *boo's* that echoed throughout the town.

"Yes, yes. It is true. If King Barbarot were liked by the gods, they wouldn't have vented their wrath on us. It's because of him and what he's done that they are upset and angry. And they're angry at you because you haven't done anything to rid yourselves of him!"

Suddenly, the people grew quiet.

"But do not fear," said Konjuur. "You may still redeem yourselves. If you follow me, I will guide you down the true path the gods want you to follow. With my leadership, you can overcome the oppression of the man who lives in *Claustrus* castle—yes, I said the forbidden name! I am not afraid to say it, and I'm not afraid of the king. It is I who can save you from the last curses predicted."

There was frenzied talking in the crowd now as all thought the omens had come and gone. There had been seven, as predicted by the *Book of Iuratis*. *Was Konjuur now telling them there were more they would have to suffer?* they thought.

Someone next to the viceroy whispered in his ear, and he nodded.

"Oh," said Konjuur, suddenly understanding the discord, "I believe many of you thought there were only seven omens and that they had all come to pass. Well, you are wrong. Your king has not told you of the omens predicted in the *second* book that, *'shall descend upon the people if they have not cast-out their evil king'.* You—we—have not cast out this evil king. Therefore, there are two more omens in the *Book of Gneima*—the second of the three great books."

Again, the crowd grew quiet.

"We must rid ourselves of King Barbarot and vanquish the threat of the disasters to come!"

The crowd roared their approval, shaking their weapons of war and readying for battle.

"Do you want to suffer another plague or disaster?"

"No!" came the unanimous reply.

"Do you want to wait for the rest of the prophecies to come true?"

"No!"

"Do you want your home and family destroyed the next time something comes through the kingdom to strike you or them down? Do you want to sit by and wait for that to happen?"

"No!"

"Do you want to do nothing? Or do you finally want to do something—to take matters into your own hands? To steer destiny in the direction you want it to go?" he yelled.

"Yes! Yes!"

And with that, the people roared their approval, clapping, whistling and waving wildly in anticipation of what Konjuur would say next.

"Then, follow *me*!" Konjuur roared. "We will retake this kingdom from the despot who has stolen it from you. We will save this land that you've worked so hard to build up for your children. I will lead you, and together, we will reclaim Rootan for all Rootanians!"

The sound of the crowd was deafening. Even the ruler's father, a short distance away in the castle, could hear it, and his eyes darted to the mob scene in the town square below.

***

"Sire!" said a castle courtier running into the throne room with alarm, "The townspeople are amassing outside the castle! What do you want us to do!"

"What do you mean? Is there a festival going on?" asked Baron Marbray, blinking robotically still in his trance. "I didn't know there was a holiday this month. The harvest is already over, and all the crops are in. So, what is this about?"

The baron was taking care of the castle and the kingdom while his son, King Barbarot, was out conquering his neighbors. He sat in a chair next to the window still gazing out but not understanding.

"I assure you, my liege, that it is certainly no festive occasion. They all have weapons, and they're acting angry—like they want to burn down the castle! What would you like me to do, sire?"

The baron rose from his chair and looked closer at the square below. There he could see thousands of peasants, merchants and farmers gathering with pitchforks, knives, old sabers and swords from wars long ago. They were chanting and shaking their primitive weapons.

"Kill the king! Bury the king! We want our kingdom back!" they cried.

The glazed look on the baron's face momentarily lifted, and he spoke in a monotone, barely raising an eyebrow at the urgency and importance of the matter.

"Send out the kujopt to scatter them," he said calmly.

"Yes, my Lord."

Marbray watched as the canine trainers walked down the narrow, stone stairway that led to the dog pen. They disappeared behind a thick, square-hinged door that closed with a deep and echoing *boom*. Then, he shifted his eyes to the pen gates, not twenty feet from where the trainers had entered. He waited until he heard the clanging of chains being pulled to lift the metal bars that kept the black beasts secured and away from the villagers on the outside.

The protestors got quiet and watched as the metal bars were being raised. They wondered what was happening, and many began running from the square, anticipating that something bad was about to be released from the pens.

As the black bars rose, the enormous, four-eyed kujopts charged out of their cages. People began screaming and fleeing for their lives. The massive dogs attacked them, sinking their teeth into arms, legs and anything else they could find. As the townspeople dropped their weapons and began running in fear, the dogs chased them. Scattering like roaches in the sunlight, the people ran in any direction they could to get away from the beasts.

The screams of terror from the mob reached the room where the baron sat, high in the castle tower. They vibrated like a timpani drum beating inside his head. He grimaced and covered his ears, wincing as though someone had taken a pickax to his brain.

"No! Stop that!" he shouted. But the yelling outside continued.

The baron shook his head to get rid of the pain, but instead of it going away, something else happened. The gray fog that had drifted over his mind, dulling his senses and muddying his thoughts, was lifting. He was beginning to think more clearly.

While the villagers ran off, the kujopts were rounded up by their trainers and returned to their pens. Konjuur and his men watched the incident from a distance. He had not started the riot, but he had certainly not discouraged it either. He wanted to see what would happen if there was a rebellion started against the king. And, he got his answer.

Konjuur had seen the baron come to the window of the castle to view the events as they unfolded. But most telling was the disgusted look on the baron's face and the speed at which he turned away from the brutality. Instead of watching, he left the window.

He doesn't have the stomach for it. He doesn't have the guts, Konjuur said to himself, grinning. *This will be much easier than I thought.*

Now all he had to do is wait. He only needed the right place and right time to seize power when the opportunity showed itself. *It will be like shooting fish in a barrel*, he thought.

***

The very next day, Konjuur had the people back in the town square, enticing them with food and drink. He smiled as thousands from the previous day returned—not scared away by what had happened.

He rose again—this time to the top of the tower to make his proclamation.

"You have seen what your ruler thinks of you! Yesterday, you were meat for his dogs. Today, I will make you masters of your kingdom. Follow me now! I will lead you to freedom and safety!"

The crowd roared as he climbed down from the tower, taking his time to absorb the praise from the crowd. It was hard work maneuvering his large body down the narrow stairs, but he used all his energy to make sure he looked as regal as possible doing it. At the bottom, a hefty volarequez was waiting for him, and he was helped up and into the saddle.

"Onward!" he yelled, shaking his fist in the air. "We shall take back our kingdom and reclaim what is rightfully ours!"

He kicked his winged steed and bolted into the air, flying toward the castle and what he felt was his own destiny.

The massive crowd out of the square and up the road toward the castle, its stone towers and its Moat of Tantalus. Flying above and at the head of the riotous group was Konjuur. He made sure no one else flew with him. Image and symbolism, he understood, were critically important. The sea of humanity fell in behind the viceroy, making him look like the *Chosen One* making his pilgrimage to a holy site. It was just the way he had planned it.

As the group reached the crest of the hill, behind them lay the now-quiet town of Emani and ahead lay the gleaming white, arondite stones of the king's castle. Even from a distance, the castle was awe-inspiring with its chromatic stones that changed color and hue. It was magnificent in its design and grandness.

The group began chanting as it descended on the castle: "Kill the king, bury the king, we want our kingdom back!"

There was little fear. With the *Chosen One* leading the way, the mass felt invincible—nothing would stop them. This time, there was no panic; there was no army; there were no kujopts. Konjuur had taken special precautions to post his knights near the dog pens to strike them down if they were again unleashed.

However, this time, there were no dogs.

The thousands continued to move, slowly, mightily, toward the castle. Eventually, they stood just on the outside of the Moat of Tantalus, cheering and jeering the name of Barbarot and his father, the baron.

"Death to the king! Death to the king!" they chanted.

From the town square, Sojourn could see what was unfolding, and he was worried. He had hoped the baron would unleash the kujopt dogs again to make the crowd turn against Konjuur. But nothing came.

Sojourn shook his head in disgust. Things were moving quickly out of his control and into the hands of Konjuur. His chances of turning the tide were shrinking. However, with age sometimes comes patience and wisdom. Sojourn had both. He realized he had to be patient—he too could wait for the right moment. For now, Sojourn accepted that this new evil would take over where Barbarot had left off—making the kingdom worse rather than better. Yet, he hoped for another opportunity to stop it before it became irreversible.

As for Konjuur, this was his time and his moment. He reveled in the attention and fawning, drawing his own energy from it.

"Baron Marbray! It is time you surrender yourself and your castle to the people of Rootan!" yelled the viceroy from across the moat. "You cannot hide any longer from us. We, the people of Rootan, demand a new leader!"

There was no reply, nor was there any movement from soldiers within the fortress.

Konjuur waited, but still got nothing from the castle. Then, he turned his winged stallion and faced the crowd roaring, "It is time we take back our kingdom!"

And with that declaration, the mass of people ran past the scared guards on the Bridge of Tantalus and converged on the Noforo Gates of the castle. By the hundreds they pushed and shoved. Those in front used battle axes to bend the iron and break holes in the doors trying to get inside.

As the doors disintegrated, Baron Marbray sat at his desk within the royal chambers overlooking the scene. He scribbled a note on a piece of parchment and attached his seal to it. He handed it to his attendant and waved him off for it to be delivered. The shock of the moment had eroded the power of the elixir and spell placed on him by his son. and he started to see things more clearly. Then, he penned another note; this one he attached to the leg of a pigmy columba and sent it on its way from his window.

Going down to the royal stables, Marbray got onto one of the king's volarequez and took off, flying low and out the back side of the castle grounds. No one saw him, and he disappeared into the hazy mist that was forming over the river nearby.

Meanwhile, as the gates started to buckle, the trumpets blared from within and a volley of arrows rained down on the people in front of the gates. Konjuur pulled his steed back and motioned for his knights to direct the crowd back as well. Suddenly, the archers stopped, and the trumpets quieted. When the Noforo Gates opened, a lone sentinel marched out, unarmed and without chain mail. Tall and valiant, there was no look of fear in his eyes as he understood his duty.

Without hesitation, he strode over to the portly Konjuur and handed him the parchment note Marbray had penned minutes earlier. Konjuur took it and studied the wax seal. Then he ripped it open and read the contents. When he had finished, he turned to the masses on the bridge and held up the paper.

"This is your pardon!" Konjuur declared triumphantly. "This is your ticket to freedom. How great is this that I have delivered your freedom to you without a drop of blood shed!"

The people roared their approval with shouting and cheering, waving their swords and rattling their shields and sabers.

"Baron Marbray, as a representative for King Barbarot, has turned over the entire castle to me and to the people of Rootan! We shall change the way you are treated in this land. You shall share in the bounties that you have helped create. No longer will you be slaves to the ruler. I shall rule you fairly and justly, and you shall call me King Konjuur!"

"King Konjuur! King Konjuur!"

Again, there was a cry of celebration throughout the town, and the people rushed behind their new leader, pushing him and his volarequez past the Moat of Tantalus and the Noforo Gates and into the castle. The tidal wave of support carried him into the immense courtyard of the castle.

Forced off his horse, Konjuur raised his hands in a gesture of triumph and, calming the crowd by motioning for quiet, he announced dramatically, "Henceforth, this castle will be renamed to its original splendor—Claustrus Castle! The castle of the Rootanian people!"

"All hail, King Konjuur!"

*****

CH 37 – Orange Flame

As Oliver and Fermat grew closer to the orange flame, they saw an animal with long, thin arms, seven fingers on each hand and a large, hairless head sitting behind the stone table on a stone chair. In fact, this creature looked like a twin of the Rebus they'd just dueled with outside the cave, except it was red in color.

"Are you a Rebus like we met outside the cave?" asked Fermat, not thinking before he spoke.

"Fermat, stop!" said Oliver scolding his friend. "We don't know if our questions count as they did before. Let's take this slowly."

"You seek the stone, do you not?" came the question from the Rebus—the tenor and pitch of his voice different from the one they had met earlier. This one was mellow and had a poetic cadence to it. Yet, the question was a familiar one.

"You are a Rebus, aren't you?" asked Oliver.

"Oliver! You just said don't ask any questions!" stuttered Fermat out of anger and fear.

"You seek the stone, do you not?" repeated the animal, refusing to answer their questions.

"We're searching for ..." started Fermat but stopped before he finished his answer. "... what exactly, Oliver? It isn't an icicle, river or darkness …"

Oliver held his breath again, as he had before. It didn't seem like it was the right answer to the question, and the Rebus looked confused.

"I don't understand," replied the creature. But rather than cast a spell on them, it simply said, "I can't help you." It immediately began to get down from its seat behind the stone table and amble away.

"Wait!" cried Oliver after him. "Don't go!"

The Rebus turned and said without emotion, "There is no reason to stay if you cannot answer my question."

Again, he turned.

"No, wait," pleaded Oliver. "We can answer your question, and the answer is yes."

"Yes? Then, I will ask you one question and one only. If you answer wrongly, you will never find the stone."

"And if we answer correctly?" asked Fermat.

"Then I will be able to help you. So, here is your question. "What is the thing that you seek?"

Fermat leaned into Oliver and whispered in his ear. "But we just told him!" said Fermat.

"It must be something else," said Oliver.

"It's a trick. It's just like when we were outside the cave."

"You're probably right, but we must play the game."

They both thought for a moment.

"We should ask about the twenty-six," Fermat said to Oliver.

"No," Oliver whispered back. "We have two clues to find— twenty-six and tomorrow. If we ask about just one, it won't help us."

"Then ask about both!"

"No. He specifically asked about one thing—not two or more."

Oliver took a deep breath and cleared his mind. *I don't know,* he thought to himself. *I just don't ...* Then, his eyes lit up. *That's it!*

"We ... seek knowledge. Can you help us find knowledge?" asked Oliver.

The Conunder smiled. "That is something I can help you with, indeed. Come with me," he said, pleasantly.

Instead of continuing down the path they had started, the Rebus took them down another that was harder to see in the darkness. However, once they entered an icy corridor, there were many more blue lights showing them the way.

"This what you seek," said the Conunder.

"What is this?" Fermat asked, looking down the iceway in confusion.

"This is the Corridor of Knowledge," said the Conunder. "You must take this if you want to find what you're looking for. I cannot go any farther with you—you are on your own from here. Good luck."

The Conunder walked halfway back up the snowy path they'd come and then pushed aside a large piece of ice, disappearing behind it.

Oliver looked down the mysterious ice hall.

"We're going down there?" asked Fermat, nervously.

"What are you worried about, Fermat? At least there aren't any spiders, and we're out of the darkness. We can see where we're going."

"That's what worries me most," said Oliver's friend.

*****

CH 38 - An End and a Beginning

Donus' memories were coming and going—passing moments of clarity and then fog. He was still having trouble making sense of them as they swirled inside his head. First, there were the images of a middle-aged woman—tall with brown eyes and blonde hair, like his own. She was a striking woman, large boned and athletic, whose smile gave him warmth and comfort. These were blurred pictures though—hazy and fleeting, as if he were remembering them as a small child. Next, he saw a large wooden table with many young men sitting around it, enjoying a feast fit for a king. However, within moments he found himself on the hard, wooden floor looking up at a man with tattoos covering his body and face. Odd images, these were, yet not enough for him to piece together his past.

Still, he was content where he was living with the new Parogild and sister, Genona, in their spacious manor in Ralop. It had been only a few days since the passing of their father, Baron Lukae 15. It was a sad time for the family, preparing for the funeral and the succession of power from father to the eldest, Parogild. Yet, it was a time when the two siblings grew closer together.

Parogild was maturing into his role quickly. Thrust into the spotlight of the family's estate and the people of the town who relied on it, he took charge of arranging the funeral and the procession through the streets of Ralop and back to the estate where the baron was laid to rest.

Thousands paid their respects, and the shepherds, in particular, were at a loss for what to do. Most of what they found of value in their lives, they had learned from the baron or from those he had brought onboard to help them on their life's journeys.

At the banquet held in the baron's honor, Parogild stood before the knights and friends who had become close to their master and mentor. He raised his glass and proposed his tribute.

Striking his glass chalice with a knife, Parogild motioned to the crowd for quiet.

"We have come to pay tribute to a great man—a man we all admired and who, in his own way and manner, was a great leader and role model for all of us."

He stopped to compose himself and then continued.

"He shared a story with me that I will tell you now," he said. "Once, there was a man who was very rich. His wealth exceeded that of everyone he knew put together. His friends were aware of the fortune he had and often asked for him to share it with them. He did so generously and without protest. Women would come for money for their children; men would come asking for loans to start their shops or trade; and children would come requesting money for candy. He gave freely and expected nothing in return.

"Then, one day, the man suffered a great loss. His son died. Inwardly, he grieved and suffered, but outwardly—to all around him—he wouldn't let them know how much he grieved and how much he missed him. He loved his daughter a great deal and made sure that she was well taken care of and that she would grow up to be a kind and caring person as he believed everyone should be.

"However, his heart had broken, and there was a wound that just wouldn't heal. Finally, he found that his dead son had been reborn—it was truly a miracle! And when his son returned to him, he asked for forgiveness. His son's death had put his poor father through much grief and sorrow, but he smiled as he saw his son walk through the doorway, alive and well. The crack in the father's heart had not healed, but the heart was large enough to forgive his son for causing him such pain.

"And when the moment came for his own end, the father reached his hand out and pulled his son close. In his ear he whispered, 'You were never lost from my heart, son ... you were always there and always will be. I am proud to call you my son, and even prouder that you found the straight path back to me and your family."

"Bless you father. You were and always will be a great man with an even greater heart."

*****

CH 39 - United Again

"I'm glad you got my message, old friend," said Baron Marbray. "I was afraid my note may not have reached you."

"No, baron, we received it, and we are very glad you have finally returned to us," said Sojourn, who was waiting for him outside the front of his manor.

The baron jumped off his ride, acting as if he were twenty years younger.

"Are you all right?" asked Sojourn.

"In many ways, better than ever," replied the baron cheerfully, "but …"

"Your son," said Sojourn.

"Yes … my son. He is a different story. As for him, I feel that I've failed. I've let him and everyone else down—everyone who depended on me for anything.

"You?" replied Sojourn, indignantly.

"Yes, me!"

"It wasn't your fault, really, Etin. Do you remember much about what happened to you or what you've been doing the last three weeks or so?"

The baron stopped to think, "No, I can't say that I do. It's a bit of a blur, honestly—like I was walking and talking in a dream. A voice kept telling me what to do and my body obeyed, whether I wanted to or not. I was a prisoner but had no cell."

"A voice?"

"Yes, there was a voice that always told me what to do. I thought it was my inner voice, you know, that tells you right from wrong. So, I was convinced that if I just followed it, everything would be fine." He paused. "It didn't work out that way. Did it?"

"I'm not sure yet, whether it has or hasn't, my friend. I still believe things—all things—happen for a reason. There is a divine purpose and path. We do what's needed to make it turn out right. I always have, and I always will," said Sojourn.

"That's what I like about you, Sojourn. You're always the eternal optimist!"

"Well, if I don't do it, who will?" quipped the old man. "But right now, we need to get you inside. Cleora and Montoi are there waiting for us."

Once inside, they found the lanterns and candles glowing brightly, as Aunt Cleora had prepared a full and luscious dinner for all. She came out of the kitchen and gave the baron a peck on the cheek.

"It's good to have you back, Etin. I wasn't so sure about you." She paused and winked. "That guy coming down the stairs there was easier to bring back," she said, pointing to Montoi. "But you—you had to be difficult, didn't you?" She laughed. "We knew you would be more of a challenge."

Montoi greeted the baron warmly, shaking his hands vigorously and giving him a pat on the back. "Welcome home, my good fellow. It's good to see you again—all in one piece too, it seems."

"It's good to be back, Montoi. Very good indeed."

They all assembled in the dining hall, and even though Aunt Cleora had fixed the supper, Sojourn's house staff brought it out to be served. Sojourn took a bite of the delicious roasted soome she had cooked for them and dabbed the corner of his mouth to absorb the extra juice.

"It is good to have everyone with us," said Sojourn, grabbing his chalice. "But I am remiss in not offering a toast." He raised his glass, smiling. "To friendship. May it give us the strength to persevere through the hard times ahead, and may it warm our hearts for however many days we are granted to enjoy each other's company."

"Hear, hear!" said the rest of the group, clanging their glasses together and taking a sip of the red wine offered.

"You are right, Sojourn," said Marbray. "I fear there will be many challenges ahead."

"Yes," said Montoi. "We've lost the castle to Konjuur. He has taken over as ruler, and we'll have to fight him in addition to Barbarot to get it back."

Aunt Cleora put down her glass of wine. "We knew that was a possibility, and if it happened, it would be very hard to unseat him. He'll use the guards to enforce his rule, and probably threaten the dukes and earls to give up their forces. Don't you think?"

"Perhaps," said Sojourn, "but most of the Rootanian army is away with the king."

"Barbarot?" said Aunt Cleora simply. "You're thinking that Barbarot will come back and successfully reclaim his throne?"

"Most certainly he will," replied Montoi.

"He *may* reclaim his throne," said Sojourn.

"*May*?" asked Marbray.

"Don't you think Konjuur has thought through that?" answered Aunt Cleora. "I'm sure he's already made plans for that eventuality."

"Yes, I'm sure he has," said Sojourn. "But then again, he doesn't know Barbarot well—or at all. He probably doesn't know about his dark powers. That's why he got the people on his side—he figured with them he would be able to defeat Barbarot's army. He doesn't think the army will attack its own."

"He's right," said Marbray, "and it takes far fewer troops to defend a fortress than to take one."

"Very true, my friend. However, again, I think Konjuur believes he is dealing with someone … well … human. Do you think Barbarot is human?"

Montoi, Marbray and Aunt Cleora looked at each other, searching for an answer.

"I don't really know, Sojourn," answered Marbray. "He certainly is not my son."

"Do you believe that something beyond the human form exists?" asked Montoi.

Aunt Cleora then piped in. "Well, I don't think any of us knows that. But there are a lot of people who believe it does. They believe in the Tribal Noque, the God of gods and that kind of stuff, don't they?"

"Sure, but that doesn't mean they believe in the kind of evil that Barbarot has become," replied Marbray. "Is it evil behind our world? Is he a demon? Or is he just a bad human being?"

Sojourn sat pensively. "Perhaps debating whether or not Barbarot is human or a demon is not relevant."

Aunt Cleora looked at him, perplexed.

"What I'm saying is—perhaps we should be discussing which is the *greater* evil?" said Sojourn quietly.

"We can only hope that the evils are equal, and they destroy each other," said Montoi.

"In one way, I hope you're right," said Aunt Cleora, "But for the baron's sake, and that of his son, I hope you're not."

Sojourn shook his head. "We can only work toward the best solution—the saving of the kingdom, and, if possible, Etin's son. There is *always* a silver lining. We just need to find it."

"How?" asked Aunt Cleora.

"I don't know yet, Cleora. As you know, I'm an optimist. When things get dark—even black—you've got to figure out a way to change things. They never get completely dark. There's always an answer, a solution. What's life without light or hope?"

Aunt Cleora used a simple white, cotton napkin to dab her lips. "All right, then what's the plan?"

Sojourn smiled at her. "Well, that's easy," he said. "I think it's time for dessert."

*****

CH 40 – In the Courtyard

It didn't take long before Konjuur had established a firm grip on the workings of the kingdom. After promising to keep Barbarot's courtiers on as "close" advisors, he threw most into the deep prison cells below the castle after they told him what he needed to know. They called it "Black Friday"—the day when all were rounded up in chains and sent down the long, narrow corridor to the prison dungeon. Many ended up where Aunt Cleora had been only a few months earlier—in the Dungeon of the Forgotten.

Konjuur hand-picked the troops who were left to guard the castle and himself as the new king. Most were his own men—those who had been with him since the failed *coup* in Dulcenou. He wanted to be sure there was no one loyal to Barbarot who would betray him. Now all he needed was to gain control of the rest of the kingdom. He already had the backing of the thousands who had marched with him against Baron Marbray; what he lacked was the support of the other aristocrats of Rootan. He needed their support—and their men.

Konjuur sent loyal knights to each township where there was an influential duke, earl or baron. There, the messengers were told to make whatever promises were needed to get the aristocrat to back the new king. But the knights were also told something else.

"Once you have the support and promises of loyalty from them and we have defeated Barbarot and his returning army," said Konjuur, "I will give each of you knights the lands and wealth of those same aristocrats. You will replace them as my closest allies in the kingdom, and they with their families will be put into my dungeons."

But not even that promise was kept. Soon, the purges began. *Anyone* who disagreed with Konjuur was labeled a traitor to the kingdom of Rootan. Notables who resisted were accused of plotting against the new king. These charges were made by the very knights sent to "befriend" them. After the charges were filed, the aristocrat was brought before the high court at Claustrus castle. There, the case was prosecuted, judgement made, and sentence passed—all by the same man: Konjuur. With mounds of faked evidence, the dukes, earls and barons were arrested, tried and convicted, and it all happened within weeks.

That left only the well-educated who were not aristocrats. They were the next biggest threat, and Konjuur knew it. He quickly issued an order to close the Knight's Observatory and followed this with orders forbidding any schooling of children after the age of twelve.

And then there was his last decree.

"Here ye! Here ye!" yelled the town crier as he made his way through the village streets.

He reached the town square and unrolled the parchment before reading the proclamation.

> "By order of the new king of Rootan, King Konjuur
>
> It is hereby ordered that all men and women having graduated from one of the kingdom's colleges must attend a meeting of the brightest minds of the land.
>
> The King wishes … commands … that each such person attend the meeting to help the king write a new constitution for the kingdom. These people will help forge a new beginning for Rootan – one based in justice and freedom for all.
>
> Claustrus Castle, tomorrow night, at dusk. Any graduate not joining the group risks having his family brought before the king's high court.
>
> Your humble servant,
>
> King Konjuur

On the surface, this looked like a chance of a lifetime. The opportunity to help mold the new order of the kingdom— something anyone within the land would relish.

Aunt Cleora happened past the posting as she walked to her store. She read the notice carefully and then reread it. Later in the afternoon, she arrived back at her brother's estate. She entered carrying one of the postings she'd ripped down from its display.

"What do you think of this?" she asked, thrusting the page in front of her brother, who was sitting quietly in his chair reading.

Sojourn took the parchment and unrolled it. He scanned its short message and shook his head.

"This isn't good. Where did you find this?" he asked, handing it to Montoi who was seated next to him.

"They are posted everywhere in town. They're making a point to be sure all educated people attend. Do you really think he cares what we have to say?"

"No, I'm sure he doesn't intend to sit and listen to a bunch of malcontents whine about what's wrong with the kingdom," said Montoi, handing the page back to Aunt Cleora.

"I agree," said Sojourn. "No, I fear something worse is going on here."

"Well, the king has ordered us to attend, so I guess we must. There isn't a way out," said Aunt Cleora.

"What's going on?" It was Marbray who had awoken from his nap. He looked weary, but the glow of life was still burning brightly.

Aunt Cleora handed him the same paper she had read to Sojourn. The baron took out his spectacles and began reading it. After he finished, he looked over the tops of them with a decidedly dour expression.

"Is this what I think it is?" Marbray asked.

Sojourn nodded his head. "It is, I'm afraid. However, it may not be as bleak as we all think. If we choose to go, we will suffer the same fate as all the others. Cleora, we will likely end up back where you found yourself not long ago."

"No!" she exclaimed. "I will die a thousand deaths before I go back there!"

"And if we don't go?" asked Montoi.

"They'll come for us," said Marbray.

"He's right," added Sojourn. "We have to go underground."

"Where?" asked Marbray.

"I'll get in touch with my old friend, Sage. He knows of a safe house we may be able to use," said Sojourn. "I'm sure he will be using it as well, if I know him."

Sojourn went to the back room where he kept his cistern. There, he went to the white, stone pedestal with the huge basin on top and put his hand on the smooth rim. He began tracing the edge in a clockwise motion, going around the basin precisely twice, then reversing the motion and going the other way once more. The clear, jelly-like liquid in the bowl vibrated, then swirled and finally steamed—a hot vapor wafting into the air before vanishing. When the liquid became still and clear as glass, Sojourn expected to see his friend. However, as he stared down, there was no wrinkled, goateed face reflecting in the still waters.

"He must not be home," said Sojourn. "We'll have to try later."

They tried later but were still unable to reach Sojourn's old friend. Aunt Cleora could tell her brother was getting worried. He paced the hallway and clenched his hands behind his back.

"He's probably just gone into town on errands," she said trying to comfort him.

Twice more they tried calling but still couldn't reach Sage.

"I'm going over there," said Sojourn, getting his things together. "I feel something isn't right."

"I'm going too," replied Aunt Cleora.

Montoi and Marbray had just entered the room when they saw the brother and sister packing their things to leave.

"Where are you two going?" asked the baron.

Aunt Cleora looked up after tying her bag. "Sojourn hasn't reached Sage, and he's worried about him. We're going there to see if he's in trouble."

"And you didn't ask us to come along?" Montoi asked.

"No, it isn't that. It's just that …" Sojourn began before being interrupted.

"… that what?" joined the baron. "I'll get my things. We're in this together if you hadn't noticed, my friend."

The trip was short, but to Sojourn it felt like hours. He dreaded what he'd find at his friend's estate. Unlike his normally optimistic self, Sojourn's demeanor was gloomy and withdrawn.

The volarequi landed in Sage's nicely manicured grounds a few miles from Sojourn's manor. And although Aunt Cleora had never been there before, she sensed something odd and out of place. With such a large estate, she expected it to be teaming with servants and attendants; however, there was no one around. It was a ghost town with only the wind making noises as it blew through the rafters of the stables.

"Is it usually this quiet?" she asked Sojourn.

"No," he said brusquely.

He kept walking, stepping on each of the large, flat stones that made-up the walkway to the front door. Reaching the arched doorways that framed the entrance, Sojourn took one of the black, iron knockers and banged it smartly against the metal door plate.

He waited. But there was no reply. Once again, he knocked on the door—this time with a sense of urgency. Still nothing.

"We have to find a way in or break the door down," said Sojourn, anxiously.

"I don't understand why you're so upset that your friend is not in, Sojourn. I mean, people go out all the time," said Montoi. "Perhaps he's on a holiday someplace and forgot to tell you,"

"You don't understand, Montoi. You see—Sage is an invalid. He can't go anywhere easily except around his estate. It's too painful for him to move too far or for any period of time. He's lived here at the manor for over eighty-five years, and I don't think he's left but for his mother's funeral."

Each of them sets out to find a way into the house, splitting up with Sojourn and Aunt Cleora going toward the west wing, while Montoi and Marbray went to the east side. The home was large and made of gray stone with heavy thatch for a roof. An orchard of orangarie trees filled the back acreage, and where there had once been farmland, the old knight had allowed the forest to reclaim it. Too old and infirmed to manage it on his own after his battle wound, Sage felt returning it to Mother Nature was the right thing to do.

"Sojourn, come quickly!" shouted Aunt Cleora, her shrill voice coming from just inside the perimeter of the orchard.

Sojourn ran to where he had heard her cry and found her kneeling over the crumpled body of Sage. He didn't have any legs, and there was no other visible means for him to get outside and onto the grounds where he lay.

"Is he breathing?" Sojourn asked.

 I think so, but just barely. Let's get him back inside," his sister answered.

Montoi and Marbray helped them carry the old man's limp body into the manor house and laid him on a long bench just inside the rear, courtyard door. There they made him as comfortable as they could.

"What happened?" Sojourn asked, seeing his friend's eyes flutter open. "How did you get to the old orchard behind the manor?"

Sage struggled to answer. "Don't worry, my friend," he said. "I'm not ready to leave this world quite yet. There is much to do and very little time."

"How so?" asked Aunt Cleora, giving Sage a sip of water.

"The throne is in chaos. There is one who is trying to take it from the Evil One," said Sage.

"We know," said Sojourn. "But what happened to you?"

"Konjuur's men came to my manor demanding that I attend a meeting he was holding at the castle. I told them to look at me." Sage's green eyes peered down at his missing limbs. "But they only spat at me. They said they didn't care if I was an invalid. They said that Konjuur had commanded that all with education attend a meeting at his castle. There were no exceptions allowed. When I continued to protest, they picked me up from my chair, took me back, and threw me into the courtyard."

"What happened to your staff?" asked Leedsom.

"They were all rounded up and taken as prisoners. I presume they were brought to the castle, but I don't know."

"We are all in danger now," said Marbray. "If we don't go to this farce of a meeting tonight, they will come looking for us."

"We are not safe here, and we are not safe at any of our homes," said Sage.

"Where do we go, then?" asked Aunt Cleora.

Montoi and Marbray looked at Sojourn, but he, in turn, only looked at Sage for an answer.

"I do know of a place," Sage began, "but we must travel from here. Do you have a strong volarequez that will take me as a passenger?"

"We will make it work," said Sojourn, "even if I have to carry you myself."

***

At that moment, Konjuur was busy consolidating his power. He knew he had little time as well—the real King of Rootan would soon find out what he had done in usurping his kingdom. But he had planted people throughout the land ready to warn him of Barbarot's return. Konjuur knew it wasn't a matter of "if" the Rootanian army returned, but rather, "when."

Yet, just as Marbray had suspected, Konjuur already had a plan, and he was working hard on putting it in place. He just hoped he would have enough time to finish it before the army returned. He was close to setting his trap; he only needed a few more days. Then, it would be ready.

*****

CH 41 - Twenty-six

"Is this the only way?" asked Fermat.

"I don't see any other," answered Oliver. "We have to keep going down this corridor until we find something."

"But we haven't found the Darkness yet," said Fermat, worriedly.

"I think that's what we just went through. You see, I think the Darkness referred to Ignorance, not the absence of light. What it meant was the absence of understanding—it's trying to show us Enlightenment. Once we entered the Corridor of Knowledge, I think we left the third and are now trying to find the fourth clue."

"Twenty-six?" asked Fermat.

"Yeah, I think that's right," replied Oliver.

The ice hallway quickly became its own maze. The cave split-off every hundred feet, making it impossible for them to retrace their steps back. At each junction, there were a series of blue and red iridescent rocks—one color on one side of the path and the other on the opposite side. Oliver always chose the blue ones and followed the path that way. When questioned by Fermat as to why he chose the blue ones, Oliver only said, "I dunno … I just like blue better, I guess."

As they walked, the temperature began to rise, yet the ice did not melt. No longer did they see their breaths in the air or feel the stinging cold that burrowed through their heavy jackets, making their bones ache. Even the walls of ice had turned from cyan blue to white and now to rose. Eventually, the corridors were lined with vibrant colors from vermillion to cinnamon.

At the end of the maze, they entered a large room lit with hundreds of blue lights. Inside they felt the floor vibrating, pulsing with a rhythmic beat that kept them off-balance. But as they looked up, to their astonishment, they saw no ceiling—yet, there was also no sky either. It was an infinite whiteness above, as if the top of the room were so high, they couldn't see it. Indeed, they felt small—tiny—by comparison. Yet, there was a strange comfort of somehow feeling a little closer to home. Ahead of them was a massive, white wall. It was wavy, and on it was a series of coiled crystals arranged in columns as if glued there by a mysterious hand.

Fermat placed his hand on one of the crystals, and it sparked to life, glowing brilliantly. A bright red, it soon turned fuchsia and then a faint pink before fading entirely. Fermat touched it again, and again it turned the same series of colors before returning back to white.

"What does that mean?" asked Fermat.

"I don't really know."

Oliver came to look at the curious crystals and put his hand on another one. Oddly, it was warm to the touch. He began putting his hands all over the wall to see if any of the others changed too, and in fact, they did. All transformed from a bright red to a pale pink before reverting back to white.

When Oliver had finished with the wall, he stood back. The crystals were arranged in rows and columns: five-by-five.

"Twenty-five," said Fermat.

"Twenty-five what?" asked Oliver.

"Twenty-five crystals. Exactly that."

"There's one missing," said Oliver, frowning. "So where is the twenty-*sixth* one?"

"It must be here. We just have to figure out how to find it."

Oliver and Fermat looked all over the wall for another crystal, another bump, another crevice, another something. But there didn't seem to be anything unusual.

"Now what?" asked Fermat.

"What if the reddish colors told us where the last one was?"

"What do you mean?"

"What did the Rebus ask us? Something about being between a square and a cube?" Oliver asked. He thought a moment, and then said, "The primes were three and five with the cube of one and the square of the other. We were to find the number in the middle. What about the middle of three and five?"

"Four."

"Of course, it's four."

"But how does that help?" asked Fermat. "We have twenty-five crystals and we need one more!"

"What if we press four crystals at a time? We have two hands each—we should be able to do that, right?"

Oliver and Fermat positioned themselves next to the wall and put their hands up, palms out, toward the rows and columns.

"When I say now, put each hand on a crystal," said Oliver. "Now."

Together, they placed their hands on four crystals. This time, they stayed bright red, not changing back to white.

"Good. Now, let's do it again."

They repeated this five more times until all but one of the crystals was a brilliant red.

"Now what?"

"That's your one crystal," said Oliver, pointing to the remaining white one.

"But that's twenty-five?" asked Fermat.

"Not now. Now, it's just the missing one we needed. Go ahead and put your hand on it."

Fermat put his hand on it. Nothing happened.

"Huh? Maybe this doesn't work this way," Fermat said.

"Let's both put our hands on it," said Oliver.

Indeed, when they put four hands on it, it too turned bright red, but then, just as suddenly, the entire wall changed from red to the brilliant blue of the lights they'd seen in the ice hallway.

"There! We did it!" exclaimed, Fermat. But as soon as he'd spoken, the wall went white once more before two crystals blinked back on—a very deep purple.

"I don't understand," said Fermat. "I just won't let us get past this."

"Remember what the Rebus said after I got that question right. He said something very odd," said Oliver.

"I don't remember anything."

"I think he said, *'y primo y primo'*," recounted Oliver, "which means something like 'and prime and prime.'"

"I still don't get it," said Fermat, increasingly frustrated and tired of playing the game.

"Primes can't be divided by any other whole number except themselves and one, right?"

"Yeah."

"Then prime and prime would refer to two *more* prime numbers after we'd already talked about twenty-six being the answer to the riddle."

Fermat nodded.

"So, I'm thinking that what the Rebus meant was the prime factors of twenty-six."

"Two and thirteen?"

"Very good," said Oliver.

Oliver looked back to the crystal wall. Sure enough, the two crystals that had turned purple were the second and thirteenth. He placed his hand on one while Fermat put his on the other; they began blinking on and off. Faster and faster they blinked, until the wall seemed to strobe with their light.

Then, the wall suddenly moved, splitting into two sections that parted precisely down the middle. Once the opening was revealed, the wall of crystals began melting in a cascade of blue and red colors that flowed onto the floor and pooled around their feet.

"Quick, Fermat. We must move inside before our feet get frozen to the bottom of this cave."

The duo leapt over the top of the colored ice flow as fast as they could before it wrapped itself around their boots and cemented their feet forever to the cave floor.

Clearing the flowing ice, they landed on the other side of the opening.

"Look!" said Oliver, pointing. "Up there on that ice shelf!"

Indeed, on a ledge above them was a large, egg-shaped crystal. It was zerobin's-egg blue and perfectly shaped. It was precisely the size and shape of the other eggs Oliver had found with the stone inside.

"It's exactly what I thought I'd find," said Oliver, smiling. "That's it! It's right there!"

"But it's an egg. What do you want with that?"

"It's not *just* an egg—believe me!" Oliver replied. "It's what's in the egg that's important. All we have to do is figure out how to crack it open. The stone is inside!"

"How hard can it be to crack an egg?" asked Fermat.

Oliver rolled his eyes. "You have no idea. Now, help me up to that shelf."

Fermat helped Oliver onto his shoulders and pushed him up toward the egg.

"Wait!" cried Fermat, stopping before extending Oliver all the way up.

"What's wrong?" asked Oliver. "What is it?"

"This seems too easy now, doesn't it?" asked Fermat. "I mean, based on everything else we've been through to get here?"

At the same time, Oliver's arms stretched out and his hands closed around the magnificent, ice egg that was resting, undisturbed, on the mantel. But it was the next few moments that happened so quickly, they only became a blur.

As soon as Oliver touched it, the egg began spinning violently. Faster and faster, it rotated, burning into the skin of his palms. He held on as tightly as he could even though the odd treasure did not slow.

"I've … I've got it!" Oliver cried out. "I'm trying to … to hang on!"

But then, the egg began moving up, floating above the mantel piece and drilling into the vaulted ice ceiling above.

"What's happening? Where's it taking you?" shouted Fermat.

"Grab my boots," said Oliver, "and hang on to me. Don't let go!"

All Fermat could do was twist Oliver's satchel around his friends boots and then hang onto it, getting lifted up as the egg rose higher into the cave ceiling. Through the layers of ice, rock and snow above, the orb drilled its way toward the surface taking Oliver and Fermat with it.

"What's happening?" screamed Fermat, clinging to Oliver's bag with all his might.

"Just hang on! It's taking us for a ride," said Oliver.

Fermat looked down. He was afraid of heights, and he wasn't sure which was spinning faster—the orb or his aching head.

*****

CH 42 - Knotsbow

Barbarot pushed onward through the thick jungles of Vinedria. The hurricane had destroyed much of his troops and machines, but not all. He believed he still had enough to conquer the small, but well-fortified, castle, and if he didn't, he thought he alone could conjure the power to do it himself.

The capital, Knotsbow, lay on the coast along the Sea of Crisium. It was well protected by land, sitting on the cliffs of an island, just off the shoreline. The rocks below were jagged, and the sea, with its violent waves crashing all around them, created swirling eddies and riptides that doomed anyone trying to cross them.

There was no harbor that made staging an attack from the sea any easier. The cliff walls rose quickly from the seabed, and the king's castle sat high on top of the precipice. Scaling the walls was nearly impossible, as the numerous turrets surrounding the perimeter were packed with archers ready to let their arrows, rocks, and hot tar loose on anyone near the base of the castle walls.

Barbarot stood on the shore across from the island castle, his boots sinking slowly into the soft, white sand beneath them. He gazed out over the strait of water that separated him from his next conquest. He had taken most of the kingdom's villages during his campaign through the jungle; now, there was just one left—the capital. Although he had lost most of his men in the hurricane and in skirmishes along the way, Barbarot still had an army many times the size of Vinedria's—something its king, Viridius, was well aware of.

As for Viridius, he had never had to fight a war on his soil before, and he was woefully unprepared for it. He still hoped his castle was unassailable. No one had ever captured the capital, and Viridius prayed his castle, perched atop this impregnable fortification, could survive the attack.

"Gather your men," said Barbarot to his commander. "We'll have to act quickly. There can be no questioning of my orders ... you must just do as I say!"

It took two days, but Commander Sterinis finally had everything ready.

"The men have completed their work, Your Royal Highness. They have taken the Tantus leaves and Navi branches to the top of the cliffs overlooking the island where the castle is."

"How many sets do you have ready?" asked Barbarot.

"They have cut enough to make three thousand, sire."

"Good. Have them assembled at once. If the winds are right tomorrow, we will begin our charge."

The next morning, the winds picked up briskly, blowing out to sea and causing the flags over his tents to snap sharply in response.

"The gusts are strong, sire. Do you wish to release the flyers?" asked the commander.

Barbarot nodded. "Yes, now is the time."

With the sound of the king's mighty conch shell, the men on top of the cliff readied for their flights. Each of them had lashed together the huge Tantus leaves to a wooden frame made from the light, buoyant bows of the Navi tree. These self-made kites were over twelve feet across and strapped onto each man by others who considered themselves lucky for not having been chosen for this part of the mission.

Across the full length of the mainland cliff stood his legion of men, wings attached, and long knives tucked into their britches. They had no other weapons, as their weight would make it impossible to cross the expansive water to the castle fortress. Nervously, they waited for the king's final command.

"Final instructions ..." said a commander to the group poised to take off. "You will fly to the castle and drop down into the city square or wherever you land. You must be quiet and lethal. You have only one hour to secure the castle and lower the draw bridge to the mainland. Our ground assault begins as soon as the bridge is down." He paused and added, "And if you refuse to launch, we have archers stationed behind you ... they will shoot you without hesitation. Any questions? ... I thought not."

The trumpeter readied his conch for the final call. Barbarot looked on at the tall fluttering flags, waiting for the right moment to launch his men. The breeze stiffened, and he watched as the flags over his tent straightened and began whipping and cracking as the tempest mounted.

Barbarot nodded and said simply, "Launch them. Launch them all."

The conch was blown, its tone low and haunting. The sound echoed along the cliffs and when its voice reached the peak where the flyers had assembled, the men began leaping out over the jagged rocks. The winds caught the underbelly of their wings and lifted most of them upward, above where they had jumped and high into the air. But some were unable to catch the wind at the right time, and they fell—ending up in the roiling waves below. Others caught the breeze but couldn't master the steering quickly enough to stay aloft. And then there were the few, who, despite knowing that they might be killed if they didn't jump from the edge, couldn't bring themselves to do it. Their fate was swift and sure.

Yet, for those who managed to get airborne, they flew high and far, buffeted by the air and cooled by the light rains that began drizzling down on them as they flew. The rain landed on their wings, making them heavier, and some began to sink. These men crashed into the cliffs of the fortress island where they met their fate. For those who were able to stay aloft, they steered their kites flawlessly and silently, circling the fortress from above and then diving quickly down into the center so they wouldn't be seen by the archers in the turrets.

It was early in the morning, and people were not yet outside in the streets on the castle grounds. It was also during the time of a changing of the guards along the castle walls, so little attention was paid to the black specks in the sky floating down into the town square and around in the corners of the grounds.

Crashing or landing, either way, the warriors hit the ground and quickly unstrapped themselves from their flying contraptions. Stealthily, they made their way toward the central guard quarters where all the inactive troops were stationed.

Tujo, one of Barbarot's lead commandos, crouched inside a doorway before dashing forward to the next, moving closer to his target—the large, wooden guard barracks. His bag was heavier than any of the other soldiers, and he was lucky he made it into the castle alive. His bag was packed with black powder—enough for just one thing.

Once he reached the side of the barracks, Tujo placed the entire bag inside the doorway and unrolled a long fuse. Then, using his ferro bar and flint, he struck a spark. It smoldered for a second before igniting the fuse. Bursting into flame, the fuse burned with sprinkles of light cascading from it as it raced toward the bag.

Tujo ran.

Within seconds, smoke began pouring out of the doorway of the barracks before …

Kaboom!

The explosion rocked the castle. Soon, soldiers came running out of their barracks, coughing and wheezing from the thick roil of black smoke. Two other men of Tujo's group waited outside and cut each man down as he came out. However, soon, others came out swinging swords of their own. Tujo whistled for his men to fall back, and they retreated, jumping over a fence that barricaded the guards' quarters from the rest of the town.

Meanwhile, another small group of commandos stood by the turnbuckles and hoists required to open and close the drawbridge. Tightly wrapped around the turnbuckles were coarse, hemp ropes. Once the leader of that small band saw the smoke pouring over the castle, he took his knife and began slicing through one of the ropes. It didn't take long before the other ropes began to give way, and when the first rope snapped, the drawbridge outside came crashing down, smashing against the stone wall of the castle. Now, the castle island was no longer separated from the mainland. Now, it was open and vulnerable to the invading army waiting just on the other side.

As the rainy fog worsened, conditions for the assault improved. The commandos went from turret to turret, taking out the sentries rapidly and without commotion. Most of the Vinedrian army was redirected to put out the fire at the guard barracks and, was distracted from the real threat outside.

As the commandos inside fought their way toward the main gate, the army was streaming across the drawbridge toward the entrance to the castle. According to the plan, the commandos who flew into the castle near the barracks were to meet up with those at the entrance where they could fight any other forces protecting the massive, wooden doors.

The Vinedrian king triggered the alarm, and the drums began beating fiercely to sound the distress signal to his troops. However, it was too late. They were busy putting out fires and trying to regain control of the front entrance. The chaos created only more chaos, and they had little chance to regroup.

Barbarot's men continued to pour across the drawbridge and the waterway. By this time, Tujo and his men had opened the thick, metal doors in front of the castle, removing the last barrier to the inside.

Converging on the gates in front of the inner palace, Barbarot's men began their fight. They swung their swords furiously, as each side struck at the other. Tujo, having only a knife, fought off attackers until he could find an abandoned sword on the ground. Picking up the bloodied blade, he carried on the fight, swinging it relentlessly trying to make headway inside the palace grounds. But just as he got closer to the gates, he felt a sharp sting in the back of his leg, and he knew he'd been hit. He clutched his leg as it began buckling under him, then he pulled away his hand and saw the bright crimson smear that he hoped was only a glancing blow. Not to be stopped, Tujo got up and continued the fighting, even though he could still feel the pain getting worse.

By then, Barbarot's infantry was streaming into the castle and then into the king's palace. The throne room was not hard to find, and when they burst through the unguarded doors, they found King Viridius and his queen waiting for them.

Within the hour, Barbarot had flown in on his mighty volarequez to survey the spoils of war and direct the final capture of the remaining holdouts. He walked into the palace and began licking his lips—it was magnificent, and now it was his.

The hallways were lined with gilded, gold leaf that adorned the thick moldings and high, coffered ceilings from which monstrous crystal chandeliers hung carrying the weight of hundreds of white candles. The tapestries were exquisite in detail, showing the great battles of the royal family through the ages. Some as large as a royal ballroom, decorated the long, vast, maze of hallways. And the artwork was of a quality, Barbarot had never seen— showing the fine lacework in the kings' and queens' portraits as well as the minute stitchwork embroidered within each garment. Even the crystal glass and china were extraordinary. Rare ruby-colored goblets, gold-rimmed china and gem-encrusted silver adorned the long and elegant dining table. On many shelves were exotic, miniature scenes of the villages and castles of the kingdom, all from hand-blown glass.

The Rootanian king moved swiftly with a few attendants down the corridor to the royal chamber. There he found the royal couple sitting quietly and bravely—not on their thrones but in the chairs set aside for the court jesters.

"I see you've found you're proper places," said Barbarot smugly. "Especially, seeing that your kingdom is now mine," he added.

"For now," replied the king. There was an impassive expression on his face.

"Take him and his lovely bride away," barked Barbarot.

"What do you wish done with them?" asked Commander Sterinis.

Barbarot looked into the eyes of Viridius and saw a proud man, a man of honor and integrity, and above all, bravery. He walked to the king, took out his knife and put it against Viridius' throat, piercing it enough to draw a small dot of blood. The king did not flinch. He sat, looking forward as if nothing had happened, and as if nothing could happen that he couldn't handle.

"This is a strong man," said Barbarot. "Like the other one, I admire him for his valor," said Barbarot. "Put the queen and him in the prison. We may have use for them later."

Jerked up from their kneeling positions, the two were dragged away through the rounded-off entrance. Barbarot pulled his black, silver-lined cape away from his side, sitting down on the king's throne. He smiled.

"One kingdom closer," he said, very satisfied with himself. "Soon, I shall be ruler of all, and then what will the empress do!"

*****

CH 43 – The Road Home

Upward they rocketed, grinding through the layers of rock and ice above. The egg glowed red, and steam hissed as the melting ice quenched the thirst of the molten fire.

"Hang on!" yelled Oliver, barely audible above the roar of the egg breaking through the last few hundred feet.

The ice on the surface fractured as the duo shot up through the ground and into the frigid air. Oliver and Fermat let go as soon as they realized they were no longer trapped below ground, but their landing was anything but soft and comforting. They hit an ice patch instead of a fluffy snowbank, sending shockwaves through their bodies and skulls. Oliver took a mouthful of snow and ice, and Fermat lost his grip on the satchel, tumbling over and over until he landed a few yards away.

"Where is it?" asked Fermat, getting up and brushing himself off. "Where's the egg?"

"It must have landed here someplace," Oliver said, starting to look around for it.

Fermat joined him in the search, and it didn't take long before they found it buried deep within another snowbank, still glowing and warm to the touch. The wide tunnel it bored into the bank was easy to spot.

"What are we supposed to do with it now?" Fermat asked. "I thought all we had to do was answer a few questions, go into the cave, find the treasure and leave. I didn't sign up for all this other stuff!"

"That's the way it is sometimes, Fermat. If it were easy, everyone could do it. In this case, it was so hard, no one had been able to do it … or at least not yet."

Then, Fermat turned to Oliver looking puzzled.

"What is it?" Oliver asked.

"We never made it to the last question: tomorrow. Is there another clue we have to find?"

Oliver smiled. "Fermat, my friend. Don't you remember? Tomorrow never comes."

"Well, let's get the stone out of it and get home—by tomorrow!" said Fermat.

Oliver could tell Fermat was getting tired. "Patience. We don't have what we need to get the stone out of this thing. The egg doesn't just crack open like a bird egg does. It's much harder. We don't have time to do it here anyway. We have to get this thing back to the castle before the deadline."

Oliver looked around. "I think the trail that led up to the cave is just down from where we are, don't you?"

Fermat opened his mouth, but before he could say anything, Oliver was halfway down the snowy trail with the egg stuffed under his arm.

"Tristyx! Tristyx!" shouted Oliver. "Here boy!"

"Here boy? Do you really think he'll come to you like a regular dog?" said Fermat, cynically.

Woof, woof.

The sound was not far away, and it was music to their ears.

"Well, I guess you were right about that, anyway," said Fermat, both surprised and amused.

Around the corner of some boulders came Tristyx, his three heads flying every which way and his three tongues outstretched and panting hard. Right behind him was his new companion, Sedah. Tristyx stopped abruptly in front of Oliver, and Sedah almost ran into the back of him, skidding with her hind legs just short of Tristyx's rear end.

"Good job!" said Oliver, patting both wolves on their backs and then rubbing their furry necks with both his hands as they slobbered their glee all over him.

320

"Oliver?"

"Yeah?"

"Where's the third wolf? We had three, remember? He's not attached to our sled anymore," said Fermat.

Fermat was right. There had been three, and now there were two.

"I don't know, Fermat. It's strange. We need to watch our backs. But we also need to get back to the start-finish line before time expires."

Oliver loaded the egg in the back of the second sled with what was left of the supplies and then climbed on board. Fermat was right behind and barely made it back on when Oliver yelled "Mush!"

The way going back was easier than it was coming, as most of the trail was downhill instead of uphill. The narrow gorge gave way to wide-open, snow fields, and the steepness of the mountains smoothed out to mere rolling hills. It was not difficult for the two cerberians to pull the relatively light weight of Oliver, Fermat and the few supplies they had left.

They had been out in the elements for two days and had only one left to make it back to Ralop. Oliver was not worried. The trip to Mt. Erebus had been filled with detours and treachery. *The way back should be straightforward and uneventful,* he thought.

The day went by quickly, and they made good time. Both Tristyx and Sedah had taken a good rest the night before when Oliver and Fermat were down in the cave searching for the stone. Their energy was high and so were their spirits. Never before had they been treated so well by their masters. Typically, they were whipped and kicked for not doing exactly what they were told or misunderstanding confusing commands of their owners. Now, their panting tongues showed their content, even if they had to push hard to keep Oliver happy. The weather was also in their favor. With the skies clear and rays from the twin suns glittering off the snow, all seemed to be going their way.

Fermat fell asleep in the back of the sled as Oliver pushed on. The jarring of the sled's movements this way and that did little to upset him or jar him out of his slumber. As for Oliver, the cold stinging of the wind on his face kept him awake, even though he would have wished Fermat to wake up long enough to relieve him. Shadows from the lissome pines were getting longer and casting themselves across the trail as the sled sped onward.

The early warmth of the day eventually cooled, and Fermat finally woke up shivering. He had taken off his scarf and hat, enjoying the suns' warmth on his exposed face and neck; however, now that it was colder, he put them back on.

"'Bout time you woke up," said Oliver, glancing at Fermat. "When are you going to take over from me, *eh?*"

"Alright, alright ..." said Fermat grudgingly, "... but, I think we should stop and rest the dogs first."

"I stopped less than an hour ago," said Oliver. "I really think we can go on for a while longer. I just need you to take over while I get some rest."

"No, I think we need to stop again. I can see Sedah panting pretty heavily, and I don't think it's good for her or Tristyx to be over worked. We may not make it back if they give out on us," said Fermat, more forcefully.

Oliver eased back on the reins and slowed the canines' torrid pace. They were approaching a thick, densely packed part of the woods where the underbrush had grown particularly heavy. The snow had begun to melt, and they could see bare patches of ground around them.

Oliver got off the sled and went to check on the cerberians while Fermat went back to the supply sled to get food for them. Oliver found the dogs panting a little harder than usual, and he thought, perhaps, his friend had been right for them to stop.

"Well, hello there Fermat! It's good to see you again. And who might your friend be here?"

The voice suddenly came out of the dense undergrowth nearby.

The man who came forward was big—over seven feet, perhaps eight—and to Oliver he looked like he was about three feet wide as well. A monster of a man, he had shaggy hair the color of burnt coffee and a heavy, scruffy beard that made him look even more menacing. He smiled, but there were few teeth to show for it—mainly broken remnants with an iron stud that was impaled into his tongue.

"Never you mind!" replied Fermat harshly, but seeming less surprised by the forbidding figure than Oliver.

"Oh, now. I thought we had a deal, you and me. Remember? You aren't acting too friendly for someone who promised to be partners in this thing," said the giant man.

Fermat said nothing. He looked down and shifted uncomfortably from one foot to another.

"So, what do you have for me there, buddy?" asked the big, hairy man, pointing a menacing finger at the sled and the bags that were strapped to it.

"Nothin'!" snapped Fermat.

"Nothin', huh? Well, let's just take a look and see what nothin' looks like, shall we?"

Oliver made a move but was cut off.

"I don't think that would be very wise, lad. I've killed men bigger than you with only two fingers of my right hand. I wouldn't have to use any more than three to snap your neck—otherwise, I'd be wastin' me energy. And the gods know that I'm gonna need every bit of it if I'm going to make it back to the castle with that stone of yours."

"Do you know this guy?" asked Oliver, staring at Fermat.

Fermat didn't answer Oliver, he didn't have to. Oliver already knew.

"And what did you do for me, Ivan? Tell me? If we were partners, then what did you do for me?"

Ivan smiled. "I didn't kill ya'," he answered, laughing.

"Well, I hate to disappoint you, but we didn't find anything, except for this stupid egg. You can have it if you want. We're just going back to see if the king will have a change of heart and let us live anyway."

The big man laughed, holding his belly as though he hadn't had a good one in a while. "That's rich, kid ... it really is! You really expect me to believe that? I don't think so. You're too smart for that. If you didn't have the stone, you'd be high-tailing it out of here to some other kingdom where de Riguere can't find you. Because you know if he doesn't find your body along the way or have proof that you were killed, he'll hunt you down. He has no mercy ... and you know that. There's no way he'll let you live if you don't have the stone. It just wouldn't look good, now would it. You and I both know you'd be dead within minutes after getting back to the castle."

"So, what's in it for you, then?" asked Oliver, understanding that the ruse was up.

The hairy man laughed at Oliver and then looked at Fermat. "He really doesn't know? You didn't tell him?" The man smiled. "So, he isn't your friend, then. You haven't cut him in on it."

Fermat shook his head slowly—sadly. Then, unexpectedly, he bolted—moving fast to get away from both Oliver and the giant man. But the mangy man only had to take a few steps before he had Fermat in his clutches and down in the snow. He struck him in the head and then took his enormous hand and grabbed him by the back of the coat, pulling him out of the snowpack. Raising his body above his head, he heaved him into the air. Fermat's arms and legs flapped wildly as if he were trying to fly, before glancing off the side of a large rock and rolling to the ground. His body broken; he didn't move.

Turning toward Oliver, the burly man walked to the sled and started ripping open the bags, pulling everything out and throwing things to the side. The cerberian dogs watched but did not move—either too afraid or too tired to come to their masters' aid.

However, Oliver was neither.

He waited until the man's head was buried inside one of the bags before he pounced, jumping onto the man's back and punching him about the head and neck. Such a beating would normally have fallen a man, even as big as this. But this seemed to be no ordinary man.

The man flipped Oliver off easily, like a purgelephant swatting away a pesky fly. Then, using the same grip he'd used on Fermat, he picked Oliver up and hurled him against the same set of rocks. However, Oliver spun in midair, missing the rocks and landing lightly in a snowbank. Still, he lay there, faking death but watching the man as he continued to rip through the sacks on the sled.

Finally, the giant pulled out the crystal egg, holding it in his hand and looking at it curiously. "This stupid egg Fermat told me about," he muttered to himself.

He held it up to the light and saw the suns' rays passing through it, splitting into reds, oranges, yellows, greens, blues and violets, all of which spread across the white blanket of snow.

But his interest was interrupted, as a deep growl and then a roar bellowed nearby him. As the man turned to look, an enormous white blur flew through the air, teeth bared and claws out. It hit its target with full force, knocking the man to the ground and sending the egg flying through the air.

"Tristyx!" yelled Oliver, getting up, still holding his shoulder.

Tristyx hit the man squarely in the chest, doubling him over before he landed in the snow. Although stunned, he threw his elbow at the wolf, which had gnawed through its restraints and was now free to circle the big man.

Oliver ran toward the man, distracting him, while Tristyx struck again—this time, sinking the jaws of two of its heads into the man's legs and swinging him from side to side. The man tried to pound on Tristyx's third head, but it refused to let go.

"Get it off of me!" he screamed.

Writhing in pain, he began punching the creature as it continued to maul him.

"I said, let go of me!"

But the more he fought, the more it only angered the wolf which bit even deeper into his leg.

Oliver's reached for a large rock beside him and hurled it at the man, striking him dead-center in the forehead. But he only shook his head and shrugged it off as if it only made him angrier.

"Sedah ... attack!" It was a familiar voice, and it came from behind Oliver.

Leaping over Oliver, Sedah tore loose from her restraint and lunged at the man's arm with one of her heads. Together, Sedah and Tristyx dragged the man out into the woods. Oliver could hear the man's screams fade into the distance and then stop altogether.

Oliver ran to his friend who was badly hurt.

"Hey, thanks, buddy. I wasn't sure whose side you were on for a while there." Then, he paused. "You *are* on my side, aren't you?"

Fermat returned the smile and said weakly, "Of course, Oliver. After all we've been through, what other side could I be on?"

"Can you help me collect the leads?" asked Oliver.

Fermat rubbed his head and neck but nodded. "Yeah, it's just that I can see two of you instead of one. Do you have a twin?" He smiled and winked.

"Close enough, my friend."

Together, they whistled for the wolves, and both came bounding through the snowy forest to be with their masters. Oliver attached them back to the sled and got Fermat comfortable in the second, trailing sled.

"We don't have any time to lose," Oliver said to Fermat. "We have to hurry to get back to the castle."

With Fermat hurt, Oliver cracked the whip, and the two canines pulled back onto the trail.

Oliver still didn't know the whole story between Fermat and the shaggy giant, but that would have to wait. At that moment, they needed to get going; time was running out before the end of the third day closed and the contest was officially over.

"Let's go! Mush!" shouted Oliver taking command as captain of the ship.

The two wolves and six heads did not let him down. They jumped with a start and powered by a renewed sense of energy and purpose. The cerberian dogs pushed on without any more coaxing, and the two friends found themselves sailing on a mast less ship across a sea of white hoping to cross the finish line in time.

In the back was the injured Fermat, sound asleep and bouncing up and down with every rut and hole in the icy trail. Daylight was fading, and they would have to slow significantly during the night if Titan didn't cooperate to give them a beacon of light and hope.

The sands in the hourglass were falling, draining the last few grains before the top half was emptied. When the first rays of Duex struck the start-finish line, the last would drop. Oliver only prayed, the nose of Tristyx would be over the line before that happened.

*****

Part III – The Unexpected Challenge

CH 44 - School Lessons

The flashbacks were happening more often, and it was getting harder for Donus to ignore them. The images he was seeing were fleeting and troubling.

He saw trees that shot long, pointed barbs at him; a girl with golden, blonde hair who looked fierce, like a knight; a silver cloud that, for some reason, seemed menacing and dangerous; and pieces of stone laying in a heap—all about the same size but different colors and shapes. He saw himself trying to pick them up and put them in certain places, but they refused to move. Whatever all this was, it didn't make it easy for Donus to sleep. In fact, he was sleeping less and less each night.

At the same time, he was growing closer to Parogild and his sister, Genona. Having no memory of his past, Donus clung to things that gave him a sense of family. Indeed, they had become the only family he knew.

The old shepherd's quarters, where Donus had taught lessons, was no longer needed for that. Instead, Parogild had a small school built next to it. Donus was a wonderful teacher—patient and caring. What he lacked in experience, he made up for in creativity. He used wonderful, creative stories to illustrate points even though he didn't know where they came from.

Once, a shepherd boy asked him what it was like to be in the army. He replied that he didn't know for sure, but that defending the kingdom was something very honorable.

"Soldiers are certainly proud to defend their kingdom," Donus had said. "They are also proud to defend their king and queen."

Then, he added, "But the hardest part of being a solider is the training. It is long and difficult. It prepares the soldier for anything that may come during battle, so he knows what to do when it happens. War and battle are terrible, but sometimes they are necessary. If you are defending your king and the kingdom, it is noble. If you are invading another country to conquer it, it is not."

Attending most of his sessions was Genona. She was his biggest fan, and she soaked up all that he could teach her. Although math was not her favorite, she tried hard. To her, it looked like he enjoyed the subject, and he seemed to like teaching it to her. But her favorite subject was literature. Her father had left them an entire room of books, most of which she had read. Often, she would make comments in the margins. Reading her little remarks and narratives, Donus felt he was reading her thoughts and her heart. The thoughts and emotions of the woman were laid out on those pages, and he relished being able to see inside her.

So, while he taught her math, she taught him much about literature and how to interpret it. He too relished in learning from her as much as she from him. They were two peas in a pod—two together in life.

Whaltooth, Blu-Ice and Sheepskin were regulars at the school and became faithful attendants to Donus. School always started in the late afternoon, after the shepherds had brought their flocks back to the manor grounds to be locked into their pens for the night. It made for a long day, but the they grew stronger, physically and mentally, as a result.

Blu-Ice got out paper and refilled each of the ink wells on the desks that Parogild had purchased for the school. He and Whaltooth cleaned the floors, sweeping the dirt that was tracked in from the previous day's session between the cracks in the floorboards. It was still cold outside, and the kettle-shaped, iron burner in the center of the school provided just enough heat to cut the chill of the air.

Parogild had also begun relying heavily on Donus to help him run the estate and assist with the business of raising the sheep and preparing them for the spring market. There was a genuine affection—almost brotherly—that had developed between them.

One day, Parogild came to Donus before he had started his lessons. He put his arm around him and drew him close.

"Well, when are you going to ask her?" Parogild said to Donus with a smile.

Donus looked puzzled, and replied, "Ask who, what?"

"Oh, come on! You know what I'm talking about ... my sister! She's very fond of you, you know."

Donus was uncomfortable. He'd not talked to Parogild, or anyone for that matter, about his feelings for Genona.

"I ... uh ... don't know what you're talking about," Donus said, looking down at the scroll he was planning to use for the day's lesson.

"I mean, you and Genona are very close. She likes you a lot, and I think you like her, don't you?"

"Yeah, of course I do," said Donus. "But there's just too much going on right now to think about it."

"What's going on right now? You're teaching at the school and you're helping me with the flocks. I know that takes a lot of your time, but not all of it," said Parogild. "Come on ... my sister *likes* you. I know she'd like to see you, well, on a regular basis."

"Did she tell you that?"

"Yes, but she told me not to tell you," Parogild said laughing. "So, like a good brother, I thought I'd tell you."

The mischievous grin gave him away; however, Donus knew he was only saying it to be a good brother, not a mean-spirited one.

Donus shook his head. "I don't know, Parogild. There's too much I don't know about myself ... that you don't know. Who knows—maybe I was a murderer--a cold-blooded killer or even worse!"

"What could be worse than that?" asked Parogild, still smiling.

"I don't know—but I'm sure there's something!" said Donus trying to remain serious.

"Somehow, I doubt that you were ever a cold-blooded killer. And even if you were, I'm sure you were pretty good at it," laughed Parogild.

"Very funny," said Donus, beginning to lighten up.

Just then, Genona entered the school. When she saw her brother talking to Donus, she gave him a dirty look.

"What are you doing here?" she asked him. "You never come around here. Wait ... are you and Benigno scheming about something? Something I should know about?"

Donus was still getting used to the name she had given him. He didn't have any other that he could recall, so it was good enough.

"If we were, we certainly wouldn't tell you, now would we, my dear," said Parogild taunting her.

Genona picked up a book and threw it at him playfully. Parogild ducked, and it hit Donus squarely in the jaw, knocking him off balance and onto the hardwood floor.

"Oh, Benigno. I didn't mean to hit you!" she cried, running to him.

"I'm fine, Genona. Really, it's nothing," said Donus. "For some reason, I seem to remember having gone through this same thing with my sister."

"You have a sister, then?" she asked, surprised.

Likewise, Donus seemed surprised at his revelation. "I ... think so."

"Yes, Benigno was just telling me about her, weren't you? I think you said something about her being your evil twin sister!"

"Oh, you're going to get it!" yelled Genona, picking up a piece of chalk and hurling at her brother. He ducked, and it broke against the wall behind him.

"That's the second time you've missed me, sis. You'd better practice a little more. Otherwise, I'll have to ban you from the army."

Genona started to run after her brother, but he ran out the door before she could get a hand on him.

"Sometimes he drives me nuts," she said.

"Yes, but you still love him ... a little anyway, right?"

"Of course, silly. But what's this really about ... a sister? You have a sister?" she asked.

"I don't know. I just can't remember ... like everything," he said out of frustration.

"It will come. It will come soon enough, trust me," she said. "So, what is the lesson today, headmaster?"

"That's master supreme, ruler of the universe, *and* headmaster to you, my lady," Donus said smiling.

She beamed back at him. The twinkle in her eye was all he needed to know that her brother was right about her. She was very special.

"But to answer your question, madam, I believe we shall ..." Donus stopped to think for a moment. Then, he too smiled mischievously and added, "... dissect a Holoditian frog."

"Ah! No! Yuck!" she cried. "You can't be serious?"

Donus winked at her. "No, I'm not. And my name is not Serious ... at least not that I know of!"

They both laughed until tears streamed down their faces and their bellies ached. But it was good. It was very good.

*****

CH 45 – Facing the Hangman

Oliver could see the glow of the first sun, Duex, wiping away the sleepiness of the dark night's sky. The chill and bleakness of the night would soon end, and the minutes were counting down until that sun would cut its rays across the plane of the horizon. When its rays struck the finish line, the challenge would be over. After that, even if Oliver and Fermat did bring back the stone for the king, it wouldn't matter; the king would likely claim they hadn't completed the challenge within the time allowed and, therefore, had failed.

"Mush! Mush!" Oliver cried out to his two canines that were pulling the sled for him. "Let's go!"

Both Sedah and Tristyx were working as hard as they could, panting and wheezing as they dragged their load through the ice and snow toward de Riguere and the king's castle. The cold mist from their breaths hung only momentarily in the air before briskly blowing back across the sled and disappearing into the inkiness of the forest behind them.

"Where are we?" came the weak and groggy voice of Fermat.

"Not sure, but I'd guess we are less than an hour outside of Icia and de Riguere Castle."

"We aren't going to make it, are we?" asked Fermat.

"Dunno. It's going to be close ... very close. I figure Duex will crack the horizon in about an hour, plus or minus a few minutes," replied Oliver, trying to be as encouraging as he could. "We still might make it."

"How do you recon that?"

"Just a wild guess, Fermat. That's all I can give ya'."

They pushed on with the wind blowing more fiercely against them and a light snow beginning to fall. Oliver had navigated all night by the stars and the helpful, reflecting light of Titan. But with the radiance of Duex, the way was made easier, and he could move faster without fear of running off the trail or off a cliff.

"Mush!" Oliver called again to his dog team.

The trees were flying past them as they slid downhill along the snowy path. Tristyx and Sedah were slipping and sliding as they found patches of ice under the thin coating of snow. But the pressure was mounting. Sweat began dripping from Oliver's brow, and he could feel his heart racing. He knew what they had to do—he just wasn't sure if his faithful leads had enough left in them to get it done.

"Mush, I said! Don't you understand '*mush*'!"

Oliver cracked his whip over the head of Sedah, catching the back of her ear. She yelped but kept on running.

"Sorry!" Oliver said apologetically.

Then, suddenly out of nowhere, two arrows split the air, inches from his head.

Ziiiiiiiiiiiiiiiiiiiiiiing! Ziiiiiiiiiiiiiiiiiiiiiiiiiiing!

"What's going on?" yelled Oliver, trying to control the wolves.

"It's the king's men!" said Fermat. "I've heard he sometimes gives orders to shoot anyone who tries to return to the castle to claim his freedom from the challenge. It's his way to make sure he doesn't lose a bet. The king can *never* lose."

"Mush! Come on! Mush!" Oliver yelled.

Now, the arrows were flying at them in thick sheets, and one struck Fermat in the side.

"*Ahhhh!*" he cried out. "They got me!"

"Hang on Fermat! We're going to get there. Now, I'm going to make sure of it!" said Oliver, gritting his teeth.

"Mush!" he yelled, continuing to crack his whip.

Oliver peered into the woods and saw figures of the king's men who were firing freely at them as they got closer to the castle. It wasn't much farther; yet, he knew the race now came down to him, the king's arrows and the first ray of light from Duex.

"Come on! You guys can't let me down now!"

They rounded a bend and up a small hill that led to a steep drop down into the town of Icia, just outside de Riguere Castle and the finish line.

Fermat began to moan. "Oliver … the arrow … it's hurting. It's hurting bad." Then he was quiet.

"Fermat?" Oliver called out. "Fermat are you still with me? You've got to stay with me ... you've got to hold on. We're almost there!"

They slid into the town before clouds began to thicken overhead and the snow came down in earnest. The orange glow from Duex started to appear as its light was just about to poke over the distant mountain tops.

The town was empty that early in the morning, and the sled moved through the main road that cut a swath through the center of town with relative ease. But the start-finish line still lay ahead, and Oliver was suddenly struck by a sickening feeling in his stomach as he watched the sun begin to rise.

He wasn't going to make it.

"Fermat! Wake up Fermat!" Oliver yelled. "We're not going to make it in time. We have to arm ourselves."

"What?" asked Fermat, only halfway conscious.

"Wake up! Arm yourself!"

But as the sled drew to the top of the hill and the finish line, he noticed something else too. Clouds laden with heavy snow were advancing in the opposite direction and were already dumping snow on the town.

"Come on!" shouted Oliver. But this time, he wasn't yelling at his cerberians—he was talking to the clouds.

If the clouds would just speed up, he thought, *they might just cover the first sun before it appears over the mountain top*. Then, he thought, technically, there would be no decisive moment when the race ended. *It just might buy me some more time.*

The sled flew past the castle walls and the guarded entrances on the way inside. Several guards had scrambled to cut them off but weren't fast enough to block the opening. By now, Duex was battling against the clouds, and it was another race that was too close to call.

It should be right there—by the castle bridge? thought Oliver, looking at where the finishing line was when they had started. But it was no longer there.

What? he thought. *Where is it?*

As they approached where the starting line had been, Oliver saw the faces of Gemma, Cori and Prima. They were huddled together to keep warm and were squinting into the eastern sky to catch a glimpse of anyone courageous or lucky enough to make it back alive. The one face missing from the group was that of his best friend, Nikko.

"Oliver!" It was the voice of Gemma. "Hurry, Oliver! The king moved the finish line back on you. You have another half-mile to go!"

He did not stop to rejoin his friends. Instead, he pressed on.

"Hurry, Oliver!" was the next thing he heard. It was the piercing scream of Cori. "You don't have much time! Duex is about to break through!"

He glanced back over his shoulder. The thick, gray clouds were close to colliding with the mountain peaks—almost ready to block the stubborn and persistent rays of the first sun. The earlier, orange glow of that sun was now a bright red and just about to turn into a brilliant ball of yellow-white.

"Hurry!" shouted Gemma.

Oliver cracked his whip once more.

"Come on guys!"

Then, as if guided by a divine hand, the clouds swirled, speeding toward the mountain peak and extinguishing the sun's rays before they could arise and speed toward the Frezia Challenge finish line. The rest of the clouds closed in behind it, snuffing out the sunrise and keeping it from reaching the challenge's final arch.

As Oliver mushed his sled across the castle bridge, he sensed victory was within his grasp.

Ziiiiiiiiiiiing! Ziiiiiiiiiiiing!

Two more arrows tried to stop him, but they failed, and rounding the final turn, he saw the newly-built stone, finish-line arch. Raising his arms, he and his sled passed underneath it in final victory.

"Oliver! You made it! You're still alive!" Gemma shouted, hurrying to him.

Pulling back on the leather reins, Oliver stopped Tristyx and Sedah and hopped off the sled. He ran to Gemma and grabbed her, lifting her in the air and giving her a hug.

"It's so good to see you, Gemma ... you have no idea!" he said. "Are you all right?"

Gemma threw her arms around him and kissed him generously. Cori looked on, smiling but feeling left out. Oliver looked over at her and pulled her into the celebration, giving her a big kiss as well. Not to be the only one standing alone, Prima tapped Oliver on the shoulder and made a pucker with her lips. Oliver first took his hand out as if to shake hers, but then burst into a laugh when she started to pout.

"Just kidding!" he said, grabbing her as well and planting a firm kiss on her cheek.

They all laughed—even Gemma, who had hoped to have him all to herself.

"Where's Nikko?" asked Oliver. "I don't see him with you."

"No, the king wouldn't allow it until you finished the mission and completed the challenge. He's still in prison," said Gemma.

Oliver looked sad, but a ray of light struck his face. He looked up to see Duex finally fight through the clouds and shine brightly down on him.

"So, we made it then, right?" Oliver asked urgently.

"I'd say you did—but just barely," said Gemma, beaming.

"You did it, Oliver!" chirped Cori.

"You do have the treasure, don't you?" Gemma asked him.

"Make way. Make way!" came a voice through the crowd. It was the royal CP.

He pushed people out of the way—even knocking some over—to reach Oliver. Moving to the center of the attention, he pulled out a frayed scroll and unrolled it.

"By the rules of the Challenge of Frezia, I declare the contest over!"

There was a cheering throughout the crowd. Finally, someone had returned from it alive.

"As such, I also declare that *no one* has won this year's challenge," shouted the short, waif-like man. "Therefore, all are condemned to return to their cells and serve out the remainder of their sentences! This is by order of the king."

*****

CH 46 - Dedman

The army Konjuur thought was approaching to take back the kingdom was nothing more than a small band of wayward Rootanian soldiers returning from a disastrous campaign in Chasmia. It was Commander Dedman who had led the party in the hot desert canyon outside of Gilabend, only to see his men disappear under his nose and unable to do anything about it.

Dedman staggered into the castle, tunic torn, boots with only the tops holding them together, and with men who looked as though they hadn't eaten in weeks. Expecting to find and confront King Barbarot, or at the very least Baron Marbray, he was shocked to see another face on the throne—one he didn't know.

"My Lord," Dedman said, bowing low and reverently to Konjuur, "I come to you to ask that you pardon me and my men. We have served the kingdom with valor and with pride; however, we failed to hold the capital city of Chasmia as commanded. For that, we are truly sorry and ask your forgiveness."

"So, why have you returned?" questioned Konjuur.

"There are things out there we can't explain, Your Royal Highness. Things that are strange and, I fear, wicked," Dedman said. "My men were snatched one by one by an evil we could not fight; an evil we could not see; and an evil we could not defeat. It came in the middle of the night, silently like the ghost of Death itself. It took my men, sire. And of the hundreds I started with, only these are left."

Dedman motioned to the handful of soldiers who had come into the palace with him. Pitiful they were—only eight—and each unlike the professional soldiers they had been when they had left the castle months earlier.

Pity was not one of Konjuur's strengths; however, when it suited his purpose, he would use it.

"I see," said the new king. "I guess I really should have you executed or, at the very least, thrown into prison for the rest of your lives, shouldn't I?"

Dedman looked up bravely and nodded. "Yes, my Lord. As you wish it."

"You tell me that you were entrusted with several hundred men under your care and you managed to kill-off nearly all them. Don't you think that's a crime against your kingdom?"

"Your decision is what we shall live with, sire," replied the commander.

"Then perhaps all of you should pay the highest price for your crimes," said Konjuur coldly.

"If that is your wish, my Lord," replied Dedman.

Konjuur could see that the man was courageous and could be useful. However, his men were not as good at acting. They stood in shock, having been told by Dedman that this was the valiant thing to do and that the king would respect them for returning and coming 'clean' rather than running as deserters.

"Then again, I suppose you didn't really have to come back to Rootan, did you?" said Konjuur coyly.

Dedman said nothing. His men looked up at Konjuur, hoping for some grace, some mercy, some kindness. But although it would be granted, it wasn't for the reasons they thought or hoped.

"All right," replied Konjuur, sneering at them. "I believe you deserve a reprieve—this time."

"Thank you, my Lord. Thank you!" said Dedman, looking up at him. "On behalf of my men and me …"

"Save it!" barked the Konjuur. "You're only getting my pardon on one condition."

"Anything, my Lord. Anything you desire," said the commander.

"Yes, it will be *anything* I desire."

"Yes, sire. We will do as your will commands."

Konjuur smirked. "Then, this is what you and your men will do for me, and if you fail me this time—I *will* have you executed."

*****

CH 47 – Re-tried

"No! That's not right!" Oliver screamed at CP. "We brought the stone back. We've got it right here!"

CP raised one eyebrow with a look of mild surprise. "I don't believe you," he said. "Show it to me, then!"

"My friend here needs help first," demanded Oliver as he went to the trailing sled where Fermat was lying, half unconscious and still bleeding from the head.

CP pushed Oliver to one side, unwilling to care for a convict he was convinced would be back in his cell within the hour. However, Cori ran to Fermat and helped him out of the sled. His knees buckled, and he began sinking to the ground. Oliver rushed to help them, getting Fermat to his feet.

"So, where is it?" asked CP, looking for any remaining bags in the second sled.

Oliver went to the supply sled and found a silver sack. He unwrapped the white cord he'd tied around the bag and pulled out the smooth egg he'd stuffed inside to keep it safe.

"It's right here!" Oliver exclaimed, holding it out for CP and everyone else to see.

"It's an egg—a stone egg, nothing more. It's not the *stone* the king said was the treasure to be returned."

But Oliver saw the look on CP's face when he had first pulled out the egg. It had become ashen and stiffened as if shocked by something he thought he would never see again.

"Oh, all right, then," said Oliver. "Well, if this isn't the stone, then it's all right for me to just throw it into the lake." And with that, Oliver stepped back to give the egg a heave as far as he could into the lake that lapped the shoreline around the castle.

"No!" cried CP holding out his hands. "Don't!"

Oliver lowered his arm and tucked the egg back under it, cradling it carefully.

"But I thought this was just some old egg ... that it wasn't what the king was looking for. Am I right?"

CP felt trapped but managed to say, "Well, it's not, but that doesn't mean it's still not valuable. You can hand it over to me for safekeeping. I'll make sure it gets taken care of properly."

"I don't think so!" replied Oliver. "It's the stone, and you know it!"

"First, you have not presented the stone in accordance with the rules of the challenge, and second, you did not get it here in time. The deadline was three days, which ended when the rays of the sun cracked the horizon."

"The sun's rays struck the finish line after I had crossed over it. You saw that with your own eyes, and so did all these people here. And as for the stone, you know very well that it's inside this egg ... it is here, just as the King's Challenge demands."

"No! You have failed! I will take that egg. Guards take them away ... all them!" ordered CP with a growl.

"You can't!" came a high-pitched voice. "You have no legal right!"

Gemma pushed her own way through the group and stood before CP with her hands on her hips.

"How dare you challenge me!" CP shouted at her. "Take them *all* away!"

"According to *The Frezia Challenge—Rules and Regulations*, by G. de Riguere, section four, subsection six, and paragraph nine-b," Gemma said, clutching the copy she had taken from the library, "we can file a protest and have it heard before the courts of the land. We can also present witnesses to the events as they occurred—and we have plenty of witnesses," she said, glancing at Cori and Prima who stood confidently beside her. "And that, my good fellow, is exactly what we are hereby doing."

CP became angry. He first bit his lip, but then let out a string of profanities that rattled all in attendance.

Then, he said, "Fine! We shall take this to the court; however, it will be the High Court which will convene this afternoon." He narrowed his eyes and added, "This should be a very quick trial indeed." And with that, he turned on his heels and went back inside the castle.

"What does all this mean?" asked Cori.

It was Prima's turn to answer. "I'm afraid there's only one juror in the High Court—our father."

***

"All will rise!" shouted the Sergeant in Arms, who policed the comings and goings of the High Court.

The room was the same one where the earlier trial was held. This time, there were no other visitors allowed—only the king, CP, Gemma and Oliver. It was only when Cori and Prima threatened to go to their mother, that CP allowed them to attend as well. A few others who had been at the finish line at the time were let in as well, under Cori's demands.

King de Riguere entered wearing a black robe that trailed behind him. He was clearly annoyed at having to spend his time to judge the protest that had been filed by Gemma. He was accustomed to the challenge ending with no one returning.

"Get on with this!" spat the king. "I have better things to do than to hear their miserable plea for an exception to our laws and rules. Did you tell them, CP?"

"Yes, Your Highness. I tried to explain that the rules of the challenge and the laws of the land are firm they cannot be changed," said CP.

Looking down at Gemma who was sitting in the front row beneath his raised dais, de Riguere scowled. He gave a quick snort to indicate his disdain and then continued, "So, what is the basis for your protest, young lady?"

Gemma rose and bowed to the king in reverence. Then she picked up a book from the table, where other books and pieces of parchment lay neatly stacked in front of her. She opened the first book—a thin, red volume with smudged pages—and lifted the long, cloth bookmark that was sewn into the binding.

"If I may, Your Highness," she began, holding the book in both hands. "Here, on page thirty-one of *The Frezia Challenge— Rules and Regulations*, by ..." Here she stopped and looked up at the ruling judge. "... G. de Riguere, the rules state, and I quote:

> 'The Frezia Challenge shall commence every other year on a day of the king's choosing. The Challenge shall begin at dawn when the first sun rises above the mountains to the east. It shall end precisely when the rays of the that sun strike the same line as the start after three days of competition.'

"... and I continue, my king ...

> 'There shall be no interference in the challenge by anyone. The competitors themselves are the only ones who may determine their own fate.

> 'The winner of the Challenge shall be the competitor or competitors who cross the finish line within the three-day period. They must return with the treasure from the mountain within the kingdom—the one known as Mt. Erebus.

> 'If these requirements are fulfilled, the king is required to grant the competitor his freedom from imprisonment or the contractual agreement made with the competitor before the challenge commenced. If the competitor does not cross the finish line within the three-day period or does not return with the treasure, the king may refuse his freedom or impose any other punishment as he deems appropriate.

'If a competitor does not return to the castle within the three-day period, he may be hunted and recaptured. It will be the king's sole discretion as to what becomes of this competitor.'

Gemma put the book down.

"You know that you have responsibilities under the rules of the challenge, do you not?" she asked.

"Of course. But no one has ever finished it before," said the king. "I do not believe I have such a responsibility. I am the king."

"But you wrote the laws for a reason. You say at the beginning of each law that no one is above it. Doesn't that include you?"

The king stared coldly at her.

"Yet, you're right. Not everyone has to abide by the rules, do they? You do what you want to do, even though you tell people that you rule by the laws of the land. Isn't that true?"

"I don't know what you're talking about," said the king.

"Isn't it true that certain prisoners were promised their freedom even if they returned *without* the stone?"

"What do you mean?" asked the king.

"There were some prisoners you put on the challenge to make sure that the few you believed who could bring back the stone would *not* come back alive if they were successful. Isn't that right?" asked Gemma.

"No, of course not. Prove it!"

"And isn't it true that even if someone did succeed, you stationed your own troops around the castle and in the woods to kill them when their sled got close to the castle?" asked Gemma, more impatiently.

"I'm the judge! I'm the king! I'm not on trial here!" de Riguere shouted, red-faced and angered.

"You didn't answer the question," said Gemma calmly.

"I don't have to answer your question! I can have you thrown in a dungeon right now if I want." De Riguere glanced around the small courtroom and saw the look of disgust on the faces of his daughters and other watching.

"You have no proof of any of those things," stated the king, backing down.

Gemma returned to her seat and picked up another book. This one was larger with a dusty brown jacket and writing on the front that had started to wear off. She opened it to a spot that she had marked with a small, torn piece of paper and began reading.

"Section one, paragraph two of the *Citizenship Loyalty Law of 2821* states, and I quote:

> 'Herewith, a citizen of Frezia is defined as anyone living within the borders of the kingdom of Frezia. This definition includes those of royalty and those holding title to land or other property within the kingdom.'

"Does that also include you, Your Royal Highness?" Gemma asked.

"Of course, it does. I am the *first* citizen of this great kingdom."

"Section four, paragraph three of the *Citizenship Loyalty Law of 2821* states, and I quote:

> 'Any citizen of Frezia who intentionally misleads another which leads to the physical or mental harm of that person shall be charged with acts against the kingdom of Frezia.'

"Who did I mislead?" bellowed the king.

"I believe in this case, you made no mention to the men you sent on the challenge that you would do everything you could to ensure they wouldn't return. You positioned your archers outside the city to shoot anyone coming in. You moved the finish line back from the starting line in violation of the rules. You promised prisoners their freedom if they would eliminate others in the race in direction violation of the interference rules. Shall I go on?"

The king smiled. "Aren't you the smart one," he said. De Riguere looked to CP for a defense, but he only got a blank stare for his trouble.

The blood was rising in the king's face, but he was not quite ready to admit defeat, especially at the hands of a woman—a young one at that.

"Two problems remain, I'm afraid," said the king. "First, CP tells me that your friend did not arrive until after the sun had risen, marking the end of the time he had to complete his mission. Second, he has not proved that he has returned with the treasure—the stone. He only has a stone egg that he's returned—not the smooth, polished stone like I have in my collection in this castle. Therefore, on both counts he has failed!"

Gemma put her books back on the table and rose to pace in front of the desk of the judge.

"I believe the rules of the challenge specify that the competitor must cross the finish line before the first sun's rays strike that line, concluding exactly three days of competition."

"Yes," said CP, "Duex had risen to start the fourth day before he reached the finish line."

"But its rays had *not* struck the finish line before then," said Gemma. "So, how can you be sure exactly when that sun rose? I believe there were clouds that blocked the rays until after he crossed, isn't that true?"

CP looked to others in the room who were there at the time. They all stared at him angrily. He knew that he would not be able to lie about it.

"But the defendant has not shown that he has the stone!" cried CP in defense of his lordship. "It cannot be opened—that egg. It does not contain the treasure specified in the challenge and by the king."

Cori ran to Gemma carrying Oliver's satchel that had been taken from him at the start of the race. Gemma took it and handed it to Oliver, who was in shackles and tied to his chair.

"Untie him!" demanded Gemma.

The guards looked at each other, not knowing exactly what to do.

"I said, untie him!"

The guards looked at the king who was shocked at the outburst. Getting no reaction from him, the guards blindly obeyed and unchained Oliver from his bindings. By the time the chains hit the floor, Oliver was rummaging inside his satchel. There he found what he was looking for and pulled it out—the Annihilation Blade. He wrapped his fingers around its handle, and it unfurled immediately at his command.

The guards came to life, drawing their own swords, but Prima came forward and motioned for them to put them away, looking defiantly at her father.

Gemma took the egg and placed it in front of Oliver, balancing it so it remained upright. She held it between her hands and looked up at him, waiting.

"Well," she said, "what are you waiting for?"

Oliver took the blade in both hands and raised it over his head. Then, he froze.

"I can't do it," he stuttered.

"What do you mean, you can't do it? You've done it before," said Gemma.

"No. If I miss the egg, I could strike you dead with it. You know how unforgiving this sword is."

"Oliver, I trust you. You won't miss. Now just slice this thing open!" Gemma commanded.

At that moment, Oliver's satchel began to swirl and whirl as if some wild animal were trying to claw its way out. Oliver's eyes grew wide, and he swallowed stiffly; perspiration started to bead on his forward even though the room was near freezing. He knew it must be his Eripio Bag, but now was not the time to be distracted. He had to show the court and the king that he had, indeed, returned with a Gneima stone.

Oliver ignored the bag, and with all his might, he swung the blade down on the top of the egg. Its razor-sharp edge hit the crown of the strange rock, sending shockwaves through Oliver's arms. It rebounded off the surface sending Oliver backwards and crashing into seats several rows back.

Gemma ran to him and helped him back on his feet. Brushing off his coat, Oliver got up holding his back.

"What happened?" Gemma asked.

"I don't know. It didn't work this time!" Oliver replied, still smarting from the strike.

Oliver looked down at his blade. It had been completely shattered by the impact—the end of the blade broken like the lance of a jousting match knight.

"My god!" said Oliver. "It didn't even make a dent in it!"

Oliver went to the egg. There was no mark whatsoever on the surface. It was as if it had never been touched.

Cori was still watching Oliver's satchel, which continued spinning wildly, feverishly, trying to get its master's attention.

"You have failed, boy," said CP smiling menacingly. "Now, it's time for you and the rest of your friends to suffer your judgment."

The king raised his hand and was about to speak when Gemma interrupted again.

"No, the law states that we have adequate time to present our case, and I say we have not yet finished our side of it."

"You have been given more than enough time to present your feeble arguments," said CP. "It is time for the king to render his judgment on all of you!"

She turned to Oliver. "See what the Eripio has for you Oliver. It's our last chance!"

Oliver reached in the satchel and pulled out the Eripio bag. It had saved him countless times before, but its quixotic solutions made him worry that he would not be able to figure what he was to do with whatever it gave him.

Tentatively, Oliver opened the top. Inside, he felt something hard and round. Pulling it out, he looked at it and then walked to the king's desk and placed it there.

"And what am I to do with this?" asked de Riguere, looking at Gemma rather than Oliver.

Gemma's face was blank. "I ... I don't have a clue," she said flatly.

However, Oliver was more upbeat. He knew there was an answer—he just needed time to figure it out.

"It is what we've been looking for," Oliver said confidently, stalling for time.

"And what is that?" asked CP.

"It's a bowl," said Gemma, unsure. "It's for ..." She hesitated, stalling.

But Oliver's smile couldn't have been broader. "I think you've got it, my lady!" he said.

Oliver grabbed the large, white-rimmed bowl from the king's desk and placed it on the floor. The bowl was heavy, made of stone and perfectly round with the top tapering only slightly to a smaller base. And although the top was white, the shades of it inside grew increasingly gray and then black toward its base.

"What are you going to do now?" asked Gemma, whispering to Oliver.

He laughed. "What does every cook do in the kitchen?" he asked.

He lifted the stone egg and held it lengthwise over the edge of the bowl. "Would you like yours easy over or sunny-side up?" he quipped.

Oliver lifted the stone egg and let it fall with a sharp crack! The side of the bowl shattered with shards of rock exploding across the courtroom floor, and when the dust cleared, everyone looked for the stone egg.

"It's cracked! It's cracked, Oliver!" shouted Cori.

"Yeah," said Oliver, grinning, "just like making an omelet."

Oliver took the fractured stone and pried it apart with his hands. It separated with some reluctance but split into two unequal pieces, showing a hollow core.

He scooped out the dust from inside the egg and with it came something else—something very special. Dusting it off, he presented a smooth stone, which was ashen gray in color. It had all the characteristics of the other stones they'd found and that the king had in his collection—small, smooth, irregularly shaped with some shade between white and black.

"I believe this is the treasure stone called for in the challenge rules, isn't it?" asked Oliver, holding up the gray stone, triumphantly.

"Bring it here, boy," said the king with his hand outstretched. "I want to see what you've brought us."

Oliver placed the stone in the king's hand and watched as the sovereign felt the smoothness and finish of the piece. De Riguere grinned. His eyes were wide, and energy was pulsing through his aged body like he was a young knight again. "Yes, I do believe you've brought back the prize we were looking for." He was smiling—almost salivating—over what was in his hands.

"And?" asked Oliver.

"And ... your freedom. You and your friends may go," said the king, now staring at his new treasure.

Gemma spoke again, "But your lordship, you also promised to give Oliver the other two stones from your collection if he returned alive and with the prize."

"I never promised that!" said the king, barking out to Gemma.

"I believe that you did, father," said Cori, standing up for her friends.

Prima was also in the room and looked uncomfortable. Her sister had just put herself in danger. Even though she was the daughter of the king, Prima knew her father would show no mercy for anyone who defied him in something that wasn't written in the laws. So, she too stood up, defending her only sister.

"Father, you should listen to what Cori is saying to you," said Prima, trying to stay uncommitted, yet urging her father not to condemn his daughter.

"What? You are siding with her, are you? How dare you two speak out against your father!" roared de Riguere.

"You always taught us to speak the truth, act honestly, and listen to those in need," said Prima. "Isn't that true? Were those really things you believed in or have you forgotten them?"

The courtroom was quiet; the heavy breathing from the courtiers could easily be heard as tensions rose.

"As our father, we always looked up to you," said Prima. "You were the one we wanted to grow up to be like—strong, wise, powerful, and, above all, honest. At least we always thought you were."

Prima paused and looked deeply into her father's eyes. She could see that this moment was tearing him apart. He was fighting inner demons that wanted to push him to do everything and anything he could to keep the stones and his power.

"You, yourself always said to obey the laws—that without laws, a civilization could not stand," Prima continued. "'There would be lawlessness and chaos—every person for themselves'. Do you remember saying that? You said, 'What kind of world would we live in if anyone did anything they wanted?'. We were only young girls then, but I don't think things have changed, have they father?"

The courtroom sat silent; now most were even afraid to breathe. Yet, all waited anxiously for the next words to be uttered from the king. He sat, stewing in the mess he had created.

He knew she was right. It was what he had taught them; however, since finding the other two stones, his pride and ego had grown, and he had found it harder to see the truth.

"I am surprised, Prima, very surprised," he said finally.

"At what, Father?" Prima asked, heroically calmly.

"I am surprised at how wise you have become. It wasn't but a few years ago that you and your sister were playing with your small toys in the royal nursery. Your mother and I were so happy. We loved you both very much. I ... I guess I've forgotten about those days. It's just that these pieces of stone are ... I don't know ... so important to me now."

"More important than your own daughters?" It was another voice coming into the room—the queen's. "She's right, you know," she said. "It's been too long since I had the king I married all those years ago. You have changed, my husband, and not for the better. Ever since you brought home those damned pieces of rock, things have been different—not only between you and me and you and your children, but also between you and your kingdom," she said. "Prima's right. Those stones have taken possession of you—over your soul. They have stolen you from us."

The king sat quietly, listening.

"You have a choice to make—either you choose to chase the stones and make your final pact with the evil that controls them, or you decide to return to your family and the people you love and who love you—you can't have both!" said the queen, coolly but firmly. "If you choose the stones, you will lose more than just your family and kingdom—you will lose yourself, forever."

Even in midday, she looked elegant and royal with her blue velvet gown flowing behind her as she entered the room. Her dark amber eyes focused intently on her husband sitting at the front of the courtroom and engaged him immediately.

"We need you back," said Prima. "We *all* need and want you back."

The king looked down at the piece of stone. He winced, but then motioned for Oliver to stand before him to face his judgment.

Then, he held out the stone.

"It is yours," said the king. "as are the other two pieces." He sat quietly, trying to think of what to say next. "It's more important for me to have my family back and that of my kingdom." He smiled. A new glow seemed to emanate from him, as if a dark cloud had been lifted.

"There are those things that can be replaced if lost or broken," the king continued. "And there are those that have value beyond measure that we are blind to and take for granted. The real treasures are those that we have right before us. Those who are near and dear to us without whom life would have little meaning. Those are our roses—those are the flowers we must nourish and protect." Then, he said, "Prima, Cori, Yamina ... you are my roses."

Cori went to him and gave him a kiss on the cheek. Seeing this, Prima and Yamina followed, joining with the king and giving him a reassuring hug.

CP, on the other hand, was agitated and fuming. He had worked hard for the king for years and had fought to protect and safeguard those stones. They had come to symbolize more than something of value to him; they had become the essence, the meaning, the purpose, of his life. He would not go quietly into the night. He was consumed. His soul was already lost.

Disgusted, CP stormed out of the courtroom, slamming the door behind him. No one paid much attention to the incident, except Oliver, who watched and worried.

*****

CH 48 - in Pursuit

Let's get our things together quickly," said Oliver. "I don't want to wait here any longer than we have to."

"But why?" asked Gemma.

"Yeah, why do you have to leave so soon? You just got back from the challenge—you must be exhausted!" said Cori, pleading with them to stay.

"Something doesn't feel quite right," said Oliver. "CP left the courtroom very upset. That didn't sit well with me. I think something is up."

He began getting all his things together, stuffing them into his satchel. "Where is Nikko?" he asked.

"He's still in the prison cell, I think," said Gemma. "They wouldn't bring him up with the rest of us."

"But now that we've all been freed, we should go get him," Oliver answered. "They can't hold him now."

"Where are they holding him?" asked Gemma.

"Follow me," Cori said, sorrowfully.

Oliver knew she was sad they were leaving so soon, but he smelled trouble—and it wasn't coming from the king or queen.

They reached Nikko's cell, and Oliver approached the bars and banged his knife handle to make some noise. Nikko was in the corner, curled up and resting. When he heard the sound, he looked up and, realizing it was Oliver and Gemma, bounded across the floor overjoyed to see them.

"Master! You all right! It so good to see you!" shouted Nikko.

"It's good to see you too, little guy," said Oliver.

Cori got the key from the guard and opened the cell. Nikko sprang through the opening and leaped right onto Oliver's shoulder as if he'd only hopped off moments earlier to pick a piece of fruit from a tree. Settling in quickly, Nikko wrapped his tail around his master's neck while Oliver stroked the monkey's blue fur, just like old times.

"Don't bother to say hi to me!" said Gemma, pouting.

Nikko jumped off Oliver and onto Gemma, using his hands to mess up her hair. Then, he leaped back onto Oliver's shoulders finally saying, "Hi, Gemma!"

They all laughed as Gemma tried to fix her golden locks.

Leaving the castle, they went to the shelter where the sled wolves were held. Oliver peered inside and walked the rows of stalls to find someone special.

"Tristyx! There you are!" shouted Oliver when he finally found his friend's stall. "I was afraid they'd put you someplace where I wouldn't be able to find you."

Tristyx jumped up, excited to see his master. He put his three tongues out and began wagging his tail, as if he were a real sled dog. Oliver climbed over the low, wooden gate and stroked the three heads as they panted happily. They all purred like overgrown puppies, licking his fingers as his hand passed by each of their noses.

"That's a good boy, Tristyx! We're going to take a little trip, you and I. That's right. Just a little jaunt out of here. Is that all right with you, boy?"

Tristyx wagged his tail as Oliver smiled at him.

He took Tristyx out of his stall and put the sled harnesses around each of his necks. Then, he led him out of the shelter. But that's where Tristyx stopped. Oliver tried to pull him, but he stubbornly refused.

"What's wrong, buddy?" asked Oliver. "Come on, we've got to get going."

But Tristyx wouldn't move. Instead, he turned and looked back into the barn-like stable, staring into the darkness. Then turning to Oliver, he began barking and whimpering, and pawing the ground to go back inside.

"Sedah? Is that what you want? You want me to bring her with us?" asked Oliver.

Tristyx immediately began jumping up and down, pulling on the harness and tethered straps. Caught off balance, Oliver stumbled and then was dragged back into the shelter by the large wolf. Up and down the rows they went, looking for Sedah.

"Sedah? Sedah, my girl. Where are you?" Oliver called out.

Cori, Gemma and Nikko helped, but they couldn't tell which dog was which.

Shortly, they heard barking in the next row of stalls and dashed around the corner to find the bright blue triangular nose of the cerberian canine. Now, barking came from six heads—from the three heads of Tristyx to those of Sedah. Once competitors, they were now good friends, and Tristyx wouldn't leave without her.

Harnessed up, Sedah and Tristyx were attached to separate sleds. Cori brought down provisions and put them in sacks, which they tied down to the top of the sled carriages.

"Do you know how to drive this thing?" Cori asked Gemma.

Gemma looked at her not knowing what to say. "Well, if Oliver can do it, so can I," she replied with confidence.

"You can do it. I know you can, Gemma," said Oliver. "Now, let's get the rest of the stones loaded and get out of here."

The day was clear, and frigid air had settled into the lake basin that surrounded the castle and town. The snowpack had hardened after melting under the previous day's suns and then refreezing overnight.

Oliver put his arm around Cori and squeezed her tightly.

"Thanks for all your help, Cori. If it weren't for you, we'd be rotting in one of the deep, dark cells back there," he said pointing to the castle.

Cori returned his smile and wiped a tear from her eye. "I'll miss you," she said choking back more that were starting to come.

"But you must wait a second," she said.

"Why?" asked Oliver. "We really have to get going!"

"Just a minute ... I promised someone something and arranged for them to be here before you left," she said.

It was more than a minute, but Cori came back down the path to the stables with Prima and a few of the guards trailing behind them.

"Someone else wanted to see you off," Cori said.

Out from between two guards stepped Fermat. He was dressed in prison garb and had his hands tied. Still, he was grinning and happy to see Oliver.

"Why weren't you freed?" asked Oliver, surprised at Fermat's condition.

"Like I told you, Oliver. The king is not always fair," Fermat told him.

"Actually, that's not quite true," said Prima. "I just heard that father signed the papers granting you your freedom. It was CP who tore them up. I'm going to go to father now to get this straightened out. Fermat will be freed soon."

Prima approached Oliver and kissed him on the cheek. "Thanks," she said.

"Thanks for what?" Oliver asked, surprised at her words.

"Thanks for giving me back my family ... and you too Gemma. It's been too long since Cori and I knew what it was like to have one."

Prima turned and retraced her steps up the path and back to the castle to have a word with her father. She left Fermat with the guards to say his goodbyes.

Sedah was glad to see her master again too and whipped her tail enthusiastically as he stroked the top of one of her heads.

"Good to see you again, Fermat," said Oliver. "I'm sure Prima will get this figured out and get you freed."

"I know. She's a good one," said Fermat. "Now, you take care of yourself, Oliver. I just hope you don't run into any more Rebuses, 'cause you know you won't have me around to give you the answers."

They laughed, and Oliver put his hand on Fermat's shoulder.

"I'll do my best," he answered.

Then, Oliver climbed onto his sled with Nikko clinging to his shoulder. He grabbed the reins and then looked over to see that Gemma was ready to go. She nodded to him, also glad to be getting out of there.

"Mush!" she shouted, cracking her reins. She prompted Sedah to take off, and she began pulling her sled with the supply sled behind her.

But Sedah got jumpy from all the commotion and became distracted by Tristyx who was having trouble with his harness— biting and fussing with a part that was irritating him. She took off with a jolt, dragging the sled helter-skelter through the snow and toward a large altimont pine tree that was jutting out into the road near the trail.

"Oliver!" Gemma shouted as she struggled to regain control of her sled. "I can't stop it! What am I supposed to dooooo?"

Gemma barely missed the tree, almost flipping the sled over, but instead whipping Sedah completely around to head back to where they started. Sedah dug in and raced off again, steering toward where Fermat was standing with the guards. Luckily, the sentries jumped out of the way, but Fermat wasn't so lucky. The sled hit him, undercutting his legs and throwing him over Gemma and into the second sled behind her.

Cori jumped onto to Oliver's sled and whipped the reins to get Tristyx going. "Mush!" shouted Cori. "Mush!"

Tristyx took off after Sedah, tearing through the snow after her. The trail was narrowing with sharp turns coming up quickly as it dropped toward the frozen lake. Even Oliver could see the danger. If Gemma got out over the lake, she could reach the center where the ice was thin. Falling through could be the end of her.

"Come on, Tristyx! What kind of friend are you to let Sedah go off like that! Let's go!" shouted Cori.

Oliver was impressed with her skills, and she began closing quickly on Gemma's sled.

"Get ready," Cori said to Oliver. "I'm going to pull the sled closer. Then, you'll have to jump."

Oliver climbed up on the supply bags and held tightly to the ropes used as strapping. The sled bumped and jostled him as it flew over the mounds and crashed over an occasional branch in the middle of the trail.

Sedah reached one of the sharp turns and barely managed to stay on the trail toward the lake. The sled veered too, nearly skidding off the path but hung tightly to the groove and continued its course, plowing ahead at full speed. The trail widened, and Cori saw the chance to pull next to the other sled, as Oliver steadied himself and waited.

"Now!" shouted Cori.

Oliver jumped the gap between the sleds and landed in Gemma's supply pile, nearly rolling off the other side. He clung to the side rails and pulled himself back onto the stack of bags.

"Hang on, Gemma!" Oliver yelled, getting behind her.

Sedah's feistiness was more than Gemma was used to, and the harder she pulled on the reins, the more Sedah resisted. Panicked, she pushed the reins into Oliver's hands.

"I can't do this," she cried, by now hitting bushes, limbs and running dangerously close to the solid rock ledge that spilled out onto the lake. "I can't get her to stop!" screamed Gemma.

Oliver yelled at the wolf, "Sedah! Stop right now!" And with all his might, he jerked the reins to all three of her heads. They snapped up and back, and she could no longer see where she was going. Quickly, she stopped.

Cori came up behind them, "*Whoa*, there Tristyx. Good boy," she said, patting the side of one of his necks.

"That was scary," said Cori, concerned. "Sometimes Sedah gets spooked like that. Usually, she's good with just about anything, but when there are too many things going on, she can be a bit funny that way."

"I guess so," said Gemma, trying to catch her breath. "She just didn't seem hear me. I thought she'd gone mad or something."

"No, she's a good wolf," said Oliver comforting her. "She really wouldn't intentionally hurt you or anyone. Would you girl?" Oliver stroked the dog, giving her reassurance and comfort that everything was all right.

But in the distance, they heard other sleds coming and wolves barking. In fact, it sounded as though the entire fleet of cerberians had been let loose.

"What's going on?" asked Oliver.

The look on Cori's face said it all.

"You must go!" she said. "I saw CP readying two teams of wolves this morning, but I didn't give it much thought. I just thought Father had a hunt planned or something. But that's not what this is."

They watched as a huge cerberian, hitched to a toboggan-like sled, appeared at the top of the hill near the castle wall. Whipping the reins madly was ... CP.

"Stop them!" he yelled as his wolf pulled him along. Behind him were three more sleds—all filled with guards carrying their swords.

Cori looked at Oliver and Gemma with alarm. "They're coming for you," she said. "You have to get out of here—all of you!"

"But what about you, Cori? He'll put you in prison for helping us. You can't stay here. It's not safe for you either," said Oliver.

"I'll be fine," said Cori. "Remember, my father is the king."

"But you don't know that he's in control anymore, do you?" said Gemma, also worried about her. "What if CP has taken control of the kingdom? Why would your father let him loose with all the sleds? It would be in violation of everything he said to us in the courtroom."

Cori stole a quick glance at the advancing sled and then at Oliver, who was nodding his agreement. Just then, four *more* wolf teams with toboggans popped up on top of the hill, following closely behind CP.

"What about Prima?"

"I don't know," said Oliver. "We can only pray that she's safe. There is nothing we can do right now anyway—especially if CP catches us and puts us *all* in a dungeon."

"You just can't take the chance," echoed Gemma. "Come with us!"

Cori shook her head. "I can't leave my family," she said.

"Get them!" shouted CP.

"What about the girl?" they heard from another knight in a sled right behind CP.

"Get them all!" roared CP.

Gemma jumped over into Cori's sled and took the reins back from her.

"You're coming with us!" Gemma cried. Then, she cracked the reins over the heads of Tristyx and dashed off.

"Mush Tristyx! Faster!" shouted Gemma to her lead dog.

Oliver echoed Gemma's call, "Mush! Let's go Sedah!"

The wolves tore down the road, veering away from the lake at the split and heading off in the direction of Mt. Erebus. Tristyx was in the lead with Gemma turning control back to Cori, who steered the sled along the course she knew would get them out of the town the quickest. Sedah followed close behind, panting but jumping higher and higher through the snow as it grew deeper with each mound and hill they found.

Fermat—riding in the supply sled now manned by Cori and Gemma—turned around to see CP and his posse were. Unfortunately, they were gaining on them. Their toboggan-shaped sleds glided more easily than the ones they were piloting making it easier to pull.

"Get them!" they heard once more coming from CP.

"Come on Tristyx! You've got to fly, *baby!* They're gaining on us!" shouted Fermat.

On they pushed with the wolves behind them snarling and snapping. One wrong move, and the posse would be on them in seconds.

Nikko could hear the heavy breaths of the wolves as they closed in. It would only be a matter of time before they were caught.

"I can't go back d'ere!" he cried. "Oliver—I can't!"

*****

Continued - Book IV – The Fires of Mt. Enat

The quest continues to the Fires of Mt. Enat in the next book, as Oliver and his crew flee from the grips of CP in Frezia.

*****

APPENDIX A

It was a time of transition between the feudalism of the past and the dawn of sovereign kingdoms. Royalty and bluebloods were still the dominant classes, but militaries were increasingly coming under the sovereign's sole control and with it, the establishment of ranks and privileges within the brotherhood of the knights.

Hierarchy of Royalty/Knighthood:

Emperor/Empress
King/Queen
Duke/Duchess
Earl/Countess
Viceroy/Viceroces
Baron/Baroness
Knight/Lady
Squire (aspiring knight)
Page (apprentice)

Levels of Knighthood

I   Grand Cordon
II   Grand Commander
III Commander
IV   Officer, Knight 1st Class
V   Knight, Knight 2nd Class, Attending Knight

APPENDIX B

Geography

Realm: Orpheus
  Ruler: Empress Sudé

Twelve Kingdoms / Rulers:

Rootan — King Portenza/King Barbarot/King Konjuur
Dulcenou — King Coraga – Queen Clytie
Sanzotur — Unknown
Frezia — King de Riguere – Queen Yamina
Vaporia — King Ferox
Chasmia — King Scorche – Queen Hollythorn
Vinedria — King Viridius

Other Kingdoms:
Vulcanage
Kavarnos
Neptom
Edenot
Sanctuia

APPENDIX C

Geographic: Map of the Realm

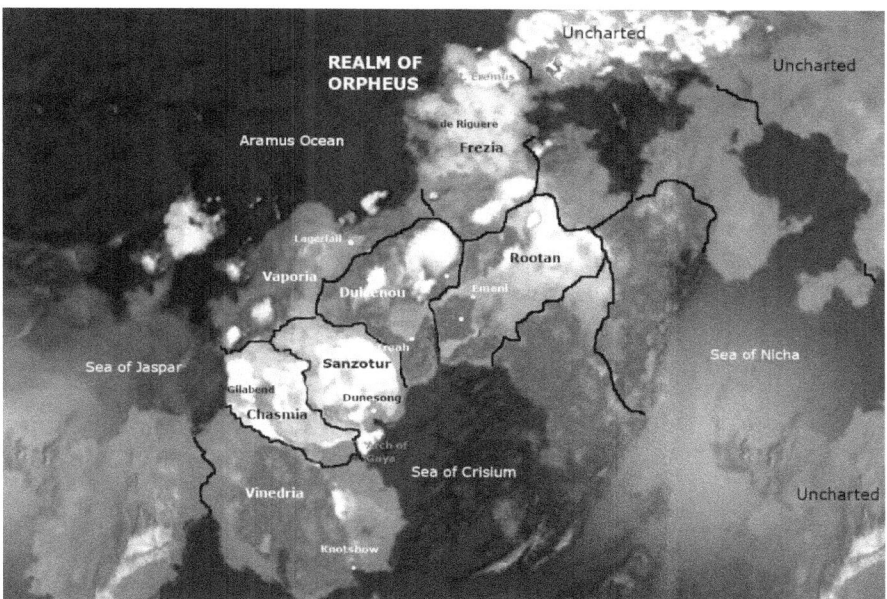

NEXT: BOOK IV – The Fires of Mt. Enat

The adventure continues …

About the Author

Alex Ross Carol is a pen name used by the author. He lives with his family near Chicago, Illinois. He began writing for enjoyment at the age of fifty.

At bedtime, Mr. Carol would often make up stories with his children to help them get to sleep. Together, they would spin imaginative yarns from random words that had to be embedded within the story. These stories started as challenges, but quickly led to quite funny or fantastic tales that often went on without end—or at least until one of them was asleep.

The author wrote the Blue Monkey Quest series purely for his children's entertainment. However, he hopes you enjoy it too.

Clues

Clues from Book III - Book Design, Marbray, Fermat, Sister, Egg